Shattered empire

Jo McCall

Jo McCall

Shattered Pieces: Shattered World Bk. 2

Copyright Jo McCall 2021
All Rights Reserved
First Published 2021
No part of this book may be reproduced, stores in a retrieval system or transmitted in any form by any means, without prior authorization in writing of the publisher *Wicked Romance Publication*, nor can it be otherwise circulated in any form of binding or cover other than that which it is published and without a similar condition, including this condition, being imposed on the subsequent purchaser. All characters and places in this publication other than those clearly in the public domain are fictitious, and any resemblance of actual persons, living or dead, is purely coincidental.

Edition: 23456789

Cover design: Kate Farlow @ Ya'll That Graphic
Editing: Beth @VBProofreads
Formatted by: WickedGypsyDesigns

THEME SONG
WITHOUT YOU-URSINE VULPA

PlayList

WARPATH-TIM HALPERINE

ON THE RISE-GENERDYN

PAINT IT BLACK-CIARA

VILLIAN-ARCANA

To the bad bitches who have always wanted to be queen.

Slay.

WARNING

The content within this book is DARK and may be triggering to some.
For a full list of triggers for this particular book go to jomccallauthor.com

PART ONE

Ava

PROLOGUE

Shattered cries surrounded me.

Tearful sobs and hushed, indistinct murmurs.

Noise came through staticky and broken like a voice through a bad phone line. Red lights danced across the water puddled on the street, droplets from the hose spray disrupting their calm surfaces as the firefighters struggled to contain the ferocious flames.

I could feel the heat of my father's body at my back as he wrapped his coat around my shivering frame. Outwardly, my body reacted to the chill of the night air, but inside there was nothing but a dull numbness spreading through my system. The flames of the ambulance were dying, leaving nothing more than a charred shell behind. I doubted there would be anything left of him to identify.

Not that I needed to.

Vas watched them load him into the back of the ambulance himself. He'd been there every step of the way except—fury coursed through my veins, hotter than boiling water as I tore myself away from Liam, my gaze sweeping the scene until it landed on the normally jovial *Sovietnik*. His lips were turned down, eyebrows drawn together, but he was safe.

Unharmed.

"Why weren't you with him?" I pummeled his chest with clench fists, hot tears spilling down my cheeks. "Where were you? Why did you leave him alone?" I hiccuped and sobbed, my mind barely registering what I was doing or who I was hurting. It was as if a part of me had snapped and taken control.

This was Vas. Sweet and funny Vas, but my mind didn't care. The monster lurking inside me wanted revenge. It wanted someone to pay.

He stood like a statue in front of me, frozen in place, his hands at his sides as he took my blows with steadfast determination. Why wasn't he fighting back? Why weren't any of his brothers defending him? He was *Pakhan* now. It was punishable by death to strike him, yet here he was, allowing me to do just that.

The punches soon lessened into slaps, and those weakened into nothing more than feeble pushes as my body lost steam and my mind shook itself from the fog of rage that had descended over it.

Warm arms enveloped me, pressing me against a hard chest as I sobbed, the scent of orange and cloves surrounding me. Guilt crashed over me, drowning me in its waves when he tugged me closer to him. "I'm sorry," he whispered brokenly in my ear. "I am so sorry."

I didn't catch it then with the crest of unconsciousness creeping into my mind as the adrenaline and shock faded, but his broken apology felt deeper than it should have. What happened wasn't his fault. Or maybe it was because he was hiding something beneath the battered exterior of his grief.

Secrets. The *Bratva* was king of secrets.

Even as I sobbed and shook in Vas's arms, the white-hot rage refused to dissipate. If anything, it grew. Vasily was not responsible for Matthias's death, but someone was.

Kenzi was not acting alone, and I would hunt down every last person who had taken part in his death.

I would tear the city apart.

Let it all burn.

CHAPTER ONE

A blazing inferno burned deep inside me.

Not a well of tears or a wall of sadness. My tears were dried, and now all that was left was a deep, jagged pit of hostility and rage. My eyes burned as I watched them lower the casket into the ground. Just a few plots away from where Vas had planted a headstone for Libby.

Her casket was empty. Void of any physical presence. Her ashes still rested in the urn Vas commissioned for her, waiting to be spread at sea. Except that the seas of Seattle were stormy, and honoring her wishes was near impossible.

Rain fell from an overcast sky in a torrential downpour. A sea of black umbrellas was spread across the cemetery. The deluge did not keep the men and women under Matthias's command from paying their respects to the former *Pakhan* of Seattle. News of his death spread like wildfire, and not just to his allies.

Rival gangs who'd been pushed out to the farthest reaches of the city were chomping at the bit to reclaim their former territories.

And they were not alone.

One week.

That was how long the planning took to safely put Matthias's funeral together, and in that time, Vas managed to keep surveillance on Christian, who was spotted numerous times meeting with the leaders of some of the most notorious gangs in the region.

Money exchanged hands, and it wouldn't be long before they made a push into the city.

A bloody one.

I drew in a deep breath and held it for a moment before releasing it. The warm air cascaded from my lips into the cold air, creating a tendril of smoky condensation, basking in the brief peace.

Grief was a fickle thing.

After my mother was murdered, the psychiatrist Elias forced me to sit down with informed me that there were five simple stages to the grieving process. Denial, anger, bargaining, depression, and last of all, acceptance.

I snorted. Simple my ass.

What she neglected to advertise about those stages could fill a library. In hindsight, however, she'd been on Elias's payroll, and she'd spent most of our time together talking about accepting my new circumstances rather than teaching me the proper coping mechanisms for the slew of nightmares that threatened to drown me at the time.

No wonder I turned to drinking the moment I was free.

In the week since my husband's death, I'd cycled through every stage and back again, repeating a few of my favorites like anger and depression. I had screamed, cried, and come to terms with his demise time and time again since his death.

And it meant nothing.

Locked away in my room at Liam's, I settled myself to cycling between anger and depression. Anger at how

Matthias shielded me from being shot. Anger at Kenzi for having fired the bullet. At Vas for not being with Matthias in the ambulance.

At myself for loving him so damn much, even in the end when all he'd done was break my heart.

When the harsh, dangerous emotion would finally subside, it was replaced with the sickening crack of depression, and with it, a wall of guilt.

Those two emotions were fucking chummy.

Guilt burrowed deep inside me as the anger lessened its hold on my heart. I felt guilty for the fury I felt at Matthias's sacrifice. A sacrifice that showed me he'd cared for me in some capacity. Then there was the guilt for blaming Vas for not dying alongside the man I loved. He didn't deserve that anger or resentment. There was nothing he could have done, and if he'd tried, there would have been two lives lost that day instead of one.

That would have been unacceptable.

There was something darker lurking beneath the surface of those *simple* stages of grief. It ran deeper than the anger and the guilt and the crippling depression. It was something more sinister. A feeling they'd glossed over in the "guide to overcoming your trauma" pamphlet the doctor so subtly handed me when I was eleven.

It was ever present and lingered at the forefront of my mind. I thirsted for it every waking hour. Dreamed of it when the call of unconsciousness pulled me under. It was a parasite digging its way beneath my skin, creating a well of darkness that stretched across my soul.

Revenge.

That should have been a stage every psychologist added to their ridiculous therapy.

I'd never thirsted for it before. Not even when Libby was

murdered. Then again, I never needed to worry about revenge. Matthias had been the sword of justice I needed. Now I needed to become my own weapon.

My rage coursed hot enough that it could burn the whole city to the fucking ground. And that was exactly what I was going to do.

Just as soon as this fucking funeral was over.

"Tomas wants to meet you," Vas whispered. He stood at my right hand, dutifully holding a large black umbrella over the two of us. "Pay his respects."

Pay his respects.

I couldn't help the derisive snort that rattled through my mind. Those were the same soft platitudes I received all day from his people. Mumbled condolences and quiet murmurs of "we stand behind you" and "we'll go wherever you lead" filtered through nearly the entire crowd as they passed us on their way to my late husband's grave.

Vas bowed his head respectively as each person strolled up to pledge their allegiance to him, the new *Pakhan*, but their eyes were fixed on me. Judging me. Pitying me. I was done with it. There was no doubt in my mind that my ties with Vas and his brethren would soon be severed. The string of fate cut short. I wasn't part of the Ivankov *Bratva*, I was simply one wife among many.

Another piece of collateral damage.

But that didn't matter.

My thirst for vengeance wouldn't stop, even if they no longer gave me their backing. Not when my father and brothers would gladly step up to the plate. They'd already promised the manpower in helping to dispatch Christian—just as soon as their own mess was cleaned up.

Leave it to my brothers to find trouble. Our family was good at that, apparently. In the week leading up to the gala, the twins managed to secure themselves a captive after she'd witnessed them take out Jimmy Burlosconi, the man who'd tried to knife me on the dance floor of their club, Clover. The man was a two-bit thug who thought he'd kill me and walk away with a couple million in his pocket.

His mistake.

Now he was lying with the fishes—or something like that. I wasn't exactly sure where the bodies went, and I didn't care to know.

The problem that hung over their heads was that the witness was a reporter and the daughter of one of the most powerful motorcycle gang leaders on the West Coast. Bailey Eriksen was a force to be reckoned with but was probably a bit dick drunk. For someone who'd been kidnapped, she did not seem to be in a hurry to leave, and from the sounds coming from their room at the end of the hall—she was sure as hell enjoying herself.

That was a mental image I could have lived without.

Whatever the three of them got up to in their spare time must have hypnotized her because less than twenty-four hours after she'd been kidnapped by them, she'd avidly agreed to be Kiernan's personal "pet" in order to gain unfettered access to the flesh auction taking place beneath the gala we'd attended.

Technically, she'd agreed because it gave her the opportunity to find her missing friend and mentor, whom we thought might have been sold at auction herself. It was also a chance for me to find out what happened to Maleah. So maybe dick drunk was pushing it.

The newest setback? Bailey was now missing.

Okay, so *missing* was a bit of a stretch. Bailey had been sold. An unfortunate byproduct of Kiernan and Seamus fucking up the operation by not identifying all the key players first. If they would have looked deeper into who ran the auction, Bailey wouldn't have been sold to the very person she'd spent countless hours searching for.

Her friend.

A betrayal of the cruelest kind, and a plan that we believe was put into action long before Bailey ran into my brothers.

Nearly a week had passed since Bailey was taken, and the twins were coming up short. Guilt gnawed at my bones as I thought about the poor girl in some brothel somewhere. I had done nothing to help them find her. Instead, I'd secluded myself in my room, letting the guilt and depression weigh me down. It felt like a betrayal now that the cobwebs of grief had thinned. Time and time again, my family proved to me they were sticking by my side, and here I was, hellbent on avenging a dead man when there was every possibility Bailey was alive.

That was going to change.

As the funeral closed and the attendees filed out of the quiet graveyard, Vas and I remained. For someone who wanted to speak with me, Tomas sure was taking his sweet ass time. Then again, he didn't get out to the West Coast all that often, and it was clear as day from the way they bowed their heads and shook his hand that Matthias's people respected him.

Fuck, this guy was the Russian version of Barack Obama with his smooth swagger and amiable smile.

"Hello, Ava." Well, shit. His voice was something akin to liquid gold. It was deep, his accent slightly thicker than Matthias's, with a rich undertone that made me wonder if the female population of Boston surrendered their wet panties to him as he walked down the street. "I've heard so much about you."

I took his offered hand, giving it a firm shake. Amusement glittered in his eyes as he pulled it away. "Likewise," I told him. "Thank you for making the trip." I might as well keep to the niceties before he throws me to the curb like yesterday's trash.

"Matthias was like a son to me." Tomas's jaw clenched, the muscles of his throat tightened, and he shook with barely contained fury as he gazed over at Matthias's grave. "There is nowhere I would rather be, but I am unfortunately short on time. I have my own problems to contend with back in Boston, and I must be getting back. Why don't we go grab a quick lunch, hmm?"

That wasn't what I was expecting.

Was the man honestly going to make me wait in dreaded anticipation while we got a meal? Didn't that just prolong the time he so adamantly said he didn't have?

"I'm sure we can have the discussion here." My eyes found his, and I held his stare unflinchingly. He searched my face, the lines of his forehead creasing slightly as he took in my tight features and clenched teeth. Could he hear my heart pounding beneath my rib cage as the fear of the looming ax above my head was drug ever closer?

Sweat collected along the back of my neck the longer the silence wore on. He was studying me, this giant man whose aged face still resembled a Greek god.

Tomas was timeless in his three-piece black suit and Armani shoes. His graying brown hair was swept up and back at the top, flanked by slick, shorter sides. His hazel eyes were piercing beneath thick lashes and bushy brows.

Long stubble was spread across his lower face, drawing my attention to his full lips and the sharp cut of his jawline. The resemblance between him and Vas was uncanny. Their resemblance was closer to brothers than father and son.

"No." Tomas's amused smile didn't waver. "This is better discussed somewhere less out in the open, don't you think?"

My brows knitted in confusion, head tilting to the side slightly as I tried to decipher the meaning.

"I don't—"

"Come." He didn't give me the chance to decline his offer or to figure out what the hell was going on. "There's this nice little piroshki shop near to here."

The fucker turned to leave without giving me a second glance. He knew I was going to follow him. I didn't have a choice, and that was the worst part.

"And I thought Matthias was a cryptic asshole," I muttered as I begrudgingly followed Vas's father to his car.

Vas chuckled. "Where do you think he learned it from?" he teased. "They may not look alike, but personality wise Matthias is a carbon copy of my father."

Was.

I resisted the urge to correct him. Matthias was—not is. It wasn't the first time Vas had slipped into present tense when referring to his best friend and former *Pakhan*. I didn't have the heart to reprimand him. It felt wrong to chastise the man who'd lost just as much, if not more, than me. Matthias was my husband, but we'd only been married for a little over a month. Vas had been his best friend and second in command for years. They were like brothers.

"How'd you turn out so normal?" I joked to ease the broiling tension beneath my skin.

Vas lowered the umbrella, shaking out the excess water before he wrapped it up and handed it to his father's driver. "I take after my mother. The only one with a real personality in my family."

"That woman knew how to get herself in a spot of trouble," Tomas cut in with a wink. "She once glued down everything on my desk because I was late for dinner."

"It was your anniversary." Vas rolled his eyes.

"And I sent flowers."

"Which she was allergic to."

"And chocolate."

"Which she hated."

"Yes, I became vastly aware of that when they ended up smeared all over my Armani and Versace suits the next day."

"How long had you been married?"

Vas snorted. He took my hand to help me into the back of the large SUV before taking his seat up front. His father ignored him and settled himself next to me.

"Three years."

I stared at the man, dumbfounded. The driver pulled away from the curb and into the flow of traffic.

"You were married three years, and you didn't know she was allergic to flowers and didn't like chocolate?"

Hell, I was pretty sure Matthias had known my blood type, the kind of toothpaste I preferred, and what deodorant I used before he even got his hands on me.

"It was a..." Tomas hesitated, "strained marriage in the beginning. We were young and stubborn, and neither of us wanted an arranged marriage. Up until that point, she'd never voiced a complaint or stood up for how I initially treated her, but with time, I learned to watch and listen. And she learned to obey."

And there it was. The mafia code for women of made men. Everything always seemed to come back to the one word that demanded so much. *Obey*.

"From what I understand from Matthias, you weren't much for obedience yourself," the man teased, his murky eyes lighting up.

I met his gaze, once again expecting to find anything other than the blatant amusement shining through them.

"I liked to keep him on his toes," I admitted with a shrug,

letting the tension in the vehicle roll away for the short ride. It wasn't long before the driver nosed us into a parking spot conveniently located in front of the piroshki shop. "But if you ask me, he's the one who kept me on my toes. That man ran so hot and cold I needed a thermometer everywhere I went just to detect the change in temperature."

My mind rolled back to all those times. Seemingly caring one moment and inexplicably standoffish the next. Tomas didn't need to know that, though. I let the reference hang in the air between us, refusing to elaborate any further. Not that the Boston *Bratva* leader seemed to care. He gave me a short nod and a knowing smile before he slid gracefully out of the door his driver opened for him.

Taking a moment, I breathed in, letting the air fill my lungs, the fragrant scent of cloves surrounding me before I slowly released it. Vas waited patiently, his brow etched with concern and his gaze softening as I exited the vehicle.

Did he know what was coming? Was he choosing not to warn me? Would he do that? Would he let his father kick me out of their lives without so much as a sliver of protest? He didn't owe me any loyalty, but I hoped we'd gained something akin to friendship since I'd married Matthias.

Only time would tell, I guess.

CHAPTER TWO

For someone so keen to talk to me Tomas, was eerily quiet at the small table we'd been seated at. The owner nearly tripped over himself when we walked in the door. He obviously knew who Tomas and Vas were by the way he smiled, shook their hands jovially, and then cleared out his entire restaurant only minutes later.

Matthias had never taken me anywhere other than the compound. I expected the people there to worship him and his men like gods. They were devoted to their boss, the man who controlled their paycheck and even their lives. But to see how the men were welcomed warmly and enthusiastically by the owner of the shop and his staff left me somewhat stunned and off balance.

I knew the *Bratva* ran this territory, but I'd never realized how well they ran it. Elias ruled with fear, and I often forgot that Matthias refused to employ fear tactics. He took care of his people and the neighborhoods. I pondered on what I knew about how he'd run his territory. Over the weeks leading up to our charade of a wedding, he'd opened up about certain parts of the business. Some he'd told me himself, but I learned most of it from watching and listening.

Now that I thought about it, the name of the shop was Piroshky Piroshky. It took me a minute to put the pieces together, but I remembered Vas saying that Maxim, who was the *Avtorvet*—brigadier—to this area, met with the locals once a week to see what was needed and to hear out their complaints. All of Matthias's *Avtorvets* did this in their own areas, even Leon.

It was one of the reasons the community didn't push back against the *Bratva*. Unlike Dante, who struggled to keep his capos under control. He'd been trying to build a new regime after his father's death, but the sinister heart of the old Cosa Nostra ran strong, and it would take at least another generation before the festering wounds of his organization were healed.

"I'm sorry." I blinked at Tomas. He'd said something, but I was too lost in thought to catch what it was. "I missed that."

Vas chuckled lowly, biting into his piroshki with gusto. Couldn't blame him, the food here was amazing.

"I asked what your plans were going forward."

"My plans?" I quirked my head to the side, brushing the crumbs from my hands on the napkin in my lap before clasping them together in front of me on the table. "What would I have plans for, Mr. Ivankov? I was under the impression I was no longer needed, seeing as my husband is dead. I assumed you were here to bang the gavel of dismissal."

Vas cringed as his father's face darkened slightly. He turned to his son; his eyes narrowed dangerously. "You didn't tell her?" he asked incredulously. Vas cleared his throat uncomfortably.

"I meant to, but between planning the funeral and her

hiding away at the Kavanaughs', there has not been a moment to sit down with her."

My gaze darted between the pair. They really did look a lot alike, but there was a softness about Vas that his father didn't possess.

"Tell me what?" I questioned frustratingly. "Will someone please tell me what the hell is going on?" Their hazel eyes snapped to me.

"How much did Matthias tell you about *Bratva* succession?" Tomas asked. Moving his empty plate aside, he wiped the crumbs from the table and leaned back in his chair, a cup of coffee in his hand.

I shrugged. "He didn't," I admitted. "Not really. Most of what I learned was from the internet. If the *Pakhan* is compromised in any way, his second in command takes the role of leadership in his stead. Or something like that."

Tomas nodded, seemingly impressed with my small amount of knowledge.

"You know," he began wistfully, pausing to take a sip of his drink. "I was sixteen when I started the Ivankov *Bratva* on the streets of Moscow." He chuckled as he recalled the memory. "I only had ten people under my command. One of which was a woman who later became my *Sovietnik*. You see, Ava, I wanted to set a different tone for my organization. For far too long, women were nothing more than second-class citizens in the *Bratva*, with little to no say in how things were run.

"It took a while, but I managed to build up an empire from scratch that saw women in the *Bratva* acquiring higher roles," he continued, and I wondered where this was going.

Was he going to ask me to stay on as a member of the Bratva?

"That's great and everything," I told him dryly. "It's a real leap for feminism, but I don't understand what this has to do with me."

Tomas smirked. "I changed the rules of succession, Ava," he educated. "If the *Pakhan* in question doesn't have a blood heir or hasn't named an un-blooded heir and is married, his role goes to his wife."

Old man say what now?

"Now, there would normally be a bit of muddied waters seeming as how you were married under duress, but Matthias's people have proven today that they are willing to stand by your side," Tomas continued, as if he did not just drop the Hiroshima of all bombs. "And he listed you as the heir in his will, so there's that."

He relayed the information so casually. Like Matthias making me his heir was no big deal. It was as if he'd been expecting it. I knew better. Divorce. That was what Matthias intended for me. Not for me to take control of his empire if he died.

So, I did the only logical thing I could think of. I laughed. Tears fell from the corners of my eyes as I struggled to rein in the maniacal sound that fell from my lips. My shoulders shook, my belly aching from the action. The painful weight that sat on my chest felt suddenly heavier, cracking through to my heart.

The two men at the table remained silent as my laughter continued until the tears and surprise were spent. When I looked back at them, their faces wore mirrored looks of shock and concern. As if they'd never seen a woman have a mini mental breakdown before. What I didn't see was any sign that they were jesting.

Tomas was serious when he'd proclaimed that Matthias had named me as his successor.

I swung my gaze to Vasily. "Did you know about this?" I

asked incredulously, the shock clearly painted across my face like a shattered mosaic. "Have you known this entire time?"

Vas nodded, his throat bobbing with unease as he shifted uncomfortably in his seat. "He named you the successor after you were married."

"And he never changed it?"

Vas shook his head.

Letting out a forced breath, I rubbed at my temples, a headache forming behind my eyes as my irritation and disbelief grew. "I don't understand," I admitted. "Matthias was planning to divorce me. Why would he keep me named as his successor?"

Tomas coughed and turned to his son expectantly.

"Why indeed, Vasily?" His father cocked an eyebrow at him as he brought his drink to his lips. The man scowled at his father, eyes burning like fiery coal.

"He wasn't planning to divorce you, Ava," Vas murmured, his eyes softening as he looked at me. "Yes, Ben drew up the paperwork before..." He trailed off.

"Before what, Vasily?" I hissed at him, my throat clenching as a sob threatened to tear through it. "Before he took Serena to the gala? Before he kissed her?" I let that sink in, noting the shame that crossed his face. "Or maybe it was before he told Liam that as soon as the gala was over, we were finished. That all he needed from me was information."

Vas took in a long breath, his hand running down his face. He let out a frustrated sigh, his jaw working, teeth grinding as he tried to put whatever he was going to say together in his head before he spoke aloud.

"It isn't what you think, Ava," he pressed, but I was done with secrets. Done with the lies. Whatever game Matthias had been playing was over.

It didn't matter anymore.

"Why don't you explain it to your new *Pakhan* then, Vasily," I growled. Tomas choked and spluttered on the coffee he meant to drink. Instead, tears gathered at the corners of his bright eyes as he struggled to breathe while hoarse laughter poured from his lips.

Vas stared at me, a sadness lining his face that I'd never noticed before. His hazel eyes darkened slightly, hands twisting anxiously in front of him. His foot tapped a quiet staccato rhythm beneath the table, his knee bouncing just enough to see.

What was he hiding?

"I can't," he breathed regretfully. "But I can tell you that the whole thing with Serena was an act. It wasn't real."

The corner of my lip turned up in a snarl. "Sure as hell felt real to me."

"And I wish it hadn't."

"If Matthias wasn't eagerly trying to get rid of me and fuck the Jessica Rabbit look-alike, then what did he need her for?"

"Information." Vas swallowed hard, his Adam's apple bobbing beneath the pale skin of his throat. He wasn't lying, but there was more to his story. He was loyal to Matthias, even in death.

"What kind of information?" Didn't mean I wasn't going to try and pry it from him.

"I can't tell you that."

"Gotta say," I breathed out harshly. "You sure are loyal to a dead man."

Vas smirked. "We all are."

Which meant I wouldn't be getting any information from the other men in his circle either. I would be lying if I said all the cloak and dagger shit didn't bother me. It did. Made my skin itch and my stomach burn like acid. Even in death, they were more loyal to Matthias than they would ever be to me.

Not that I expected anything different. Respect and loyalty were earned. Matthias taught me that. And even though we'd been married, and they knew me, had fought for me when my husband thought I betrayed him—I still needed to show them they could rely on me as much as I relied on them.

Silence fell over the table as the three of us sat with our own thoughts. Vasily looked as if he wanted to say more, but his promise to his friend, his *brother*, was holding him back. Out of all the scenarios I went through on how our conversation would go, this was not one I envisioned.

Pakhan.

I was now the most powerful woman in the city. The first female to ever lead a faction of the *Bratva* in mafia history. There was an army at my back who were all just as bloodthirsty to see Matthias's death avenged as I was. Hell, probably even more.

That gave me power.

True power. Something Christian would never have.

I thought back to the horrid night. The night the one I called sister shot the man I'd fallen in love with. The man who'd shown no sign of loving me back. The man who adamantly stated he was incapable of loving me. It was a weakness. He was also the man who'd taken the bullet for me.

He was right. I was his weakness, and I was the reason he was dead.

I shut that shit down real quick.

Kenzi was the reason he was dead.

Kenzi and Christian and all those who plotted to take his empire. She'd been aiming for me, but I wondered now if she knew Matthias would jump in front of me to take the bullet.

Killing me did nothing. Killing the leader of the *Bratva* in Seattle could have potentially destabilized the underground hierarchy, causing chaos and disruption.

Disruptions that would have been easy enough for Christian to slink in and take advantage of, but he'd never be able to hold on to that power. There wasn't enough left of Elias's empire to successfully keep control of the underground. That did not mean he didn't have help.

The man with the silver cane.

My grandfather. Seamus McDonough, the man my brother was named after. Libby had written about him in her diary. *The silver cross cane.* My mother had been a spitting image of him. I was reticent to approach my biological father about my grandfather. So buried in my grief, I never bothered to crack open the book that would soon decipher Libby's rashly written code in the back of her journal.

It meant going back to the penthouse, and I hadn't been ready. I was too cowardly to face the space we once shared. The memories it invoked.

Now, I was more than prepared to face what lay ahead.

"So," Tomas broke the silence. He leaned forward, elbows braced on the table, a small smile tugging at his lips. "What is your plan?"

"Kill them all."

CHAPTER THREE

The funeral had wrecked me, but my conversation with Tomas had done far worse damage over the past week. Everyone was looking to me for answers. Answers I didn't have. There was so much to do on a daily basis that I barely had time to think about plotting revenge. Right now, I was just trying to keep the snakes at bay.

Pakhan.

I was the motherfucking *Pakhan* of one of the most powerful *Bratvas* in the United States, but it all felt too fantastical. Too fake. As if it would come crashing down at any moment. The bastard never told me he had made me his heir.

Fucker probably thought he'd live forever.

News flash, he didn't.

Now I was expected to seek revenge on his behalf. Not that I had an aversion to seeking justice for his death. I'd planned on it long before the nuclear bomb dropped on my head. Exhaling harshly, I quietly stalked down the lower passages that snaked below McDonough's, toward where Seamus had set up an operational center for finding Bailey.

"The old witch herself," my father muttered darkly as I

walked into the room. He was staring at a picture of an older woman talking with Kiernan. Immediately, I recognized her as one of the women who worked for Elias. "Quite the social climber, that one. What did she say to you when you were talking?"

"She knew who I was," my brother Kiernan divulged. "She was asking about Bailey's sale price. I thought she worked for Lina."

"She does." I spoke up from behind them. The three men turned around, surprised to see me standing in the doorway, peering over their shoulders. Being invisible had given me some pretty neat ninja skills over the years. "So does Bailey's ex-fiancé, Drew."

"And you know this because..." Kiernan let the question hang in the air. I smiled at him, the gesture not quite reaching my eyes. "Well, we know Drew works for Christian. His logo is on the side of the containers he was using to ship his cargo."

"All right, that was a gimme," Seamus laughed, lightening the mood. I chuckled, but after the day I'd had, it came out sounding more wounded than I would have liked. Jesus, they had been working down here for the last two weeks trying to find her, and where was I? Trying to control an empire I had no business leading.

I ran my gaze over the board. Shit, maybe they would have found her sooner if I'd been here helping.

"That woman." I pointed at the picture of a woman I recognized. "And that one." I pointed back to the tall woman my father had called an old witch. "Are the ones Elias placed in charge of strip clubs and brothels."

"How progressive of him," Kiernan drawled.

I chuckled darkly. "Elias believed that he'd have less trouble with a woman in charge than a man," I elaborated.

"Said that men think with their dicks, but a woman thinks with her bank account."

My father laughed. "I'm putting that on a T-shirt," he snorted, and I couldn't help the laugh that followed. We spent another hour going back and forth on why Lina would take Bailey in the first place. Kiernan and Seamus believed that Bailey had been set up long before she'd caught them in the alley.

Elias had a history with the two women that went back further than any of us had anticipated, and I dreaded the moment my brothers had to tell Bailey the truth about her mother. In a way, it would have been a relief for her, but there was a darkness to that truth that would taint her forever.

It didn't matter. We were her family now, and that was all that mattered.

Once we all decided on a course of action, we planned into the wee hours of the morning. Sometime in the middle of the night, I brought in Vas and Maxim to assist in our coordinated attack. My men and I would hit Drew at Bailey's old penthouse while the twins and my father took out the brothel where we'd learned Bailey was being kept.

Lina was smarter than her coconspirator. Sarah Eriksen was as dumb as a box of rocks. She'd led us straight to Bailey with her car GPS system backlog. My father told me he took those out of every vehicle he and his men used. They were easy to hack and easy to subpoena in a court of law.

"I'm sorry," I murmured to my brothers as we left the confines of the room to head upstairs for a few hours of sleep before the raid.

"For what?" Kiernan asked, perplexed.

"I should have been here with you sooner," I admitted sadly. "Bailey is important to you, and maybe, if I had helped sooner, she would be back here already."

Seamus, the hugging hippie that he was, wrapped an arm around my shoulders and pulled me tight to his side. "You," he emphasized, "have nothing to apologize for. We know your pain and how hard it is to lose someone you love. The gala was one big fuckup after another. It's our fault we didn't do better research on the attendees or on Lina. Our guts told us not to take her down there, but we ignored them. Plus, I don't think we could have stopped her from going even if we tried."

Kiernan snorted. "She probably would have climbed out the window and gone, anyway," he pointed out, eyes dancing with amusement. "Bailey wanted to save her friend. There was no stopping her once she put her mind to it. No matter how much we tried to dissuade her." He nudged my shoulder and winked obscenely.

Oh gross.

"I think I threw up in my mouth a little."

The twins laughed merrily, and I found myself joining in. God, it felt good to laugh and let go. I hadn't done that since Matthias was shot. Family had a way of healing you, no matter how deep into the darkness you sank.

The building had been easy enough to clear out with our fire department contact, who slipped door to door, warning everyone of a possible hazardous leak. Each floor held two penthouse-style condos, and the one across from Bailey was thankfully vacant.

Looking down, I double-checked the safety on my Smith & Wesson M&P, making sure it was off, before giving Vas the go-ahead. There were only four of us. We didn't need an entire contingent of men for two measly people who were a threat less than zero.

Maxim was posted in front of the door, his gun aimed at the lock, waiting. Vas counted down quietly from three. The man had barely reached one when Maxim shot out the door and Leon kicked it in. The three men created a barrier around me, with Vas taking point at the head of their little V-shaped safety net.

It was frustrating going from being the protected and constantly guarded wife of a mafia boss to being the protected and guarded mafia boss. It was like nothing had changed besides my nameplate.

Oh, I should get one of those.

Wood breaking, followed by a shrill scream, rent the air.

"What the fuck?" That was Drew, Bailey's ex-fiancé. I recognized his voice from the schmoozing he'd done at the gala when he found out my last name was Ward. Matthias had me revert to my maiden name, which was easy enough, since I had never officially changed my last name when I was forced to marry him.

No papers or ID.

Mark was working on that for me just to make things easier. I doubted they would be real, but that didn't matter. As long as I had something, that was what I needed.

"Oh, I could have lived without seeing this," I grumbled, scrunching my nose up at the two naked bodies before me. We'd interrupted sexy time. *Gag.*

None of the men looked happy about it, either.

"Okay, let's get this over with so I can stop having to look at the Amityville horror show before me."

The girl, Brittany, I believed was her name, sniffed the air like she was miffed I had insinuated she was ugly.

I didn't want to insinuate anything. So, I straight out told her.

Vas and my men laughed. She didn't. Neither did Drew, who looked like he was about to wet the bedsheets.

Tilting my head, I brought my gaze to him as I studied him. He wasn't anything special. Average height. Average size. He reminded me more of an underdeveloped college freshman than a man. Then again, I could say that about anyone if I compared them to the hulking muscle standing around me.

"What the fuck do you think you're doing?" It might have sounded demanding and strong if his voice didn't waver like a little bitch.

"I want you to tell me about the money you've been shipping from the Middle East for Christian Ward." Might as well cut to the chase.

"I don't know what the fuck you're talking about, bitch."

A low growl permeated the room, and Drew's eyes widened as my men took a collective threatening step toward him, their lips raised in a snarl. They didn't like him insulting their new boss.

"Do you know who I am?"

Taking his eyes off the surrounding men, he sneered. "I've heard about you," he spat. "Christian Ward's little whore."

I smiled at him, my eyes lighting up as I let out a small giggle.

Then I aimed my gun and pulled the trigger.

The girl behind him screamed, jumping back as Drew howled in pain, clawing at his exploded kneecap.

The two men behind me shared a quick glance, their eyebrows raised in surprise.

That's right, men. There's a new Ava Dashkov in town. And she's the fastest draw in the west.

I really needed to get out of my head more.

Once his screams had died down, I stepped forward, gun aimed at his other kneecap.

"My name is Avaleigh Dashkov," I informed him calmly. His eyes widened at my last name, no doubt understanding the power behind it. The violence. "I'm the new boss in town, and when I ask you a question, I expect you to answer. So, let's try again, shall we? Tell me about the money you've been shipping from the Middle East for Christian."

Without hesitating, he curled his lips up in disgust, shot me a hostile scowl, and hissed, "Fuck you."

He screamed.

The girl screamed.

There went the other kneecap.

"I could do this all day, Drew," I told him, shrugging a shoulder. "You either tell me what you want me to know, or the next bullet hits those family jewels."

Crickets.

"Okay then..." I aimed my gun, finger resting on the trigger when he cried out for me to stop.

"Wait. Wait." He covered his limp noodle dick with his hands. Not that he needed two hands to cover the little gherkin. "Look," he swallowed hard against the fear and pain, tears streaming down his face. "We spoof the ship port numbers, all right? But I don't have anything to do with that. My company just provides the muscle and the containers. That's it."

"You expect me to believe that?" I chuckled mirthlessly.

"It's true, I swear," he pleaded, a desperate, feral look in his eyes.

"How did you get into business with Christian?" That was a fairly simple question. Should have started with that one, he might still have both kneecaps if that were the case.

Not as fun, though.

"His father did dealings with my father," he panted, sweat dripping down his forehead. His eyes were beginning to flutter slightly as the blood loss set in. "I started working with Elias a few years ago when I first started up. He had a man that funded my entire operation."

Now that piqued my interest.

"What man?"

"I don't know," he grimaced. "Some older guy with a cane. Odd accent. Not quite foreign but not quite American either."

"Name." I demanded harshly.

"I don't know!" he wailed.

"Okay." I shrugged as I processed what other information he might have. Nothing came to mind. I pulled the trigger without a second thought, Drew's head exploding over the weeping Brittany, who was kneeling behind him. "Then I guess you're of no further use to me."

I lowered my weapon, letting it settle at my side. Brittany wept, her bottled blond hair a rat's nest, her makeup sliding down her face like a clown who'd been out in the heat. I expected to feel a pinch of remorse at having just killed a man, but it wasn't there. Rather, there was this widespread apathy that settled beneath my skin and calmed the churning fire.

"You fucking whore!" The weeping hag finally spoke, breaking out of the fear she'd imprisoned herself in.

"I'd be careful who you call a whore," I taunted. "Who sleeps with their best friend's fiancé?"

Brittany scoffed. "Please." Her lips turned up in an ugly sneer, her face twisting darkly. "She never had him. We'd had this planned for years with that bitch, Sarah. Sell her and split the profit. Of course that stupid slut had to go and—"

Well, that was enough of that. The words of the viper had begun to bore me, and now she was dead silent. Literally. Her blood and brain matter joined that of the snake of a man she'd had between her dirty thighs.

A match made in hell. Now they would rot there.

"Well, that wasn't part of the plan." Leon sighed, holstering his gun. "Now there are two bodies to clean up."

"Why are you complaining?" Vas quipped as he too holstered his weapon. "It's not like you're the one cleaning it up."

"True."

"Still," Maksim hedged. He was the only one, besides me, who hadn't put his gun away. "We don't normally kill women."

"Eh," Vas shrugged. "Can't say she didn't have it coming."

"But..." Maksim pushed. His shoulders were stiff, jaw clenched tightly enough that I could see the muscles in his throat tightening. He didn't like what I'd done.

"She wasn't an innocent, Maksim," I reminded him sternly. "Do you really believe that if we had let her live, she would have just hidden? No, she would have talked to anyone who would listen. She wasn't some pawn or coerced. That viper was an active, willing participant to kidnapping and selling a girl she duped into being her best friend."

Maksim huffed as he stowed his weapon before he crossed his arms against his chest.

"You aren't judge, jury, and executioner, Ava," he growled. I lifted my head to meet his thunderous gaze. Had he so patiently told this to Matthias, too? Been this forward? I knew they were close, and I had no intention of ruling like Elias did. Through fear. And now, in the comfort of our circle, he could vent his frustrations, but something about it was off. It felt more like he was blustering. Blowing hot air.

"Listen to me, Maksim," I warned him, stepping into his space, my eyes never leaving his. "I don't expect you to agree with all of my decisions. I'd be worried if you did. But let's get one thing straight. I *am* the judge, jury, and executioner here, make no mistake of that. Now, I understand we don't go around killing women and children, and I plan to 100 percent uphold that.

"Unless you come after my family. And then all bets are off. Feel free to air your concerns or file a grievance, but anyone who maliciously and purposefully raises a hand against me or mine will suffer the consequences regardless of gender. Understood?"

The three men smirked, eyes shining as they looked down at me.

"Understood," they all confirmed, laughter in their voices.

Fuckers had been testing me.

"Same go for your sister?" Vas asked after a moment.

I let my gaze slide to his. The warmth of his hazel eyes did nothing to heat the frigidness in my own.

"My sister was murdered the night of my wedding. I don't have another one." I told him as I turned on my heel and strode out the door, almost missing Leon's whisper.

"This is why we should have told her."

What did he mean by that?

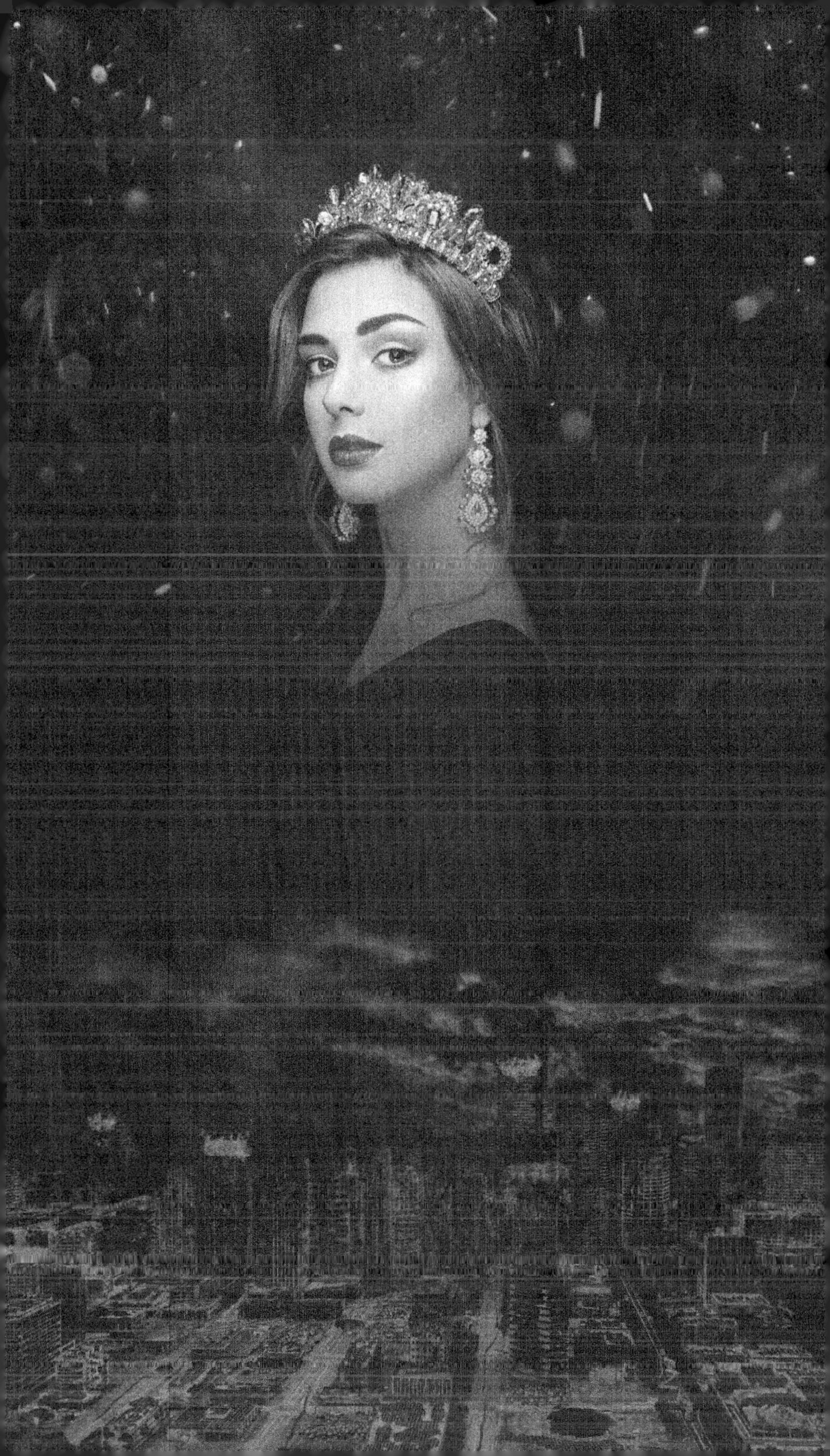

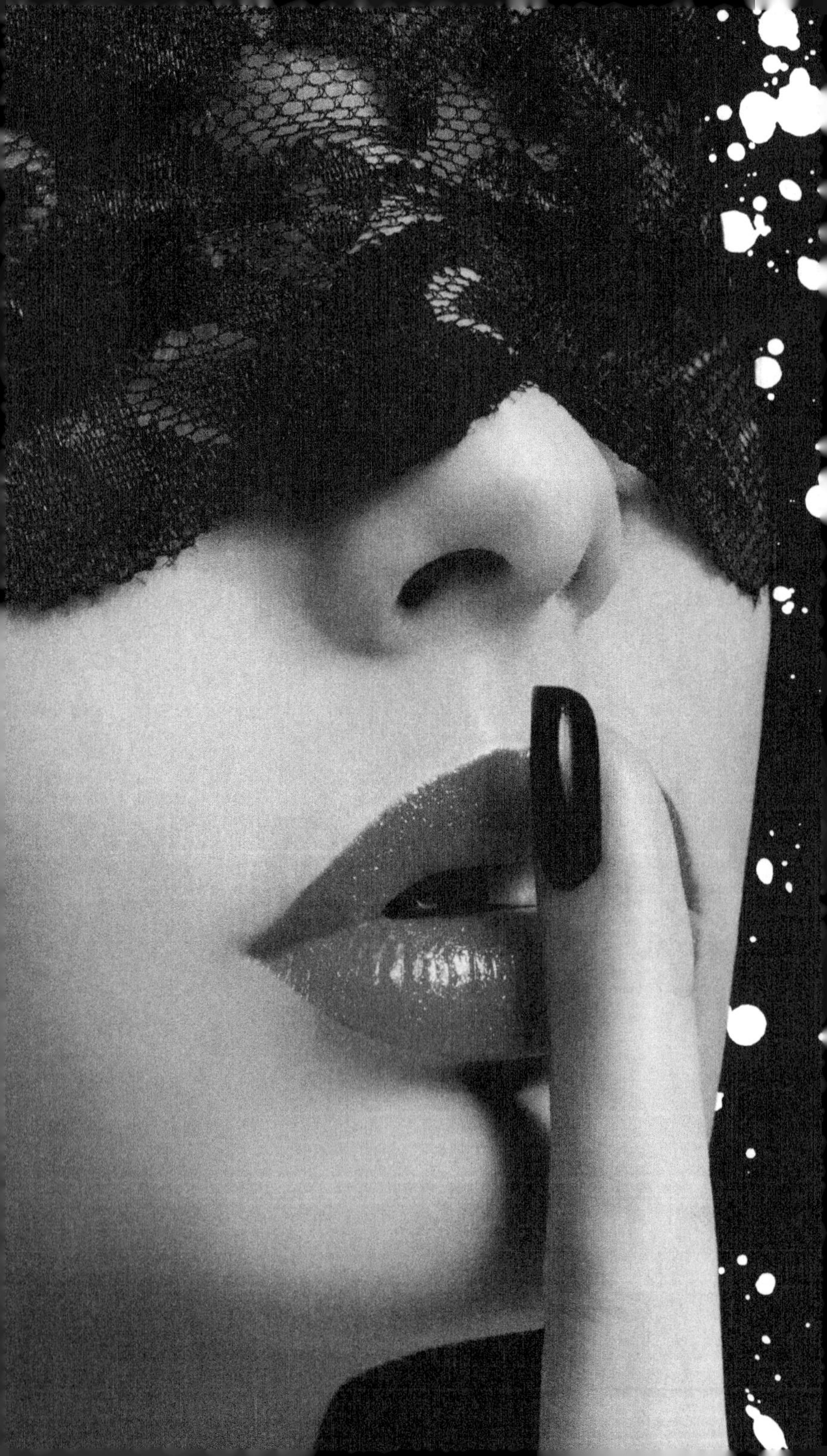

CHAPTER FOUR

I stared down at the numbers written in Libby's journal.

1-3-6
14-3-1
19-1-7-2 (3)

Each number represented a specific part of the book. The page number followed by the paragraph on that page followed by the word in that paragraph. Flipping through the pages at the beginning, I turned to the page labeled as the first. My finger slid gently to the third paragraph and over until it found the sixth worth.

Well.

Easy enough. I repeated the process with the second cipher.

Far.

I could already see where this was going, but wanting to be absolutely sure, I followed the cipher one last time. This one was different. It contained four numbers instead of three and had one in parentheses. So the seventh letter in and two of those three letters made the word, which was 'ago'. Since "ag" made little sense, I went with "go."

Well far go.

Didn't take a genius to know she was talking about the bank. It was simple, and she didn't attempt to obscure the name or make a riddle out of it. No one other than Kenzi would have known what those numbers referred to. You had to have the book to decipher it, and not just any version of *The Hobbit* would have gotten the job done. It needed to be this specific edition.

If it was a bank she was leading me to, that meant that the numbers she listed below were a bank account. 1974762095230091. Were the remaining numbers, 091322, the passcode? Or something else? And what did the hastily scrawled name of *Demeter* mean?

A passphrase?

Ugh. I closed the laptop screen and leaned back in my chair, closing my eyes as I rubbed my temples. Libby could have left clearer instruction. Like what Wells Fargo she was talking, for example. Since there were approximately fifteen in Seattle. If it was just a bank account, then it wouldn't matter which I chose, but if it was a safe deposit box, it would. Luckily, only a handful of Wells Fargos had safe deposit boxes.

"Everything okay in here?"

Cracking an eye open, I looked at my *Sovietnik* and shook my head, letting out a rough breath.

"That bad, huh?" he asked, taking a seat in front of me. We were in Matthias's office. His old office, since it was now mine, but everything in it was still exactly as he'd left it. I couldn't bring myself to change anything. It still smelled like it. The light scent of tobacco hung in the air, mixing deliciously with the warm spiced aftershave he always wore.

"Libby's secret code leads to a Wells Fargo bank," I informed him. "But she doesn't say which one or whether it's an account or a lockbox. Nothing. I've got the account number, but that's it."

"What about the name and the other set of numbers she listed?" Vas questioned. "Any clue what those mean?"

I shook my head. "The six digits could be a passcode." I sighed. "It couldn't be a historical date because it's dated for September of 2022, and it's February."

"What if it's not a date?" he suggested.

"Then it has to be a passcode."

Vas's mouth turned up, and his shoulders shrugged. "Maybe. Maybe not."

"How very clear of you, Vasily," I told him dryly. "Please, be as vague as you possibly can. It thrills me."

Vas grunted his amusement, his eyes shining. "Could it be another cipher?"

"If it is, then it isn't with this book." I gestured to the battered copy of *The Hobbit* on my desk. "There aren't thirteen paragraphs on page nine, and she wouldn't have mixed up the cipher."

The man before me tapped his chin lightly as he contemplated what to say next. "What if it is a date?" he wondered aloud. "What if the numbers are mixed up? Instead of September of 2022, what if it was September of 2013?"

"We'd have to assume that whatever it was took place in Seattle," I pointed out. "There would be too much data to go through if we included every event that happened that year worldwide."

Silence fell over us.

One would think that the six digits were a passcode of sorts. Or a password. However, a password for a bank account wouldn't be simply numbers. It would need to contain letters as well. The passcode theory was applicable, but only if it was for verification. If she had been pointing me to a lockbox, then she would have needed to lead me to a key, not a bank code.

What was Libby up to?

"Here." Vas's deep voice interrupted my thoughts. When I looked up from where my eyes were glued to my desk, he was standing in front of it, holding out a whiskey-filled tumbler. Not my favorite, but I would take it.

"Thanks," I murmured, taking the glass from him. The ice clinking around in the glass sounded heavy in the enclosed space.

"I love how you redecorated," Vas drawled as he looked around. "It's really you." The teasing smile he held at the edge of his lips was infectious. His bright eyes lit up when I smiled at him from behind my glass.

"Couldn't really bring myself to touch anything," I admitted. "There's this...gut feeling I have that says he'll be back. Stupid, I know, but I haven't been able to bring myself to change anything."

"Ava—" Vas began hesitantly.

"Pfft." I waved him off. "I know it's stupid. Just humor me, okay? I'll get around to changing it sooner or later, but right now...right now—" I let out a sigh and shrugged. "I just like how it makes me feel."

"And how is that?"

"Like at any moment he'll walk through that door."

Except he wouldn't.

He was dead.

Vas sighed. It was deep and sad. Leaning back in his chair, his ankle crossed over his opposite knee, he said, "I know what you mean. I've been going through the reports on his laptop and feel like I'm snooping."

"What reports?" I asked curiously.

"We keep all of our dealings on an encrypted black box that is nestled just inside the laptop," Vas explained. "Unless someone took the laptop apart piece by piece, no one would ever know it was there. Plus, it's linked directly into a program. So as long as you insert the right username and passcode, it leads you to the box. Any other combination will take you through the dummy program. It allows the operation to keep everything off paper as well as make sure there isn't any electronic trace either."

That had me stunned. It was pretty advanced thinking for the mafia. Not even Hollywood movies had come up with that.

"When you say dealings," I questioned, leaning forward in my seat. "Do you mean like the *Bratva's* black book?" Vas nodded.

Snapping my fingers excitedly, I stood, the chair rolling out from beneath me and hitting the shelves at my back. "That's it," I exclaimed, rushing from the room.

"What's it?" Vas trailed behind me, hot on my tail.

"Libby mentioned snagging a few of Elias's black books from his office when you took her back for some of her things," I told him, pushing the door to Libby's old room open. "I went through her room, and I never found anything."

"I can sense a *but* coming." Vas sighed.

"But—" I kept going, ignoring his snide remark. "If you all managed to think about having everything electronically, so would Libby. She was nothing like Mark, but Libby knew her way around a computer. What if she translated everything electronically and locked it up?"

The lightbulb went off in Vas's brain. His shoulders straightened, and a feral smile crawled across his face. "Damn, she was smart."

"No doubt."

Opening her bedside drawer, I pulled out the sleek black laptop she was given when she first arrived so she could still complete her schoolwork while they hunted down Elias and Christian.

I flipped open the top, and the laptop whirred to life.

"She didn't have it locked?" Surprise tinted his voice. "Who doesn't lock their laptop?"

I shrugged. "Someone who has nothing to hide that isn't already secure?"

It made sense. Libby would have only ever had her schoolwork on the computer, which she completed from the safety of the penthouse after Vas had her switched to online classes. She wouldn't have needed to lock her laptop. But she would have protected the information she copied over from Elias's black books.

The question was—where would she put imperative information on her laptop? A subdrive was possible, but I wasn't seeing anything popping out at me other than her normal school documents. I thought back to what I read in her journal. The hastily scrawled numbers and name. I assumed Demeter was a username I would enter to access a specific file, but there wasn't anything in her files that didn't just open. No passwords were needed for any of them.

Where the fuck did she put it?

"What if it isn't to a file?" Vas asked. "What if it's to a site or even another account on the laptop?"

"Worth a try." I logged out of the current account to get to the main screen. Nothing. There wasn't even an option to log in to another one. "Wait." The lightbulb clicked. The dawn was rising. It was all coming full circle. "What was Demeter's daughter's name in the Greek myth?"

"Um," Vas thought for a moment before the lightbulb dinged. "Persephone."

"Persephone's Web." We both said aloud. Persephone's Web was an underground chat room and dark web encryption hosting platform. Unlike most of the dark web, Persephone's Web was created to help people in need find and store vital information on taking down organizations like Elias's. Libby and I had learned about it from Mark before I pulled a Houdini and disappeared in the dead of night under Elias's nose.

Persephone was a legend. Having exposed more sex trafficking rings and shady government officials and deals than any law enforcement agency in the world. It was a safe space for victims or families of victims to find justice without all the expenses.

My fingers moved lightning fast, clicking back into Libby's primary account. I had missed it. There had been a small black symbol that blended in with the swirling of her wallpaper in the top right corner of the screen. It was Demeter's symbol in Greek mythology. Flush stalks of grain.

I double clicked.

And waited with bated breath as the rainbow icon of the mouse shifted and turned.

"Yes!" I grinned broadly when a subscreen popped up before my eyes, requesting a password. Entering the digits I saw in her journal, I pressed enter.

Bingo.

"Holy fucking shitballs, Batman," Vas murmured under his breath as file after file popped open on the screen.

"I really hope she labeled these," I muttered. There was enough data on the screen that it would take weeks to sift through.

"Well, that's why there is more than one of us." Vas winked at me and stood. "Let's get this back to the compound. We can get the others to help."

The others.

Maxim and Nikolai had been scarce since I took up the mantle of *Pakhan*. Dima was apparently out of the country on personal business, and Leon was busy helping build alliances with my Uncle Dante and the Cosa Nostra.

I thought.

Or he was out assassinating them. Vas hadn't made it super clear.

At this point, I couldn't care less.

The drive to the compound took longer than normal thanks to the heavy flow of traffic. I hadn't been back since the first time Matthias had taken me here, and I missed it. Mark's smiling face greeted me as I stepped out of the vehicle. Vladmir, my driver and secondary guard, nodded at me as I closed the door to the SUV and led me up the stairs to the underground bunker.

He was tall and muscled. The pristine white dress shirt he wore was stretched tightly over his chest, the seams straining at his broad shoulders. I was waiting in silent anticipation for the buttons to suddenly burst off. His accent was thick and deep, his skin covered in tattoos from the Cyrillic Russian letters on his knuckles to the ink scrawled up his neck.

Vladmir was one intimidating mother fucker, and if he wasn't on my side, I might have shit my pants when I first met him. No joke.

"I'll wait here, ma'am." His *W* sounded like a soft *V*.

"Ava," I corrected him. The big man blushed, the red creeping up his neck.

"Ava."

Vas shot me a disapproving look, but I simply winked and

walked right past him into the somber darkness of the tunnels that ran beneath the compound. A lump of sadness threatened to emerge when my thoughts turned back to the last time I was here with Matthias. We'd been a team then, taking down Elias's port access and bringing his illicit dealings into the light.

We'd been in a bubble those few weeks that were later shattered by my perceived betrayal.

I wanted him to be here with me. I wanted to rule together, side by side. That was all I had ever wanted from him. What a fairytale that had been. A dream that would never be reached. A goal that could never be achieved.

There was only me to lead, and just the mere thought of that darkened the surrounding colors.

"You doing okay?" Mark questioned hesitantly while we walked. I nodded and turned to face him, a smile on my face that didn't quite reach far enough. Skepticism burned deeply behind his eyes. He didn't believe me. "If you ever need anything..." He let the invitation hang in the air between us.

"I know," I assured him. "Thank you."

He took a deep breath and nodded, accepting that I wouldn't be spilling my guts to him anytime soon. Emotions weren't new to me, but growing up, I had learned to limit them, hide them, secure them away so they couldn't be used against me.

Show fear, and they made me more afraid. Show pain, and they reveled in increasing it by tenfold. The rage was beaten out of me, the defiance whipped from my body, sadness had been starved, and happiness barely existed enough for them to bother with. Matthias had been the first person I truly opened myself up to emotionally. He took them and shaped them into armor for me. Carved weapons from the very things that had burned me, drowned me, and carved me into pieces.

"There she is." Nikolai stood from his seat, a toothy grin cracking his normally grumpy exterior. "Welcome back, ma—Ava." The cold glare I gave him stopped the formalities dead in their tracks.

"Hello, Nikolai." I beamed back at him and took the chair he offered me. "Maxim." I nodded at the burly Russian.

"Ava."

"Let's get started." Vas inclined his head to Mark. A moment later, the screens before us were filled with the files Libby had been collecting on Persephone's Web.

"So," Mark began. "I've been digging through these files for the last two hours, and I have got to say—Libby was a fucking genius. Not only did she use Persephone's servers as a way to hide the files, but she also encrypted the hell out of them. The NSA and CIA would be proud."

"I wonder who taught her how to do that," I mused teasingly.

"Surely you don't think I would teach her such naughty things." Mark held his hands up in a gesture of innocence, but the smirk on his face spoke to his guilt.

"Moving on," Vas grunted. Mark winked at me before turning back to the screen. Cheeky bastard.

"I was able to decrypt a good amount of them, but there are a few my program is still working through due to the amount of data stored within them," he continued. "From the size of the files, I would favor a guess that they are probably MP4s." He turned his gaze to Nikolai and Maksim. "For the vintage models in the class, that means they're videos."

"Fuck you," Nikolai growled, throwing his pen as hard as he could at the hacker. Mark laughed and danced out of the way of the flying object. "We're not that old, you fucker."

"Could have fooled me," Vas murmured beneath his breath. I laughed, tears gathering at the corners of my eyes when Nikolai threatened to dismember Vas's family jewels with a rusted spoon.

"Okay. Okay." I wiped at my eyes. "What have you got from the ones that have been decrypted?"

Mark's smile turned feral.

"Well, your instincts about your grandfather are spot on," he told me. "Seamus McDonough has been a naughty senior citizen, and I am not just talking about him running the Irish in Boston. On top of the usual drug and weapon distribution, he has invested a huge sum of money in ground transportation companies over the last ten years secured by—"

"Knightman Security."

"Exactly." He nodded. "Five points to Hufflepuff."

There went the beer I was about to drink. Right out my nose and onto the polished wooden surface before me.

The room roared with laughter while I struggled to relearn how to breathe. *Assholes.* The lot of them. My stomach clenched and my chest ached as I joined the raucous strings of hysterics going on around me.

Times were hard, and war was looming on the horizon. We had suffered losses our hearts could barely cope with. Blood would be spilled on both sides going forward, there was no getting out of that, but that didn't mean we couldn't enjoy life while it lasted.

No one in this room could even begin to guess the outcome of our battle with Christian and the unforeseen puppet master who pulled his strings. We could hope that we came out on top, but there would never be a guarantee.

All we could do was pray to see the sunrise tomorrow as we watched the sunset tonight.

Taking these moments in was vital. Without hope and

laughter, we would be nothing more than zombies trudging through life unaware. Broken. Dead. It was the little things that kept us going and kept us fighting. The small smiles and comradery. The chuckles and games and beers. It was knowing we had a family to fight for. To survive for.

We all needed someone or something to live for, and the men at this table were mine. Liam and the twins were mine. The need to see them come out on top of this was greater than my thirst for revenge. I would sacrifice myself before ever sending them to die for me.

My gaze traveled to the lit-up faces of the men who stood by my side, and for the first time since I'd met Matthias, I understood the weight he once carried on his shoulders. These men and the many other men and women who followed him were his responsibility. They had families and friends. They were sons and daughters. Mothers and fathers. Nieces and nephews. They had people to go home to each night.

Now, they were mine to protect.

"Settle down. Settle down." Nikolai chuckled, tears streaming down his face at the impression of Harry Potter Vas had been trying to mimic. His British accent was horrendous, and the stitch of laughter in my side was worsening.

Still—on to business.

It took at least another ten minutes before the overgrown men-children were ready to start the meeting again. Another round of beer was handed around, and we got back to work. The sudden breakdown was forgotten, like it was a distant memory.

"Most of the files that have been decrypted involve finances," Mark informed us as he flipped through the screen. "It will take me a few days to sort through the numbers and associate them back to dealers and cargo, but it isn't an impossible job."

"Did you find anything on Maleah?" My heart flipped at the thought of finding my best friend. Archer had lied to me when he said he knew who Maleah had been sold to. Christian told me the truth died with Elias, but I refused to trust his words. Even if Archer had lied, Elias would have kept some kind of record of the sale.

I hoped.

Mark's lips turned down, and he shook his head. "Nothing, I'm afraid." His tone was grim, his eyes darkening. "If he kept a record of where she went, he didn't list it outright."

It was worth a try.

"I did, however, find a reference to your sister."

My forehead puckered. "Libby?"

"No." Mark swallowed hard, his Adam's apple bobbing beneath the skin of his throat. "Kenzi."

"Was it her college tuition bill paid with drug money?" I sneered, not caring even one iota about the sister who'd betrayed me. "Because I couldn't care less."

"No," Mark snapped. My gaze snapped up to meet his. His light eyes were swirling with barely contained irritation. They bored into mine, frigid and cold. "It told me she'd been sold."

That was news to me.

"Impossible." My lip turned up in disgust. "Libby talked to Kenzi almost daily."

"For how long?" Vas turned to me. Not him, too. He couldn't possibly be thinking that Elias had sold her. Shooting and then blowing up my husband, then taunting me about it didn't exactly scream *captive*.

"I don't know." I threw up my hands, exasperated. "Five

or so minutes. Libby always said she sounded rushed. Said she was busy."

"And you never found that odd?" Maxim butted in. Fucker was against me, too. "Twin sisters who were hardly ever separated, always had time for each other no matter what, and suddenly one of them can't find the time? That doesn't sound odd to you?"

Of course it did. I wasn't an idiot, but I had chalked it up to Kenzi finally being free. Without Elias or Christian to dictate her every move, she'd found a chance at having a real life, and I wouldn't have blamed her for not wanting to be dragged into it again.

"If Elias *sold* her"—the sarcastic air quotes I put around that word should win an Oscar—"then how did she end up becoming the next American Sniper? Did he send her to assassin school?"

They all exchanged a look I didn't like. It was the kind of look that meant they were holding something back. They knew something about Kenzi, and that pissed me the hell off.

"Someone start telling me what the fuck is going on, or so help me god, I will empty every single bottle of alcohol here and in the penthouse."

Threatening to lop their heads off wouldn't have gotten them talking as fast as they were about to. They knew me too well. I didn't believe in the threat of death or dismemberment as proper motivation, but that didn't mean I couldn't make their lives miserable, and they knew it.

"Elias made a note in one file under Kenzi's name," Mark blurted out, breaking the stagnant surprise of my sudden threat. "I found the file under her social security number."

"Okay..." Talk about drawing out the punch line.

"Did you ever hear Elias talk about something called the Chameleon Agency?" Nikolai asked from his seat two chairs

SHATTERED EMPIRE

down. He was dressed casually tonight in a pair of black jeans and a fitted black tee. Then again, it was normally Leon who dressed to the nines, even for something as simple as movie night.

Elias had never mentioned that name. Not in front of me, at least. Who would want to? That name was horrible.

Shaking my head, I waited for him to elaborate.

"From what we've been able to gather, the Chameleon Agency is responsible for more than seventy-five percent of trafficked humans in the US and ten percent worldwide."

Jesus, that was a startling amount.

"We think that, until recently, they've been slinking in the shadows." Maksim leaned forward on his elbows. "Slowly building their empire underground. Most likely, their operation is dissected into multiple parts so that if one sector goes down, it doesn't affect the entire operation."

"Like terrorist cells." That made sense. Many terrorist cells operated on a similar premise so that one cell couldn't corrupt another. Most terrorist cells had an overseer. One person or a group of people who knew each and every operation. They were the only ones to know the final plans. It was easier to sacrifice pawns that way.

"Exactly like a terrorist cell." Vas smiled approvingly. "We think each cell has their own agenda. One cell might be tasked with retrieving the cargo. Another cell might be tasked with selling at auction, etc."

That was both disturbing and disgusting.

"What does this have to do with Kenzi?" It took everything in me to say her name without sounding like a complete bitch.

Vas licked his lips nervously and took a deep, calming breath before speaking. "We believe Elias sold Kenzi to the Chameleon Agency, who then sold her to another operation

53

that buys and trains women and men and even children to assimilate and assassinate."

What kind of bullshit was this? It was so far-fetched that I could almost believe it.

"This isn't a fucking Natasha Romanoff movie, Vas." My voice pitched higher, and I pushed back my chair as I stood. "That is some Red Room bullshit."

Mark snorted. "Funny, that's what"—Vas shot him a nasty glare, and Mark coughed uncomfortably—"that's what I said when I found out."

"How else do you explain her sniper skills?" Vas pressed, his gaze settling back on me. What the fuck? Was there something they were keeping from me? More fucking secrets. This was ludicrous. Did they honestly believe that my sister was *La Femme Nikita* or *Kill Bill*? Kenzi barely stood up for herself, and violence made her sick. "Knowing how to blow up the ambulance? Get past what you knew about her. You haven't seen her in three years, Ava. That is a lot of time for someone to change."

Three years.

That was how long it had been? It didn't seem like that much time had passed since she left for college at sixteen. The nerd graduated before everyone else and bounced her ass out the door to college like there was no tomorrow.

Had she been sold, or was she a willing participant?

Why?

What did Elias think he had to gain?

"Do you know who she was sold to?"

"It's a place called the Dollhouse." Mark switched the screen again. The image that appeared was of a stunning woman in her late forties or early fifties with pinched red lips and a sharp face. Her gray hair was swept back in a bun that rested at the nape of her neck, and in her hand was a cane.

A cane with a silver cross.

"A covert underground training facility that no one has ever been able to find. That was all I was told until I found these documents that listed the name of the woman buying up her unwilling recruits. Madam Therese."

That was a name I did know.

"I know her." All eyes turned back to me. "I mean," I hesitated. "I've never seen her until now, but Bailey said her name. She said that before she was ushered on the stage, they let that woman backstage to pick from the lineup before they were sold. The only reason she didn't pick Bailey was because she'd already been sold. Her entire bid was a farce."

Nikolai leaned forward, his powerful jaw clenching tightly. "What else did she say about what happened?" If there was anyone who hated those who forced others into killing and fighting for a living, it was Nikolai. Matthias once told me that he met Nikolai in an underground fight ring in Moscow. He was a willing participant in the fights. Nikolai was not. If he ended it too quickly and didn't give a show, he would starve. Drag it out too long? He would be punished. Lose? Losing wasn't an option. Each fight was to the death.

"Uh," I thought back to what Bailey told me, "her accent was different. A soft European, but not Russian. Same with the men she was with. She said they sounded almost German, but softer, like they hadn't been there in a long time and their accents had started to fade."

"What else?" he prodded.

"Two of her assets went rogue, which was why she was getting the new women from a sex auction," I recalled. Then it hit me. "And that Ward provided the best assets."

I was going to be sick.

Elias had sold his daughter into being an assassin, and Christian was taking up that mantle to provide capable women. That meant he wasn't just grabbing up homeless women and prostitutes like he did for the sex auctions. No, he was grabbing up women from their everyday lives. Elias had sold Kenzi because she was of no use to him. Without the ability to bear children, he couldn't make an alliance. Which meant that Christian was searching for and taking women just like Kenzi. Barren. Unable to conceive.

Shit.

Then there was Madam Therese's cane. It was a replica of the cane my grandfather had with him at the gala. I might have chalked it up to being a coincidence—here were plenty of silver cross canes out there in the world to buy—except for one small detail. The tiny emblem that was carved into the wood of the cane just below the knob at the top.

That crest had been on Seamus McDonough's cane as well. It had also been stamped on the paperwork that listed my mother as being sold. Elias never ran the trafficking rings.

Seamus McDonough did.

My own grandfather possibly had my mother kidnapped and sold.

And he had help because there was one other place I had seen that emblem, and if I was right—I might never be forgiven.

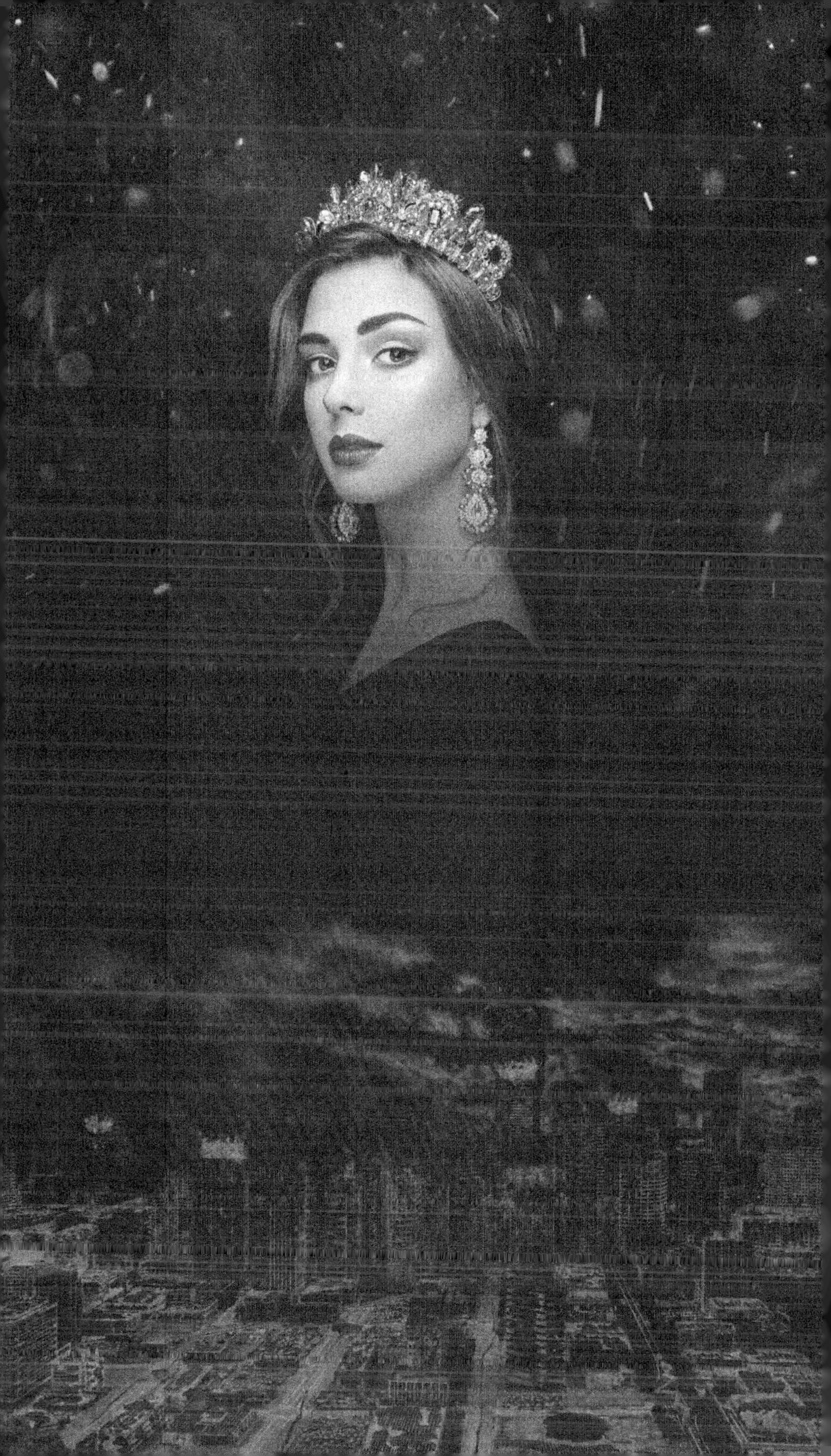

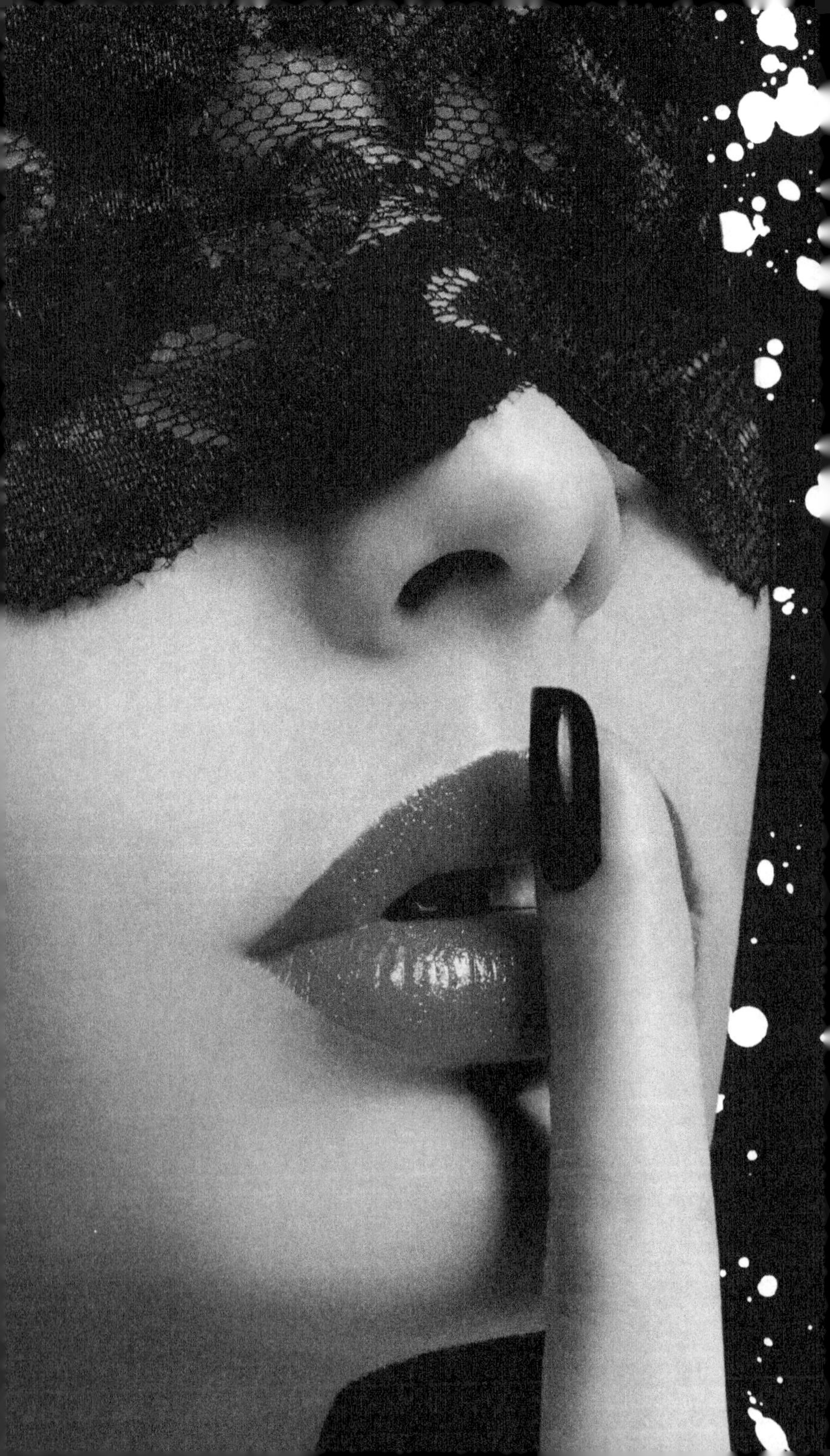

CHAPTER FIVE

The day had faded into a shady night. The cold breeze wrapped around me, seeping into the wool of my coat and the thick hide of my boots. I needed a break from the confines of the bunker. The walls were closing in on me, each new layer of information pushing them that much closer.

I had suspected on numerous occasions since Libby's funeral, but it wasn't until Mark had shown me undeniable proof that it sank in.

How could she keep such a thing a secret?

Fuck.

It drove me bat shit crazy thinking of my sister feeling that she needed to keep such an important thing to herself. The revelation would have shattered her world. I know because when I learned of my true parentage, it had done the same to me.

Libby was there for me when I learned the truth.

She was alone when she discovered hers.

Dante Romano was the twins' biological father.

Had Elias known? Is that why he'd so easily sold Kenzi?

Kenzi.

Just thinking her name caused the grip on my sore and battered heart to tighten painfully. It felt as if someone had wrapped a tourniquet around it and just kept tightening and tightening. Sooner or later, it would explode under the torturous pressure until nothing remained but the cold, dark abyss.

"Gonna freeze my balls off out here," Vas mumbled, stepping through the open doorway that separated the tunnel system from the forest that surrounded it.

"You didn't have to follow me out here."

"Pfft." Vasily snorted through his nose. "I didn't follow you," he insisted. "I love being out here in the cold. Reminds me of Russia. So nice...and cold. Freezing."

"I get it," I deadpanned. "It's cold."

Vasily shivered dramatically. "So cold."

I couldn't help but smile at his attempt to cheer me up, but it didn't lighten my soul like it normally would have. There was too much weighing it down. So many secrets.

"Do you think he knows?"

Vas didn't have to ask who I was talking about; he'd been in the same room as me when Mark dropped the bomb.

"I would be surprised if he didn't at least suspect," Vas admitted.

"All this time and I never suspected that anyone other than Elias was their father," I breathed. I thought back to everything I could remember about the twins from the first time I came to live with them. If Elias knew, he hid it well.

"No more secrets," I whispered to him, the bleak, silent dawn of the early morning wind carrying my words like a promise. "I mean it, Vas. I'm done with it all."

Vas hesitated, his face contorting painfully. "There are things I won't betray, Ava."

I scoffed. "Like where Dima is?"

Vas let out a frustrated sigh and looked heavenward, as if praying for patience. "He's on an assignment. I told you that."

"An assignment that you can't tell me about," I pointed out. "Your *Pakhan*."

"I made a promise to—"

"A dead man." I didn't let him finish. "You made a promise to a man who is now rotting six feet under, and as much as I admire your loyalty, I need to know what goes on in *my* operation."

Vas smirked. "This has nothing to do with the *Bratva*. It's a personal thing."

"Then why can't I know about it?"

Vas shrugged. "There's no need for you to."

"Just so you know," I told him. "I'm picturing your sudden demise in ultra 4k right now."

"Whatever helps."

His nonchalance was going to get him a bat to the back of the head. Or pushed off a cliff.

"What about Leon?"

"With the Cosa Nostra," he replied simply.

"You didn't think to tell me one of my men is working with my former uncle?"

"I said Cosa Nostra."

What the fuck? "Yeah." The look I shot him was somewhere between "duh, you dumbass" and disbelief. "You do not remember that Dante is the head of the Cosa Nostra in Seattle?"

Vas snorted in amusement. "He wishes. Dante is the head of the American Mafia, not the Cosa Nostra."

Huh?

"They're the same thing."

Vas's forehead raised, and he quirked an eyebrow at me. "No, they are not."

"Yes." I nearly stomped my foot in protest. "They are."

Vas chuckled and ran his hand through his mussed hair. His manbun had fallen out at some point, and now his hair hung just below his shoulders in beachy waves most women would kill to have.

"Cosa Nostra is the Sicilian mafia," he said. "They operate in the US directly from Sicily. Most of the members aren't US citizens and travel back and forth, operating on both grounds."

When I said nothing, he kept going.

"The American Mafia are the descendants of the Cosa Nostra," he continued. "They no longer have direct ties back to Sicily and operate on an independent base. American Italians, basically."

Well, shit.

"You still have a lot to learn, Ava." Vas smirked. "You may have grown up with Elias and heard his bits and pieces of the business, but that doesn't mean you know this world."

"Why is Leon with the Cosa Nostra?"

His smirk disappeared, replaced by a dangerously handsome Cheshire grin. "Can't tell you that."

I really stomped my foot that time, my arms crossing against my chest as I stared up at the six-foot Russian with a petulant frown that would rival any toddler's. If there was a competition, first place prize would be mine.

"I'm your boss."

Vas shrugged. "True."

"You can't keep secrets from me about my own men."

Vas's mouth tugged downward, as if he was thinking about what I told him.

"You don't need to know about it."

"Vasily!" God, I sounded like a toddler who hadn't been given her morning snack.

Vas smiled, the expression lighting up his eyes as he stared down at me. Suddenly, he patted the top of my head softly and winked.

"You're just so adorable when you get worked up."

"Ugh!" I groaned in frustration, swiping at his hand. "Stop that."

Vas laughed, the sound easing the tension of the night. I loved that about them. The men who had stood with Matthias for years and offered unconditional loyalty. They never came across a situation where they couldn't laugh or find some form of merriment. Even at the expense of their own humiliation. But mostly at others'.

"Sorry." The look on his face told me he was anything but.

"Sorry enough to tell me about Dima and Leon?"

"Nope." He popped the word dramatically before he turned to stroll back inside.

"Dammit, Vasily." I growled as I followed him, the sound of his laughter echoing off the tunnel walls warming the bitter cold that had begun to set in.

He was holding himself back again.

The monster inside. The one that told him to take me and fuck me until he'd proven to me who owned me.

Him. Heart and soul.

It was foolish of me to give him so much when I doubted I would get a return on my investment. Sometimes that was just how life played its cards.

"Ava." My name was a pained groan on his lips. His voice thick, eyes darkening as he stared into mine. Conflict danced across his stormy gray irises like clouds just before the rain.

I touched his lower lip with my thumb, surprised at how

soft it was, so different from the pleasant roughness of his three-day scruff. Matthias didn't wince or pull back as I gently caressed the split on his lower lip. He was a beast after a battle and wired from the adrenaline rushing through his system. But I didn't care.

I wanted all of him.

He was watching me carefully. Looking for signs of unease or apprehension. He wouldn't get any of that from me.

Lacing my hands behind his neck, I whispered my plea. "Just touch me, Matthias. Don't think."

I rested my ear against his defined chest and listened to the steady, dependable beat of his heart as I waited for him to make his move.

My patience was rewarded when he placed one hand on my hip so he was holding me, his fingers hesitant as he squeezed me tightly, his fingertips digging into my flesh, thumbs grazing the waistband of my pajama shorts. He pressed me forward, gently, as if he was afraid he would break me.

I wasn't so easy to break.

I let the line of my body meet his, and even through his all-consuming warmth, a shiver bubbled down my spine, my nipples hard against the thin fabric of my silken top.

He wasn't moving nearly fast enough for me. Finally, when I could no longer stand the anticipation and tension that wound tight around us, I leaned on the tips of my toes and brought his head down so I could press my lips against his.

Matthias growled low in his chest, the vibrations running straight to my already soaked core.

With a burning need and deep, unsatiated hunger, he devoured my mouth with his. Taking control.

"This isn't going to be slow, Red." His gravelly voice, low in my ear, hardened my nipples further until I was sure they

would tear right through my silken top. "I'm going to fuck you, and you're going to take it like the good girl you are."

Breathless and wanting, all I could do was nod.

"Words, Krasnyy," he warned.

"Yes," I whispered breathily.

Desire pooled in his eyes. Oh, he liked that.

In mere seconds, he had me stripped of my flimsy pajamas. Hands on my waist, he twisted me, and my stomach hit the black glossed lacquer of our dresser. He forcefully bent me over the pristine wood, my chest coming down on its top, scattering the few trinkets decorating it.

His hand connected with my ass, and I let out a long, sultry moan.

"Yes, what?"

Biting my lower lip, I remained silent.

Another smack, and then another.

"Yes, what, Red?"

"Yes, sir." I gasped when his hand came around to pinch my clit.

"Good girl." I preened under his praise.

Matthias entered me with zero hesitation and tenderness. I cried out at the force of his aggressive thrust, but he didn't stop, and I didn't want him to.

He was savage and unrestrained as he thrust in and out of my wet heat, filling me wholly and completely.

His hand buried itself in my hair and pulled, eliciting a whimper from my lips as my back was forcibly bowed, the move pushing him deeper inside me.

"Matthias." I cried out his name as the sharp pain of his unrelenting thrusts drove through me harder and rougher. Could a pussy be bruised? Was that a thing? If it was, I was sure as hell going to have one tomorrow. "I want to feel all of you."

The pain had begun to fade into a steep euphoria. Unadulterated desire clenched inside me, the coil in my belly tightening more and more.

His free hand snaked around to my throat, cutting off my air as he used me for his own pleasure. I wanted him to use me to work off the devil lurking underneath his skin. The one he often tried to hide.

He'd once told me I didn't need a knight in shining armor. He was right.

I needed a monster, and as the sharp edges of bliss rolled through my veins, so potent I could barely think, I knew he was right.

Rest for me was fitful that night as I lay in the bed Matthias and I had truly bonded in. It was the place he and I both put everything on the table. Like the day he told me that I never needed a prince charming. That a monster would do.

He was my monster.

A monster I would do anything to get back. Every night was the same. Visions of him dancing through my dreams. Memories of our time together. Each time I woke with my hand between my legs, I wondered if there would ever be anyone else, or if I was doomed to lust after a man buried six feet under.

A soft reminiscent sigh fell from my lips as I pushed away the fading desire left by my dreams and readied myself for the day. There were several files that still needed to be decrypted, but Mark had made headway on hacking into the Wells Fargo mainframe to find out the owner of the mysterious bank account number.

Bank account numbers were assigned based on availability and branch locations. The sixteen-digit account number originated at a branch based in Boston. A creeping sensation slithered up my spine when he informed me of the account's origins. There was only one person I knew who would have a bank account that originated in that city.

My grandfather.

Libby had done her research into Seamus McDonough not long after she had encountered him with Elias. The dates go back nearly a year. Right after I ran away. Her notes stated that she suspected we were somehow related.

The most disturbing part?

My sister had managed to link him back to my mother's abduction.

Unable to acquire Katherine Moore's case number. Managed to hack crime scene photos, but the evidence has obvious signs of tampering, as does the coroner's report. There are things that aren't lining up, and they all lead back to the man with the silver cross cane. Detective on case

Full stop.

It was her final note on the subject, and it wasn't even finished.

"Have we gotten any packages in from the Portland police?" I asked Maksim. He was usually the one who dealt with deliveries.

"Nyet," he answered in Russian. They had taken to saying small words in Russian here and there to assist me in learning the language. A small step, Vas had said, to help me connect with the men and women I commanded.

Not that all of them spoke Russian. There were more than a few Italians and Greeks in the mix, too.

"*Spasiba*," I murmured, dejected at still not having the shipment the woman promised me. It had been nearly three weeks since she told me she would send the documents, and there was nothing. When I tried calling the precinct again, they told me she wasn't in. Vacation or something like that.

I was calling bullshit.

"What did you order?" Vas queried, his eyes not moving from his cell phone as Maksim drove through the compound and away from the administration building.

"Case file and evidence from my mother's murder," I admitted with a sigh. "She was supposed to send it three weeks ago, and now she's on vacation."

"Stinks of something foul."

I nodded my head in agreement.

"She mentioned that there were some big names who had a hand in my mother's case file." I thought back to the phone conversation I'd had with her. "She didn't say who. Just that the detective on the case, Jonny Morelli, was as dirty as they come."

"Why would they send you the files on an open case?"

"According to her, the case was closed."

"Did they ever find out who did it?" Maksim eyed me through the rearview mirror.

"Well, no."

Now that he pointed it out, I don't remember anyone being arrested and charged with my mother's murder. Nothing. If that was the true, how had they closed the case?

"Stop the car."

Maksim growled as he slammed on the brakes. Vas grunted, his phone flying from his hands, his body jolting forward with the force of the stop.

"What the fuck?"

My eyes drifted out the window as we spoke, landing on

the capacious grass courtyard that sprawled across one part of the compound. It was eleven in the morning, and it was already crawling with people.

Not just any people. Kids.

Teens, to be exact.

They were dressed in workout gear and paired off in groups of two or three.

"Why the hell aren't they in class?" I snapped, throwing the door of the car open and stepping out.

"Ava..." Vas called, but I slammed the door on him before he could finish his sentence. "Wait."

Fucker got out of the car.

I surveyed the scene before me with a fearful trepidation I'd never experienced before. Pain zinged across my chest, my heart lurching as I imagined the innocent faces of the children before me dying in a war they had no right being a part of.

The students were focused, our sudden halt not even registering on their radars as they dutifully performed maneuver after maneuver. Roman, their instructor, called out. Some of them I recognized as ones Kiernan and Seamus had drilled into me when they first taught me to defend myself. The longer I watched, the more complex and dangerous the moves became.

"What are you thinking?" I hissed at Vas when he came to stand beside me.

"They're training," he said, pointing at the obvious. "We're readying them for war."

"They're children."

Vas shook his head sadly. "They haven't been children for a very long time, Ava. You should know that."

He was right. I did know that. Most of them had grown up just like Matthias and me. There was no doubt in my mind that some of them had endured much worse.

"They need to focus on their grades and graduating," I reprimanded harshly. "Not being forced to learn how to fight in a war they don't belong in."

Vas chuckled mirthlessly. "You still have so much to learn." His voice was tinted with sadness, and I could hear the disappointment dripping from his tone. "These are the top students about to graduate. They all exceed expectations in every aspect of learning and training."

"They still shouldn't be forced to be out here learning to kill people."

"None of them were forced."

Eyes wide, I turned to him in surprise before shifting my gaze back to the students.

"They all volunteered to defend their leader and their home and avenge Matthias's death." Maksim came up behind me, his voice filled with a deep pride as he overlooked the courtyard. "We never force our students into anything. Hell, this was their idea."

"Why?"

"Many of them owe their lives to Matthias," Maksim informed me. "They want to repay a debt in the best way they know how."

Tears gripped the edges of my lash line. I dashed them away before anyone could see. "They could die."

"If it wasn't for Matthias and the *Bratva*, they would be dead already," Vas pointed out logically. "This place is their second chance. Their second life. You need to accept and honor their dedication and, as it may be one day, their sacrifice."

But I didn't want anyone to sacrifice anything for me. I never had and never would. If it came down to it, I was more than happy to be the one to sacrifice my life for them. These students who had carved their bravery and survival onto my soul.

"I can't do it!"

The sudden shrill proclamation caught my attention, and my eyes followed the sound back to a small brunette who faced off against a giant Roman.

"You can," Roman growled. "You aren't trying, Amika. You're holding back. You're hiding."

"Coward, more like," her partner, a boy I recognized by the name of Vadim, sneered.

"I. Am. Not. A. Coward," Amika, shrieked. I saw the move before she made it, and so did Vadim. Amika leaped at him with a war cry, her body bouncing slightly off the grass as she surged forward, her fist clenched and ready to strike.

Amika missed Vadim's face by a mile. He'd easily sidestepped her attack. Grabbing her wrist midair, he twisted it behind her back, using the momentum of her lunge to slam her hard into the ground.

Ouch, that had to hurt.

Amika cried out, a mix of pain and frustration as she wiggled and writhed beneath her captor.

"Let me go, you fucking egghead."

Vadim chuckled.

"You gonna calm down, princess?" he taunted her. Amika growled and swung her free arm back at him. He caught that one with ease as well, locking it behind her back with the other.

"You're going to regret this."

"No," I stepped forward. "You are if you think you can fight with all that pent up anger."

"*Pakhan*," Vadim instantly released Amika as if she were hot coal and stood, his shoulders tightening as he came to attention before him.

Then he was flat on his back.

I suppressed a small chuckle when Amika took Vadim's legs out from under him.

"First lesson," I smirked down at him. "Never turn your back on an enemy. Even in training." Vadim took my offered hand, shooting Amika a freezing glare.

Damn. Polar ice caps, that one. I could feel the frost from here.

"Second lesson." I turned my attention to Amika. "Getting angry will get you killed. Taunts and digs can only hurt you if you let them. I doubt he's the first to call you a coward, and he certainly won't be the last."

Amika's eyes widened as she stood and dusted herself off. "Yes, ma'am." She came to attention. The entire training session had stopped, their eyes on me.

"He's beating you so easily because you're telegraphing your moves." I noticed several times how easily predictable she was when she moved. "You're dropping your shoulder before you strike, and your emotions play over your face like a newbie at VIP poker night."

"Vadim is bigger than me," she whined. I raised my brows at her statement, my eyes narrowing at her.

"And you think that's what?" I hardened my voice. "Unfair?"

Amika lowered her attention to her feet and scuffed her shoes in the dirt, looking uncomfortable.

"Size doesn't matter, Amika," I told her. "What matters in a fight is using every tool you have available against your enemy. If he's bigger and brawnier than you are, then he's slower. So be quicker. Move your feet more. Wear him out before striking at him.

"Fighting is like seduction," I continued. "Watch them. The way they move. The way they talk. Does he have light steps that will tell you how quickly he moves or heavier ones to tell you how slow? If you pay attention, everyone has a tell. Even Vadim and Roman. Find that tell, that weakness, and then exploit it without exploiting yourself."

Amika's throat bobbed. "I'll never survive out there. I'll lose." It was a whisper on her lips. An admission to herself more than to me. I'd thought the same thing at once.

"As long as you have something to fight for," I assured her. "You've already won."

"Not many of us have anything to fight for," a boy toward the back spoke up. "We're poor. Homeless. Our parents either died or gave us up. Many of us used and abused. What is there to fight for?"

"Justice." It was a simple word to give him, but a powerful one all the same. "You are fighting to end the very thing that put you here. You're avengers. People who understand what it means to be powerless and feel victimized."

"We are victims," Amika spat.

"No." I smiled at her affectionately. She reminded me of Maleah, who had once told me the same thing I was about to tell her. "You're survivors. You did what you needed to do. Every day you went on living, you survived. Look at all of you." I swept my hand in front of me, gesturing to the crowd. "Look at how far you have come. You could have easily given up. Given in to death and pain and sorrow. Another nameless kid on the street. Another drug addict or prostitute. Another no one. But you chose to live and learn and survive."

"What do you know of survival?" a man in the back I didn't recognize spat. He wore a black shirt with the word trainer printed across the front. "Posh bitch from a posh home. You don't know anything about suffering or survival."

"Watch your tone, Malich," Vas hissed. He stepped forward, hazel eyes turning a burnt gold with his pent-up ire.

"Leave it," I ordered Vas. He looked down at me in surprise before nodding his head submissively and stepping back. This was my fight.

"I grew up in a house filled with riches," I admitted coldly. "A place I believed was my home. Raised by a man I thought was my father. A man who beat me and made me watch as he killed those who were disloyal to him. He ruled through fear. Not with loyalty and compassion. He stole me and called himself my father for years. Locked me in a cupboard of a room for days with no food or water. Only letting me out when he thought I was about to die.

"And trust me, there were many times I'd wished I had," I sneered. "I finally managed to run away, and when he caught me, he had my best friend raped in front of my eyes for assisting me. He sold me to Matthias as collateral so his precious son would survive. Should I keep going? Most of you know the rest. Will my word suffice, or should I show you my scars, Malich?"

Now he looked downright contrite and mildly fearful.

"We all have stories to tell that would give even the darkest soul nightmares." My gaze left Malich to draw over the crowd. "But the most important story you must tell is your future. The past is gone. Don't forget it, but don't let it drown you. You can't control it any more than you can control the weather. But what you can control," I paused. The dramatics heightening the moment. What could I say? I was a sucker for theater, "is your future. You determine who you are and who you want to be.

"You decide where you want to go from here. No one else controls what lies ahead."

Silence fell over the courtyard; the only sound was the mild shuffling of the bodies who couldn't remain still and the wind singing through the trees. This was a moment for them.

A moment they needed with the battle looming on the horizon. The faces before me had still been living in the past, and they let it dictate where they were going.

The past was just a guide to a better tomorrow. We accepted that it shaped us, and the moment we realized it had no control over us was the moment we were free. We all had two lives. The second one began the moment we realized we only had one.

Or so Confucius said.

He seemed legit; I'll take it. Better advice than a fortune cookie, if you ask me.

"Let's go everyone," Roman whistled. "Back to training. The *Pakhan* is very busy, and we have more drills to run."

With a low groan, the students filed back to their original positions, some of them waving at me as they went. Compassion and kindness bred better loyalty than fear could ever hope to.

"Ma'am." Amika looked over at me with a hopeful expression in her obsidian eyes. "Will you..." she bit her lip, a slight blush sweeping across her cheeks, "will you train with us tomorrow?"

"The *Pakhan* has better things to do than—" I cut Roman off with a wave of my hand.

"I look forward to it."

Amika's broad smile was all I needed to know that I'd made the right decision.

Loyalty was earned; not demanded.

Built and not forced.

I wouldn't let them sacrifice their lives for mine like Matthias.No. My life would be laid down first.But not before I painted the streets with blood and burned the city to the ground.

Hades and hell weren't ready for me yet.

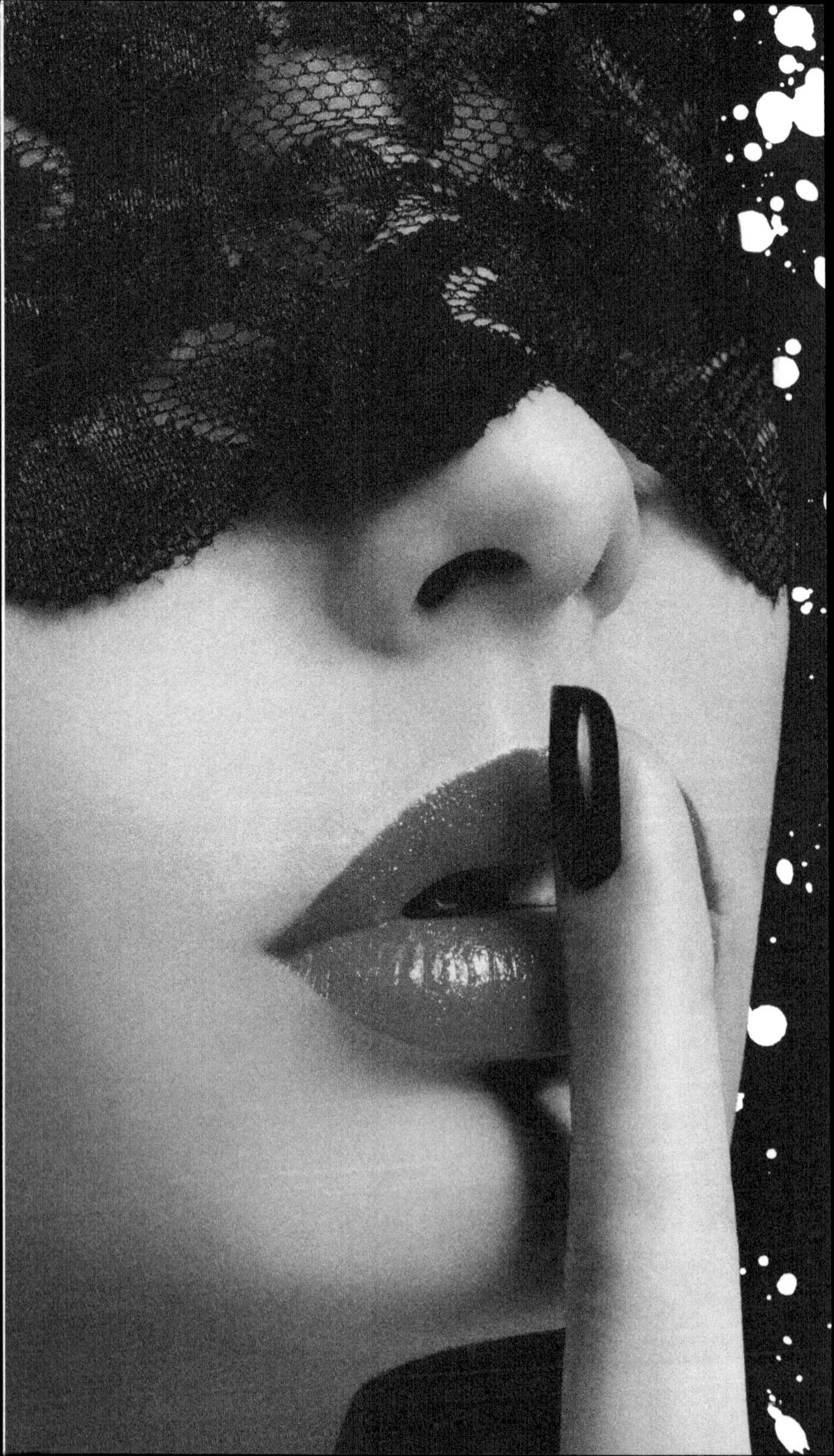

CHAPTER SIX

Sweat collected along my palms, and I wiped them nervously on my pants as I walked toward the empty dock. We'd told each other to come alone. Not that either of us would. My men littered the area, blending in with the general population, and I suspected Dante had his men doing the same.

What he wouldn't suspect is the secret weapons I had. If he tried anything, he would be surprised where the attack came from. My capacity for trust was a thin thread, fraying in the middle as more tension was applied. It wouldn't take much for the thread to break under pressure.

"Hello, Ava." Dante's low voice came up behind me. I turned to face him, the wind whipping at my hair.

"Hello, Dante." I smiled up at him, but it didn't reach my eyes. "Thank you for coming."

He smirked. "I was surprised to get your call."

"Now that I know," I murmured, reaching my hand out slowly to trace my fingers along his face. "I can't believe I ever missed their resemblance to you."

Dante stiffened at my words, but he didn't make any move to remove my curious fingers.

"Kenzi inherited your nose," I told him with a small, authentic smile as I traced his furrowing features. "But Libby got your fire and that blazing look in your eyes."

Removing my hand, I took a small step back, waiting for his next move. His throat worked, blue eyes brimming with tears he wouldn't dare to let fall. There was more emotion playing across his face now than I had ever seen before. He was always so stoic and put together. Even when he smiled, but now, that carefully erected barrier shifted beneath the moving sands.

"How did you find out?"

I swallowed back my own lump of emotion. "Libby."

Dante's eyes widened at her name. "She knew?" he asked incredulously. Nodding sadly, I held out a large manilla envelope to him. He took it without question, peeling it open to reveal the contents. It was everything Libby had managed to acquire on Kenzi, my grandfather, and a few other shady deals that Mark managed to decrypt.

"She knew a lot more than just that," I told him, watching his expression closely. The further he dug into the files, the redder his face became, until anger was all he seemed to know. Mark had added in some special footage of the "fake" wedding as well.

"Motherfucker," he growled dangerously, his knuckles whitening as he gripped the evidence tightly in front of him. The papers crinkled under his fierce grip, bending to his power. "You should have told me. The fucking *traditore*."

"I told you to look closer to home," I reminded him bitterly. "You just didn't want to listen."

Dante lifted his head and sneered at me. "I don't like games, Avaleigh. You should have been straight with me."

"Sure," I scoffed, crossing my arms defensively. "Blame the kidnapped victim for not spilling her guts to you in the middle of a funeral where my enemies surrounded me. Makes sense. Christian ordered Eduardo to rape me as punishment for our discussion already. What do you think he would have done if he'd found out that I outed him to you?"

Confusion tilted his face, making him look older than his forty-five years.

"What do you mean, kidnapped you? Dashkov is the one who took you from Elias."

Laughter spilled from my lips, tainted with disbelief at his naivety. He honestly believed that? Had Elias told him nothing?

"Elias *sold* me to Matthias to save Christian," I told him, bitterness coating my tongue at the memory. "I helped them take down Elias's shipping port. That was my idea. Then we staged the fake wedding to draw Elias out. Libby was shot by a sniper. One who worked for you, by the way. Paid off by Christian. It's all outlined in the file I gave you."

"You're telling me Christian killed not only his sister, but his father?" he scoffed. "Come on, Ava. You really expect me to believe that?"

"I don't need you to believe it when the proof is right before you," I snapped. "I've outlined everything to a T. These are all records you can scrounge up yourself. You don't have to take my word for it."

"Why?" he pushed. "Why would Christian kill them?"

"Elias got in the way." A heavy weight was lifting from my chest as I told him about the puppeteer Elias had been working with all these years. The man behind the curtain. I didn't care if he believed me. That wasn't what would cleanse the bitterness that had clung to me since childhood. No, all that mattered was I was finally able to tell him. The one man who had been kind to me when no one else but my sisters were.

"And Libby?"

"She betrayed him," I admitted. "The fake wedding was her idea to draw them out. But he had plans to kill her long before that because he didn't need her. Her final use to him was framing us for her murder."

"Us," Dante murmured. "Wedding wasn't so fake, huh?"

I chuckled. "I married Matthias weeks before the fake wedding. It's why I am *Pakhan* now."

"So, is this why you asked me here?" He gave the file a slight shake. "To air out all of Christian and Elias's dirty laundry to me?"

"Part of the reason," I admitted with a shrug. "You deserved to know what happened to your daughters. You'll find one marked Kenzi as well."

"Kendra told me she is doing well at college." He seemed puzzled that I would have anything to hand over when it came to the daughter he believed was on the other side of the pond living a normal college student life.

"Kenzi never made it to college."

Dante swore.

"Kendra either has her head buried in the sand or was complicit in her own daughter's sale."

"Sale?"

"Elias sold her to the Chameleon Agency."

Dante's face paled beneath his Italian coloring. It was apparent he knew who they were or had at least heard the name.

"You're wrong," he jeered. "He would never do that. Elias knew their reputation. Why would he...?"

"Get rid of the one daughter who was of no use to him?" I

mocked. "Did you bother to even contemplate whether your brother suspected an affair? That maybe he knew that Kenzi and Libby weren't his? He kept Libby because she was useful. Kenzi wasn't, and Elias only kept around things that were useful."

"So why did he keep you around, then?"

Well, that stung like a bitch. Rage thundered through me at his callousness. I almost walked away. Almost.

A new wave of anger swept over me as I thought back to all the times he knew about my predicament and never once thought to help.

Nope. This useless bitch was gone. Sayonara, fucker.

"Wait," Dante called out as I turned on my heel to begin walking back toward the shore. "I'm sorry. That was uncalled for."

Turning, I raised a brow at him, incredulity written on my face easier to read than a neon stripper sign.

"You think?"

"I'm trying to wrap my head around all of this, Ava," he fumed. Dante ran his hand angrily through his hair, stressing the roots, his jaw clenched. "You're telling me my own nephew not only murdered his sister but also committed patricide, and my brother sold off one of my daughters. That's a lot for anyone to take in."

My lips curled into a snarl, gaze hardening as I thought back to all the information I had been slammed with in the last few months. "Oh?" I bared my teeth at him and let the bottled-up rage unleash itself. "You mean like finding out the man who had called himself my father since I was eleven, who beat me and tortured me, was in fact, not my father but the one who abducted, sold, and then bought my mother? That he raped her and used her. The man who sold me so that his precious son could live?"

Dante stood stunned before me, unable to form any words, his lips pressed into a thin line.

"How about how the man I thought was my brother would brush up against me time after time when I was growing up? How he threatened to rape me? You want to know what he did to me when he told you he had 'rescued' me?"

That fucking word got air quotes and everything.

"He would wake me up with a stun gun. Or a cattle prod. Sometimes with a whip. Hell, one day I woke up to him trying to drown me." My voice had risen, silent tears tracking down my cheeks. The look of horror on his face didn't help. He honestly had no clue what Christian had done to me. "After the funeral, he told Eduardo to rape me so I would learn my place. You want to know what I did?" I didn't wait for him to answer. "I smashed his skull in with a rock. I killed him, Dante. Ended him. And it wasn't enough. Because every person involved is going to bleed."

Might have left out that one of those people was going to be Kenzi.

I doubted Dante would take well to me wanting to kill his only remaining daughter.

"Is your mind scrambled yet, Dante?" I mocked. "Heard enough? Because I've got more where that came from."

Dozens of possible things he might do were running through my head in that moment. Scoffing and brushing me off were among them. Attempting to kill me was another. Maybe he would simply nod his head in acceptance and take it all in stride.

Stumbling into his chest as his arms wrapped tightly around me, the soft scent of leather and smoke ensconcing me was not what I expected. One hand cradled the back of my head while another rubbed soothingly down my back.

"I should have done more," he croaked. Guilt and regret were choking him. Something wet hit the top of my head, and I belatedly realized he was crying. Dante Romano, head of the Italian Mafia, was crying. "I'm sorry. I am so, so sorry, *piccolina*."

Shit. Now I was crying even harder.

It was cathartic.

Cleansing.

Exactly what I had been needing. To know that someone who'd known me as a child cared. That it wasn't all a carefully placed façade.

"What do you need from me?" He pulled back, his thumbs wiping at the tears along my cheeks. Fuck, had any of my men seen me crying? My gaze darted around the docks. "No one but Vas saw anything," he assured me.

Oops.

Dante smiled proudly. "I knew you didn't come alone, Ava," he said. "It was expected. I am not alone either." I let out a nervous laugh that was wobbly and wet from crying.

"So," he started again. "What do you need? I am at your service."

"This man," I pulled out a picture of my grandfather from the stack of papers I gave him. "His name is Seamus McDonough, he's—"

"Your biological grandfather," he finished for me.

Nodding, I kept going. "In her journal, Libby mentioned Elias talking to a man about me. She identified him as the man with the silver cane."

"What does that have to do with Seamus McDonough?" he queried, looking at the picture again.

"At the gala, I saw him and my grandmother." I took out another picture that Mark had managed to obtain from the gala's security cameras. "Look at what he's using."

"Okay..." Skepticism colored his voice. "There are plenty of canes out there that have a silver cross on them."

"That's true," I admitted. "But look at the emblem just beneath it carved into the wood."

Dante still didn't look convinced, and I hadn't expected him to be.

Not yet, anyway.

"Now," I flipped to the photograph of Madam Therese, "look at this cane."

His forehead puckered, his eyes darting between the pages as he took in every detail he could.

"Do you recognize her?" I asked him. "Or the symbol?"

Dante shook his head. "No." He sighed. "But I've met Seamus McDonough before, and he never had a cane. Certainly never needed one, but shit, it's been nearly twenty-five years since I last saw him."

That got my attention.

"Where was this?"

Dante thought about it for a moment, his eyes flicking up as he recalled the memory. "In Boston. My father was still alive and running *la familgia* at the time. He wanted to show me the ropes and help to secure a new merger."

Merger?

"What year was this?"

"It was 1996, I think."

The year my mother went missing.

"Was your father looking at merging with McDonough Shipping Corp?" Part of me already knew the answer.

"Yes," he answered slowly, curious to see where my train of thought was going. "Elias never found out, but my father had been underbidding him for years. Taking his clients and spreading rumors and planting evidence for the FBI to find."

"And then you killed him."

There was no regret on Dante's face. Nothing. Not that I would judge him for that. Dante's father was a horrible man.

"Did Seamus McDonough want the merger?"

"It was his idea."

"I sense a but coming..."

Dante clicked his tongue and let out a breath. "But when we arrived in Boston to negotiate with him, he had no clue what we were talking about. Told my father he would never align himself with anyone whose shipment involved human cargo."

"Is that how the war started?"

He gave me a grim nod.

The Italian-Irish war was carved into Seattle's history as the bloodiest gang war on the West Coast. There were so many lives lost on both sides as hails of gunfire littered the streets day after day. Nowhere was safe. The police were at a loss, and gang violence rose until the day Dante had put an end to it.

By putting a bullet through his father's skull.

"Here's the thing." Dante rolled his shoulders back to ease the tension that was no doubt gathering there. "The initial conversation took place here in Seattle. In person."

"Wait..." I blinked rapidly several times, trying to process what he just told me. "But you said..."

"That's why my father was so upset," Dante told me with a small shake of his head. "He had a face-to-face encounter with him. Sat down and had coffee. Fucked a few whores."

Well, I could have lived without that information.

Wait.

"No, it couldn't have been him."

"Trust me, Ava," he assured me. "It was. I saw him myself several times over the two days he was here in June 1996."

"You don't understand," I argued as I combed through my

phone. One of the crime scene pictures Libby had of my mother's trashed dorm room held a photo. It hadn't meant anything before, but now that I was putting dates together, it couldn't have been him.

"What were the exact dates?" I asked frantically as I pulled up the photo.

"June fifteenth was the day he arrived. He left two days later." He frowned. "Why is that important?"

"Because—" I turned the phone around to show him the photo. "This is my mother's graduation photo, taken with my grandmother and grandfather." I zoomed the phone in so he could see the date on the bottom of the picture.

"It's dated June fifteenth, 1996."

Dante checked and rechecked, as if what he was seeing might disappear if he kept looking away and back again. "That's impossible," he whispered. "If that's him...who the fuck met with my father all those years ago?"

"That's what I need you to find out."

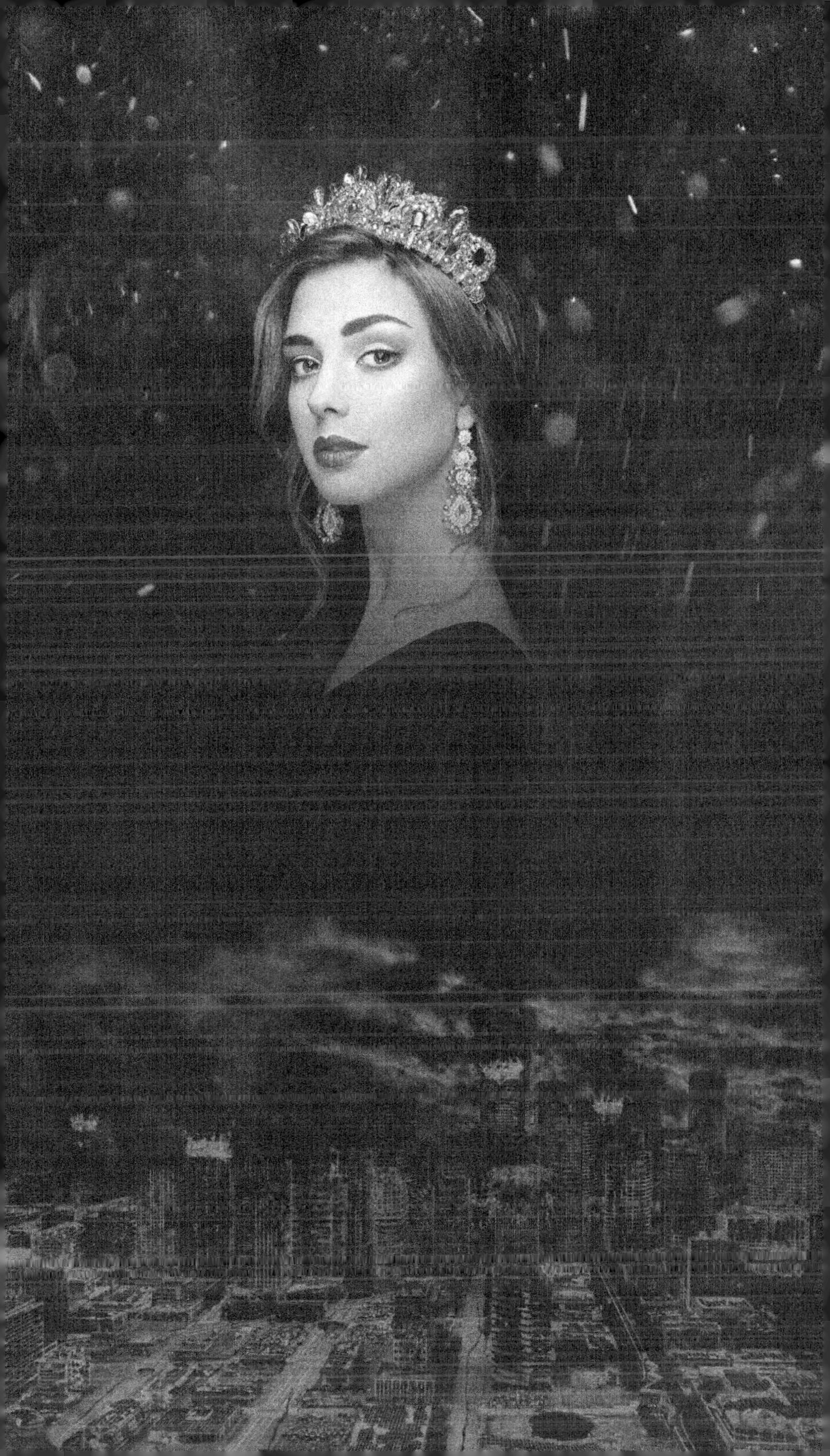

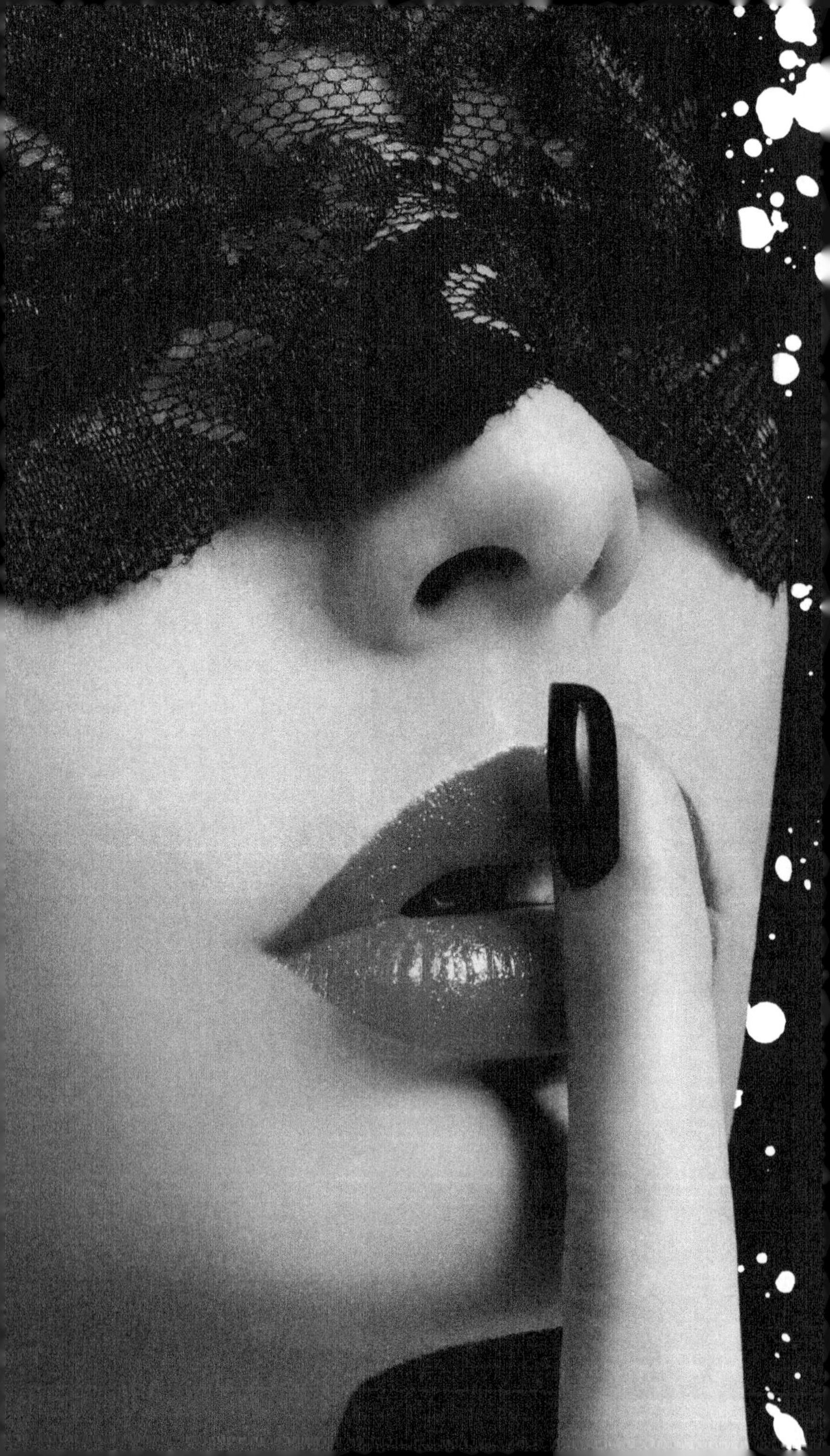

CHAPTER SEVEN

"Five. Three. Seven. Nine." Seamus called out number after number as he worked me through the paces in the gym beneath McDonough's. It had been nearly two weeks since my meeting with Dante, and still nothing but radio silence. To keep Christian from getting suspicious, we agreed not to contact each other unless it was absolutely necessary.

He wanted Christian dead for what he'd done to Libby. As much as I didn't want to stop him from putting that asshole's head on a spike, we needed him alive still.

Only for a little while.

"Focus, Ava," Seamus reprimanded when his kick made contact with the side of my head. I stumbled to the side, wincing at the pounding pain before cracking my neck and hunkering back into position. "You've been too distracted lately."

"Got a lot on my mind," I mumbled before throwing my uppercut at the pads.

"If you lose focus in a fight," Seamus scolded, "you die."

My lip curled into a snarl. "And if you keep pushing me," I taunted, "so will you."

"Feisty today." Kiernan laughed from the doorway. I kept my focus on Seamus, but a slight movement from behind my brother drew my attention.

"Fuck."

I was pretty sure I saw stars when Seamus landed a punch to my jaw, knocking me off balance and sending me careening to the floor.

"Seamus!" Bailey's voice was panicked. "You need to be more careful."

The motherfucker shrugged as he watched his girlfriend peel me off the floor.

"She should have been paying attention, *astoré*."

Bailey rolled her eyes at my brother, then turned back to me. "Ava, there's a delivery for you upstairs."

"Wait," Seamus called out. "I'm not done kicking your ass yet."

I flipped him off as I headed up the stairs to the main floor.

The bar was empty at this time of day. No one but my father, the twins, and Bailey were usually around, except the few kitchen employees who came in early to prep for the night's crowd. Marianne was blissfully never around unless my grandmother forced her to help, which wasn't a lot because Liam couldn't stand the bickering between the hotheaded pair.

A small, unmarked box sat on the bar top. I wasn't expecting any packages except the one from Portland, but it was too tiny to be filled with evidence.

"Came by special courier." My father spoke up from behind the bar where he was polishing glasses. "O'Malley's boys dropped it off. Said it was urgent."

I winced. My father wasn't on the best terms with the O'Malleys.

"Want to tell me what is so important that it has them risking their lives to deliver it here?"

There was only one person it could be from. The officer from Portland where the O'Malleys were based. No one else knew I was here.

"It was supposed to be evidence from the night my mother was murdered."

Tilting his head, he studied the box for a moment before he frowned. "Seems a wee bit small for that."

A smile tilted my lips.

We really were alike.

I shrugged. "Might as well find out what she sent me."

Liam nodded and grabbed a pair of scissors, cutting away the tape in a few quick slips. I opened the flaps to reveal a small black burner phone nestled among some foam.

I picked it up and turned it on.

There was only one number programmed into the directory. Before I could second-guess myself, I dialed it.

"Jesus, those couriers are slow," a woman huffed as she picked up. "Took you long enough to call."

"Took you long enough to send something my way," I shot back. "I didn't ask for a phone call. I asked for a box of evidence."

The woman on the other end of the line snorted and chomped her gum.

"Yeah, well," she sighed again, "things came up, and that's why I'm calling."

"Please tell me you didn't lose my box of evidence."

She chuckled on the other end of the line.

"Hell, no," she assured me. "Who the hell do you think I am? My precinct is dirtier than a fat man's undies on cardio day." That was an image I could have lived without. "I sent out a false package to see what would happen to it. My instincts were right. Some fucker grabbed it up, shot my courier, then tried to come after me."

"Hope the motherfucker is dead."

"Oh, he is." She paused, the gears in her mind working overtime as she thought through what to say next. "Look...you sure you want to go digging around in this, Ava? Whoever is trying to get this evidence, they mean business. I can help but..."

"You want something." There was no anger or resentment in my voice. I understood where she was coming from. The woman cleared her throat uncomfortably.

"My uncle wants a sit down with you and Liam Kavanaugh."

"And who is your uncle?" Seeing as how it had been the O'Malleys who had delivered the phone I could almost guess, but I wanted to hear it from her.

"Sully O'Malley."

"Please hold." I put her on mute and turned to my father.

"Sully wants a sit down, doesn't he?" I nodded, not even bothering to ask how he knew who I was talking to. My father had been in this business so long he didn't need me to tell him what was going on. He'd put the pieces together the moment the box was delivered. "It's smart."

"I don't care about smart," I told him. "What do you want? He's most likely going to want to build an alliance with you."

"Us," my father corrected. "Sully knows it's a smart move to side with the first female head of the *Bratva*. I'm just a consolation prize."

"Do you want to?"

He shrugged a shoulder. "Wouldn't be the worst idea. The O'Malleys, although brash, would make powerful allies.

They know everything that goes on in their territory. You might find some answers from them."

Unmuting the phone, I said, "You have a deal."

The woman sighed in relief. "Thank you," she said. "How is tomorrow at two p.m.? There is a warehouse in the Eliot district we use. That's where I put the evidence for safekeeping."

"Text me the address."

"Okay."

"What's your name, by the way?" I asked her. "Should probably know it if we're going to be doing business together."

"Aine," she told me. "Aine O'Malley."

"Well, Aine O'Malley—" I shifted the phone to my other ear. "It's nice to meet you officially. Let's talk about that precinct of yours."

Things were fishy with Mark and Dima. Mark had been on edge when I walked into his office at the compound to find him on a video call with Dima, who still refused to tell me what he was up to. The two of them looked guilty as they interacted with me, rushing me out of the room. Mark all but pushed me out the door like a madman after I asked him to dig up some dirt on Sully O'Malley for our meeting today.

We left him to watch over things remotely from the compound. The warehouse address Aine had given me was now fully covered by surveillance cameras, satellite imagery, and a few dozen soldiers. We weren't taking any chances. I didn't doubt Aine's sincerity when she informed me that her uncle was truly looking for an alliance, but just because she believed him didn't mean I had to.

Sully O' Malley was nothing like what I expected him to

be. From the long list of dirty laundry Mark aired out about the man, I expected him to be older. Closer to my father's age than my own. He sat at the head of the small metal table, head held high like he was the king.

We were certainly not his subjects.

The man had short black hair and brilliant blue eyes. The angles of his face were outlined by a rough stubble that gave his features a dark edge. He looked like the young pirate Hook from that silly modern fairy tale show Bailey insisted I watch with her.

Aine, or who I assumed was Aine, stood next to him, her head bowed slightly as she whispered angrily to her uncle. Her soft features didn't match the rugged tone of her voice when we'd spoken on the phone. I half expected her to be wearing ripped jeans and an AC/DC top. Instead, she stood demurely next to Sully, wearing a collared lace blouse with peasant sleeves tucked into a gentle peach tulle skirt with a pair of white flats.

Her long raven hair was braided back loosely, a few strays framing her gentle porcelain face. When she looked up at me, her ocean blue eyes were anything but submissive, and I loved it. Aine O'Malley may have been forced to play dress up, but that didn't mean she liked it.

"Welcome." Sully's voice was strong, dripping with honey. His gaze roamed over me. Not leering, just curious. He tilted his head and studied me. My red hair hung in loose waves around a makeup free face. I'd chosen to wear black leggings that I tucked into a pair of low-heeled leather boots. A loose olive wrap completed the ensemble.

Stylish but also loose enough that if we were attacked, I could easily move and bend.

I approached the table, my father on my right, and Vasily on my left. Both dressed to the nines in Armani suits and gold

Rolexes. The woman at Starbucks this morning had a field day with them when we ordered our coffees.

Neither of them noticed, of course. They just smiled, placed their orders, and moved to surround me as if a barista attack was imminent. One of them had been eyeing me with thinly disguised hate when Vasily all but brushed off her obvious advances.

Sully stood and reached out his hand to me with a disarming smile. I took it with a smile of my own. Once we all exchanged pleasantries, we sat.

"Thank you for coming." Sully leaned back in his chair comfortably.

I glanced at my father and then at Vas. Smirking darkly, I said, "I was under the impression I wouldn't get the box of evidence I wanted if we didn't. Not the best way to start relations, is it?"

Sully chuckled. "No, I suppose not," he admitted. "You'll have to forgive me. I have been trying to get your father to agree to a sit down for years now."

Father snorted derisively. "Then you shouldn't have been trying to push into my territory."

"And I have tried telling you that it wasn't us."

"Men bearing the mark of the O'Malley clan don't lie," my father snarled. He pointed his finger at Sully. "Each of them was selling your drugs stamped with your mark, and so were they."

Sully waved his hand at him dismissively. My father growled. "Do you honestly believe I would be that careless? Also, if they were truly my men, I would have retaliated."

"You did."

Sully snorted. "I never retaliated, and that is why I've been trying to sit down with you," he explained calmly. "Your territory is nice and all, but I don't need it. I have my own, and

I like it here. Why would I want to give that all up for a territory that's three hours away?"

"Shipping ports," Liam said confidently.

"I don't need your shipping ports, Kavanaugh," he told him. "I run one of the most successful ground transport companies in the nation. Boats aren't my family's thing, and you know that. It's why my father turned down your offer all those years ago."

That caught my attention. Liam had been out of town on my grandfather's request to scope out a trucking company here in Portland. It was his alibi.

"You never bought it from him?" I asked my father.

He shook his head. "No." The muscles in his jaw clenched tightly. "Nearly got me killed coming down here. Luckily, Owen O'Malley didn't have an itchy trigger finger, or I would be dead."

"He set you up," Sully deadpanned.

"You don't know what you're talking about," my father snarled. Vas and I exchanged a knowing look. "That man raised me."

"No, he didn't." I said at the same time as Sully.

Well shit.

Sully looked at me with mirrored surprise. "Looks like I'm not the only one who's been digging where I shouldn't."

"What the hell are the two of you going on about?" Liam roared, his face turning red. "Seamus McDonough raised me. Arranged for Katherine and me to go to college together."

"I am not contesting that." Sully's voice was low and calm, like he was talking to a spooked animal. "What I am saying is that the man who sent you to buy my father's trucking company wasn't Seamus McDonough."

"And neither was the man at the gala," I spoke up. My hands twisted nervously in my lap. This was a conversation I had been avoiding. He never believed me when I voiced my doubts about him, and I was not up to feeling that sting of rejection again. As a result, I avoided talking to him about anything related to my mother and grandfather. The only reason he was here now was because Sully wanted the sit down.

Liam groaned. "Not this again, Ava," he chastised. "We already put it to bed."

"No," I growled. Pain lanced through my heart at his words. We hadn't *put it to bed* as he said. He chose to ignore what was in front of his eyes. "You refused to acknowledge what is right in front of your goddamn eyes. I understood your reticence when it was just me, but now you have someone else telling you the exact same thing. Something isn't right about Seamus McDonough. If that's who he even is."

"You don't know what you're talking about, Avaleigh." He stood his ground. "This isn't some—"

"Actually, she does," Sully interrupted. "Whoever is setting us up is using Seamus McDonough as a patsy."

"It's more than that," I whispered. "Whoever he is, he's pretending to be Seamus, down to his very looks."

"That's insane." Liam shook his head. "There is no possible way that someone is impersonating your grandfather."

"I have proof."

"Let's see it then."

The pain in my chest deepened. The knife Liam had shoved into my heart twisted deeper at his stubborn refusal. I told him once that I refused to be the daughter of a man who dismissed my cares and worries as if they were nothing more than dirt underfoot. I warned him of the strain it would cause. He was proud to call me daughter, he told me, but he wasn't acting like it.

At this moment, I wasn't proud to call him my father.

Vas, who had been sitting by my side, hands clenched into fists as his anger rose, shoved his phone at Liam. Both photos were time stamped. One was the photo of my mother's graduation, and the second was an airport security photo.

The man in the photo was an exact match to Seamus McDonough with one glaring difference.

The silver cross cane.

Liam stared at the evidence, eyes wide, searching for proof that we were wrong. He couldn't deny it anymore, however. The truth was before him, plain as day, and he would be a fool if he attempted to refute what was before him.

"This..." The disbelief in his voice killed me. The hurt and sadness reflected in his eyes made me want to hold him. Comfort him. But now wasn't the time. Over time, his face hardened, his eyes narrowing at the man in the picture. He was coming to terms with the truth. "Tell me more."

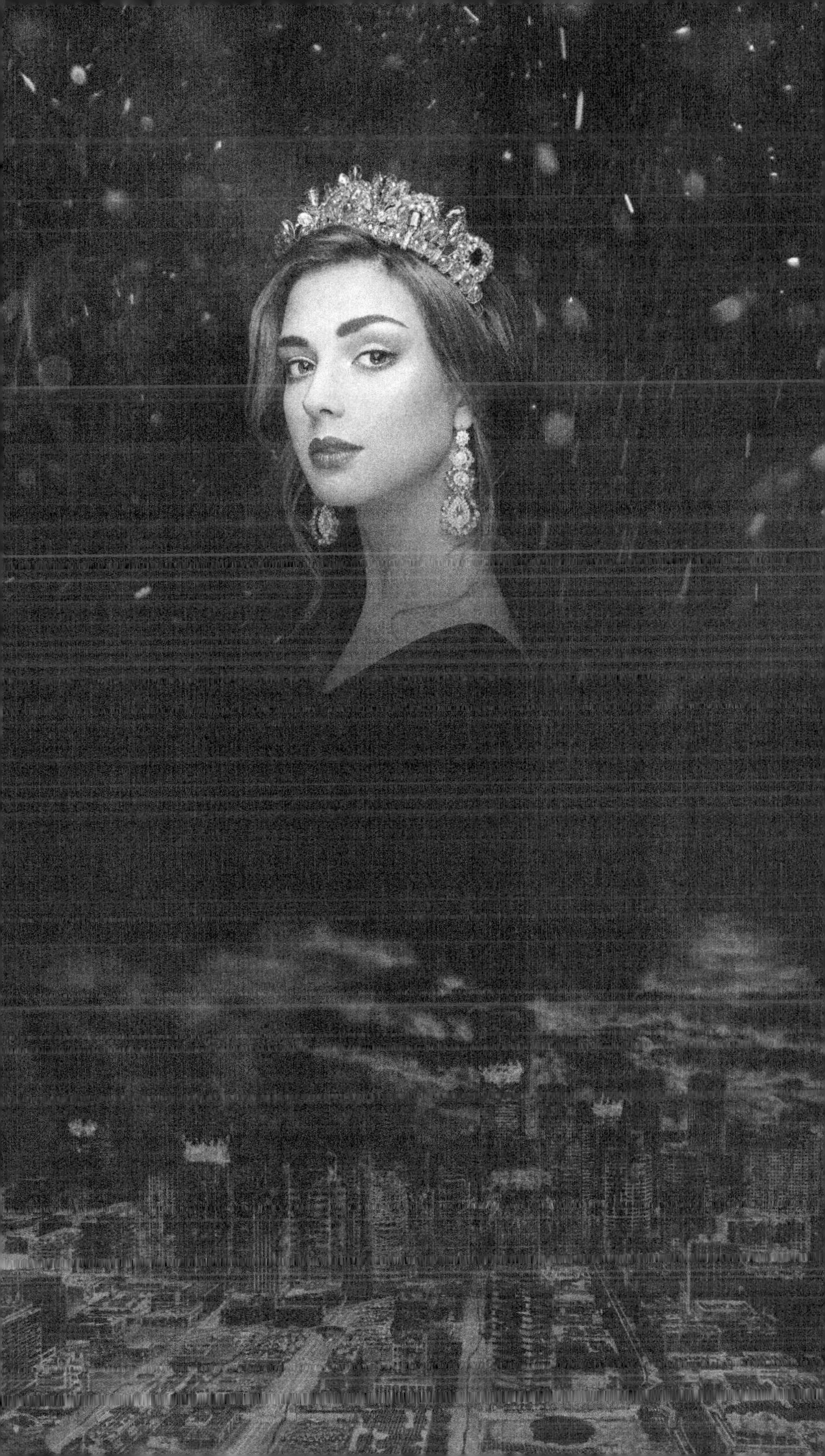

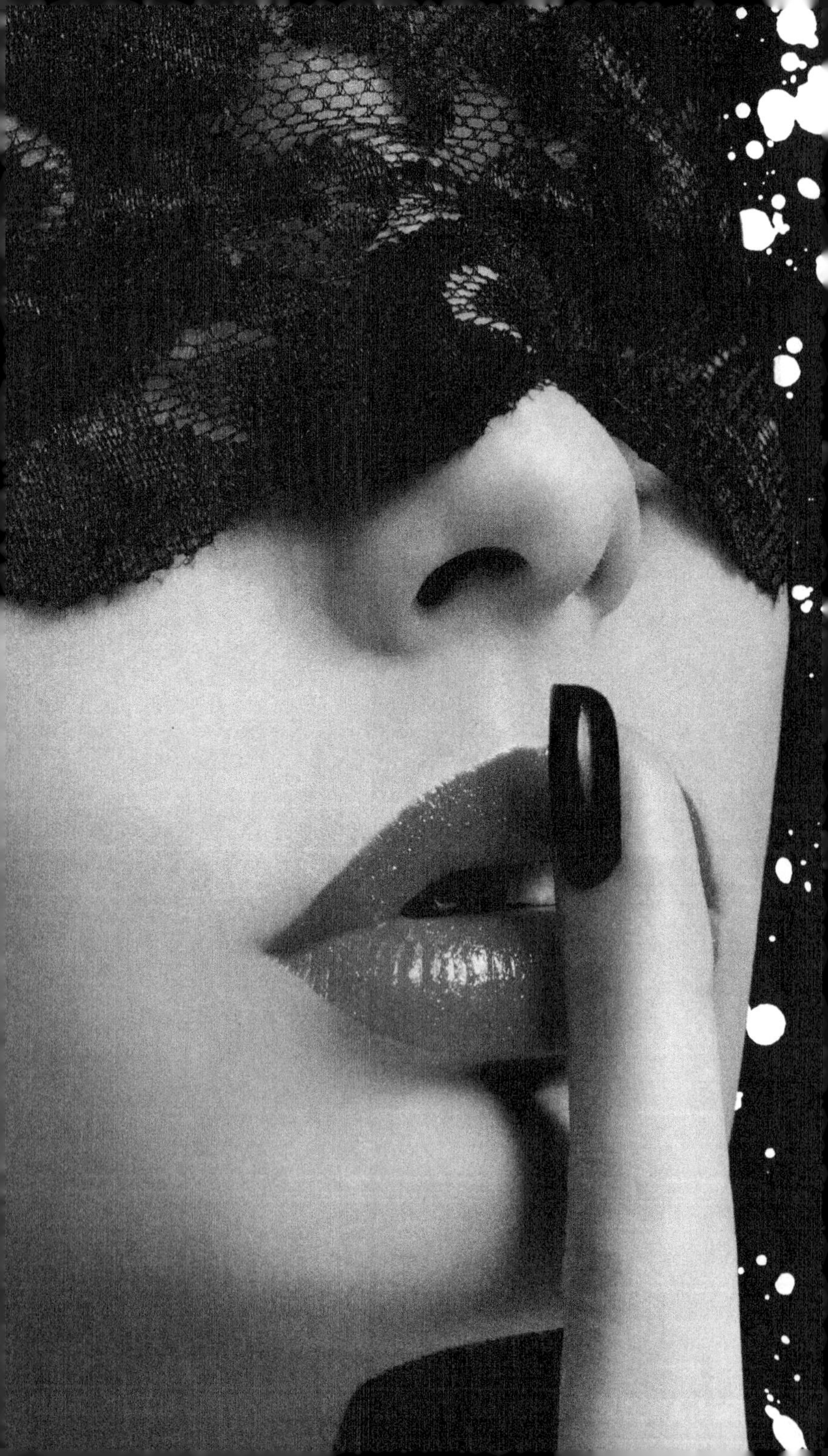

CHAPTER EIGHT

It was several hours later when the truth was finally hashed out and the facts were laid bare. Disbelief and pain lingered behind my father's eyes. We both knew what it meant if the man at the gala hadn't been Seamus McDonough.

I recalled the fear in Sheila's eyes that night when the man parading around as my grandfather approached us. She knew he wasn't who he said he was. How long had she known? Was she aware of his true identity? I highly doubted she was involved willingly. The panic and horror she displayed that night were real.

So why was she playing along? What did he have over her?

I knew one thing for sure. If Sheila knew that man wasn't her husband, then there was very little doubt in my mind that he was dead. From the crestfallen look on Liam's face, he'd made the same conclusion.

"I don't understand." Tears shone in his emerald eyes, refusing to fall. "How many years has this been going on? Why? What purpose..."

"There might be someone who can answer that for you," Aine told us gently. "She'll be able to tell you her story."

Brow creasing, my gaze fixed on the woman who'd been nearly silent the entire conversation.

"Who?"

Her eyes met mine and without hesitation she said, "Your mother."

I barked a laugh, the sound tainted with icy bitterness. "She's dead," I reminded her.

"But the evidence left behind tells a story she can't." Aine gazed at me, her eyes soft and understanding. "We needed to be sure, though."

"About?"

Her gaze turned to Liam. "That everyone would go in open to the truth," she told us sadly. "Because if I'm right—the truth might break one of you."

"Show us," Liam demanded.

The streets surrounding me were oddly familiar. Flashes of my childhood stretched out before me, but there was nothing concrete. I might have played on that playground. Is that where my mother took me for dinner one time?

Gradually, the memories that had faded over time resurfaced the closer and more familiar the neighborhood became. There wasn't much that had changed. Houses were repainted. Streets were re-paved, but it seemed as if everything was the same.

Including our house.

It didn't pass my notice that my childhood home was in O'Malley territory. I doubted it was a coincidence, either. My mother knew where we needed to go. Not that it had helped much.

"I wasn't the leader at the time," Sully said as we exited the SUVs. "My father was. When Aine mentioned your mother's name, I immediately recognized it from a file my father had stashed away in his desk. I thought it odd when I found it a few years after I took his place. Not that there was a file, but that it had been hidden in a false bottom of a locked drawer I never found the key for.

"At the time, I paid little attention to it," he admitted. "I had a rising mutiny on my hands, and the IRS and FBI were coming down hard on my transport business. But the file gnawed at me." He stopped to fetch a key from his pocket. It was covered in worn butterflies and flowers, the coating nearly gone from the test of time. "Then I came here." He handed me the key.

With trembling hands, I took it from him. The key that I once used dozens of times after coming home from school. The porch was worn but maintained, with no sign of rot or disrepair. It was like stepping back in time. The shadows of my past pushed in on me. The cage around my heart squeezed tightly, my chest heaving as the memories of that fateful day resurfaced. A tsunami of emotion swept up, bubbling to the surface, disturbing the calm waters of my soul.

"We laid out each piece of evidence where it was found," Aine whispered gently from beside me. "The crime scene photos weren't tainted. Maybe something will help jog your memory."

The muscles in my neck tightened as I gritted my teeth against the painful sweep of despair flooding over me. The walls I'd built over time were crumbling, and grief threatened to overwhelm it. I thought about my mother's death every day for years, but I never expected to be back here, confronting my most painful memories in the house where I was the happiest.

A warm hand on my shoulder centered me, dragging me up from the depths of despair. Tears painted my face. I turned the key, the lock disengaging easily, and the door slid open noisily.

The air was slightly musty, and dust settled on every surface. Elias refused to allow me to bring any of my mother's belongings when he took custody of me. Everything was left behind, except the book I managed to hide beneath my faded, oversized hoodie.

I stepped inside, the cherry wood floor creaking slightly beneath my weight. Everything was exactly as it had been the day I was taken away. From the tipped over bookcase to the blood-splattered walls. My mother put up one hell of a fight that day. Carefully, I treaded through the house with ginger footsteps. Afraid to disturb the past. As if I would somehow change it.

The kitchen had always been the center of this house. My mother often spent hours in here, dreaming up new recipes and teaching me to bake. It was our favorite activity on nights when we both felt restless. She had dreamed of opening her own bakery one day. Dreamed of giving us a life of freedom.

It wasn't until I discovered her past that I truly understood what she had meant.

I ran my hand along the cool marble of the island, my eyes drifting closed as I let the past overtake the carefully constructed barriers of my soul.

"Do you know the most important ingredient in making cookies?" my mother asked me as I stood on my little stool at

one side of the island, flour dusting my face and hands as I worked the gooey dough into balls.

"Love." *My nose scrunched as I smiled at her. She smiled back softly.*

"Always love."

"Who do you love, Mommy?" *I asked, placing one of my misshapen balls of dough on the stone cookie sheet.* "Do I have a daddy you love?" *She reeled back slightly, as if the words I uttered had slapped her. Sadness was etched in every line of her face, and her eyes swam with a pain so deep it made me want to cry.*

"You do have a daddy I love." *Her voice was hoarse, full of regret.* "Very much."

"Can I meet him?" *The thought of meeting my daddy sent a thrill of excitement through me. Timmy and Mary had a daddy and a mommy who took them camping and tucked them in to bed. They both looked happy. Maybe Mommy would be happy if I had a daddy here.*

"Maybe one day, moy a chroí."

I preened at the Irish nickname. My heart. I had a daddy somewhere. Someone Mommy loved. Where was he?

Tears welled in my father's eyes as I walked him through the house, recounting memory after memory as best as I could. Over time, Elias had conditioned me to forget these memories. They became tainted with the blow of a hand or the crack of a whip. Even now, as I conjured them to the forefront of my mind, hoping to give my father a glimpse into our lives before her murder, the phantom pain swept over my skin.

"We had hidden areas all over the house," I whispered as I opened a small hatch at the end of one of the cupboards. Just big enough to fit my eleven-year-old frame.

"She never told me why, just that when the time came, she would utter our safe word, and I was to find the nearest one."

"What was your safe word?" my father asked quietly.

"*Mo réalta*," I murmured.

"My star." It came out choked, hoarse, and full of pain. "I used to call her that all the time. My beautiful star."

"Where were you that night?" Sully asked, his voice soft, as not to disturb the quiet contemplation that settled over the room. "We didn't find any evidence of a child living here."

My laugh was small and breathy. "You'd never find it if you didn't know where to look."

I led them up the staircase at the front of the house, my fingers trailing up the dark cherry wood of the railing, the steps creaking under my weight as I ascended to the last place I'd seen my mother alive.

"You cheated." My eyes narrowed at my mother, a pout forming on my lips. "You win every time."

My mother smiled. It was soft and comforting, but there was a hint of mischief behind the emerald green that caused the gold tint in her eyes to light up. They looked otherworldly against her porcelain freckled skin and fiery red hair.

"You're just not patient enough, my love." She winked at me as she settled the game back into its box. "You don't take the time to consider your moves and the impact they might have later down the road. Think before you act."

I screwed up my face as I looked at her. "You sound like a fortune cookie." She laughed, melodic and low.

"Maybe life would be better if we all sounded a bit wiser."

It was my turn to laugh. "I never said you sounded wise," I teased her. "Just old." She growled low in her throat before launching herself at me, hands prepared to grab me. I squealed with laughter and took off like a shot.

"I'll show you old." She ran after me, barely missing me as I darted past her and scrambled up the stairs. There was no way out on the second landing, but plenty of hiding spots. Her room alone had several. One of my favorite places was beneath the pile of clean clothes in her overly large laundry basket.

Unfortunately, she would see that coming. I chose to hide beneath the mountain of pillows on her bed instead. Curling myself up against the headboard, rearranging everything over me as if it had never been moved.

Let her try to find me now.
Except—she never did.

"I heard her screaming at the top of her lungs," I choked, refusing to look down at the pictures Aine had laid out on the floor on the landing. The combination of them together, laid one on top of another, created a life-size portrait of my mother's last moments. "Heavy footsteps thudded up the steps after her as she screamed our safe word again and again. One of the safe spots was in her room."

"The police report said there was no sign of forced entry," Aine told me softly. "She knew her killer, Ava, and she let them in."

"Doesn't narrow down a suspect pool," Liam commented bitterly.

"Actually," I told him, leading them into the master bedroom. "It does." He didn't need to ask what I meant. He knew. Seamus McDonough. Well, the man who masqueraded as him, anyway.

Taking a calming breath, I searched for the spot I had hidden in for hours before one of the officers finally found me.

JO MCCALL

The house had been crawling with people, and any noise I made was lost to their heavy footsteps and loud voices.

Then, out of nowhere, the door opened, and a saddened but caring face appeared in the darkness. His name was Officer Finn, and he'd done everything he could to take care of me before social services whisked me away without warning.

"No one will hurt you, a chroí," he uttered the safe word my mother had drilled into me to accept.

"They will call a chroí," *she told me. "Always trust that word, my star."*

"I remember staying with him and his family for almost a week before social services found us," I told Sully. "Finn..."

"Kelly." Sully smiled at the name. "He was a good man. Good soldier."

"He isn't still alive?" I cocked my head to the side, concerned.

Sully shook his head and said, "He was killed in October 2007 in a drive-by."

"That was less than a month after I was taken," I said. "Did your father think anything of it?"

"He wrote down a couple of theories." Sully nodded. "But nothing he could prove. Whoever did it was a ghost."

I was getting tired of ghosts.

Bending down, I felt along the wooden floor near the edge of my mother's old dresser and pressed down when I felt the wood change from rough to smooth. The wall to the right of the dresser slid open, revealing a dark, musty crawl space.

"Several of these were built into the house on my father's orders." Sully bent down to admire the craftsmanship.

"Why would your father protect her mother?" Vas wondered. "Was she paying him for protection? Or—" Sully growled and stood, turning on Vas in a second.

"Be careful what you say next," he snarled. "My father would never exploit a vulnerable woman like that."

My *Sovietnik* held up his hands in a gesture of peace. "Okay. Okay," he backed off. "But the question remains. Why would he protect her without anything in return?"

"What if she did pay him?" Liam wondered, not the least bit upset about the two men talking about my mother trading sex for protection. His eerie calm bugged the shit out of me, and I wanted to ruffle the surface just to see what lay below. "With secrets."

"That explains a lot, actually," Sully agreed. "We saw a huge intake of drugs and guns that year. At least on paper. I wasn't old enough to remember what was taken in."

Liam smirked. "McDonough pulled out of Portland within a few months of putting a huge chunk of money into a ground transportation company. He said it was because there wasn't any money to be made there and moved the transport company back into Washington."

"But you think it was because of all the shipments my father and his men lifted."

Liam grinned. "Katherine was smart. A genius. And she could hold a grudge like no other. She would have found a way to screw him over."

Realization hit. She hadn't been trying to screw Elias—she had gone after her own father.

"She knew," I murmured brokenly. "He's the one who sold her."

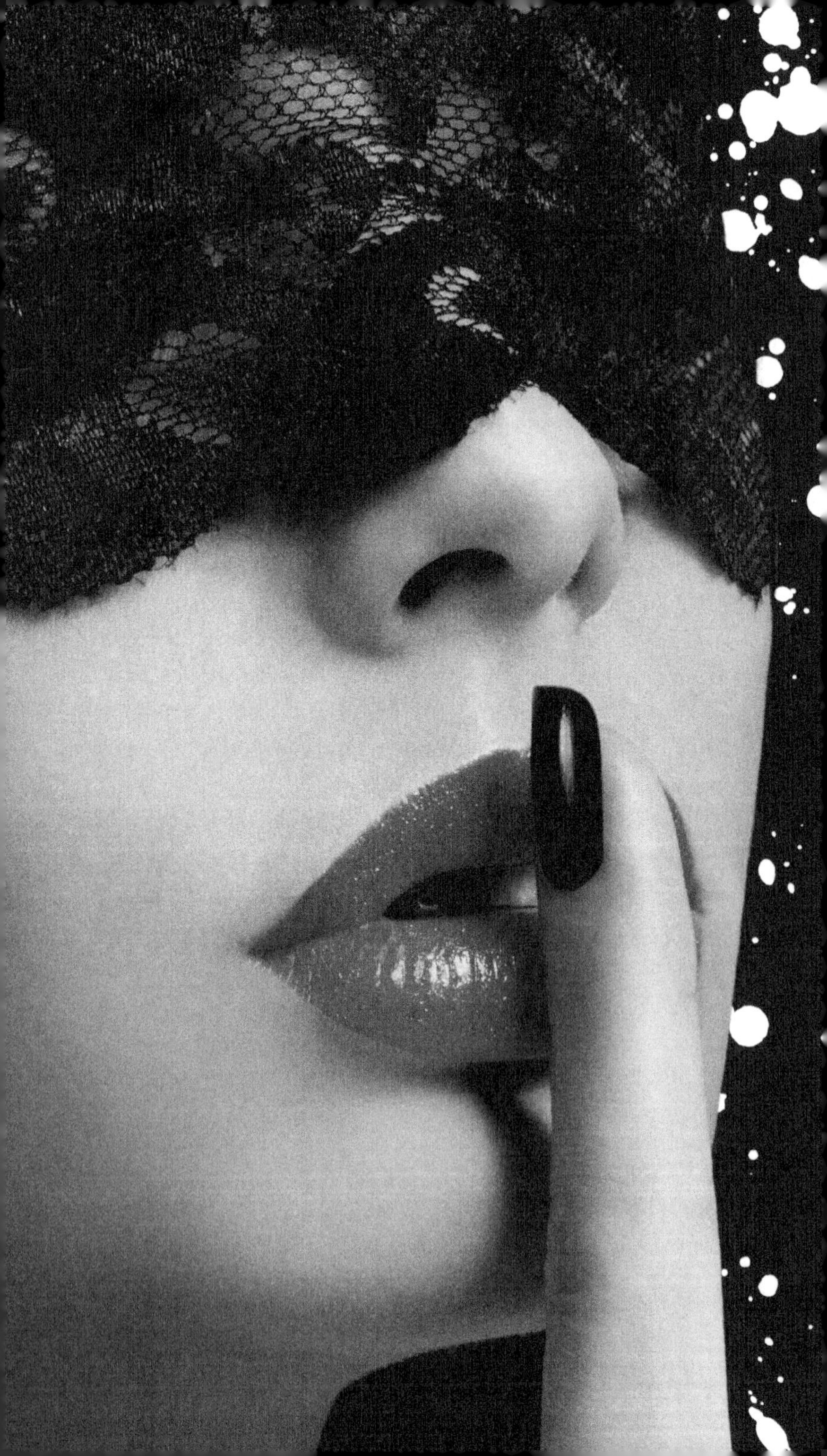

CHAPTER NINE

It was all coming together. The morbid pieces of my mother's death slipped into place section by section. Piece by piece. There were so many years of my life I had let slip by, never wondering about her death or the mysterious appearance of my "father." I questioned none of it as a child, and even as I grew, I simply accepted the life fate handed me.

Until Matthias pulled the wool back from my eyes.

Well, Mark did, but I would never have had the opportunity if Matthias hadn't bought me.

Semantics.

My teeth dug into my lower lip hard enough to bleed as the scene came together. The pictures strewn cohesively on the floor made up my mother's dead body as it had been found the day of her murder. Crouching down, I inspected every inch of every photo until I found what I was looking for. A bruise, just barely visible on her cheek due to the poor lighting of the photo.

A bruise in the shape of a cross.

Libby had written that the silver cross man had sent a

woman after Elias's *obsession* years ago and then ranted about how he came back with her *spawn*.

He was talking about my mother and me.

So the man we hadn't identified yet didn't know at the time my mother was murdered that she had a child. How did Elias find out? And who was the woman he sent to kill her? The presence of the bruise shaped like a cross told me that it was someone in the upper echelon of whatever secret society Madam Therese and the McDonough doppelgänger were a part of.

Another player we needed to identify.

"This," I pointed out the weird bruise to Aine. "I didn't see this documented on the autopsy report."

Aine shook her head. "No," she confirmed. "There were several anomalies with not only the autopsy but also the crime scene itself."

Liam frowned. "What do you mean anomalies?"

"Well," Aine started. "Besides the cross-shaped bruise, both the detective on the case and the coroner left out that it was a woman who committed these crimes. Not a man."

"A woman did all that?" Vas waved a hand at the photos of my mother. Aine nodded.

"Whatever she was hit with was long and cylindrical," she informed us. "Something covered in a black lacquered paint and metal."

"Like a cane." She didn't need to confirm what I already knew.

"Like a cane," Aine confirmed. "Then, there was this." The Irish woman pulled out her cell phone and pressed play. The footage was old and grainy, but there was no mistaking the size and height of the figure getting out of the car and walking up to our door. "This is an Irish neighborhood, and there are cameras everywhere. The police got this off the house across the street, but it never saw the light of day. It wasn't even documented as being in evidence."

"Why does she look so familiar?" I wondered. The black and white footage made it difficult to determine hair color or car color, and the distance and angle of the camera didn't help in identifying any traits that might stand out.

"There's a license plate, but we haven't been able to link it back to anything yet." Sully sighed. "Your hacker might have better luck."

I nodded, but my mind was completely on the woman in the video. There was a tugging at the back of my mind that spoke to familiarization. Like I had somehow met her but had never seen her. A face in a crowd of hundreds you think you see again a few days later. Déjà vu was another word for it.

"Was Jonny Morelli the only officer on this case?" I turned to Aine. "You said he was dead."

"Yeah, fucker committed suicide a few years ago," she said. "IA found him working for some Italian Mafia type here in the city. Caruso."

Vas snarled. "Fucking Cosa Nostra," he spat. "Leon's been working on getting info from the Seattle Don, but it's been slow going, even for him."

I turned to my *Sovietnik*. "Why do you say, *even for him?*" I asked suspiciously.

"Well," Vas rubbed the back of his head, looking a bit uncomfortable, "you know that Leon is Italian..."

"Yeah? So? I thought maybe he used to work for Dante."

Vas flinched.

"No." He sighed heavily. "Leon's last name is La Rosa."

And you could hear a pin drop.

That was how quiet the room became as everyone around me stared at Vas with utter shock painted across their faces.

And there I stood, like a fucking idiot trying to figure out what the fuck was going on.

"Who are the—" I didn't get a chance to finish my sentence.

"La Rosa?" My father's eyes were wide with disbelief. "Your *Obshchak* is Leon La Rosa? Son of Augustu La Rosa? Don of the West Coast Cosa Nostra? The butcher? The—"

"We get the point, Dad." I'm not sure which part startled him more. Leon's family tree or my calling him Dad.

Either way, he was left speechless for a few minutes while his mouth hung open like a guppy fish.

"Is that where he's been this whole time?" I questioned Vas. "Is Dima with him? Or is he out visiting his own family with prominent mafia roots as well? Who's his father? Putin?"

Vas didn't find me amusing.

Whatever. It was a good line.

"Don't worry about Dima," he scolded. "He is fine, and yes, that is where Leon has been. We discovered some ties between your *grandfather* and the Portland Cosa Nostra. Leon thought he could gain some insight and maybe even an alliance, but he's having a hard time of it."

"Why?"

"His father is only willing to help if he gains from it."

"What does he want?"

"An alliance."

"With us?" I asked. "I have no problem with that."

"A marriage alliance."

Nope. Nada. Wasn't happening.

"I'm taken."

"You're widowed."

"And not into a man who came out of the womb wearing a suit."

"Could be worse." Vas shrugged with a smile. "Augustu could have wanted you to marry him instead."

I think I just threw up in my mouth a little.

"I'll pass."

Vas chuckled.

"It's okay." He shrugged playfully. "You were never on the table, anyway."

I blew out my lips. "Whatever," I huffed. "I'm a great catch. Tell him about how many crazy psychos I have after me. He'll change his mind about me being a hot commodity."

"I thought you said you'd pass."

"Well, I mean, yeah." I shrugged. "But I don't like not being considered. That's just rude."

"Okay." He drew the word out, sarcasm leaking from every syllable. "I'll write him a formal rejection letter for you."

"Much obliged." I grinned up at him, forgetting that there were other people watching our banter.

"It's good to see you two work well together." Sully smirked. "There were many of us who wondered how having a woman as a *Bratva* leader would affect the pyramid of power."

"Women can lead just as well as men," I pointed out. "Even better if you pay attention to the history books."

"Hey now." Sully held up his hands. "That wasn't what I was saying. Just that you are the first female to hold the title of *Pakhan* in *Bratva* history. Not surprising, though. Your mother was set to inherit the Boston Irish from her father. Leadership runs in your blood."

Now I was confused.

"I thought she was going to be here with you." I turned to my father. "Weren't you set to inherit the Seattle Irish?"

"There was no Seattle Irish, Ava," he said. "I built it up after your mother disappeared."

"But you said you inherited it from your father."

"I did." He stared at me. "Your grandfather, my father, was Seamus's top lieutenant. I begged Seamus to bring me men, but he wouldn't have any of it. In hindsight, I should have read more into that. Seamus loved your mother. Doted on her. So did your grandmother. But I was drowning in pain and sorrow."

"And booze," O'Malley muttered. There was a story there I would get my father to tell me later.

"That, too," he admitted shamefully. "I missed them. All those fucking signs being waved in front of my face. I missed every single one. When he refused to send aid, my father defected and took more than half of McDonough's army with him."

"Half?" Pride and warmth bubbled in my chest. "That had to be more than a hundred people." My father and brothers now had more than five hundred loyal soldiers.

"More like two."

"But why?"

"Because your mother was a beacon, Ava." Sully spoke up. "It wasn't just information your mother gave to my father. Your mother was pure Irish Mafia. Straight from the homeland. Your family, the McDonoughs, have led the Boston Irish since its inception."

"So? How did that make her a beacon?"

"Because she wanted change," my father answered for him. "Genuine change. More opportunity for Irish immigrants. She wanted to make us legit. All of us, across the country, making legitimate livings."

"No more drive-bys," Sully listed somberly. "No more being knifed in a dark alley or shot at while delivering dope. No more prison sentences. We would still work in the shadows, but instead of running guns and drugs, we would build casinos. Launder money."

"So not quite legit," I deadpanned. But it didn't bother me. You can domesticate a lion, but the savage beast would always lurk just beneath the surface.

"More legit than we've ever been."

"Even more motive than before." Aine pondered a thought, her finger tapping against her chin thoughtfully. "Did the file contain the names of everyone at the north precinct who worked on her mother's case?"

Sully nodded. "Yep," he confirmed. "Some of them are dead. Tragic accidents, according to my father. But the coroner, the chief of detectives, and the evidence officer are still alive and thriving. In fact, they lead some pretty cushy lives now."

"How cushy?" my father asked suspiciously.

"Chief of detectives is now the chief of police. The coroner is now the chief medical examiner, and the evidence officer owns a security company here in the city."

Vas perked up at that.

"Which one?"

"Platinum Security."

Vas's smile dripped with malicious intent, his eyes flashing dangerously.

"Excellent," he crowed. "I've been needing a reason to take them down."

"Would you like to fill me in?"

Vas's smile dropped.

"Well..."

Liam barked a laugh. "You didn't tell her, did you?"

"Tell me what?" Why the hell did I always feel like I was out of the loop on everything?

"Um..."

"Start talking, you hippie haired Russian," I snarled.

"Platinum Security is our firm's greatest rival in the security industry."

"Our firm?"

"Yeah..." Vas hesitated. "Arctic Security and Associates."

"I thought that company was just a cover?"

"In a way it is." He winced.

Liam snorted. "It's a multi-billion-dollar cyber and protective security agency with contracts in over fifty countries. The associate part is the law firm they run as well."

"What the hell, Vas?" I screeched at him. "When were you going to tell me I inherited a billion-dollar company?"

"Multi-billion..." Liam smirked at Vas, who glared at him like he could shoot laser beams from his eyes and melt him into a pile of goo.

"Tomas wanted me to wait," Vas explained, his eyes still narrowed at my father. "He didn't want to overwhelm you with too many responsibilities. Being *Pakhan* was more important first. Maksim and Nikolai have been running Arctic behind the scenes for a while. Before you even married Matthias."

"Oh."

When he put it that way, I could see how letting me adjust to one role before taking on another would be wise. I was barely keeping up with being *Pakhan*, and adding public CEO to my list would only make things harder for me. Especially since we were in the middle of a war.

"Well," I beamed at him and slapped him on the back. Vas turned to me bewildered, "now that we have all this settled. Let's go torture some people and make them pay."

"After we get answers, of course," my father, the killjoy, reminded me.

"Yeah." I shot him a "duh" look. "Torture them...that's what I said."

"Torture is never highly effective for getting answers," he educated me. "But—" He shrugged, ignoring my icy glare. "Okay."

"And I thought our family was messed up," Aine grunted, amused. Sully laughed as we all made our way out of the house.

"Oh, kid." He shook his head. "You have no idea."

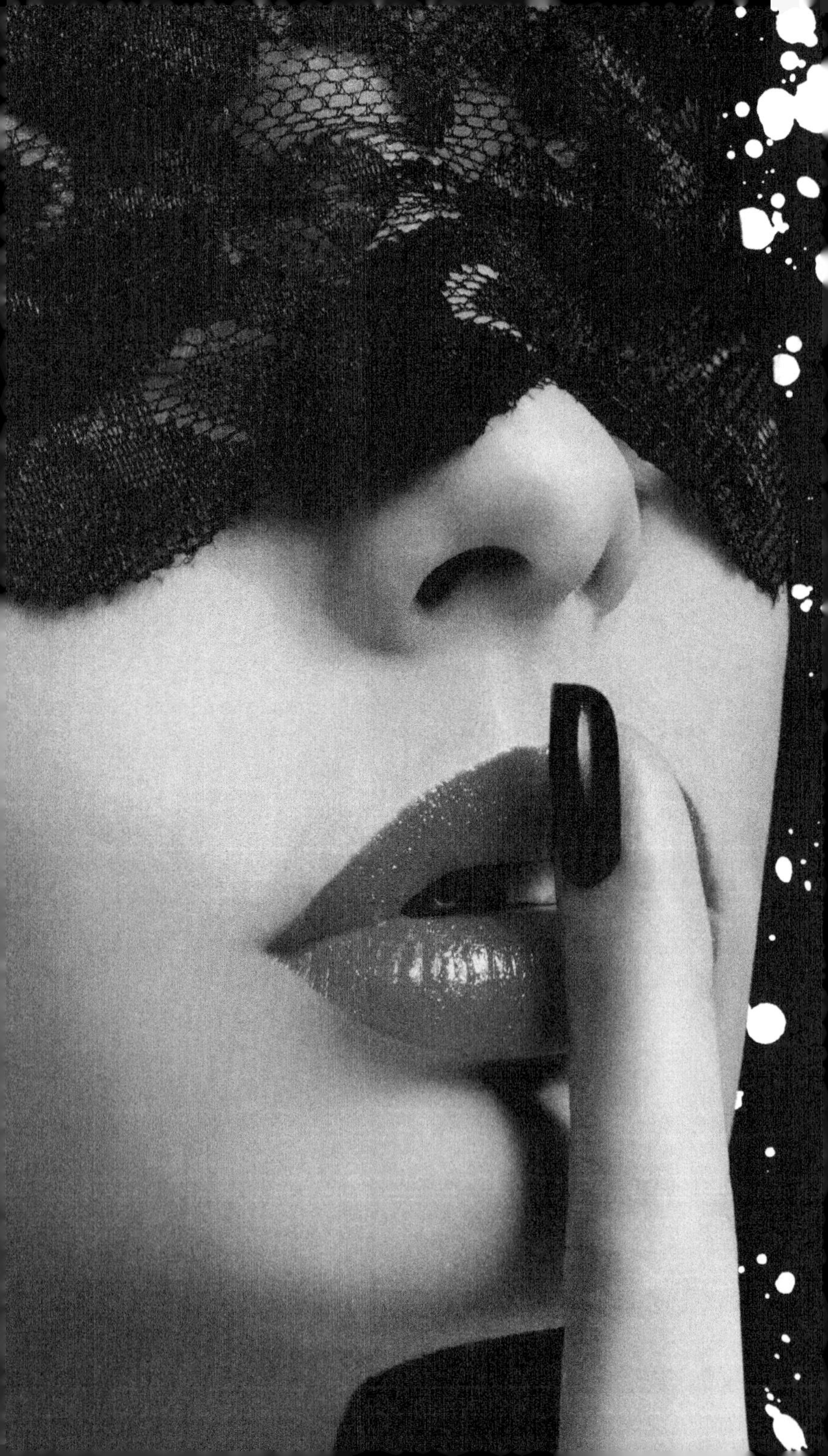

CHAPTER TEN

Sleep was a nonexistent little bitch.
In fact, over the past two days, it had been making me its bitch.

Apparently, my body thought I didn't need it, because it sure as hell hadn't shown its face in the last four hours. Sighing, I glanced over at the neon red lights of the hotel alarm clock. Midnight. I had to be up in five hours. Groaning, I slung an arm over my eyes.

This sucked donkey balls.

I was still wired from today. Being back at the house I grew up in left me unsettled and with far more questions than answers. I wished Matthias was here. He would know what to do. Or at the very least, I would have someone to talk everything out with.

There was a constant ache in my chest every night when I lay awake, wishing for the warmth of his body beside me. Behind me. On top of me. What a fucking fool I was. The man was planning on divorcing me. I had his empire on a technicality.

But that didn't mean I could easily forget how he made me feel. How his hands had played me like a violin.

Leaning my head back farther, I melted into the feather softness of the pillow. Even with him gone I could feel the ghost of his touch on my skin and in every part of me. My senses were branded with the familiarity of his touch.

Letting out a small, breathy sigh, I ran my hand leisurely along my body, mapping where he had been. My hips jerked, and wetness pooled between my thighs at the gentle touch of my fingertips I pretended were his. Every neuron singed with electricity, my body remembering what my mind wished it could forget.

"Forget the food, Krasnyy," he whispered in my ear as he bent me over the kitchen table. The cool marble of the countertop sent a shiver through me as my nipples pebbled even further at the juxtaposition of the cold marble and his hot mouth breathing down the side of my neck. "The only thing I'm fucking starving for is you."

The hand on the back of my neck kept me subdued as his free one glided down my back, brushing one of my ass cheeks before snaking around and gripping the soft nest of curls just above where I needed him. I jerked as he yanked on the sensitive hairs, the sensation sending a spike of wanton desire shooting through me.

"Matthias," I pleaded breathily. "Please."

"You want me to lick this cunt, baby?" he asked, his fingertips teasing my clit. I thrust my hips forward, but his fingers simply danced away. The countertop pushing into my stomach prevented me from moving any farther. He was in complete control.

As always.

"You want me to make you come?" He nipped at the top of my ear. My body shivered.

"Yes," I breathed. "Matthias..."

He left soft kisses down the back of my neck and shoulder. Nipping at the skin every now and again, causing me to cry out before he laved the wound with his tongue. His hand left the back of my neck as he knelt behind me. I turned my head to look, but a sharp swat to my ass put me back in position.

"Eyes forward, Ava," he warned. "Don't make me tie you down." My cheeks flushed, and I bit my lip at the thought of being entirely at his mercy. "Oh, my kinky little slut likes that, huh?"

Shit, why was him calling me a slut so hot?

Fuck.

Matthias chuckled and dragged his nose along my center, inhaling deeply. If I wasn't so turned on, my body thrumming, I might have been embarrassed. He growled, the sound making my pussy clench, and then dove in.

Gasping, I gripped the edge of the countertop when his mouth latched directly on to my already swollen clit. There was no gentleness, and he certainly wasn't taking any prisoners as he sucked and nibbled on the sensitive bundle of nerves until I was a writhing mess.

"Oh, god." I swallowed hard when his index and middle fingers slipped inside me. My back bowed, hips jerking back against his face, begging for more. Matthias hummed his approval as I pushed back against his fingers.

"That's it, Red," he growled. "Fuck yourself on my fingers while I suck on you."

With a loud moan, I did just that. I fucked myself wantonly on his fingers, feeling him curve them inside me as I did so, stroking my inner walls while he tongued my clit. He added a third, stretching me even farther. The pain melded *with the pleasure as I pushed back harder and faster, my moans filling the empty, cavernous kitchen.*

"That's it, baby," he urged me forward, the wave of euphoria just beginning to crest. I was so lost to the sensation of his fingers and mouth that I barely heard his zipper. His mouth left my clit, but his fingers were still working overtime. "Now," he breathed in my ear again, "scream for me, little whore." Without preamble, he shoved himself inside me in one long, hard thrust. Buried to the hilt.

"Matthias." I was lost to an endless sea of bliss as my euphoria crested. He rode me through my high, his grip on my hips bruising as he set a brutal pace.

"Fuck," he gritted, jaw clenched. "You feel so fucking good, Red. I want another." One arm snaked forward, and he tugged at my clit again, the nerves oversensitive.

"I can't," I cried. Tears tracked down my face at the stimulation that felt so good, but at the same time was pushing toward the edge.

"Yes, you can," he snarled. "Be a good little slut and come for me again. Grip me tight, baby." One more tug, and a hard, bruising slap on my ass, and I was a goner. The coil in my belly snapped, and I once again plummeted into the depths of ecstasy like I'd never known before.

I screamed his name, my fist pounding on the counter as he held me down. Wave after wave crashed over me as stars lit up my vision. I had never come so hard before.

"Shit," Matthias groaned as he emptied himself inside me. He braced himself over me, panting and sweaty, his face buried in my neck. "Good girl." I groaned lightly, those two simple words causing my pussy to pulse, even after the beating it had just taken.

. . .

I came down from my high, the orgasm I had just given myself nothing compared to the one in my memories. Tears slid down the side of my face and onto the pristine white pillow beneath me. Matthias was my first. There was a time when I had hoped he would also be my last. He'd ruined me in all the best ways. How was I supposed to forget that and move on?

There would come a day I would have to. If I survived the war ahead, I would need children to secure the Dashkov line, but they wouldn't be his children, and I doubted I would love any man as deeply as I loved Matthias.

Only time would tell what the tide of fate had in store for me.

Children were the last thing on my mind when vengeance was so much closer.

Closing my eyes, I let my mind wander to the past and the security it held. Because the future was nothing but a distant unknown.

This sucked.

Really. Really. Sucked.

"Can we do something now?" The petulant sound of my voice made me cringe. Not that I cared. The car was small and cramped, and the muscles in my legs were screaming at me in protest from not having moved in over an hour.

"You asked that twenty-minutes ago," my father scolded. Huffing, I blew a strand of hair out of my face.

"Get used to it." Vas smirked. "The word patient isn't in her vocabulary." The men in the car snickered.

"No, but the word beheaded is." I stuck my tongue out at him. It was official. I was a child. "As well as castrate." Vas widened his eyes in mock horror.

"Settle down, children," Sully scolded playfully. "We need to wait here until he arrives, otherwise, he will see us coming."

"You sent him a note that said, 'We know your secret. Do you really think those files are safe? Give them up or your family dies,'" I reminded him, with air quotes and everything. "He probably already knows we're waiting for him."

"He'll think we're at the meeting point I designated," Sully explained. "Dr. Martin believes he will have the drop on us, but in reality, we hold all the cards."

I shrugged. "If you say so."

"He will never give us those files," my father pointed out.

"Speak of the devil," Vas murmured.

Dr. Abram Martin was a tall, gangly motherfucker with round wire glasses, wearing a tailored Armani suit and driving a Benz. Two things a medical examiner shouldn't be able to afford with his salary. A dive into his financial records indicated he had received a two-point-five-million-dollar payout three days after my mother's death and smaller subsequent payouts throughout the years that we tracked back to the suspicious deaths of local trucking company owners and even a few cops.

The man looked over his shoulder nervously, causing him to take several extra moments to properly unlock the doors with his shaking hands.

"That's a go." Sully nodded his head the moment the good doctor stepped inside the office. He hadn't locked the doors behind him.

"Bet you the first things he goes for are the false files."

Vas scoffed at Sully. "I'm not taking that bet. Do I look stupid to you?"

Sully's mouth turned down as he thought about that. "Eh." He made a so-so motion with his hand. "A little, yeah."

"Fucker," Vas growled and grabbed his gun from the trunk before handing me mine.

"Come on." I nudged his shoulder with mine. "You can hit him for that later."

Vas grinned. "Promise?"

Laughing, I nodded and assured him, "Yep. All yours, big guy."

"Dreams really do come true."

"I heard that," Sully muttered as he walked past.

"Good." Vas winked. "I wouldn't want to have to say it louder for your old-ass ears."

Giggling, I shook my head in amusement and strode up to the office door.

"You know the drill," Vas reminded me. "Stay in the center of us and—"

"Don't take any unnecessary risk or try to be a hero," I drawled.

"Exactly."

"Fun ruiner," I muttered behind his back as the men surrounded me. Jesus, it was like being the president of the United States, but worse. I could defend myself. Not many presidents could say that. The current one would probably have a heart attack if he had to.

Quietly, on soft footsteps, we made our way through the darkened building toward the good doctor's office. Papers were being shuffled around, the sound echoing into the hallway. He cursed, a hard, heavy object falling to the floor with a distinct thud.

"Where is it?" the man muttered to himself in a panic.

"Looking for something, Doctor?" The two men in front of me parted to let me through. I strode into the posh office, head tilted up as I studied the man who falsified my mother's death report and who knew how many others.

"You..." He trailed off, the blood draining from his face as he stared at me, eyes wide.

The corner of my mouth tilted dangerously. "Cat got your tongue?" I sneered. "You look like you've seen a ghost."

"How can...you're..."

"Dead?" I raised an eyebrow, eyes flashing darkly at the word. He thought I was my mother. The ghost of his past coming back to haunt him. That was something I could work with. "Funny thing about death. Never really sticks when you want it to. Does it?"

"What do you want?"

I let out a harsh puff of air tinged with a dark chuckle. "I want my life back, doctor," I told him. "The one you stole from me. Tell me, how much was your soul worth? A couple of million?"

"I...it wasn't..."

"Personal?" I sneered. "Sure as hell felt like it. But don't worry," I bit my bottom lip, eyeing him like a lion does her prey, "when I kill you, it will be very personal to me."

"You don't have to kill me," he pleaded, dropping the file in his hand to the desk. "I'll give you whatever you want. I promise. Name it."

"Who gave you the hush money?"

The man visibly swallowed, his Adam's apple bobbing dramatically as fear welled in his eyes. His chest heaved, once. Twice. I could see the war going on in his mind through the minute facial tics he was unable to hide.

"I can't..."

"Wrong answer." The doctor screamed, his left leg collapsing beneath him as my bullet tore through his patella. The silencer kept the gases that propelled the bullet through the chamber quiet, muffling the sound of the bang.

Vas grimaced. "What is it with you and kneecaps?" I

shrugged. It was just an easy target to hit that I knew wouldn't cause him to bleed out or pass out.

"Let's try that again, Abram." I crouched down in front of him, gun dangling loosely between my legs. "Who gave you the hush money?"

"They'll kill me," he sobbed. "Please."

"You're going to die either way," I told him. "How painful your death will be is up to you."

"Please…" His cries and pleas for mercy fell on deaf ears. Just like my mother's had.

"How about this?" I lifted the barrel of my gun, pointing it at his stomach. "I can shoot you in just the right spot, you know, the sweet spot. The one that will have you lying here on the floor for hours in agony before your body finally shuts down. You'll be begging me to kill you, but I won't. I'll sit here and listen to your pitiful cries, and then I'll go find that sweet lil family of yours and do the exact same thing." I wouldn't go after them, but he didn't need to know that.

"No!"

"Or"—I tilted my head, eyes wild—"you can tell me what I want to know, and I'll leave your family alone and give you a nice, quick death. You decide."

"I can't…" He shook his head mournfully. "You don't know who you're dealing with."

"I'll give you to the count of five."

"Listen…"

"Five."

"Their organization runs deeper than you can imagine."

"Four."

"If I give them away, they'll come after my family. Even if I'm dead."

"Three."

"You don't know what they do to women and children."

I gave a throaty, venomous laugh. "You don't know what I do to women and children." My finger slipped over the trigger, ready to pull. "Two."

"Mercy. You have to have mercy."

"One." My finger began to pull on the trigger.

"Magnus Cartwright!"

Abram sighed in relief when I lowered the gun.

"Who is Magnus Cartwright?"

"The new chief of police," Sully answered for him. "Fucking bastard of a man if you ask me. Dirty as they come."

Abram nodded.

"Why would he want to cover up my mother's death?"

"Because whoever wanted it to look like a robbery set him up for life," Abram rasped. "I can see it now." He smiled sadly. "You look so much like her it's uncanny."

"The only time you saw her was when she was dead on your table," I snarled. The doctor nodded solemnly and huffed a sad breath.

"Whoever killed your mother," he told me. "It wasn't a robber."

"Why do you say that?"

"Because the wounds were too personal." He hiccuped. "Someone without attachments to her would have stabbed her or shot her and gotten it over with. Whoever killed your mother went into a fit of rage doing it."

"You had everything I wanted. Everything. Why couldn't you just lose for once in your fucking life?"

Another memory. Another mirage of the past. A woman's voice cutting through the haze of memories I'd locked away.

"What else did you lie about on the report?" My father gritted his teeth, hand clenched tightly around his gun. His knuckles were white, the tendons of his neck taut as he held himself back.

"Cartwright wanted the report to reflect that it was a man who'd killed her," the doctor divulged. "But it couldn't have been. The blows were too weak to be a full-grown man."

"What about an older gentleman who walks with a limp and a cane?"

Abram shook his head.

"Another set of evidence that had been suppressed was a pair of bloody shoe prints on the stairs," he continued. "Pointed toes with no heel."

"Stilettos," I breathed. It was starting to come together. The puzzle pieces fit snugger and snugger as more of the picture was revealed. There was only one woman I could think of who had the means and motive to kill my mother.

Marianne.

My mother confided in her once, and then suddenly Elias found her again. I knew the note my father said she had left was utter bullshit. Even without seeing it, there was no way my mother would have left him. She loved him.

Looking back now, at all the times she discussed the love of her life, I knew it was him. It was always him. But why did she run to Portland instead of back to him?

What made her flee? Or more precisely, who?

Marianne could have easily driven the two hours to Portland to kill my mother, and no one would have been the wiser. She had the motive, too. Years of living in my mother's shadow. The mafia princess with her fairy tale life and prince charming.

I glanced at my father out of the corner of my eye.

Nope. He wouldn't take that well. I needed concrete proof before I could bring that bombshell to him. He hadn't taken it so well the last time I brought my Marianne theory to him. Better to wait.

"What about the other cases you fudged?"

Abram sobbed, still clutching his bleeding knee. "They're on the table. Every case I've ever manipulated. I kept proof in case they went back on their word."

"Did you meet with anyone other than Cartwright?" Sully questioned.

"Jameson O'Neill," he admitted with disgust. "Owns Platinum Security."

"Anyone else?"

Abram shook his head. "No one I would know by name," he said. "There was an older gentleman with a cane I ran into a few times when I met with O'Neill or Cartwright, but he never introduced himself."

Flipping through my phone, I found what I was looking for. "Does he look like this?" I showed him the screen.

Abram nodded. "That's him."

"Good." I tucked the phone away. "Thank you for the information." I aimed my gun at him.

"Wait," he pleaded. "My family."

My eyes softened. "I was never going to hurt them."

"They will, though."

"Then know I will protect them," I promised. "But no one can protect you."

The trigger gave way under my finger.

Abram was dead, and I was one step closer to avenging not only Matthias, but my mother as well.

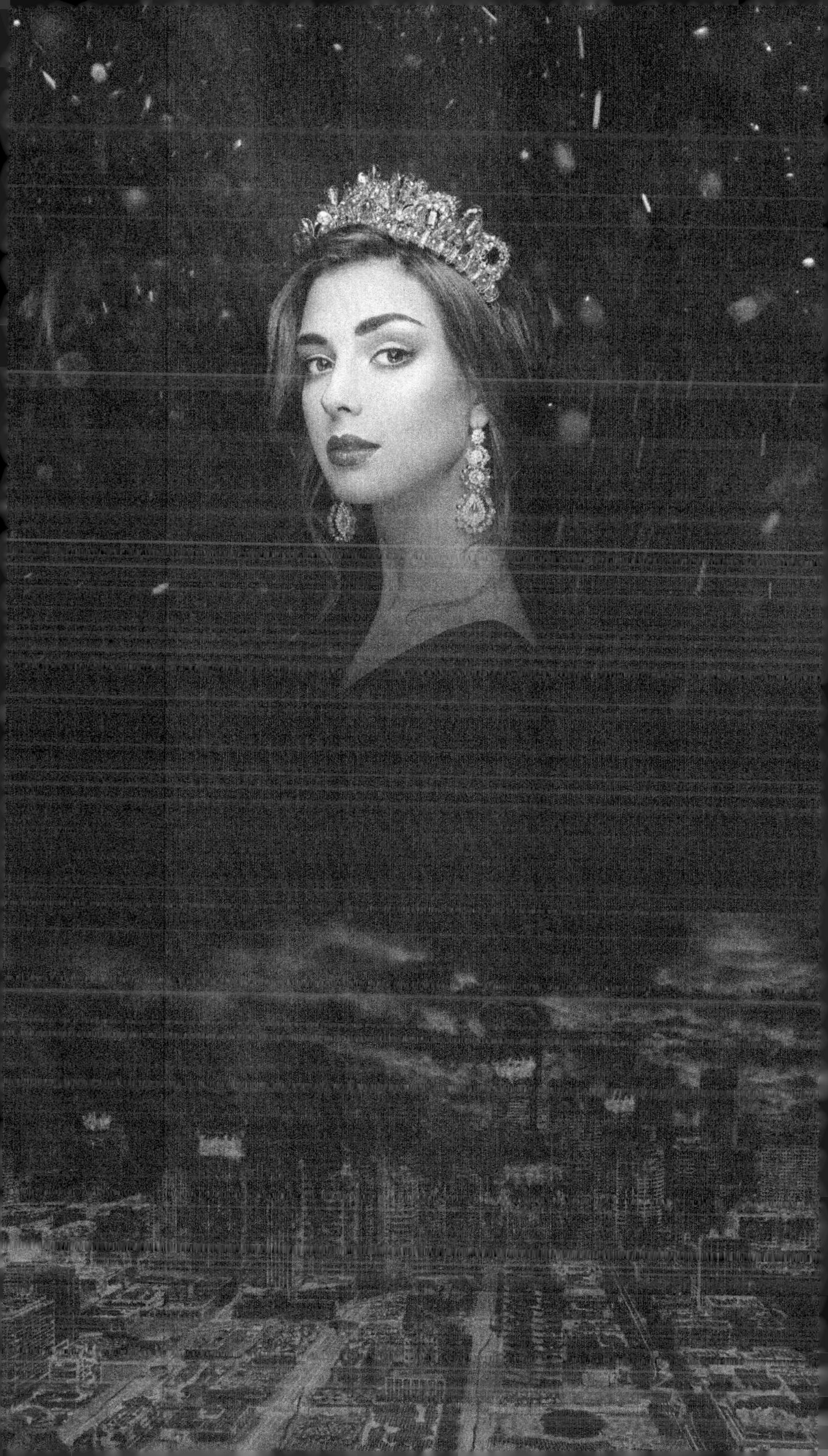

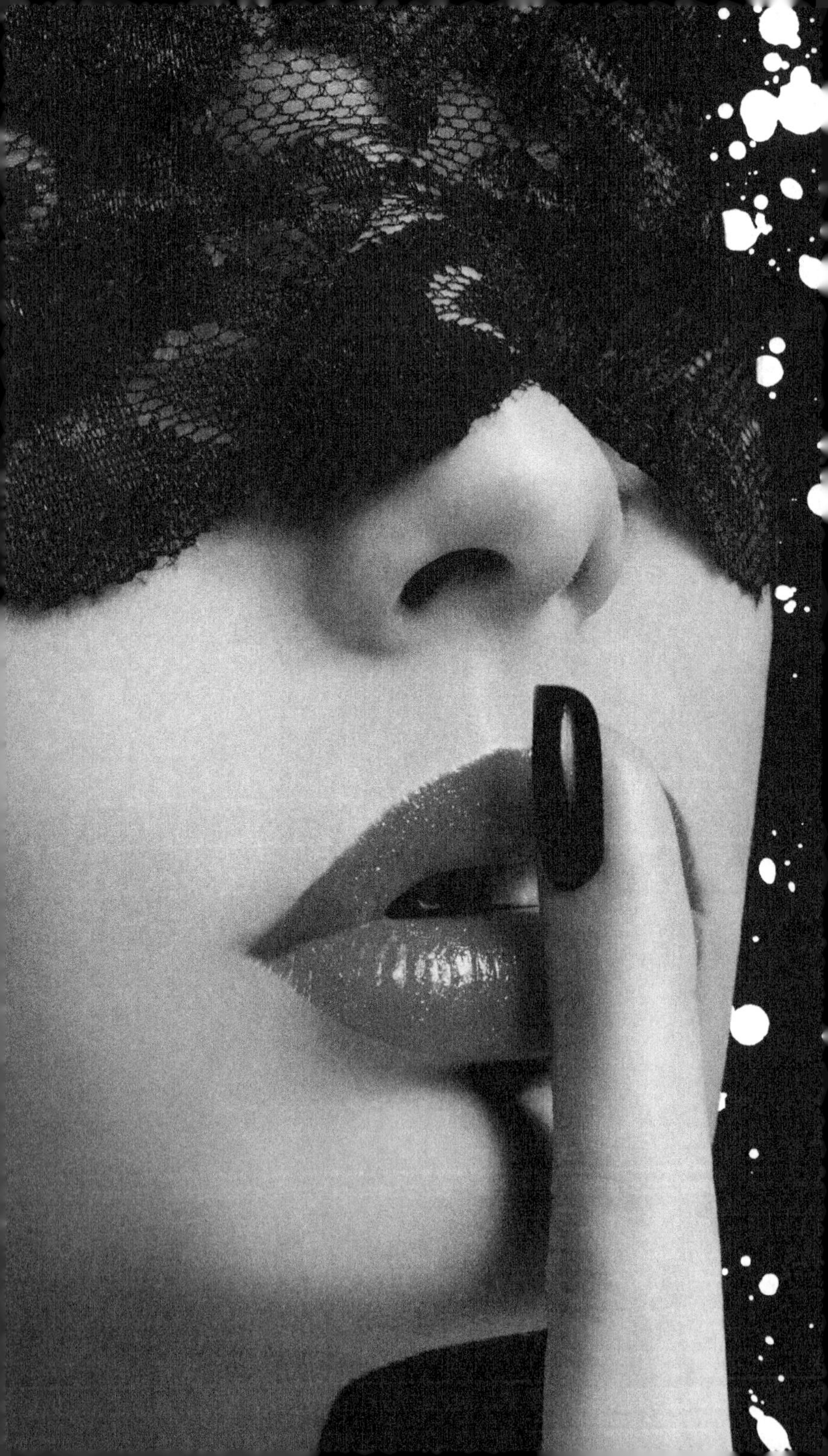

CHAPTER ELEVEN

"She was flirting with you." I scrunched my nose in disgust as the woman in question walked away. Tall, blond, and stacked. It was definitely his type before he married me. Even if they were mostly Vivian's paid whores. My husband was sex on wheels. The flesh version of Adonis, all muscle and sinew. He was a machine. Powerfully built. Women were going to stare.

Few of them had the nerve to approach him directly. This one had the gall to proposition him while I was sitting at the table. It had taken everything in me not to skewer her with my Christian Louboutin's. Matthias clearly saw my irritation. He winked at me and turned on the charm. Fuck, I was waiting for the woman to hand over her panties.

"I'll be in room 403 if you decide you have some free time." The falsetto mocking made me sound like a child, but I didn't care. She sounded like she'd been sampling the helium from the fake peckers her surgeon put in her chest.

"You're jealous." Matthias beamed at me. His stormy eyes shone with amusement, twinkling in the lights. Fuck yeah, I was jealous. I wasn't going to tell him that, though.

JO MCCALL

"Pfft," I huffed and took a sip of my champagne. *"No."*

He hummed like he didn't believe me.

"So, if I was to meet her upstairs in her room later?"

"See how far you get before I stab a knife through your testicles."

Matthias grimaced at the image, his hand going to his groin.

"And you say you're not jealous."

I scoffed. "There's a difference between jealousy and not wanting to catch one of her many, many diseases. Like entitlement. Or the obsessive need to see a plastic surgeon on a daily basis."

Matthias threw his head back and laughed. A full, deep-throated laugh that had my toes curling and my pussy clenching. Jesus, I wish he would do that more often.

"Shit." I'd knocked my fork off the table. Scooting my chair back, I bent down to pick it up, but it was still slightly out of reach. Well, damn. I knew I could wait for a waiter to get another one but leaving cutlery on the floor didn't sit right with me, so I did what any well brought up woman would do.

I knelt to retrieve it.

"Where did your friend go?"

Oh, that bitch was vapid and stupid. All those bleach products to her hair had fried her brain.

"She's," he paused for a moment, chuckling a bit, "around."

Biting back a laugh, I maneuvered myself under the table while the blond bimbo from planet Barbie told Matthias all about herself. My daddy's this and he bought me that. I got a pony on my twelfth birthday and named it Sparkles Pancakes.

Okay, that last part was made up.

Matthias's legs twitched slightly when I put my hand on his knees and leaned into him. The tablecloth was so long that no one besides my husband knew I was under here. Without hesitation, I unbuttoned his slacks and pulled at the gold zipper. My mouth watered when I saw he was going commando. He was already half hard.

His pelvis jerked when I took his length in my hand, and I could feel him hardening in my grip.

And men thought they had all the power.

He groaned. The feeling of my hot, wet mouth on his cock too much for him to contain.

"Are you all right?" the blonde asked, concerned.

"Just getting comfortable." He was clenching his jaw; I could hear it in his voice. "You were telling me about your pitbull?"

"Oh gosh no," the woman exclaimed. "My poodle. Hypoallergenic."

Laughing to myself, I took him in my mouth, and he stiffened beneath me, twitching against my tongue. We hadn't been married all that long, and until tonight, I had never been the one bold enough to initiate anything. Especially not in public. Matthias was always the one to take control and lead.

Most of the time, I was too anxious to try anything, afraid he would reject me, but now, as I sucked him down and felt him harden even further in my mouth, I knew I had nothing to worry about.

I could feel my abdomen tightening, and my core flushing with heat at the prospect of being caught servicing my husband under the table at one of the finest restaurants in the city. The thrill of excitement and the thought of being caught lit my body on fire.

Pulling back, I flattened my tongue along the underside of his shaft until there was nothing but the crown left in my mouth. I swirled my tongue along his girth, licking the slit at the top. His knee jerked, catching the table.

"Are you sure you're okay?"

"Fine," he gritted. *"Continue."* The tablecloth folded against his lap lifted slightly and I could just make out the glare he gave me. One that promised retribution. Grinning up at him, I sucked him back into my mouth and, wanting to show him exactly who was in charge, I started a relentless pace.

"Blyad," he murmured. The woman didn't seem to notice his sudden Russian. She was too busy talking about herself. He fisted my hair in one hand but didn't take control. Barely able to swallow half of him, I added one hand to the base of his cock, stroking him in tandem with my mouth while the other hand gripped and fondled his balls. His pelvis bucked harder into my mouth, causing me to gag, but I didn't relent as I continued for several more minutes.

"It's time to end this," he said, and the woman audibly pouted her disappointment, not realizing Matthias wasn't talking to her. Without warning, he gripped my hair tighter, yanking me against him until his cock hit the back of my throat, causing me to tear up.

I sucked harder, hollowing out my cheeks, allowing my teeth to slightly graze the underside of his cock. It wasn't much longer before warm liquid spurted down my throat, his hips jerking as he released the last of his pleasure into my mouth.

Swallowing it all down, I dragged my mouth off his softening cock and tucked him neatly back into his pants before straightening my dress and discreetly climbing out from under the table. There was no way to escape without her noticing, so I simply cleared my throat to gather her attention.

"Where did you come from?" She stared up at me with thinly veiled distaste.

"From," I smirked, "around." I winked over at Matthias, who coughed a laugh before taking a long sip of his whiskey.

The woman's gaze darted between the two of us before she gave a disgusted snort and stormed off.

"Well," Matthias grabbed my hand and drug me toward him, "that was entertaining."

"Definitely not something tits for brains over there would do."

Matthias hummed, tilting his head a bit to look up at me. His hand snaked around my waist to grab at my ass and pull me into him. Even sitting, he was still nearly as tall as me, and I was in heels. The distance between us was minimal. The other hand grabbed at my jaw, firm but gentle, and then he was devouring me.

"Ava," he murmured, pulling away, and the past faded with him.

"You had the men move Abram's widow and children?"

Vas nodded as he prepared himself a cup of coffee at the hotel's continental breakfast. One look at me, and he handed me his cup and poured another. Damn. Did I look that bad? Sleep had been negligible at best. Haunted by memories of the past. Didn't help that it was all one large porn dream that had me waking up hot and heavy with a growing need pulsing between my legs.

My hand wasn't the same as Matthias's. That was for sure.

"Sully and his men cleared them out this morning," he informed me. Taking a sip of his coffee, he continued. "Seems like Abram had a contingency plan in place in case things went to shit. She wasn't even surprised when we showed up on her doorstep. Had suitcases ready to go and everything."

"Good," I murmured, my eyes closing as the taste of pure

heaven seared my tongue. It was cheap, but that was fine with me. I'd spent a year downing cheap coffee and booze. "Sully said we can't touch Cartwright. Not yet, anyway. What about O'Neill?"

Vas's eyes twinkled with mirth. "Oh, I have just the plan for that."

"Why do I have a feeling I'm not going to like this?" I groaned.

"Depends." He shrugged, grabbing a plate and helping himself to a hearty helping of eggs, bacon, and grilled veggies. "How quick of a study are you?"

"Pretty good," I told him. "What are you having me learn?"

"How to be the CEO of a billion-dollar security company in less than," he looked at his watch, "six hours."

"Great," I muttered. "'Cause that's something I've done before."

Vas grinned at me as we sat down with my father at one of the tables situated in the back. "Did you tell her the plan?" he asked.

I turned to him. "You're in on it, too?" I pretended to be appalled.

"It's not like it's a real date." My father shrugged casually. "It's just business."

Pump the brakes.

"I'm sorry." I stared at the two men incredulously. "Did you just say date?"

My father shot Vas a look. "You didn't tell her that part?"

Vas chuckled lightly. "Hadn't gotten that far."

Liam cursed under his breath.

"You want me to go on a date with the guy who had a hand in covering up my mother's murder?" Disbelief was written over my entire face in red permanent marker. "He's old and crunchy."

The two men choked on their breakfast.

Served them right.

Vas coughed, pounding on his chest to dislodge whatever was stuck. His fucking ego, probably. Devious bastard.

"With his son," my father placated in a hoarse voice. "Jaysus. What kind of father do you take me for?"

"Eh," I shook my hand side to side. "So-so."

"So-so?" he repeated slowly. "I am not so-so."

"Then where's my pony?"

Vas snorted into his coffee cup and coughed.

"You want a pony?" he asked seriously. "I'll get you a pony. Fuck, I'll buy you an entire stable."

Throwing my head back, I laughed.

"I don't need a pony."

He didn't look convinced. Shit. What if he actually bought me a stable full of horses?

Wouldn't be the worst thing.

Except—I didn't know anything about horses.

And I was pretty sure I was allergic to hay.

"All right," Vas interceded. "Moving on."

"Fine," I grumbled. "Why do I have to go on a date with Crusty's son?"

Leaning back in his chair, Vas fixed his gaze on me. "It's not a date, Ava," he assured me. "It's a business meeting. Matthias has always vocalized his disdain for Platinum Security publicly. We need you to convince him we want to partner with him."

"Why? What's the endgame?"

"Jameson O'Neill built his company with money stained in your mother's blood," Vas explained gently. "Not only that, but there is evidence that his company is working with whoever has been shipping women for auction."

That was suspicious. Where had he come up with that information?

"Who told you that?"

"Mark's been digging into their background and clients." Vas waved his hand dismissively. A sure sign he was hiding something from me. But why? "If we can make him believe that you don't have the same scruples as Matthias, maybe we can get some insight into who they are working for."

"The Dollhouse." Why was he repeating information? We'd already been over this.

"We think the Dollhouse is just one facet to something larger that we can't see," Vas informed me. "Have you ever heard of *Potestas Omnis*?"

I snorted. "Impotus Omnis sounds more appropriate, if you ask me."

They both groaned. "*Potestas Omnis* is Latin for Power Over All. We believe it's a secret society going back more generations than anyone could count. Possibly even as far as the fall of Rome."

"We?"

Vas's lips parted slightly. It was the only tell he gave me that hinted at his duplicity.

"Mark and I."

Shrugging, I nodded. "You and Mark discovered a sudden link to a secret society?" Vas nodded. "By yourselves?" Another nod.

"Right." I stood from the table. "Look, I'll go on your stupid business date with Crunchy Jr. But, until you start telling me the fucking truth, Vasily Ivankov, feel free to step down as my *Sovietnik*."

"Ava," my father cautioned gently.

What the hell?

"No." I slammed my hand down on the Formica tabletop. "I'm done with the lies and subterfuge. How am I supposed to trust my own men when they can't tell me the truth? Do you not trust me to be your leader? Was you backing me with your father all a lie?"

"It's not like that, Ava." Vas pushed his chair back and stood. He leaned toward me, hands on the table. "I need you to trust that I can't tell you everything. Not right now."

The laugh that left my lips was mirthless.

"That's not how this works, Vasily," I told him. "Matthias and everyone kept me on the outside. Hell, I didn't even know I would inherit the *Bratva*. Or that his security company was an actual thing and not some showboat site. How can I trust someone who has never once trusted me?"

"I do trust you."

My eyebrows disappeared into my hairline. "Then where is Dima?" I crossed my arms against my chest and stared at him expectantly. Vas sighed and hung his head. "That's what I thought. Send up what you need me to learn."

Then I walked away.

"Shit," Vas raged behind me. My father whispered something to him that was too low for me to hear. Whatever he told him didn't appear to have any effect on Vas. Not at first. But slowly, he submitted and sat back down in his seat.

What the hell was going on?

One thing I knew for sure, I was going to get to the bottom of whatever they were hiding.

Even if I had to do it myself.

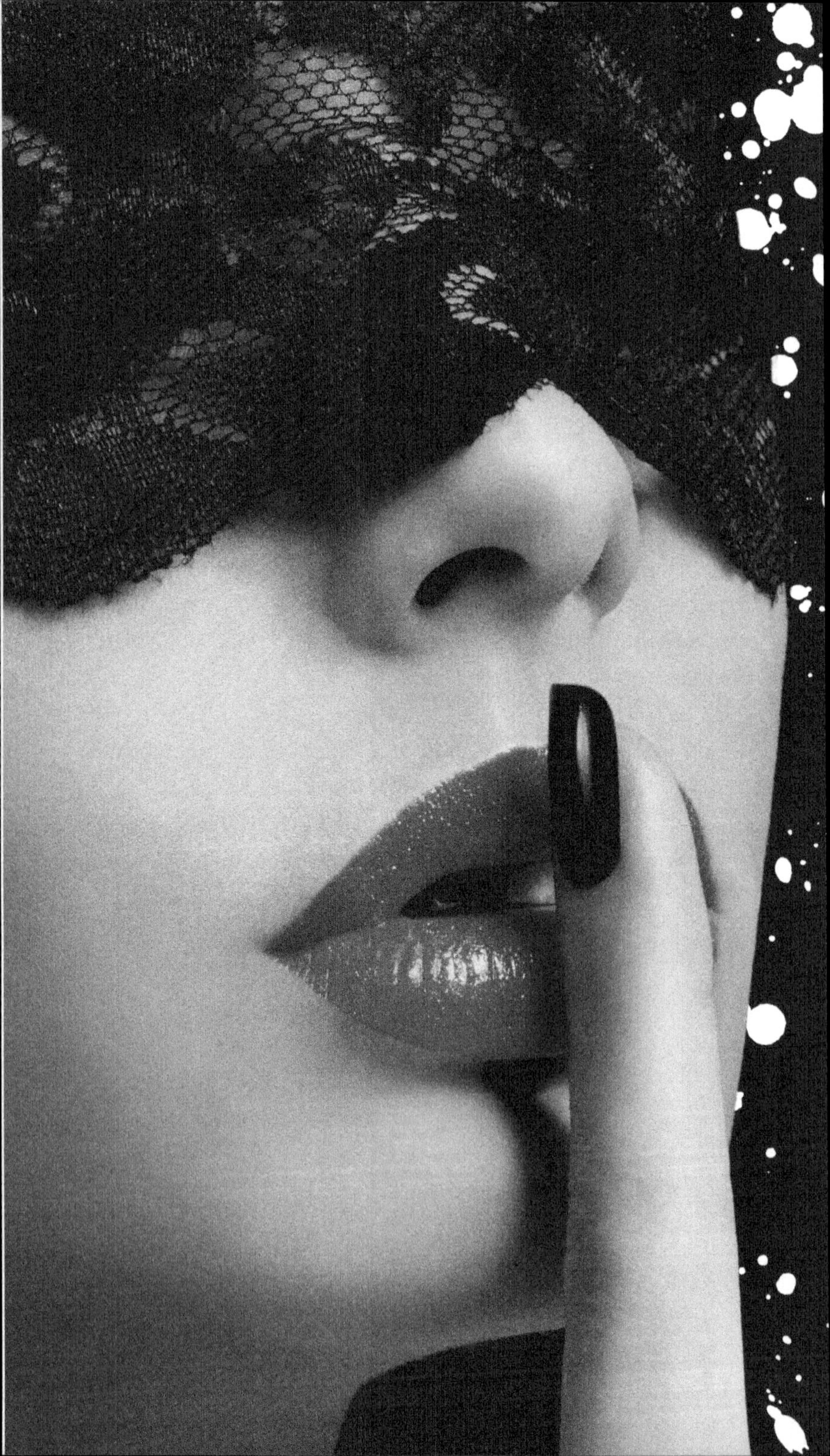

CHAPTER TWELVE

This was ridiculous.

Stupid.

Certifiable.

Groaning, I swept my untamed curls into my signature messy bun and took a step back from the bathroom mirror. Tilting my head, I surveyed the outfit, wondering what was missing.

Ah.

My gun.

Using the new holster Bailey had bought me, I secured my weapon at the small of my back, shifting my oversized knitted cardigan to cover it.

There. Perfection.

"Is that what you're wearing?"

Great. Just what I needed. An appearance by a Tim Gunn wannabe.

"Is there something wrong with what I'm wearing?" I quirked an eyebrow at him through the mirror.

"No." Vas dragged the word out, his voice pitching slightly with his lie. "Just seems a bit...casual is all."

I turned to face him. "You said it was a date." I pointed a manicured finger at him. "Is this not a date outfit?"

"It's a business date," was his rebuttal.

"Well, I don't want to sit all night in business attire."

"Your top is too low."

Looking down, I took in the soft, silken tank top I was wearing. It was white and fringed with a lace sweetheart neckline that prevented me from showing any cleavage unless I was leaning over. I'd tucked it into my black jeans and paired it all with black ankle booties and a red wine cardigan.

I thought it looked cute.

"My top is fine, *Dad*." I rolled my eyes. "Why are you suddenly so fussy, anyway? You're the one who set this up."

The corner of Vas's lip twitched. "I'm beginning to regret that."

"Whatever." I dabbed a small amount of perfume on my neck and the inside of my wrists. "Too late to cancel now."

"Don't be so sure."

Sighing, I slammed the perfume bottle down on the bathroom counter. "What is your problem, Vasily?" I demanded angrily. "You're the one who told me this was important. Now you're acting like a scorned lover."

Vas scoffed.

"I am sick and tired of your bipolar, shit attitude," I told him. "It's giving me whiplash."

"Ava..."

I held up a hand. "Stop," I snarled. "The only time you say my name recently is when you're about to make up some fucking excuse about why you can't tell me something or to apologize. I'm done, Vasily. You're relieved of your duty. My father and Igor can take it from here."

"You need to understand—"

"I am tired of you telling me that!" Brushing past him, I

picked up the small satchel from the couch. Purses of any size weren't my thing, but I wanted to be sure I had my phone and money easily accessible in case something went wrong.

Which it always did.

"The only thing I need to understand is that you don't trust me," I snarled. "And I don't want a *Sovietnik* who doesn't trust me. Want to keep your spot? Then man up and tell me what the hell you've been hiding. Show me that you think more of me than just Matthias's widow who's in over her head."

Crickets.

Well, that was slightly heartbreaking. Vas was one of the few friends I had. Or thought I had, anyway. It appears I put more stock in that friendship than he ever did. To him, I wouldn't be anyone other than a mafia widow. Someone he couldn't trust to keep the secrets he was holding on to.

"Okay then." Turning, I stalked out the door of the hotel room before he could see the tears gathering in my eyes and the broken shards of my soul.

"Moving those assets around was pertinent to keeping the Saudi prince safe," the man pontificated. "He was so grateful he gave me one of his diamond encrusted turbans. The Portland Museum was honored to have us add it to their collection, of course…"

Jesus. Was this guy for real?

Conrad O'Neill, or Crunchy Jr., as I was referring to him in my head, hadn't shut his useless trap since I'd sat down for dinner. Vasily didn't have to worry about me memorizing facts about our company. This asshat didn't care what I knew about Arctic Security. He was more interested in telling me how wealthy he was and how many people owed him a debt.

I wondered if it was bad manners to slit his throat before the appetizers came.

"Good evening." The waiter approached with a smile. "Have we decided on our orders yet?"

Pushing back a laugh, I smiled and nodded. The poor man had been trying to take our order for the last ten minutes, but each time, he was ignored in favor of another boring tale of how Crunchy Jr. had saved everything from disaster.

The man should write a book.

If he hadn't already.

"Yes." Conrad barely gave the waiter his attention. "I'll have the sixteen-ounce ribeye, rare, with potatoes and asparagus. Also, a glass of your best red."

"Very well, sir," the waiter acknowledged before turning to me. "And..."

"She'll have the house salad with light dressing and a white wine."

Poor man. The waiter's gaze shifted nervously between the two of us as he scribbled down our order. Well, Crunchy Jr.'s order. It sure as hell wasn't mine.

"I can order for myself, thank you." I put on my best Kendra smile. Fake and plastic. "I'll have the Bourbon Chicken and Shrimp with fondant potatoes, please. And your best top-shelf whiskey."

Conrad sneered. I caught the look out of the corner of my eye. If he thought I was the same level of bimbo as his previous dinner dates, he would be sorely mistaken.

"Don't you think you should have something lighter?" he asked, taking a sip of his wine as I tucked into my dinner. The man hadn't shut up about my eating habits the entire time it had taken the waiter to bring out our food.

"Well," I smirked, taking a sip from my glass of whiskey and eyeing his bloody steak, "if you don't have to watch your figure, why should I?"

Oh, he didn't like it when a woman fought back.

If looks could kill.

"You're rather hostile for someone who needs to do business with my company," he sneered. "I was rather surprised at the dinner offer, honestly. Had I realized I was meeting with the company whore instead of the CEO, I would have suggested we skip dinner and go straight to my hotel room."

Vas said I can't kill him.
Vas said I can't kill him.

"Oh, honey." My laugh was low, sensual, and full of the promise to do bad things. "I'm no one's whore. I am the CEO. Maybe you should have paid attention when they told you my name."

That had him slack-jawed and silent for a moment.

"Yeah." I wrinkled my nose at him and smiled. "Should have thought about that before popping off at the mouth. And as for my company's *need* to do business with yours? There is no need. In fact, from the look of things, you need my company more than I need yours."

"We don't—"

Holding up a hand, I interrupted him. "Now, now. There's no need to lie, Mr. O'Neill," I assured him, injecting as much condescension in my voice as I could. "Your shares are dropping, and your investors aren't happy with you overspending your budget every quarter."

He went to talk, but I didn't give him the chance for a rebuttal.

"Must have something to do with the fact that you've been doing some naughty side jobs." Taking a sip of my whiskey, I continued. "I wonder what the FBI would think about the money you've been shunting through an illegal account that has been funding the Aryan Nation, a well-known domestic terrorist group."

His grip tightened on the wineglass in his hand, his face turning a rather fetching shade of purple. Like Violet Beauregarde in *Willy Wonka*, just angrier.

"I mean," I chuckled breathily, "if that isn't enough, I'm sure that the CIA and Interpol would be ever so interested in the many items you've acquired and moved for your clients. Or how about the Department of Defense? Do they know you were helping Knightman Security move all that lost cash through the Middle Eastern ports? That one took me a while to figure out, but I do have one of the best hackers in the business."

"You don't know what you're talking about," he hissed, but sweat was beading down his immaculately botoxed forehead. "My company is perfectly above board."

"And I'm Cindy Lou-Who," I scoffed. Wiping his mouth with a white linen napkin, he threw it down on the table in a huff and went to stand. But I wasn't finished with him yet.

His high-pitched scream was music to my ears as my steak knife slid like butter through the middle of his hand, embedding itself into the wooden table beneath the silken cloth. People were staring, but that didn't matter. Let them see what happened when you crossed a Dashkov.

"Did I say you were dismissed?"

"Fucking psycho bitch," he spat angrily, tears rolling down his face.

"Heard worse," I admitted casually. Leaning in, I whispered, "But we're not here to discuss me. We're here to discuss you and your sick fuck of a father who started your little company with the blood money he got from suppressing my mother's case."

"That's what this is about?" he asked incredulously. I swatted his hand away when he went for the handle of the knife that was still buried in the table. "Get over yourself. It was a long time ago, and from what I heard, the whore deserved it."

He paled, his eyes widening in fear when he saw the fury of storm clouds etched across my face. I tsked, shaking my head in mock remorsefulness.

"Wrong thing to say, Crunchy Jr.," I scolded him. The restaurant was silent. All eyes were still on us. No one moved. Or breathed. Not that it mattered if they did. The only people in this restaurant that weren't Sully's or mine were the staff, and they'd been well compensated for their trauma.

I mean time.

Circling the table, I let my fingers graze over the soft table cloth before clutching the hilt of the knife. Conrad hissed at the contact, the serrated edges digging further into his skin.

"I was hoping you were nothing like your pig of a father." Disappointment colored my tone, and I tsked again. "Luckily, my hopes weren't too high. I do hate to be disappointed. Now," I twisted the knife slightly, and the man howled, "one of your clients caught my attention, and I want to know who the owner is."

Silence.

Conrad's teeth clenched together, his lips turned up in what I suppose he thought was a snarl, but it was more of a grimace. He wasn't going to tell me without a little more motivation.

"Okay, then." Grabbing the other steak knife on the table, I embedded it into his other hand. He wailed and cursed and cried, but it didn't matter. "Sorry about that. Some people were complaining that I go for the kneecaps too often, so I thought I'd try something different. But don't worry. A little bit of surgery, and you might regain some use sooner or later. Who. Is. The. Owner?"

"I don't..." He swallowed back the pain and sobs. "There wasn't a name attached, but I've seen him. Older man. Irish. With a cane. He was my father's first client."

Seamus. Or whoever the hell was pretending to be him.

"Why wasn't there a name?"

"Guy didn't want anything traced back to him," Conrad told me breathlessly. "We kept him anonymous."

"What about—" Movement at the door to the restaurant caught my attention. It was subtle, and no one else in the room appeared to have caught it.

Blue eyes beneath a wide-brimmed hat burned into my soul, the hatred bubbling up around me at the smug smile that was shot my way.

Kenzi was here.

Then, before I could blink, she was gone.

A ghost.

"Let's continue this later, huh?" Without a backward glance, I strode out of the restaurant, ignoring the people calling my name. This was more important. The revenge I had been searching for was at my fingertips.

The street outside was nearly empty, save for a few pedestrians.

An engine revved to my left, tires squealing as it broke to a sudden stop in front of me. The window slid down. Betrayal seared my soul when she smiled at me and winked from behind the wheel of her Aston Martin.

"Come and get me, big sis," she taunted before revving the engine again. Snarling, I ripped my father's car key from my pocket and darted to it before she could get too far ahead of me. It was pure luck that I had insisted on driving myself to the restaurant.

The door opened automatically at the push of a button, sliding up and out of the way. Once I pressed the keyless ignition, it closed, and I was off like a shot. The Ferrari F60 America glided through the slick streets of Portland with ease. Its compact body allowed it to take the sharp turns of the city, weaving through traffic smoothly.

Kenzi managed to continually stay out of range. She was leading me somewhere. Probably a trap, but I didn't care. This was my chance. Matthias was dead, and she was the reason why. I didn't care if she had been tricked into it or was ready to apologize.

All I wanted was for her to bleed like my heart bled every damn day.

Rain began to pour from the open sky. The Ferrari's wipers were working overtime as I followed Kenzi's trail down a long dirt road just outside of the city limits. Despite the mud beneath the tires and several near wipeouts, I only inched the gas pedal down farther.

Kenzi had disappeared from my sight. Not that it mattered. There was only one place this road led. An abandoned barn surrounded by a field of trees. Because that wasn't creepy at all.

"Bit dramatic, don't you think, Kenz?" I hollered over the howling wind, the rain instantly soaking me as I stepped out of the car. Unease blitzed through me when I peeked at the depreciating structure before me. Summoning what little bravado I possessed, I stalked toward the dilapidated building.

"Come on, lil sister," I mocked once I had stepped through the open door that led inside. It smelled of mold and musty hay, and the air hung heavy with disuse. "You got me all the way out here." I let my hand rest on the gun tucked into the small of my back. "You just gonna hide?"

The echoing laugh was mordacious and dark. It made my skin crawl and my jaw clench.

"You used to like to play and seek." Her voice was distant, and the capacious space made it hard to pinpoint where it was coming from. "Remember?"

I rolled my eyes. Oh, I remembered all right. The twins knew the inside and outside of the house. The secret hallways, the servants' wings, everything. I'd spend hours looking for them, only to realize Kendra had taken them out for something special while leaving me home.

Yep. There were no forgetting memories such as that.

"That's not exactly how I remember it," I returned. "But let's not quibble over such trivial things." Not that those memories were trivial. They were branding. A reminder of where I truly sat in that family growing up. "Why don't you just come on out? Let me shoot you. Get this over with nice and quick."

More laughter.

"I always knew there was a mentally unstable psycho lurking just beneath that ridiculously naïve façade of yours."

I snorted.

"If I'm a psycho," I told her, "you made me so by murdering my husband. The one man who cared for me."

"Oh please." Her voice echoed around me, full of pity. No remorse to be heard. "Libby and I cared about you far longer than he has. We were always there for you."

"You weren't there for Libby, were you?" It was a low blow. Really low, but I was angry, and angry, rage-filled Ava didn't make the best decisions. "Had her believing you were off at college this whole time. Where were you really, Kenzi? Learning to be Christian's lapdog?"

"Shut your fucking mouth, Ava," she hissed. "You don't know anything about what I've been through."

"And you turned a blind eye to everything *I* went through," I shouted back. "Pretend all you want, Kenzi, but you always knew more than you were letting on."

Silence greeted me. I doubted it was because I hit a nerve. More likely she was—

"I did." I froze at the sound of her voice. Her hot breath on the back of my neck. "But do you honestly think I could have done anything? My father was a monster who didn't need me and sent me away the first chance he got. But you? The whore's daughter? You might not have been treated as precious, but he wanted you. He was obsessed with you."

Snarling, I yanked on my gun, but it was too late. Kenzi had it in her hand and pointed at the back of my head before I could say "fuck you."

"I've learned some tricks, big sis," she mocked. "Don't make me use them on you."

I scoffed. "You're not the only one with tricks."

If she thought I was going to let her take me to Christian or kill me, she was about to get a reality check. As soon as I felt her body shift, I twisted out of the way of the gun. Kenzi hadn't had a physical grip on me, and it was easy to duck out of the way of the barrel. I gripped the wrist holding my gun and twisted it over quickly. The move threw her off balance, and she dropped my gun onto the hay-covered floor.

Spinning around, I swept her legs out from under her. She landed hard on her back with a groan. With lightning-fast speed, she recovered, flipping back to her feet like a ninja. Where the fuck had she been? League of Assassins? Training with Oliver Queen?

Her gaze on me was askance. I smiled at her and winked. Kenzi hadn't expected me to be able to go toe to toe with her.

Bitch didn't know I'd leveled up.

"I don't want to hurt you, Ava," she cautioned as we circled one another. "There's a lot that needs to be explained."

"I'm not letting you take me back to my psychotic brother," I hissed at her. "You'll have to kill me first." I paused and shrugged nonchalantly. "Or I'll kill you."

"Really?" she huffed. "You'd kill your own sister?"

"You stopped being my sister the moment you killed the man I love." I growled and lunged at her. My arms wrapped around her waist in an attempt to tackle her. I was slightly bigger than her, but I could feel the muscles beneath my grip. She wasn't the only one who had underestimated her opponent. Using my momentum against me, she wrapped her arms around my upper chest and rocked backward even faster as she let us fall to the ground.

Fuck.

Kenzi bucked her hips when we landed and sent me crashing over her head in a heap.

That hurt like a bitch.

Taking advantage of my momentary disorientation, she grabbed one of my arms and twisted it painfully behind my back, driving me facedown into the ground.

"I didn't kill him." Her words were a mere breath against my ear.

"Liar!" I roared, my head snapping back to catch her in the face. Kenzi yelped, loosening her hold on me. She rolled onto her back, clutching her nose for a second too long. Her moment of weakness was my time to strike. "You taunted me!" Getting to my feet, I landed a kick to her side. Kenzi grunted. The force of my strike sent her rolling onto her stomach. Another kick, but this time she was ready.

Reaching out, she snatched my ankle in her grip and pulled. The move sent me careening to the floor on my back. She was on me, straddling my waist as she delivered a blow to my left side. *Ow*. I hoped I still had a spleen after that shot.

"There's more at work here than you know," she wheezed through her broken, bloody nose. The droplets of blood dripped down her face onto my chest. "I'm not your enemy."

I spat at her.

"You weren't there!" I snapped, bucking my hips to dislodge her. It didn't work. I needed to distract her again. "You blamed us for killing her, but you weren't there."

"That was the point." She said it so matter of fact. "You needed to believe what I was telling you."

"You still murdered him," I cried, tears leaking from my eyes. "You took him from me and left me all alone. Everyone always leaves me. First my mother. Then Libby. You took the last good thing I had in my life and blew him to hell."

Kenzi threw her head back and laughed.

"And look what you became," she pointed out with a broad, blood-filled grin. "A warrior. A queen. You would never have become that in his shadow. You needed to grow. To learn what you were capable of. All your life, you've lived in the shadows. One person's pawn after another. A tool. Now you are the master. You decide your fate. No one else. That is what *I* gave you."

"You. Gave. Me. Nothing."

It was small. A glint of silver among the darkness. I barely recognized it for what it was. There wasn't any time to analyze the psychobabble she was spewing to me.

A trick.

A ploy.

Thrusting my knee into her stomach, I rolled our bodies, snatching the small silver hilted knife from the inside of her boot as I laid her out on her back. The knife was to her throat before her back hit the ground.

"You. Took. Everything."

Kenzi's nostrils flared, her lips parting slightly as the pupils dilated. Her body shook infinitesimally beneath me. For a moment, she was truly afraid.

"Then do it." She bared her teeth and leaned in toward the blade. My hand trembled, nicking the soft, vulnerable skin of her outstretched neck.

"Enough!"

The command caught me off guard, and I hesitated.

Strong arms wrapped around me and tore me off my sister. Surprise shook me, and I dropped the knife to the ground as the scent of fresh pine and old leather assaulted my senses.

No.

It was a trick.

He was dead. I'd watched him die.

"Enough." His lips brushed the shell of my ear, and his warm breath cascaded over the chilled skin of my cheek. "*Krasnyy.*"

"Stop." I shook my head in denial, my hands covering my face as I let out a sob. "Stop. Please."

"Red." His voice was as soft as supple leather, his grip strong and tangible. But it couldn't be him. He was dead.

"This isn't real." I wrenched against his hold, twisting and turning as I kept hollering. "This isn't real!"

Chest heaving, I struggled to take in air. Black dots etched across my vision. Numbness and tingling spread like wildfire through my limbs.

The world shifted in and out of focus. He was talking to Kenzi, and she said something back, but it sounded like they were underwater, their speech distant and garbled.

Did they know one another?
How?

She killed him.

He was dead.

"This isn't real."

"I'm very real, my love." Had he uttered those words, or was it my imagination? Was it all my imagination? Would I wake up and find myself back in Elias's shed, starving and close to death? It wouldn't be the first time I'd been subjected to hunger-based hallucinations.

Was any of this real?

There wasn't time to contemplate further as the darkness washed me under, and both imagination and reality ceased to exist.

PART TWO

Matthias

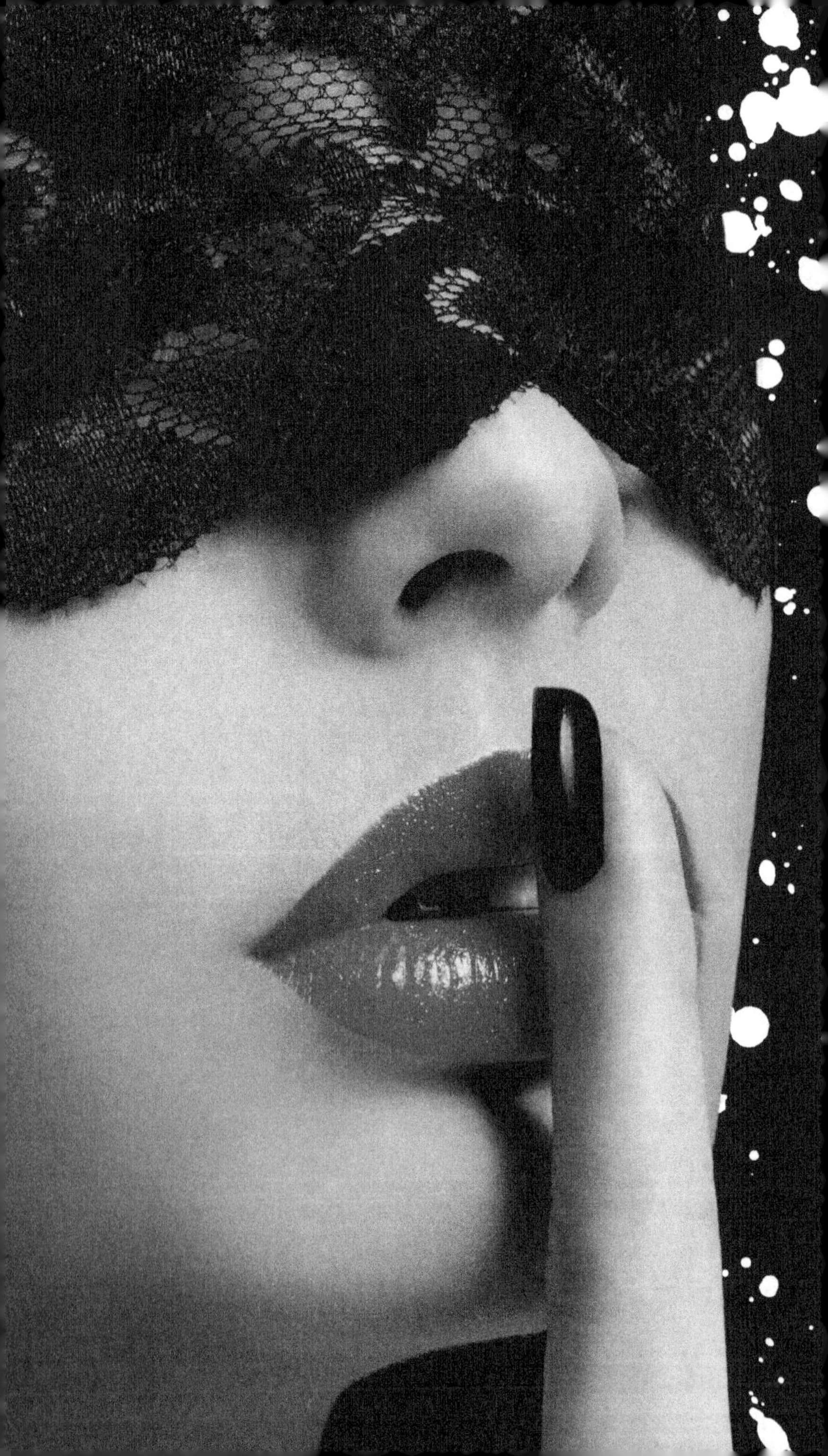

CHAPTER THIRTEEN

I watched from beneath the cover of a coppice of pine and willow as they lowered my empty casket into the cold ground. There was just enough room between the crowd of people to make out the face of my most trusted men. Their heads were lowered respectfully as Father Michaels presented my pre-planned eulogy.

It was short and concise, and the priest was known for epigrammatic ripostes that kept the crowd from falling in too deep a melancholy. I never wanted people to cry at my funeral. Fake or not. Death was something to be celebrated and not mourned.

My gaze wandered, searching through the faces as they swept past me with an almost concerning amount of unawareness. They wouldn't recognize me. Not with my disguise, but that didn't make it any better. How easy it would be for someone to penetrate the unassuming crowd and open fire.

Even with the cemetery highly guarded, my gut churned. That could also be the gunshot wound that was still healing. One week was barely enough time to recover after having major surgery, but I was insistent. Maxim shifted in his spot just behind my wife, his head tilting slightly to the right as he tugged on his earlobe nonchalantly.

Everything was clear.

I took my place at the back of the receiving line, my black umbrella allowing for just enough coverage to keep me from looking suspicious as the rain dropped against it, the sound loud among the silent mourners. I kept my gaze from wandering too much and drawing suspicion. There were only a handful of people who knew I was still alive, and drawing attention to myself was something I didn't need in case I was recognized.

The line trudged forward, and I took the time to simply look at her. My wife. The woman I had taken a bullet for. *Technically*. Her jaw was clenched, her emerald eyes hard as she clenched and unclenched her fists at her sides. A sign she was expecting something bad.

Vas hadn't informed her of what was in store for her. Ava was no doubt under the impression she would be cast aside once the funeral ended. That wasn't the case. She'd just inherited the largest, most powerful criminal organization on the West Coast. Soon she'd learn more about who I was. What I did.

That I wasn't merely just the leader of the *Bratva*. I was also the founder and CEO of a multi-billion-dollar security company.

We'd discussed the company before, but in the short time we had been married, I never fully discussed with her just how far of a reach I had, both legally and criminally. The world's largest target was now painted on Ava's back. All because I needed to fake my death.

There was a threat out there worse than Christian, and it needed to be taken care of. Something I could only do if everyone believed me to be dead.

My wife was stunning in a pair of high-waisted black trousers that clung to her shapely legs. She'd tucked a cream silk blouse into the waistline and covered herself with a brass buttoned Armani blazer. I was slightly miffed that Vas hadn't made her wear a thicker jacket. It wasn't fucking summer out here.

Ava shifted slightly from side to side uncomfortably, her heels sinking into the wet earth beneath her feet. She'd left her hair down, the luxurious red curls framing her porcelain features that were highlighted by a minimal amount of makeup.

She didn't paint herself up like most women her age, but she did try to appear stronger and more resilient than she felt. It was easy to spot in the way she held her shoulders erect, her spine stiff. Her emerald eyes were hard as she quietly greeted the men and women who came to pay their respects to the new *Pakhan*, no doubt believing the soft platitudes were meant for Vas.

Ava would soon come to realize what I left her.

What I would be back to claim.

Just as soon as I took care of my own problems. Starting with Kirill Kasyanov and that fucking bastard who called himself Jonathan Archer. He might have been an FBI agent, but everything from his name to his background was false. I knew it from the moment I saw him on the video feed Neil provided me of Ava while she'd been held captive by Christian.

It was the reason I'd turned to Serena the night of the gala. Her family's involvement with my father went back long before I had been born. I needed that information, and so I put the plan together the minute I learned about Kenzi. It pained me to keep what I knew about her sister secret when

Ava had been nothing but worried for Kenzi, but I couldn't risk putting my wife in danger even further.

"Isn't spying on your wife at your own funeral a bit morbid?" The voice was light, but there was a hardness that tainted it, an edge she couldn't quite hide. I barely heard her approach. Her footsteps were light on the grass, her shadow barely visible due to the dim clouds crowding the sky. I wondered what my wife would think if she knew the truth about the woman who had so casually snuck up on me. How she had spent the last few years of her life training to be an assassin. A ghost.

"Isn't showing up at the funeral of the man you killed a bit stereotypical for a psychopath?" I shot back, my eyes never falling from my wife. "It's terribly predictable, don't you think?"

"Sociopath," she corrected calmly. As if it made any difference what you called it. Crazy was crazy, and wherever she had been had given that to her in spades.

Keeping my eyes forward, I shifted slightly, drawing her into my periphery. After all, one should never turn his back on a serial killer. A paid one at that.

I couldn't help but point out one thing, though. "If my wife sees you, Kenzi," I smirked, "she'll kill you."

The sociopath shrugged nonchalantly, her jacket rustling slightly.

"Vas even told me she has a picture of you with your eyes scratched out pinned to her wall with one of my knives," I continued, just to see if I could get a rise out of her. "The tip goes straight through your throat."

"Sisters disagree all the time." Kenzi smiled widely, her lips parting to reveal pearly white teeth. Fuck, she resembled a *Strzyga*. A female demon in Russian folklore that was much like a vampire. At least she wasn't a rotting corpse, but that didn't mean she wouldn't drink the blood of her enemies.

Hell, the bitch probably bathed in it.

"She'll get over it." Kenzi sighed softly, her light tone dipping slightly before she pulled it back in place like nothing had happened. "Especially once she finds out I didn't, in fact, kill you."

"Still shot me, though," I muttered a bit petulantly, the pain in my abdomen flaring at the memory. I could still hear Ava screaming my name. Her wail haunted my dreams.

"You told me to make it look real."

"And you did." My lips curled in distaste. "By blowing up the ambulance. You could have shot me in the shoulder."

The woman fell silent for a brief pause before she snorted the thought away. "Nah." She scrunched up her nose at the thought. "Needed to make it believable. No one would have panicked as much if you had been shot in the shoulder."

"That was what we agreed to."

"And I altered our agreement," she pressed on. "Stop being such a big Russian baby about it. It's not attractive."

We lapsed into silence, which wasn't all that uncomfortable, seeing as how we were two predators standing side by side. Two people who had violence thrust upon us without our consent. We were kindred souls in that aspect.

Compared to her sister, Kenzi was an enigma. I wondered if she'd had the same knack for lying before she had been sold to the Chameleon Agency, or if it was the result of her training. I'd talked to her several times, and her ability to switch her emotions on and off at the drop of a hat was something both awe-inspiring and concerning. She was obviously trained to fit into any situation she could, flipping from one personality to the next like she was turning the pages of her favorite book.

Little was known about the secret underground agency, but from the intel I managed to gather, they were a mediator of sorts.

Who had given themselves a horrible name.

The Chameleon Agency.

Pfft.

There were rumors floating around the underground about a group that had been buying up women left and right before they ever hit the sex auction. Whispers ladened the streets these days, hushed conversations on missing girls of all ages. Ones no one would care about and the police would never search for.

It all led back to one place.

The Dollhouse.

Kenzi mentioned the name a time or two, but beyond that, she refused to give up any information. Not out of any sordid, twisted loyalty that I could glean from her, but from the one thing that motivated people the most to keep their mouths shut.

Fear.

Kenzi, the serial-killing sociopath, was afraid.

And rightly so. Since learning their name, I'd connected the Dollhouse to more than a dozen high-target assassinations in the last ten years. Congressmen, presidents, Al-Qaeda leaders. The list went on, and those were only the ones I could find. Who knew how many more people they had murdered or how many events they had controlled?

"You don't have to go back, you know," I whispered. The receiving line was dying down, and it wouldn't be long before I was noticed. Maksim scratched his nose. Another signal.

It was time to go.

With a heavy heart, I turned from my wife and walked away. She was the woman I had once called my weakness and

SHATTERED EMPIRE

the chink in my armor, but I had been wrong. Ava made me stronger without even knowing it. I was blind to it for so long.

Slowly, I made my way toward the modest-sized SUV parked at the far end of the cemetery.

"They're already suspicious," Kenzi admitted with a bite to her lip. She followed just behind me, her body angled mildly toward me. It was a smart move. If I or one of my men made to incapacitate her, she could easily knife me between the ribs as she made her escape.

I had no plans to betray her.

Not that she knew that.

Like me, Kenzi dabbled in the art of paranoia and knew what it meant to let her guard down. It was a matter of life or death. I could understand her reticence. Without having to look at her, I already knew that her gaze was sweeping the cemetery for threats. Her eyes were counting the shadows, judging the distance of the people behind her by how close their shadows loomed.

"If Christian doubts that I believe him, you'll have another host of problems on your hands that you can't afford," Kenzi pointed out. "Plus, I wanted to kill him the night of the gala, remember? You're the one who was adamant about letting him live."

"Christian is just a pawn," I reminded her. "If you kill him, we risk not finding out who the man behind the curtain is."

"Is that a *Wizard of Oz* reference?" she teased. I grumbled half-heartedly at her, cursing her name. "I knew you'd watch it, you big softie."

Some of the real Kenzi was coming out to play.

"It was our favorite movie growing up," she admitted, a twinge of sadness lacing her words once again, but this time, she didn't pull it back. "Every Friday night, we used to do movie night together. Me, Ava, and—" She paused, her breathing growing rapid as memories of her dead sister pushed and pulled at her fragile mind. For just a moment, she was a vulnerable nineteen-year-old again. "Anyway..." The false Kenzi was back. "I knew you'd like it."

"Never said I liked it," I mumbled.

"People don't quote movies they don't like."

God, give me strength.

"I'll admit I liked the movie if you tell me more about the Dollhouse."

"Nice try." She rolled her eyes. I knew it. I had a sixth sense for those things. "I already told you what I know. I thought I was going to college like he promised. Instead, when I arrived in England, they took me. The moment I stepped off the plane, they grabbed me. No one batted an eyelash. Not one person in that terminal lifted a hand to help me. That is how much power they have."

"Then what?" I pushed. I needed more information; I couldn't fight an enemy I couldn't see or find. Information was power, and Kenzi had that information. She just needed to see the power it gave her. "Where were you taken?"

"It was all very Red Room," she admitted. The false Kenzi faded away to something new. Someone devoid of emotion, her voice sounding far away. She was disssociating from her memories, protecting herself against the trauma she endured. "The very first day, they stripped us of our clothes. Made us do everything naked. They said it would desensitize us. They wanted to get us used to being naked, and if we pushed back —" She shivered slightly, her cold, detached persona dropping minutely before her shell fixed itself back in place. "They showed us just what they would do to ensure we understood what it meant to not comply."

I stopped once we reached the SUV and gazed down at

the woman standing with me. In many ways, she was still just a child. Then again, growing up in a household like Elias's, was she ever really a child? Trauma and pain were two key essentials in casting childhood aside, like a wet rag that could no longer be used.

From what I learned from Ava; Kenzi was an outcast in her own home. In the game of chess, she was the first pawn to be sacrificed. How many times had Elias told her she had no worth? No meaning because her womb was barren and she couldn't be married off? Even if she could, I doubted that Elias would have fetched a worthy enough alliance with another family when she couldn't bear an heir.

That would explain why he sold her. With no chance of an alliance, money was the only other use she had.

"Get in," I murmured, opening the door for her. Kenzi's gaze flickered to her surroundings before she slid into the running vehicle. Leon was already behind the wheel, waiting.

"Here." He reached back to hand Kenzi a small black tablet that had been sitting on the passenger seat. "Mark said he loaded everything for you."

"Thanks." Kenzi nodded as she took it and powered it up.

"We're not done with this," I warned her. "You're holding back."

Kenzi huffed and reached forward to dial Mark on the small screen attached to the seat in front of her. The seat in front of me had one as well that would mirror hers, so there was no need to lean over and share. "We'll see."

I grunted. We were not done with this, and that was a promise. The Dollhouse and the Chameleon Agency presented a big problem. I couldn't have families selling their children for cash to fund underground assassination agencies or worse, selling them to brothels or perverts.

"Kenzi," Mark's warm voice greeted from over the crisp

video feed. He was sitting in the office we'd given to him, his guards visible in the background. He'd needed to earn our trust back after the incident with Archer, and he was well on his way to doing so. "Sir."

I nodded my head in greeting and left the rest to Kenzi. The pair had been working closely for the last week to find the information I requested. The pair of them were like the nerd hacker wonder twins.

"All right." Kenzi placed the tablet in the cradle that sat between us. It allowed for me to view the information without having to pass it back and forth. "You gave us quite the task when you asked us to search for this Kirill Kasyanov guy."

"Shouldn't have been all that hard," I drawled. "I even provided a photo."

Kenzi blew out her lips. "Yeah, the only problem is that Kirill Kasyanov doesn't exist. At least, not anymore."

"So, he is dead." This is what I had hoped for, but the look on Kenzi's and Mark's faces told me another story.

"Nope." Mark shook his head. "The problem is that Kirill Kasyanov literally doesn't exist. His surname isn't Kasyanov, it's Tkachenko."

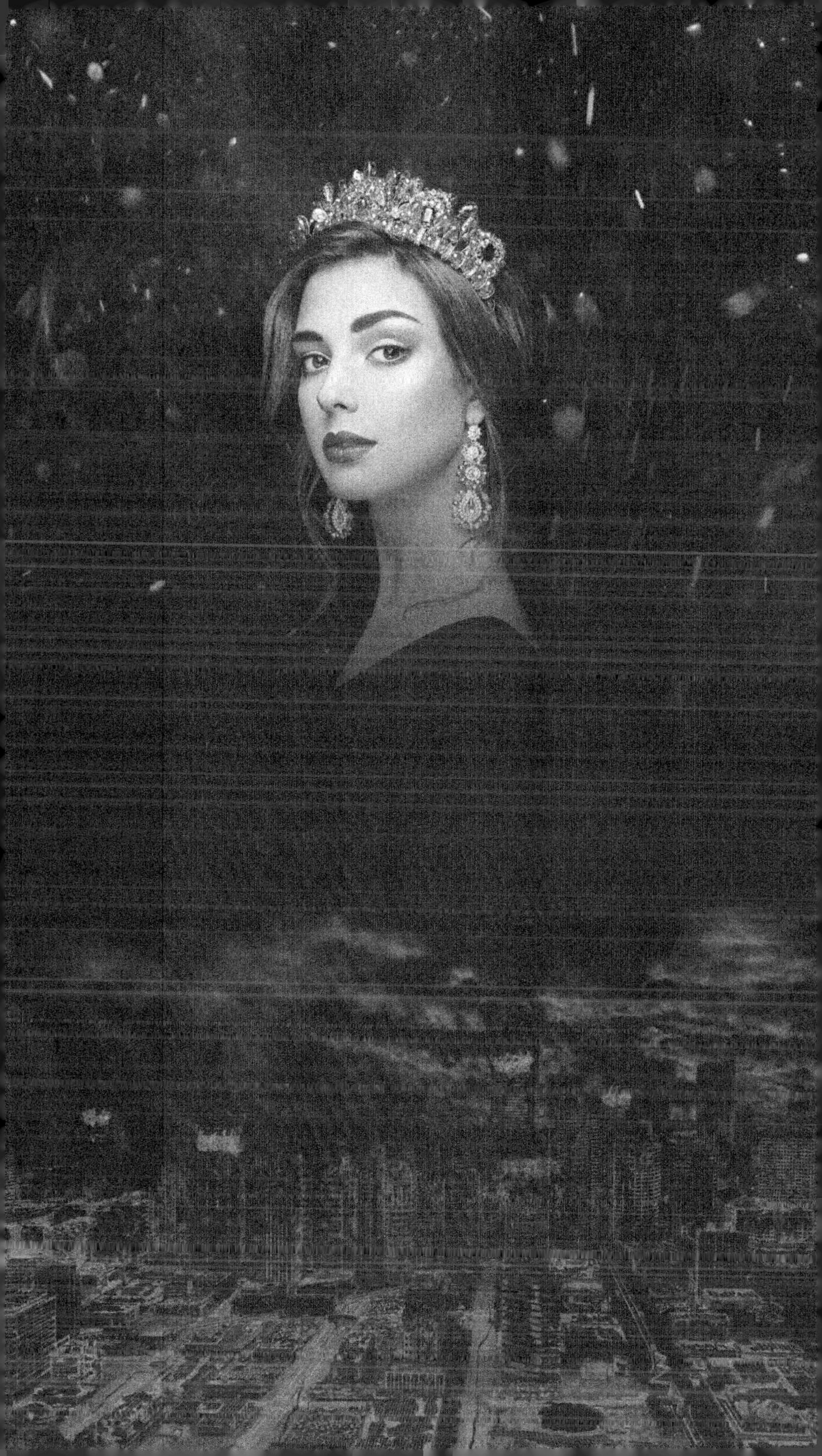

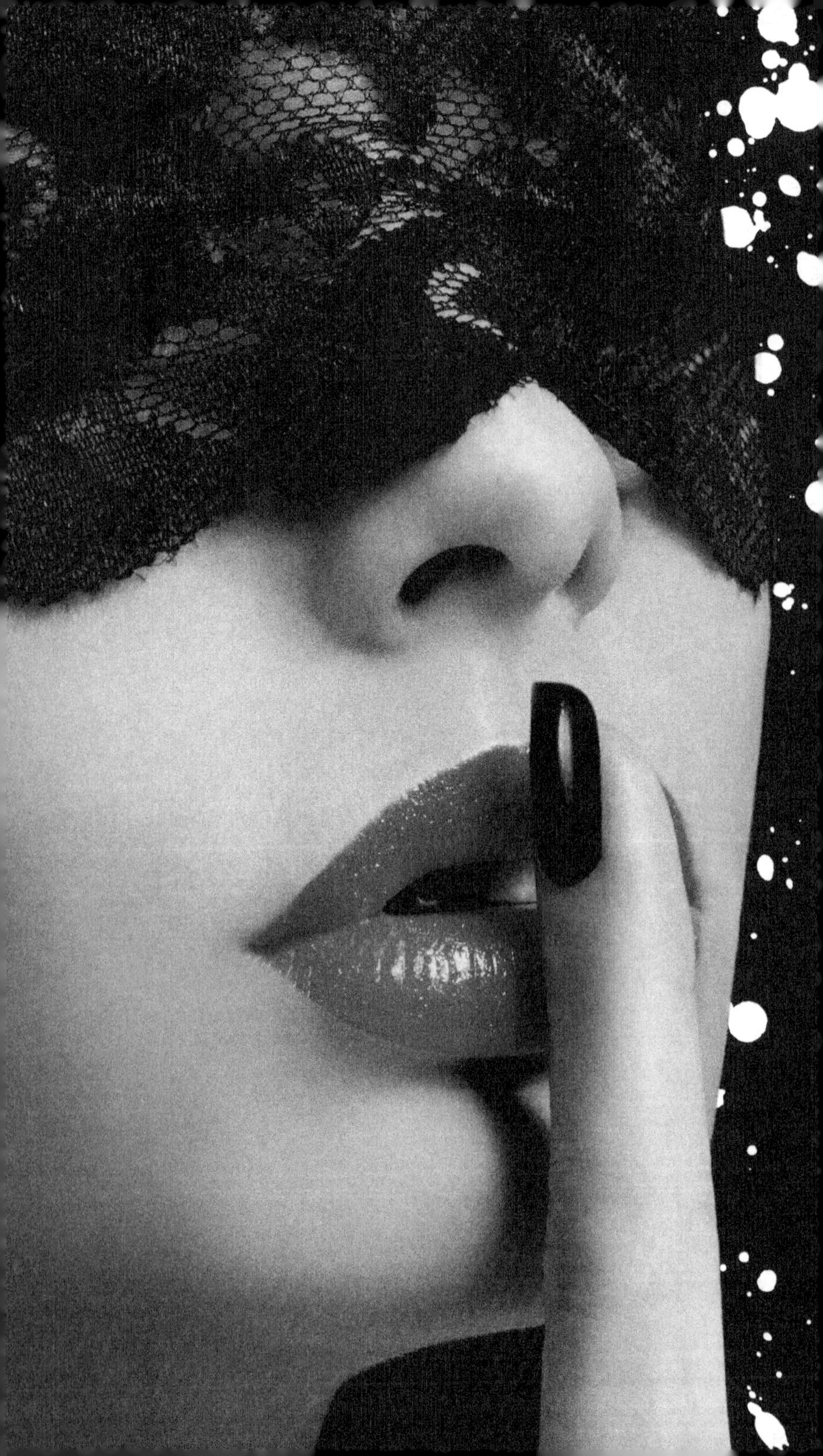

CHAPTER FOURTEEN

That name sounded familiar, but I couldn't place it. Where had I heard it? Before I had a chance to think too long on it, Leon answered instead.

"Like the Tkachenko *Bratva*?" His voice was laced with suspicion and disbelief. He knew about my father; I'd told him and the others everything there was to know about Kirill Kasyanov's pathetic life. Never once had I associated him with the name Tkachenko. "The *Bratva* of all *Bratva*?"

"Geesh," Kenzi snorted. "Drama queen much? Yes, that *Bratva*."

That didn't make any sense. My father was a low-level runner, not *Bratva* royalty. "You must be mistaken."

Kenzi pursed her lips and shook her head. "Nope." She popped the *P*. And here I thought that was just an annoying trait Ava had when she wanted to test my patience. "Kirill Kasyanov was an alias. He was born Kirill Malikovich Tkachenko, September of 1965, to a Yelena Morisov and—"

"Malik Tkachenko," I snarled.

"Um, yeah..." Mark hesitated briefly, his forehead drawn up. "How did you know that?"

"Russian middle names are patronymic," I explained. "Meaning that they are drawn from the father's first name. My middle name *was* Kirillovich. Vas's middle name is Avtonomovich. In Russia, it is common to introduce yourself or greet someone else with their first and middle name."

"From what we could uncover," Kenzi crept on, her lips turning up in a sneer at the mention of the Russian patriarchal traditions of introduction. Couldn't blame her for that. Her whole life had been controlled by men. "He was illegitimate. Yelena was a maid in Malik's household. He took a shine to her. She got pregnant, had the baby, and then mysteriously disappeared."

"The baby was kept in the household and raised to be an enforcer," Mark cut in. "Never legitimized."

"Malik was a purist," I spat distastefully. The man had been a royalty supremacist and believed in not tainting the Tkachenko bloodline. "He saw illegitimate children as cockroaches."

Mark huffed. "Didn't stop him from having a host of them. Most of whom died working for the mafia or were purposeful sacrifices."

"How did Kirill end up in St. Petersburg?" I questioned. The Tkachenko *Bratva* was run out of Moscow, and even though there was a presence in St. Petersburg, I couldn't remember if he worked for them or not. I blocked out much of that time in my life, refusing to dwell on what I couldn't change. "And why under a different name?"

"There aren't a lot of records from that time," Mark admitted sheepishly. "We had to go old school and find the few people who were alive during Malik's reign. Let me tell you, there weren't a lot."

"From what we gathered, Kirill made a lot of mistakes that cost Malik a shit ton of money." Kenzi clicked the button in her hand. A new image appeared on the tablet. It was a younger version of the man I knew. He was eighteen when he was banished to St. Petersburg to work under a man named Vlad Morozov. Kirill went from an enforcer to a drug runner. No one could verify it for sure, but it appeared Malik forced him to use an assumed surname. One that couldn't be traced back to him."

"Makes sense," Leon piped up from the back seat. "He may have let him keep the last name Tkachenko as an enforcer, but the moment shit hit the fan, he made sure no one was going to know who Kirill was and how they were related. Finding out he had an illegitimate son was one thing, but that same son being responsible for some of his failures? That would have had him in a rage."

"So why not just kill him?" Mark wondered. "If he was such a purist, why keep him around and involve him at all? He didn't involve any of his other offspring."

I had a few theories, but none that I was willing to share now. The churning in my gut told me that there was more to the story than just him bedding a random maid. Malik hadn't produced any more male heirs after his son Andrei was born. Kirill, although illegitimate, was a spare heir.

"Why did Kirill leave St. Petersburg?" Kenzi wondered aloud. "It seems a bit coincidental that your mother overdoses and then soon after that, he kicks you out on the street, never to be seen again."

"Wasn't there a big civil war that ended around that time, too?" Leon asked. "I remember hearing Tomas speak of it a few times. Said it was the reason he got out. Malik's people were dying left and right. It was carnage."

"Give me a sec." The sound of Mark's fingers popping over the hefty keyboard filled the car. "Bingo. There was a civil war from early 1986 to late 1996 after Andrei

Tkachenko's wife mysteriously went missing. One of the men Sasha interviewed told him that all fingers pointed at the boy's father."

"Why would Malik even care?"

"Because it wasn't a marriage alliance," Mark told us. "He fell in love with her. She was a waitress. No money. No connections. And no one ever found a body. Andrei raged war for years until he finally killed his father with a knife to the throat in 1996, ending the bloody war. More than six hundred soldiers died in that war."

Mark hummed in surprise as he filtered through the data our informants had provided. "Funnily enough," Mark continued. "The year he kicked you out on the streets was the same year Andrei Tkachenko legitimized Kirill."

"What's the significance of that?" Kenzi questioned, confused. "If he was willing to legitimize Kirill, he would have no problem with a child born out of wedlock."

"One, Kirill already had a family and a wife that probably didn't know about his extracurricular activities," Mark elucidated. "And two, I don't think he wanted the burden of another child. He was already in hot water, and his pockets were practically empty. But none of you are asking the right question."

I sighed, running a hand through my hair, which was still damp from the rain. "And what is the right question?"

"Why assassinate a thirteen-year-old you could have just killed when he was eleven?" Mark noted.

Kenzi bit her lower lip, her eyes sinking to the bottom left. She was trying to conjure up a reason as much as anyone else. I'd asked myself that same question so many times over the years, and I'd never found an answer.

"Well, if Andrei was willing to legitimize Kirill, maybe Kirill thought he'd legitimize Matthias without asking?"

There was skepticism in her voice. The scenario didn't fit. "I mean," she shrugged, "if he was worried about his wife finding out. That could be a reason."

I shot her a sideways glance, one eyebrow raised, conveying just how little confidence I put in that statement.

She held up her hands. "Okay, so probably not the reason. Geesh," she muttered petulantly. "Just trying to brainstorm here."

"Until we can come up with some solid evidence, why don't we move on to where the hell he is?"

"Oh, that's easy." Kenzi winked as she pressed the control to move the tablet's viewer forward a few slides. "He's in London."

That was a hell of a lot farther from Russia than I had thought he would ever get. The man had firmly believed in what it meant to be Russian. I never thought he would leave the country.

"What the hell is he doing there?" I wondered, my tone darkening. Kenzi's brows buried in her hairline as she took in my sudden demeanor change.

"He's *Pakhan* of the local *Bratva* there," she informed me, her eyes narrowing, waiting for me to explode. I wouldn't, but that didn't mean I wasn't pissed off. I was in an information overload. The man I thought was dead was still alive. Kirill Kasyanov was the only name I had ever known him by. I never thought it to be an alias.

Fuck. All this time, he was alive for me to interrogate. To kill, and I missed it. And to learn that he was *Bratva* royalty. Even illegitimately...

Shit, I had family. An uncle and cousins. Not just the brother I had murdered in self-defense.

"He was made *Pakhan* around ten years ago," Mark

informed me. "But from the looks of his books, it's not going well. He's hemorrhaging money and not in a good way."

"There's a good way?" Leon teased, trying to lighten the mood as we neared the private airstrip on the outskirts of Tukwila. My private jet was waiting for me, fueled and ready to go. Apparently, our trip would be leading to London rather than Russia, as I initially thought.

"He isn't losing product to turf wars or thieves," Mark clarified. "The money is just...disappearing. It's in small enough amounts at a time that unless you were a forensic accountant, you wouldn't even notice it. I doubt the home office has even blinked an eye until recently."

"What happened recently?" I questioned.

"He couldn't afford to pick up product from the cartel."

Leon whistled. "Yep, that is bound to draw attention."

He was right. Wars had been started for less. The cartel ordered their product off how much each client was willing to pay. Usually, a couple of million. If Kirill had been unable to pay for the product the cartel had already ordered, he would be in some serious shit. The cartel would refuse to shove off the debt. They'd come after Kirill and his men until he was able to pay. And knowing the cartel, they wouldn't just kill *Bratva* soldiers, but their wives and children, too. Until either no one was left, or they paid.

Either way, it would be bloody unless Andrei stepped in for his brother.

Fuck. Andrei Tkachenko was my motherfucking uncle. That was going to take some time to wrap my head around. Leon pulled the SUV into one of the spots near the hangar. Dima stood at the bottom of the flight of stairs with the pilot. When he saw us park, he gave a slight nod to the pilot, dismissing him before heading in our direction.

Dima was the obvious choice to take with me. He was

young and smart and could easily blend into any given environment. Leon had been my runner-up, but his presence would too easily be noticed if he was gone. That, and he was going to be needed if shit hit the fan with the Italian Mafia here. Dante Romano had been MIA since our run-in with him at the small shipping port where we found the cash and shipping container.

It was thanks to the miscreant reporter Bailey that we managed to put a few more links in the chain on figuring out how Ward had been getting money into the United States from the Middle East. American dollars, at that.

"There's one more thing you should see before you go." Mark nodded through the screen at Kenzi, who dutifully changed the slide on the tablet.

"Recognize him?" she asked curiously.

My jaw clenched at the sight of the man before me on the screen. He was tall, almost as tall as me. The silver hair he'd sported was gone, replaced with a rich dark brown that screamed fake but somehow suited his face. I wondered which color he'd faked. He appeared younger than the videos and photographs my men had gained since I learned of his involvement with Ava.

When I first saw him on the video feed outside McDonough's, his suit was two sizes too big, a cheap department store fabric that wrinkled with the slightest movement. Now, he wore a gray tweed Sebastian Cruz original that fit him like a glove. The wolf had shucked away his sheep costume.

"Jonathan Archer," I sneered at the screen. "Tried to frame me for Elias's murder."

Kenzi shook her head.

"His name is Ivan Tkachenko and—" she informed me as she flipped to another slide. My blood froze as I stared at the image before me. The man's hand was outstretched, the skin of his wrist barely visible, but I could still make out the familiar deformation that every man in my family carried. "He's your cousin, and he's been on your tail for the last ten years."

Ten years? He'd been after me for ten years, and the first time I'd had any confirmation of this was in the past few months. What had taken him so long to make a move?

"It explains why he wanted that video." Mark cleared his throat uncomfortably at the reminder of his betrayal. One I didn't have the heart to hold against him. Most betrayals were met with a swift hand. A bullet between the eyes, and it was done. There was something about Mark, however, and whatever it was, I couldn't bring myself to view his betrayal as malicious. Not like I had Ava's.

"He was searching for proof," I growled.

"Maybe not," he told me.

"He must have just arrested me for fun, then," I deadpanned.

Mark huffed impatiently. "The video clearly shows you acting in self-defense," he stressed. "And the video wasn't the only thing he was after. He wanted a whole bunch of documents, too, remember? I kept a copy of everything I found and have slowly had a program deciphering them."

"You could have just asked," I reminded him dryly. "Most of us speak Russian." Mark shrugged a shoulder.

"You were all busy," he sighed. "I started deciphering the documents he went through most. One was the death certificate and autopsy report of Inessa Kasyanov and the other was your birth certificate." He paused for a second, bringing a copy of the paperwork onto the tablet's screen. I snatched it from the cradle to get a better look.

"I scoured the web for an Inessa Kasyanov," Mark continued. "But there is nothing on her. No birth certificate, no fingerprint files, no parking tickets—nothing. She was like a ghost. Inessa Kasyanov didn't exist. Which means—"

"She was made up," I breathed, my brow furrowing as anger and sadness rushed through me. A geyser ready to erupt.

"Do you know her?" Kenzi asked tentatively, taking in my expression.

I nodded.

"She was my mother."

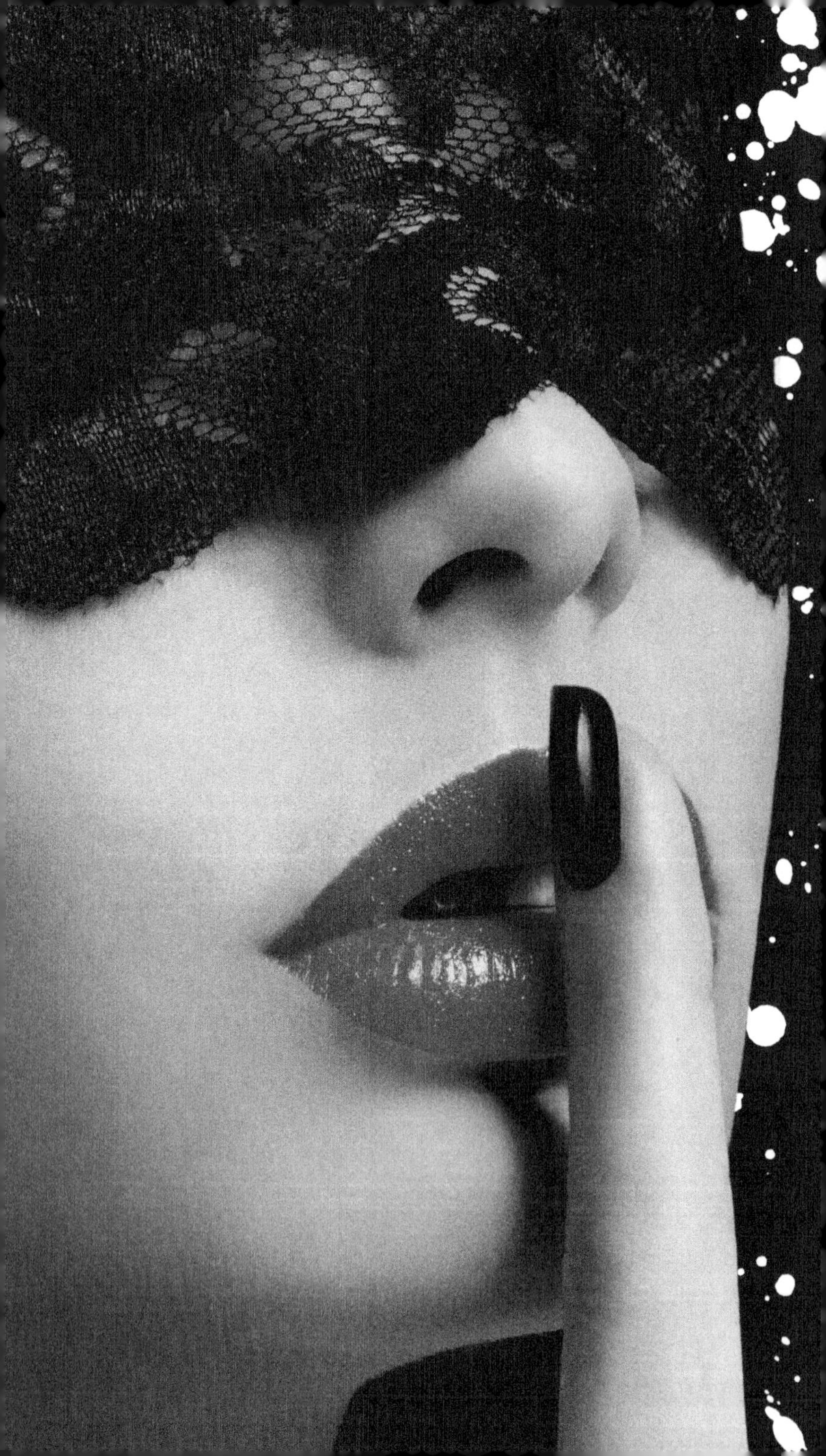

CHAPTER FIFTEEN

Dima was making himself busy with the pretty, petite stewardess at the back of the plane. The bedroom at the back was nearly soundproof, but her porn star-worthy moans managed to seep through the carefully crafted walls.

Blyad.

Her moans sounded practiced, not authentic. Images of my sweet wife writhing and moaning beneath me had my body tightening and cock hardening. Groaning, I released my belt and freed my hard cock. My eyes closed as I conjured up a vision of Ava before me on her knees, her emerald eyes shining up at me innocently as she took my cock in her hot, wet mouth.

I fisted myself, pumping it slowly as I let the fantasy take over.

Fuck.

Ava kissed my cock, swirling her tongue along the smooth, wet head. I let out a throaty groan, relishing in the soft feel of her tongue as she flattened it at the base of the tip before her hot, delicious mouth engulfed my length.

She sucked, and I moaned, my eyes closing, my hand burying itself in her ginger curls.

I bucked into her mouth as she dropped down farther, taking more of me into her warm, wet hole. It took everything I had not to take control and force her head down until her nose touched my stomach. Instead, I massaged my fingers along her scalp, reveling in the way she preened against my steady action.

Rough, feral sounds escaped my throat as she lapped at my cock. It wasn't long before she added her delicate hand to the mix. She squeezed the base of my cock roughly, the pressure causing my hips to jerk the tip farther into her mouth as she worked the two in tandem.

Pleasure built, my balls tightening the more aggressive she sucked and stroked. On her knees before me, Ava held all the power. My hand grasped her hair tighter as I chased the euphoria she was creating inside me.

Fuck.

Wrenching her hair back, I pulled her mouth from my cock. My free hand squeezed her cheeks, forcing her mouth open.

"Stroke me hard until I come," I growled, her obedience nearly sending me over the edge as she reached her hand out and stroked my painfully hard member. It took just a few strokes to send me barreling over the edge. I cursed, groaning her name as my release spurted over her mouth and cheeks.

Ava was perfect.

A high-pitched scream sent me careening from my fantasy and back to the hellish nightmare of reality. I let my hand fall from my softening cock and took a deep breath. Then I cleaned up and tucked myself away.

When I got my hands on her again, there would be no saving her. I'd fuck her until we were both too exhausted to go on, and the moment she thought she was free, I'd do it all over again. She would remember who owned her.

Me.

Ava was mine, and the minute I returned, I would remind her of that fact.

Hinges squeaked. The woosh of a door opening alerted me that Dima was finished with his business. He had been only sixteen when he came to me, begging me for a job and a way out of the toilet he called a life. He came to me as a junkie with only the clothes on his back. His girlfriend packed up her shit and ran, and his crew got wasted after a raid gone wrong. Dima was left with nothing, and I helped build him into the man he was today.

Strong. Resilient. But a coward when it came to confronting the woman who'd sold his crew down the river. Instead of finding her, he buried his dick in easy, disposable pussy. Not the best way to deal with trauma, but I wasn't going to judge him for it.

"I really wish you would stop fucking the stewardesses." I shook my head and sighed. "Do you know how hard it is to find good ones who keep their mouths shut after the ones you fuck get their heart broken and quit?"

Dima shrugged.

"If it helps, I'll hire the next one," he volunteered.

"After this one quits, I'm hiring men," I threatened lightly. "Beefy men."

Dima crowed with laughter, his head thrown back at the absurd threat. "Those are always the most fun to dominate." The fucker winked at me. The gall of this kid.

"You could just confront her," I told him. "We know where she is."

Dima sneered. "I have nothing to say to that traitorous bitch."

The urge to roll my eyes had never been greater. So was the urge to choke this motherfucker. "You may not. But your dick surely does."

Dima growled.

"Shut it."

I chuckled. "Did I hit a nerve?"

The glare my enforcer sent me was enough to reduce a grown man to tears. Luckily, I happened to be immune to his charms.

"We should be landing in half an hour, sir." Stephanie, the stewardess, smiled coyly, batting her fake eyelashes at me. Any appeal she might have held washed away with her desperation. "If you need anything before we land, please let me know. I'm happy to assist." Another bat of her fake lashes, another teasing grin as her eyes roamed my body.

"Your resignation will do."

Dima coughed, the vodka he just sipped spewing over his lap.

"I'm...sorry?" Stephanie's face twisted into a state of confusion and panic, her eyes widening as her drawn-on eyebrows buried themselves in her hairline.

"This will be your last flight with us," I snapped, handing Dima my handkerchief. "I employed you as a stewardess. Not a whore. Fucking Dima was one thing. Blatantly hitting on a man you know is married is another. Seek employment elsewhere, Miss Wise. It'll be in your best interest."

Her red lips wobbled uncertainly, her pleading eyes darting to Dima, hoping he would save her.

He wouldn't.

With a subtle shake of his head, he turned his attention away from his latest conquest and onto the screen in front of him.

"You were shitty lay, anyway," she sneered at Dima and stalked toward the front of the plane, her heels stomping against the lush carpet.

Dima cackled delightedly once she was out of sight. I ran a hand down my face and gave a frustrated sigh. "Male fucking stewards," I mumbled, which just caused Dima to crow louder. "Stop fucking laughing, *Svoloch'* and tell me what the fuck we're looking at when we land."

"Okay. Okay." Dima's laugh settled, and he straightened his shoulders as he scrolled through the data Mark had sent over about Kirill. "Looks like he took over the old *Pakhan's* house on Old Queen Street. It's a luxury townhome, built in 1775. Georgian style architecture, five bed—"

"Dima," I snapped. "You're not the house's real estate agent."

"Right." Dima's cheeks took on an uncharacteristic blush. I was trying to be patient with him since he rarely got to be point man on anything like this. He was an enforcer, not an intelligence gatherer. This situation was new to him, and I tried my best to remind myself of that.

"What's his schedule like?" I asked. He was frozen, searching through the information Mark had provided, his confidence wavering as he tried to find the exact information I wanted.

"Creature of habit," Dima informed me. "He rarely deviates from his routines. Leaves for the warehouse every morning at seven in a black Mercedes G-Class with two guards and one driver. No decoy car and no extra security."

"Bold," I murmured. Dima nodded in agreement.

"It's like he thinks he's untouchable."

Kirill would. His ego rivaled the greatest cities. Even as a meager mafia runner, he always walked and talked as if he was a king among men. A Caesar among the Romans. Learning about my father's heritage explained why he always thought himself better than the men he worked alongside. How he would puff out his chest and crow at them, flaunting authority he didn't have.

Only, he did. It was that no one knew of it, and if they did, they didn't care. It was one thing that constantly made him angry when I was growing up. He would take his anger and aggression out on my mother.

"You were right," Dima admitted. "The moment he heard you were dead, he dropped all the extra security measures."

I smirked. Kirill was anything if not predictable. It was no surprise that my death would lessen his hold on the strenuous security protocols he had in place. Satisfaction bloomed in my chest, knowing I'd caused all his fear. How many times had he jumped at the surrounding shadows, believing I hid behind them, ready to strike? Had his life been fraught with nightmares of his death, just as mine had been?

No matter.

Soon the bastard would be dead, and I would be free. Justice for my mother and brother would be served, and I could rush home to bury my cock in my wife's tight cunt.

"What are we going to do about Archer?" Dima asked. "He's here in the city. Could be coincidence, but I'm thinking we aren't the only ones who know about Kirill's dirty laundry."

Jonathan Archer.

A.k.a. Ivan Tkachenko, my cousin.

Who I thought to be my brother before Mark had hit me with Kirill's true parentage. I winced at the implication. It meant that Roman was not my cousin by blood. Kasyanov was the surname of the man I knew as my uncle. There were only a handful of times I had seen him before Kirill kicked me to the curb. It wasn't until I began fighting in the underground that we reconnected.

It was a weary connection, full of distrust, and then later filled with disgust when Roman came begging for me to take him in. I was working as Tomas's enforcer by then. My uncle hadn't wanted an Italian-Russian hybrid for a son. Said his Italian side would make him too soft.

Now he was one of my most ruthless killers.

If his father wasn't already dead, I would have brought him along to do the honors.

"We might be able to use him," I surmised as I leaned back more comfortably in my seat, crossing an ankle over my knee. "If Kirill really is cheating Andrei out of money, he isn't going to take it lightly. There's a chance we could use Ivan's connection to his father while exploiting mine."

"You gonna tell him you're related?"

I blew out an amused breath. "I'm pretty sure he already knows from his research. There was no way he would have missed it."

"True, but looking back, nothing he's done makes sense," Dima contemplated as he too got comfortable. We'd be landing soon. "He took on the guise of a deceased FBI agent for years and never once went after you. Then he suddenly teams up with the Wards? For what?"

"He wanted to use Ava to get the video." The statement wasn't as confident as I wanted it to be. "Frame me for Elias's murder."

Dima shot me a skeptical look.

"Really?" he questioned. "Because from where I'm sitting, that makes no sense. Christian's betrayal of his father was spontaneous. He didn't plan it out. Not to mention, he had

Mark involved long before he solicited Ava. Using her was just an excuse. He didn't need to. He *wanted* to. Nothing he had Ava do was necessary. Mark could have easily slipped him that information via a secure server without any of us being the wiser. He *chose* to use her. The question is—why?"

I reflected on what he said as Stephanie's broken voice announced that we were descending into London. I stared out the window, a sneer painting my lips at the sight of the city below me. London was a cesspool of the worst crime families. Boys playing at men. They were reckless here, and most of the underground was run by dirty corporations instead of blue-blooded mafia families.

Despicable.

George landed the plane with the same finesse as always, the jolt barely detectable as we hit the runway and coasted toward the hangar. When he powered down the engines and Stephanie released the staircase, we were off like a shot in the Ferrari F12 Berlinetta I had procured several years ago when I was still traveling back and forth from this hellhole.

The Ferrari weaved through London traffic, handling like a wet dream. I thought about having it shipped to the states just so I could fuck Ava in it. The machine had power, and I had customized the interior from Ferrari's standard nude leather to black, adding in hand-stitched red thread to compliment the exterior.

This Ferrari wasn't just built for speed, it was made to be street legal until the city limits faded away and you could let loose. I bought it for the aerodynamic design. The engineers structured the car so well that air seemed to slip right down the flanks of the car, making for smoother turns and transitions.

The yellow-coated attendants outside the car whistled as we pulled up to the valet of the Savoy hotel. A place, I'm told, where Guccio Gucci once worked as a baggage porter. I tossed my keys to the one attendant who hadn't been vying to get to my car and handed him a two-hundred-dollar tip.

"Not a scratch," I threatened. "Or I break fingers."

The boy audibly gulped, his carotid pulsing as he nodded emphatically. I patted his cheek and then made my way through the hotel doors with my bag in hand.

"Welcome." The woman at the front desk smiled broadly at us, her eyes shining as she took in our expensive suits and polished demeanor. "Can I get your name for the reservation?"

"Pavel Kasyanov." I gave her my dead uncle's name. Using my own meant showing my hand, and I wasn't ready for that. Not yet.

"Oh, yes." The woman's smile brightened even further. "You're in our River View Suite. Here are your cards." She handed me the small envelope containing our room keys. "I can show you to your room if you like."

Jesus.

The woman's eyes were hooded, pupils blown open with lust as she gazed up at me from underneath her lashes. It was bold and brazen. At one point, I would have taken her up on her offer and brought her up, fucked her, and dismissed her. But not anymore. The only woman who made my cock twitch was currently mourning my death on the other side of the world.

"Well..." Dima smirked and moved to push past me, but I wasn't having it.

"You just fucked our stewardess," I reminded him, watching the woman's face fall in disgust. "I think your dick needs some recovery time first."

"But..."

"Nyet," I hissed before dragging him along after me. "Stop

acting like a boy and thinking with your damn dick before I castrate you to solve the problem."

Dima didn't say anything, but it was hard to miss the pull of his lips.

Fucker was messing with me.

"Come." My voice was less harsh as we stepped into the elevator. "We have work to do."

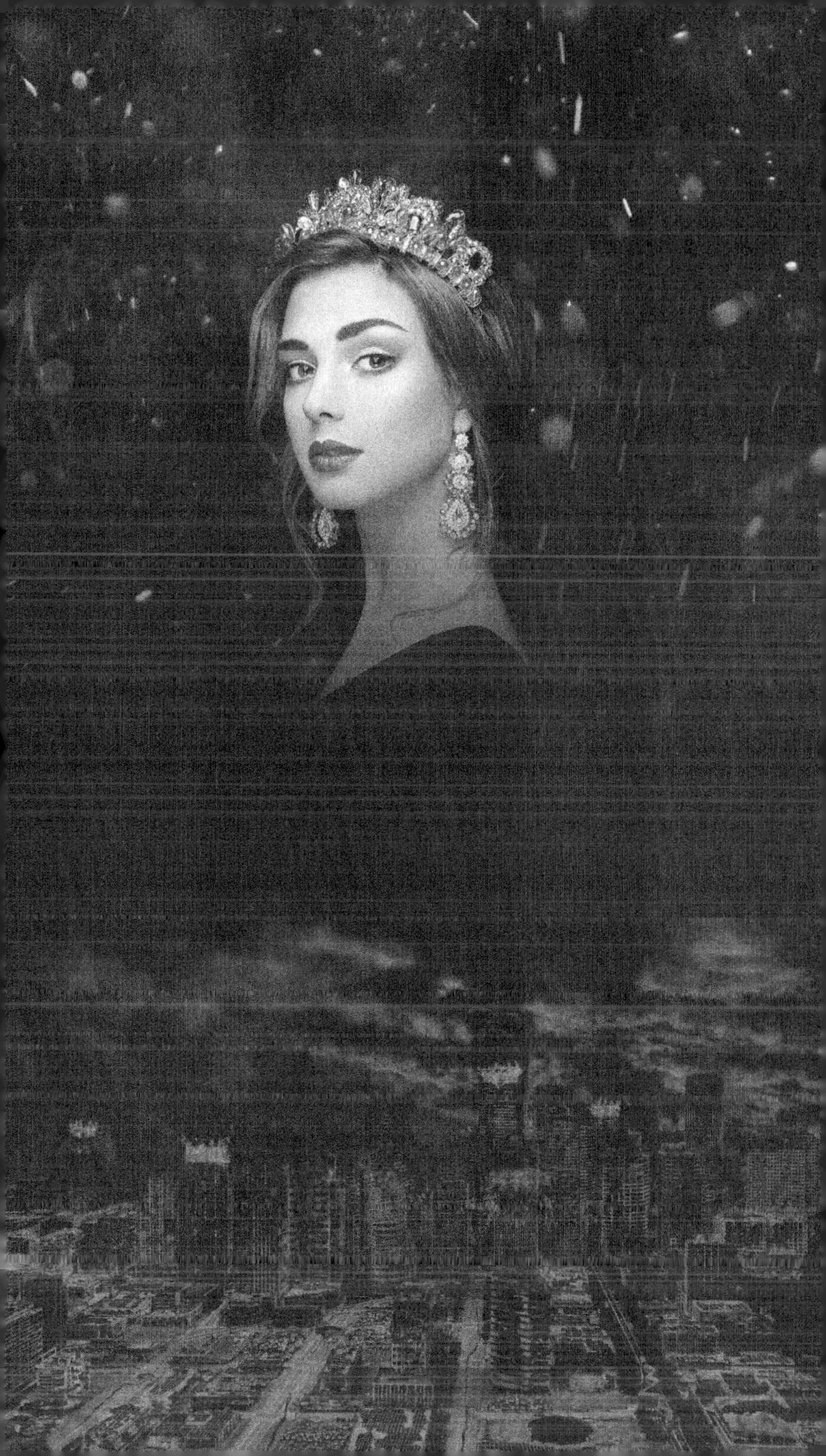

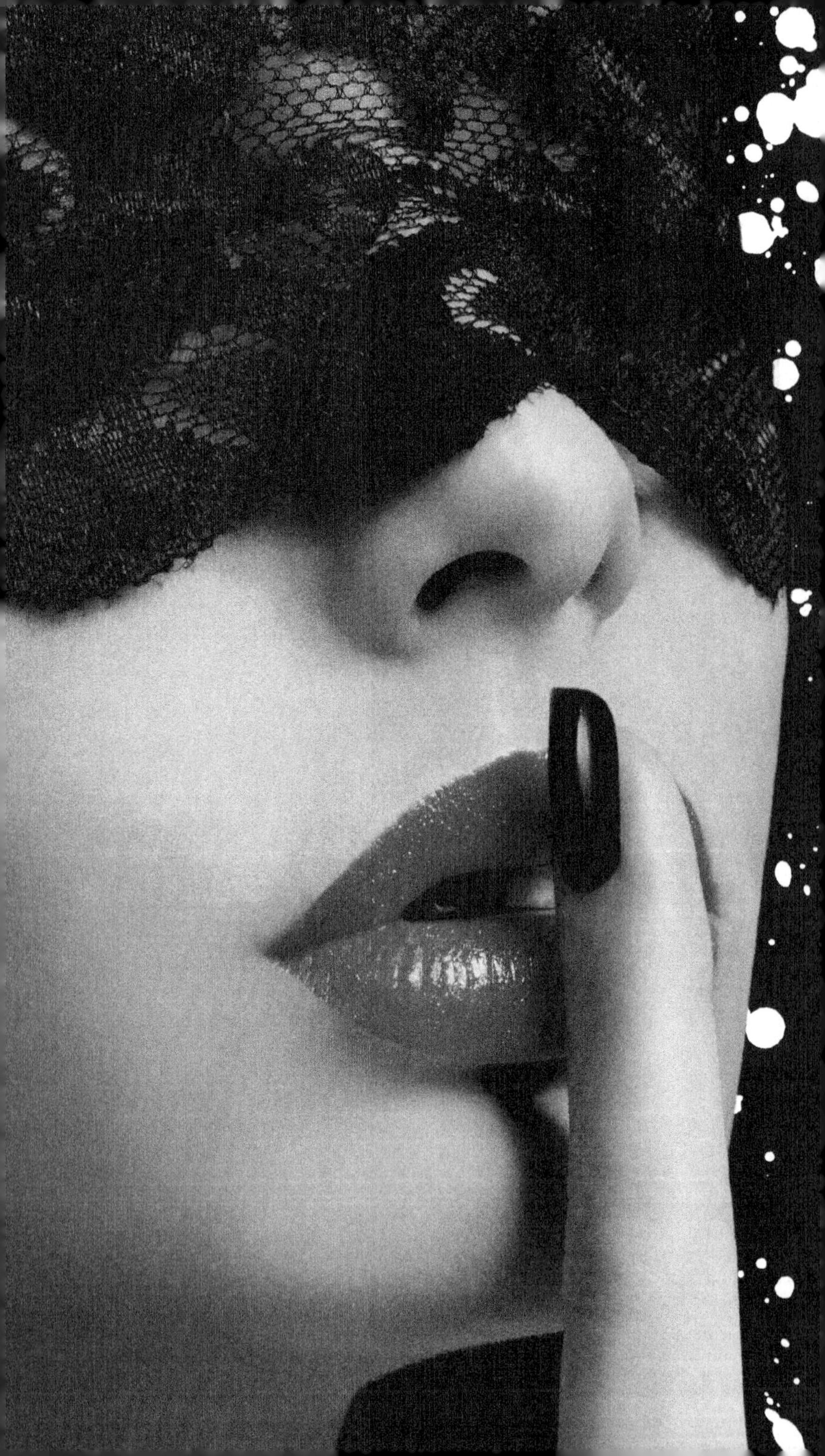

CHAPTER SIXTEEN

"I'm not as stupid as you think I am."

A snort escaped my lips at the insinuation. "I never said you were," I placated. "I simply wanted to be sure that the pretty brunette at the service desk wouldn't be a distraction for you."

Dima blew out his lips in frustration, and I couldn't help the chuckle I released. Here I was sitting like a fucking creeper in the middle of a blacked-out apartment, stalking my target. It was long past midnight, and the fucker still hadn't shown his face. We'd come here for Kirill, but he wasn't the only one I was after.

My backup man was currently pouting outside in the car like a dejected puppy. I made sure to crack a window for him. Maksim had been the holder of Dima's leash for as long as I could remember. I would say it was something kinky, but while my young associate might flex and bend with gender, Maksim had no such flexibility.

"I know when to take my balls out of the game."

Wasn't quite how the American phrase went, but I would let it slide.

JO MCCALL

For now.

"Then prove it," I commanded him. "Prove that you can be a reliable asset, *brat*, and maybe I will think about allowing you more freedom in the future."

Should have brought fucking Leon or Roman with me.

Problem was that both were easily recognizable as being associated with me.

Dima was my ghost man. My thief in the shadows.

"Got him," Dima informed me. Hacking into the hotels Wi-Fi had been horrifyingly easy. "He's heading into the elevator with two security guards."

My hand clenched on the gun in my lap.

"Security got off on the floor below him."

Rookie mistake. I smirked darkly. Never leave yourself open without easily accessible backup. I waited patiently, the soft pad of footsteps my reward some minutes later. Rolling my shoulders back, I tilted my head up and prepared. The lock beeped, and the door handle clicked. Moments later, it closed, and the snick of the lock sounded.

Time for business.

"Privet, *dvoyurodnaya brat*," I greeted my cousin coldly, the muzzle of my baretta aimed at his chest. Ivan, the man who paraded himself as Jonathan Archer, froze in his tracks. Flipping on the lamp, I expected to see fear creeping into his silver eyes. Instead, his own gun was aimed at my head, a smarmy smirk goading his lips.

Pizdets.

"Matthias." I wanted to punch that smirk off his face and watch that smug glint in his eye fade to nothing as I choked the life from him.

"Archer." I nodded my head at him, my eyes never leaving his face. "Or should I call you Ivan?"

"Took you long enough." Again, the man showed no fear,

only expectance. "I thought you would have found me sooner, honestly."

I sneered.

"Know me so well, do you?"

Ivan grinned broadly, showcasing pearly white teeth and a more youthful face. The graying edges of his hair were gone, and he was clean shaven, making him look years younger than the man he portrayed. Hell, even his eye color was different. Gone were the hazel contacts, replaced by the familiar silver glint.

There were very little traces of Jonathan Archer left. He'd hidden behind his façade so well that I barely recognized the man standing in front of me.

"I know more about you than you think." He lowered his gun as a show of good faith, tucking it into his waistband.

"Well," I tipped the muzzle of my gun back and forth, "not surprising with your stalker tendencies." The man looked like he wanted to smile, but he kept his face somewhat neutral.

"You should tell your man downstairs to come on up for a drink," Ivan informed me. He gave my gun a quick glance before walking to the bar that sat to one side of me. Dima cursed over the comms line. I winced at the volume. "He's good." Ivan smirked. "My men are just better."

"Indeed," I grumbled and put my gun away as I barked at Dima to stand by in the lobby. "How long have you known?"

Ivan chuckled darkly. "Since the minute you stepped off the plane."

I swore.

"Give me one reason why I shouldn't shoot you right now, then."

That fucking smirk. I wanted to wipe it off his face.

"I want Kirill dead."

That wasn't what I was expecting.

"He's your uncle. Why would you want that?"

Ivan turned toward me, jaw clenched, the muscles in his throat tightening around his pulsing carotid. The man was angry, eyes burning with uncontrolled hatred.

"Antony Tkachenko was my brother."

I shook my head slightly, gun lowering. Brother. That was impossible. He called *me* brother before he died. Antony had been a Kasyanov.

Right?

"Impossible," I murmured and took the glass of scotch he offered.

Ivan scoffed. "I think I would know my own brother."

I thought back to that fateful night. The one where we fought, and I killed him.

"I'm sorry, brat."

Those were the words he said to me.

Unless they weren't meant for me. Maybe they had been meant for Ivan?

"How much do you know about Kirill?" he asked me. Ivan sat across from me in one of the other chairs, making himself comfortable as he sipped on his vodka.

"Seeing as how he is my father," I sneered at the term, "a lot."

And out came the smirk again.

"Is he though?"

This *mudak* was playing with fire.

"You think I don't know my own father?" I growled. My hand tightened on the glass I was holding. "The pig of a man who got my mother addicted to drugs. The scum of the earth who kicked me out on my ass when I was eleven. The scourge of my life who sent one assassin after another for years until they were too afraid to come after me. That man? I know that man."

There was sadness and regret in Ivan's eyes. His gaze was fixed on me. The tension in his shoulders had released, and he seemed at ease. Off guard. I could have killed him then, for everything he had done, and he would have been unprepared.

Except I didn't want to.

The longer I studied him, the more I noticed the similarities beyond the familial platinum eyes and dark hair. They had been hidden before, purposely altered beneath the carefully crafted face of Jonathan Archer. We bore the same sharp angular jawline and high cheekbones. His voice, when not altered, was deep and gravelly.

At one point, I thought he had been my brother, not my cousin. My first instinct when I saw the mark on his arm flash across the video feed from the Ward stables had been accurate. The revelation that I spent my entire life hating someone who was absolutely nothing to me was startling. The rug had been pulled out from under me. The wool falling from my eyes.

"You said Antony was your brother as well." Suspicion laced my voice. Things weren't adding up, but I didn't raise my gun again. I would keep the peace that had settled between us.

For now.

"Yes," Ivan affirmed. "He and I were born two years before you. When they first were married. Mom was eighteen and working at a diner in America when he met her. Seduced her. Married her. It was a whirlwind romance," he said.

"I assume Malik didn't take too kindly to that."

Ivan snarled. "I do not believe our senile old grandfather had anything to do with it, at least not completely."

Now I was puzzled. "Why else would Kirill take her?"

JO MCCALL

None of what he was saying made any sense, but at the same time, it did. The pieces of the puzzle were blurry, but slowly, as I shifted everything I thought I knew aside and focused on the facts he was giving me and the ones I had begun to dig up myself, everything was beginning to fit together.

"Her name was Amalia," Ivan told me, a wistfulness to his voice as he remembered her. "I was only two when she was stolen in the dead of night with you still in her belly. Antony and I would put our ears to her stomach to listen. It would put a smile on our faces whenever we could feel you shift. She would sing to us our favorite lullaby. Her voice soft and sweet."

Tears swam in his eyes as he told me the only things he remembered about her. The memories of a two-year-old were so fleeting. Finite.

"Bayu Bayushki," I chuckled. "The lullaby about a wolf dragging a child from bed for sleeping on the edge. She used to sing that to me as well. I remember the first time I was able to properly understand the words—I was too scared to sleep for days."

Ivan laughed. "Father used to try and sing it to us, but his voice sounded too much like a dying *koshka*. Antony would beg him to stop, but he would just hammer on, anyway. Louder, if that was possible."

The two of us laughed, the jovial sound fading away as sorrow and regret cinched our hearts and souls. I had grown up without the love of a father. My only glimpse of what one was truly supposed to be like coming from the kindness and compassion Tomas showed me many years later. Many years too late.

Ivan and Antony were forced to live without the tender care of a mother. Their memories just wistful dreams. Even in her worst times, when Kirill had her hopped up on drugs, she never stopped being the loving mother I knew when she was sober.

"Her favorite color was green," I told him, the lump in my throat growing as I dredged up memories I buried long ago. "And not like the forest or the grass. It was lime green. The kind you found on walls of homes built in the seventies."

Ivan's eyes lit up as I told him about our mother. Her favorite foods and how she liked to settle down and read to me in the evenings. She was fierce and protective. Loving and kind even in her darkest times.

Gradually, over time, the happiness of my tale melted into anger, then rage. Now that I had all the pieces, I could see the proper flow of time.

But there were a few questions that remained unanswered.

"If Malik wasn't behind the plan to take our mother?" I questioned, thinking back to everything I knew. "Who did? Kirill? There is no way he was smart enough to pull it off on his own."

Ivan shook his head softly.

"Have you heard of a man by the name of Pavel Kasyanov?"

I nodded.

"He was the man I grew up believing to be my uncle," I told him. "Died a few years ago."

Ivan smiled darkly. "Horrible accident with a knife in his gut." He shrugged nonchalantly. "Drug deal gone wrong."

I chuckled. "Couldn't say he didn't deserve it."

"Kirill and Pavel grew up together," Ivan continued. "Both bastard sons of high-ranking members. Pavel blamed it all on Kirill before I killed him. Said the bastard wanted to be *Pakhan*. Since he wasn't a legitimized heir, there was no way he could."

"Unless he got someone to legitimize him."

"Pavel and Kirill made sure all the evidence pointed back to Malik," Ivan kept on, his breathing growing rapid as he recalled how the mother he barely got to know was taken. "Kirill and our father were friends, but according to Pavel, all Kirill wanted was Andrei's seat of power. So, he started a war. Offered his brother his support as a spy."

I held up a hand to stop him. "How could he have done that if Malik had banished him to St. Petersburg?"

Ivan raised a brow at me. Of course, he would have falsified everything to cover his tracks. "Kirill and Pavel's job in St. Petersburg was to gain support. Kirill manipulated everything so that he could be there to make sure our mother never escaped."

"So, what?" My jaw clenched so hard I could hear my teeth grinding. "He thought he would help Andrei overthrow Malik, and then what? He still wasn't the heir."

"Until our father legitimized him as a reward for his service."

Blyad.

That would make Kirill the next heir, but if he sought to kill Andrei and gain the throne, then why wasn't he dead?

Ivan knew what I was thinking and voiced his answer before I could verbalize my question. "Until recently, he hasn't tried to make a move directly on our father. He started with us. The heirs."

Us. The heirs.

"Why the façade, Ivan?" I looked askance at my brother. "You join with Christian Ward. Blackmail my wife. You've spent the last how many years impersonating an FBI agent. For what? To get revenge on me for killing Antony? For letting our mother die? Honestly, I can't figure out what the hell you've been playing at, *brother*." I spat the word out. "Why should I trust anything you're telling me right now?"

Silence simmered in the air between us. Volcanic activity bubbling beneath the surface, waiting for the right moment to explode. There was bitterness between us. A tight rope strung to the point that the threads were fraying. One harsh pull, and it could sever itself forever, and there would be no repairing it.

Ivan's throat bobbed before he spoke. When he did, his voice was quiet, broken. It was the voice of a man who had lost everything he loved. Something I knew about all too well.

"I hated you at first," he admitted hoarsely. "Antony disappeared one night, and he never came back. Kirill told me..." Ivan choked, his throat clogged with overwhelming emotion. "He told me that Antony had found you, our little brother, and that he was going to bring you home. When he didn't return with you, Kirill showed me a picture of you stabbing him." Standing, he ran a hand through his hair. Ivan paced the small space between our chairs, still holding his drink as he told me his story. "There was so much rage and pain. I couldn't imagine why you would want to kill your brother."

"I didn't do it by choice," I assured him gently. Ivan came to a sudden halt and hung his head, shame coloring his cheeks.

"I know," he whispered brokenly. "Over the years, more and more things just were not adding up. Conversations I would overhear. Meetings he would have. Our father gave Kirill so much power for his loyalty, and he never saw how much his brother was abusing it. Still doesn't. Losing our mother made him mad for revenge, but when the war was over and the bloodshed ended, he was broken. Despondent. The more time went on, the more he withdrew from his duties as *Pakhan*. Especially after losing Antony."

"How did Kirill become *Pakhan* of London?" I wondered.

"Wouldn't he be wanting to sit closer to the seat of power in Russia?"

Ivan snorted. "The one good thing our father's *Sovietnik* has done was send that fucker here," Ivan spat. "Vlad couldn't prove it, but he was beginning to put things together as well. Our father put an end to the Tkachenko human trafficking ring when he took power. It disgusted him. Suddenly, not long after Kirill started gaining power, there were new rings popping up and women going missing again."

"Did you ever find out a name?"

"No," Ivan sighed and sat down in his chair, utterly defeated. "Just an emblem of some kind of lizard or something on the top of some papers."

Bingo.

"The Chameleon Agency."

Ivan sat up straighter, the slump in his shoulders straightening.

"You know who they are?"

"We've had a run in or two with them over the past year," I told him. "They take women and put them in auctions all around the globe. Sometimes they sell them directly to high-profile clients. Have you ever heard of The Dollhouse?"

"Rumors and whispers," he admitted with a shiver. "But nothing else. Some say the organization is older than most countries. That every large-scale assassination attempt in history is thanks to them. Caesar, Lincoln, Rasputin, Alexander, Ghandi, King—the list goes on and on."

"Pfft." I rolled my eyes. "That is a bit presumptuous."

"But not altogether without merit," Ivan pointed out. "Who knows how long an underground organization like that has gone unnoticed. Been renamed. Do I believe they orchestrated the assassination of Julius Caesar? No. But Lincoln? King? It is a distinct possibility."

"Both of those figures were assassinated by men," I rebutted. "From the research we've been doing, that isn't their target for forced recruiting."

"It isn't *now*," he said. "But women hold more power now than they did in 1865 and in 1968."

He did have a point.

"Look," he sighed. Pinching the bridge of his nose, he closed his eyes for a moment to regroup. "I'm not going to give you the highlight reel of why I've done what I have. But I am sorry for some of the things," he admitted. "I never should have involved Ava, and for that I am sorry, brother."

Brother.

I had brothers. Vasily, Roman, Maksim, Leon, and Nikolai were my brothers. Even that shithead Dima. They had been for years. But there was something in the way Ivan uttered that word, with reverence and respect, that stirred the shattered parts of my soul.

"Why did you?"

"Because she meant something to you," he sighed with regret. "Even before you realized it yourself."

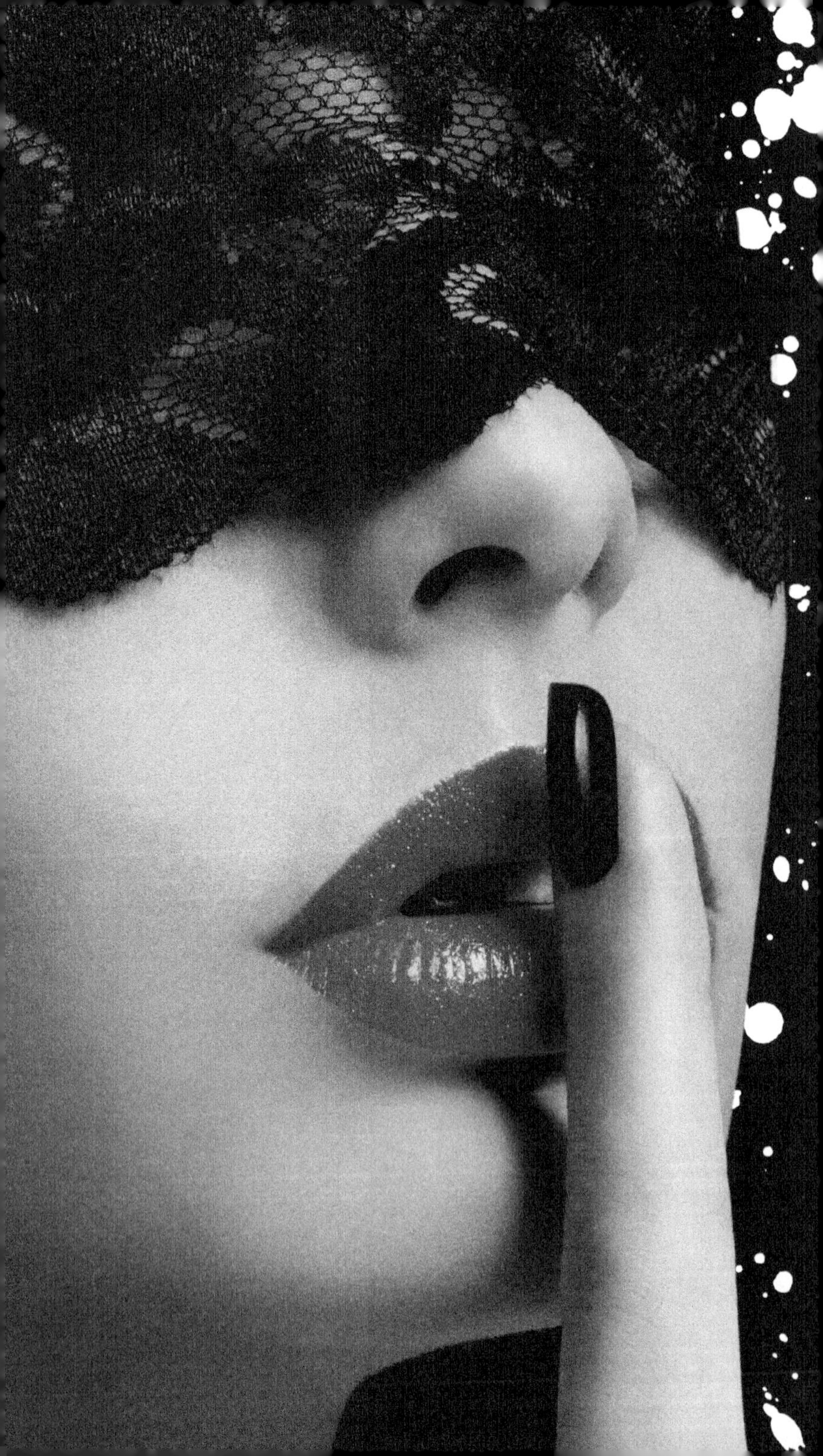

CHAPTER SEVENTEEN

"The London *Bratva* has been hemorrhaging money," Mark droned over the video chat. He was briefing Ivan on everything we had learned so far. I searched through the new images Mark had sent over. My brilliant wife managed to break Libby's code and obtain at least a terabyte of new information we never had before. We'd been in London for nearly two weeks, and we still weren't any closer to bringing Kirill down.

I frowned. Thoughts of Kenzi popped into my mind. We'd left her with Leon at the airport, but that was the last thing I had wanted to do. Kenzi could easily take care of herself. The training the Dollhouse had provided her with was extensive. I was worried she would be blindsided by her relationship with her brother. Afraid she wouldn't see the killing blow coming because she underestimated him.

Libby had been the gentlest and sweetest girl I had ever known. Vas fell head over heels for her kindness and love for others, and Christian killed her for her perceived betrayal. She stood in the way of what he wanted.

Ava.

"What's that?" Ivan leaned forward for a better look at whatever Mark was showing him. "Her cane, can you zoom in on it?" Mark snorted.

"Can I zoom in on it?" he mocked Ivan. There was still salt in the wound. "Of course, I can zoom in on it. An ape could zoom in on this." He paused, his eyes flitting to Ivan. "Well, most apes." If my brother caught the insult, he didn't respond, too focused on the photo in front of him.

"Ava was curious about the cane as well," Mark added. "Especially this." The photo grew larger, focusing on the small crest etched into the wood of the cane, just below the silver cross.

"That is odd," Ivan murmured. "I recognize the cane."

"How is that odd?" I asked.

"Not odd in the sense that he has the same cane," Ivan explained. "But this is the Eye of Providence." He pointed to the lidless eye in the middle of the symbol. "And this is the Seal of Solomon." His finger swept around the rest of the symbol, which was depicted as a pentagram inside a perfect circle.

"Isn't the Seal of Solomon a legend?" Mark inquired. "An alchemic symbol thought to control demons and such?" Ivan nodded.

"It has had many meanings throughout history," he breathed. "Same as the Illuminati symbol. It all depends on who you ask and what time-period you are sifting through. The Eye of Providence, as it is attributed to the Illuminati, is the all-seeing eye. Meaning that they have eyes everywhere. Can see everything."

"Big brother is watching." Mark smirked.

"Something like that," Ivan agreed. "In other parts, it means wisdom and protection. Some believe it is a variation of the Eye of Horus in Egyptian Mythology, which is restoration and protection." I listened intently, pride spreading warmly through my chest at hearing my brother's depth of knowledge. He was smart. Obviously well-educated, and the passion he exuded caught me up and held me hostage.

"You know a lot about this."

Redness crept up Ivan's neck. He shot me a small, bashful smile. "I've always had a passion for history and symbolism."

I nodded and smiled at him.

"Do you have other pictures of people with this cane and symbol?" Ivan questioned, turning his attention back to Mark, who nodded.

"A few," the hacker confirmed. "The cane itself is rather common, but there were very few I found that had that exact symbol. The first one is this lady." An image of a woman they'd identified as Madam Therese filled the screen. "From what we've gathered, she's a buyer for the Dollhouse."

Ivan took a moment to study the picture before announcing that he knew her.

"I have seen her meet with Kirill on several occasions," he admitted. "That explains a lot, actually."

Puzzled, I asked, "What do you mean?"

Ivan swallowed, his throat bobbing as a slash of anger cut through his features before disappearing. "Kirill has that same cane. With that exact symbol carved into the wood."

Crickets.

"Do you think he is a buyer?"

"Or a client?" Mark added.

"Both," Ivan whispered, his gaze turning to me. "If he's involved with the Dollhouse, I think he is more than just a client. I doubt clients are given a special decoder cane, and I highly doubt Kirill could afford their services if he wasn't part of the inner circle. Which means he's helping supply them while skimming off the top."

"The assassination attempts." Everything was becoming clearer. The threads of fate weaving the tapestry of my childhood were starting to come together to reveal Kirill's grand design.

"How many were there?"

I scoffed. "More than anyone should have to count," I told him, bitterness coating my tongue. "After Antony, they came every few months. The older I grew, the more frequent the attempts became."

"He was growing desperate. Why?"

"Matthias was the only one who could identify your mother." Dima spoke up from the doorway. The three of us missed the unlocking of the hotel room door. "Think about it." He stepped into the room, handing out the bags of food we ordered. "If it was about straight-up succession, he would have made an attempt on your brothers."

"He did," Mark pointed out.

"Eh," Dima scrunched his nose. "Not really, though. Yes, he manipulated your brother into hunting down Matthias. How he did that, you'll have to ask him yourself, but I honestly don't believe that he expected Matthias to kill him."

Dima made a valid point. If Kirill wanted to remove the obstacles in his way of direct succession, he could have taken out Antony and Ivan long before he came after me.

"Antony was collateral," Ivan snarled. "Either way, Kirill won. Our brother either killed you and his secret was safe, or you killed Antony and that was one less person in his way." The gears in Ivan's head were turning, his anger building as he recounted every moment Kirill had control over. Then he exploded.

"Son of a bitch!" Ivan roared, his fists clenching and unclenching as he fought the urge to destroy the room in his rage. "That motherfucking asshole."

Kirill was playing a long game. Building an army for his war, but he was ill prepared. If the information we had gathered was accurate, it meant that Kirill was slipping. Or it was all a ruse, and we were walking into a trap.

"What are you doing?"

A feminine voice crackled through the speakers of the tablet.

Ava.

Closing my eyes, I let the familiar sound of her voice wash over me. Fuck, I missed her. Mark stuttered something, his back keeping us from her view.

"We're heading to Portland." Her soft voice was like a drug to me. "Can you gather some information for me? Sully O'Malley wants a sit down, and I need some dirt to take with me."

"Yeah," Mark told her anxiously. "I can do that. Just give me half an hour. I'm finishing up with a few things."

"What are you doing?"

"Uh, nothing." Mark panicked as he tried to keep Ava from viewing our video feed. Growling, Dima shoved Ivan out of the way of the camera and sat down, food in hand. "Look it's..."

"Privet, Dima," Ava's face popped into view. I stood sat just off camera so that her view of me was blocked, but I could see everything. "*Kak dela?*"

Fuck, why was her asking how Dima was doing in Russian such a turn on?

Ivan stared at me, his gaze wandering to the tent in my jeans, and raised his brows.

"Really?" he mouthed. I narrowed my eyes at him and quietly readjusted myself.

"Fuck off." I mouthed back. He snorted.

"Who's there with you?" Ava asked curiously, peering

closer to the screen, as if it would make her see farther into the room.

"No one." Dima waved a hand at her. "Television."

Ava scrunched her nose. "You don't like to watch television."

She had him there, but Dima just shrugged it off.

"Thought I'd try it while I was here."

"Well," Ava sighed despondently. "All right then. When are you coming home?"

Home.

"Soon," Dima promised. "I'll be coming soon, *Pakhan.*"

Ava smiled at him through the screen.

"Okay then." She let out a wistful sigh, but otherwise left it alone. "Be safe, Dima."

Dima nodded and gave her a small smile. Then she was gone.

"That was close," Mark muttered underneath his breath a few moments after the door clicked shut behind him.

"Too close," I growled.

Ivan chuckled. "That is what you get for not including her in the plan."

Fuck him.

"Trust me," Dima muttered petulantly. "We've all told him the same thing. But honestly, it was very last minute, and Ava has a horrible poker face."

Ivan tilted his head. He couldn't argue with that. He knew from experience just how bad Ava was at lying.

"We need to get back on track here," I chastised them. "What are we going to do about Kirill?"

My brother sighed and ran a hand down his tired and worn face. For years, he hunted and searched for the truth behind Antony's disappearance. I could not begin to imagine what he would have to do in order to gain the necessary information.

I had to hand it to Ivan. He was creative and willing to get his hands dirty. He was smart and cunning. Devious and brave. That didn't mean we were suddenly going to have sleepovers and bond over sports, especially after his involvement with Ava's kidnapping, but it was a foundation.

Plus, slitting Kirill's throat would be a great brother bonding activity, in my opinion.

"I can't touch him without our father's approval." The carefree way he said *our father* both warmed and tightened my chest. Tomas had always been my father. He raised me from a savage, rage-filled boy to the man I was today. Those times were hard, yes, but I recalled those halcyon days training under him with Vas as the best days of my life.

I still remember the first time he called me son. Vas and I had successfully taken down the inner-city gang that had been controlling parts of north Boston. They had been terrorizing the residents, stealing women and children from the streets to sell, and forcing businesses to pay an insane protection fee that nearly bankrupted half their territory.

A territory that had once belonged to the *Bratva*.

We took it back.

"What kind of proof do you need?" Mark's fingers flew across his keyboard, and moments later, document after document popped onto the screen. "I don't have any proof regarding your mother," Mark hedged nervously. "His tracks were too well covered. But these all prove he's been skimming off the top for years."

"That might not be enough," Ivan admitted sadly. "Kirill is one of our father's most trusted advisors. He was there for him in his darkest times. Even if he was the cause of it. Our father isn't aware of that."

"He won't believe his own son?"

Ivan's face fell, hurt shining through his platinum gray eyes.

"We had a falling out many years ago," Ivan told us. "It is why I went undercover as an FBI agent. To prove what Kirill had been doing. That he was the cause of all our misfortune."

Putting my hand on my brother's shoulder, I gripped it tight, giving him my silent support. We needed to prove to Andrei that the evidence against Kirill was true.

"Kirill thinks you're dead, right?" Mark's lips turned up mischievously.

"Yes. Why does that matter now?"

"Because he finally got what he wanted after all these years."

"I'm not following."

"The one piece of evidence that could tear apart all of his plans," Mark explained, "he believes to be dead. Which means—"

"He won't see me coming."

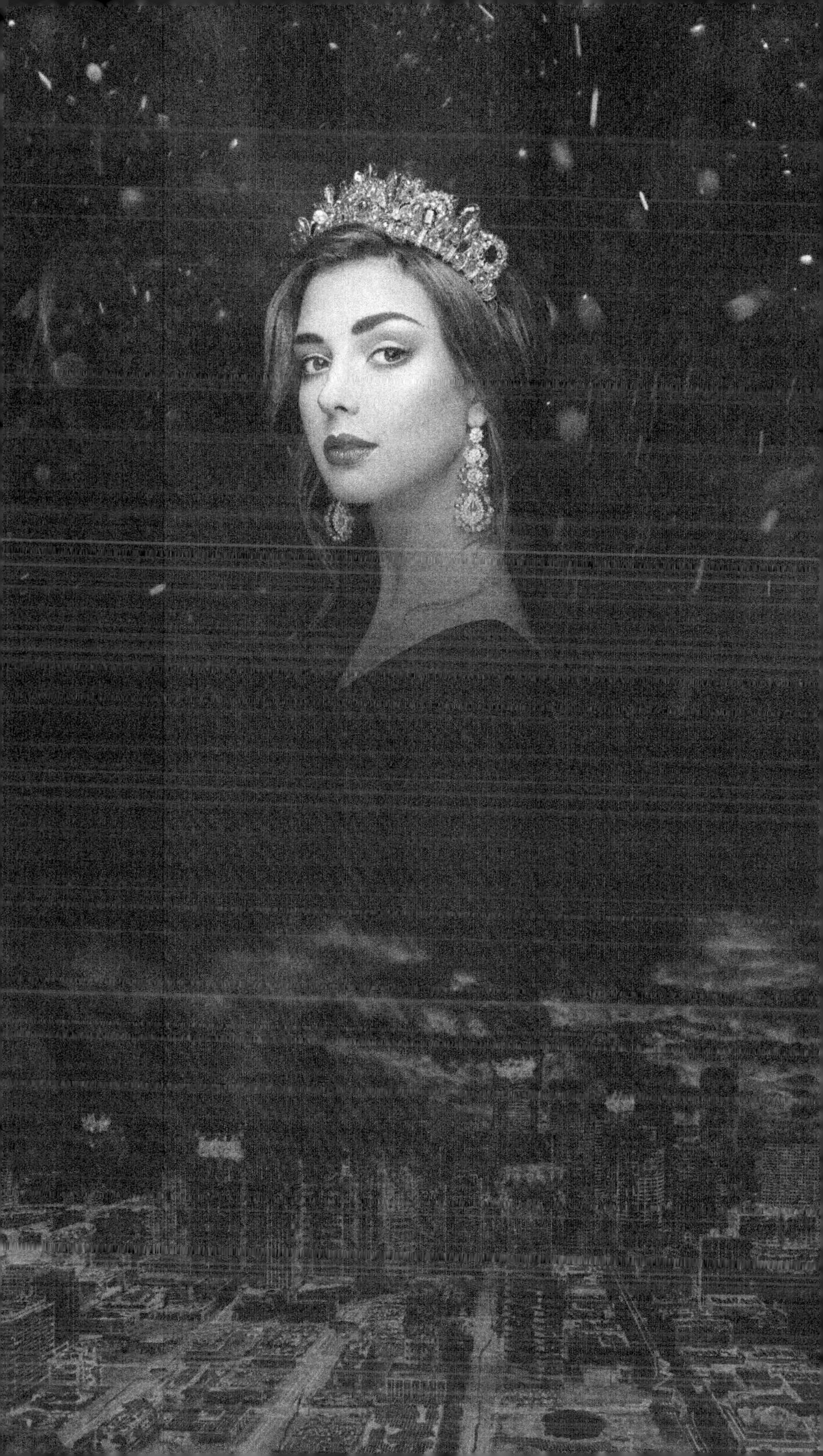

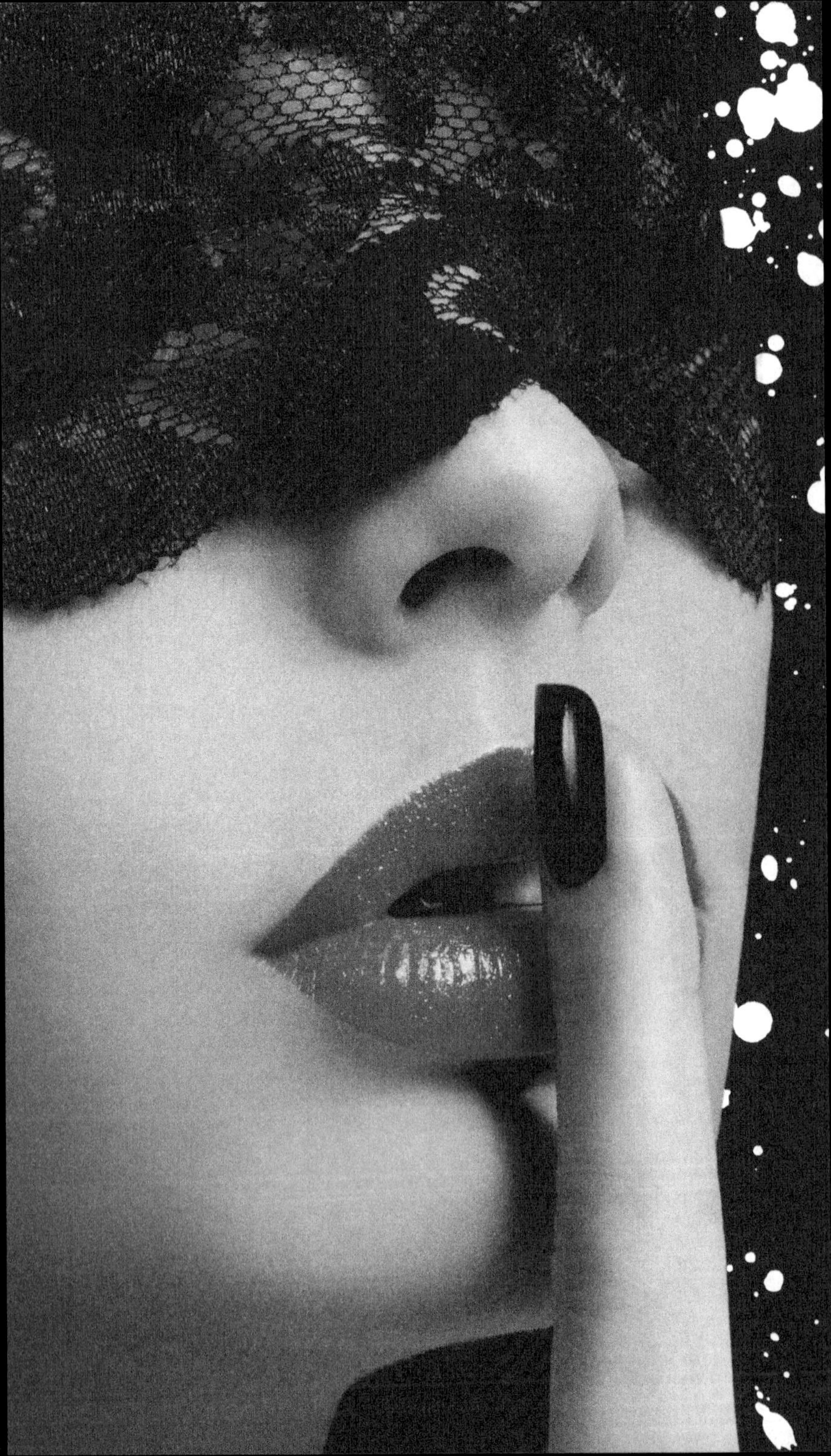

CHAPTER EIGHTEEN

"Jesus," Ivan muttered over the comm unit. "I forgot how boring he is. Kirill has barely left the house most of the week. How is he running the city like this?"

Two fucking weeks. That was how long it had taken to spread the seed of doubt through Kirill's men and put together all the information we could on him. I felt like a damn private investigator. Then again, this was what my company did.

I just didn't.

Sitting in a car, waiting for hours for someone to make a move or not was not my idea of a good time. That was why I hired others to do it for me. I was a man of action. Not a spy.

"He had a few whores delivered this morning that still haven't come out." Dima smirked. "I wouldn't say he isn't having *any* fun. Who would want to leave that? One of them had breasts the size of watermelons."

Ivan retched. "I didn't need that particular image in my head, *idiot*."

Dima chuckled. "Maybe I can grab one on their way out," he pondered theatrically, tapping his chin. Not that Ivan could see him from his position at the back entrance. What scared me was that he sounded serious. "You know, interrogate them a little."

Ivan groaned dramatically.

"Do you really want to be sticking your dick where he did?" I asked my enforcer, who sat next to me in our stake-out car. "You don't know how many whores he has fucked or what kind of diseases he may have. Used pussy isn't always good pussy."

Another groan from Ivan.

"Eh." Dima shrugged, tipping his hand back and forth, undecided. "I'll risk it. I doubt he stuck it in all her holes. I'll just utilize the ones he didn't."

"*Khristos*," Ivan swore. "Gag him, will you?"

I snickered.

"*Oh*," Dima lifted his eyebrows. "Someone has a kinky side."

"All right, children," Mark scolded through the video screen. "Don't make me put you on separate comm lines."

Dima winked at Mark while Ivan grunted. "Please do. Before I shoot him in the face."

My enforcer gasped, drawing his hand to his chest like some Shakespearean actor. "Not the face, *mudak*. It's my moneymaker, you *glupyy malen'kiy gnom*."

"Who are you calling a stupid little gnome, you…"

"Enough." My voice thrummed dangerously inside the car. "For fuck's sake. I thought I was supposed to be the younger brother, Ivan?"

Dima sniggered, and I went to round on him next before I was interrupted by Mark's amused voice. "He's got a call."

"Patch it through so we can all hear."

Silence, a few keyboard clicks, and then the car was filled with ringing.

"Kirill."

A bolt of hate raced up my spine at hearing his voice for the first time after so many years. The man who'd kidnapped and murdered my mother. Who tossed me on the street without a second thought to further his own greed and need for power.

His voice was hoarse and grating. He coughed, his lungs wet and rattling like a pack a day smoker.

"What the hell have you done, Kirill?" the man on the phone line snarled viciously. "How long did you think you could get away with playing me, *brother*?"

"Our father," Ivan whispered through the comm line.

"I don't know what you are talking about, Andrei." Kirill sounded shocked; panicked. He hadn't known this was coming. We had taken everything Libby and Ivan acquired over the years on Kirill's work and association. From his involvement in trafficking girls under the Chameleon Agency to his current profit skimming. Every nook and cranny had been swept out from under the rug for Andrei Tkachenko to see.

"Don't lie to me," Andrei roared. "This was your last chance, Kirill. I'm flying there to settle this. I gave you one last shot, and you ruined it. Again."

"It isn't what it looks like," Kirill began. "I swear I had nothing—"

"Are you telling me it is all lies?" Andrei hissed. "Because I am holding some pretty damning evidence."

"It is fake," Kirill insisted. "Men who want to drive a wedge between us, brother. They know we are stronger together."

Dima snorted derisively. I agreed with him. The honey buttered bullshit spewing from Kirill's mouth was as much amusing as it was frustrating. There was no doubt in my mind the man would seek to worm his way out of his crimes with Andrei. Pin them on an unforeseen enemy. Play on his loyalty to him. His help in winning against his father.

It wouldn't do him any good.

Not this time.

"You better hope so." Andrei was cold, his tone dropping dangerously as he continued. "I'm flying down there. You better pray I don't find any more evidence of foul play, *brat*." The sarcastic edge to the Russian word for brother wasn't missed. It seemed tension between the two had been riding high for a while it seemed.

"You won't," Kirill swore. "I promise you that."

Then the line went dead.

"Well," Dima's brow shot up, "I expected something a bit more."

"Don't go anywhere just yet," Mark told us. "He's making an outgoing call."

"To where?" Ivan questioned. A few more clacks of the keyboard later, and he had it.

"Seattle."

There was ringing, and then, "You better be calling for a good reason."

The hair on the back of my neck stood up in awareness at the harsh, feminine voice on the other end. It sounded familiar. Too familiar, but I couldn't place where I heard it before.

"We need to move up the timeline." Kirill's voice was shaky, unnerved. He was afraid of this woman, whoever she was. "Someone is working against me. Sending him information."

"It isn't my responsibility to clean up your messes, Marius," the woman hissed. The way she tilted her words told me she had an accent she was attempting to hide. It was slight, and I couldn't place it, but one was certainly there.

Where the fuck had I heard this voice before?

"My messes are your mess, Caesar," he growled. "Remember that. If I lose my position here, we no longer have the foothold we need to the docks."

Caesar? Marius?

"Fucking Roman general names, really?" Dima muttered beneath his breath. I shot him a look. He shrugged. "What? I paid attention in school."

Ivan's soft laugh filtered through the comms.

"Don't threaten me," the woman snarled. "If you hadn't been so careless, this wouldn't be an issue."

"Just send one of the legionnaires." Kirill sighed heavily. "It must look like an assassination. Otherwise, there will be too much digging when I ascend as leader."

Ascend. What a pompous asshat.

"And what about your nephew?" the woman questioned. "Ivan? He is next in line to inherit."

Kirill brushed her off. "He is nothing," he insisted. "Nothing but a disgraced outcast who hasn't been heard from in years. I made sure he appeared to be nothing more than a disgruntled son after his father's money. Andrei cut him off."

"But he didn't cut him from his will," the woman pointed out. "Or from succession."

Kirill brushed her off. "It is nothing. He is nothing."

Or so Ivan led him to believe.

"You better hope so, Marius." The venom dripping from the phone line was obvious. As was her disdain for him. "Otherwise, you might regret what is coming for you."

"And what is that?"

"Ghosts of the past."

"All my problems are dead," he gloated. "Your legionnaire made sure of that."

The woman hummed. "That may be so, but his wife sure is causing a commotion over here."

Kirill grunted. "She won't be a problem for much longer," he dismissed. "Sulla will make sure of that. He took care of Elias with no problem; he'll take care of her."

"We'll see," the woman sounded skeptical. "As for your request, I'll send 848 to take care of it. She's proven to be efficient at taking out pests."

"She did it in spectacular fashion for me," Kirill agreed.

Kenzi. They were talking about sending Kenzi to take out Andrei.

"Get her on the phone," I hissed at Mark. "Quick."

Another beat of silence. Another moment of holding our breaths, waiting in anticipated suspense for Kenzi to pick up the phone.

Nothing.

"She's not answering."

Dima swore.

"Who are you trying to reach?" Ivan questioned.

"Kenzi."

"Ward?" he asked incredulously. "What does she have to do with this?"

My forehead raised in mock surprise that my older brother didn't know about the remaining Ward twin.

"Guess you didn't do your research all that well, brother." I snarked.

"Shove it and tell me what you know," he huffed over the comm line. Dima laughed.

"Kenzi Ward was sold to the Dollhouse by her father," I told him. "Convincing everyone that she had gone to college overseas instead."

"She told you this?"

"Yes," I responded. "Originally, she'd been tasked to kill

Ava. Luckily, an old friend of mine had an interest in the Dollhouse as well and had been monitoring certain chatter."

"The three of them had a strong bond," Ivan stated. "Why would Kenzi willingly kill her sister? The Dollhouse must have known Kenzi wouldn't follow through."

"They twisted Libby's death to make it appear as if Ava and I had her killed." That organization knew no bounds. "It took some...convincing to get her to see the truth."

"And you trust her?"

"Yes." There was no hesitation in my reply.

"Okay." Ivan took a deep, calming breath. "What do we do next? If we can't reach Kenzi and she isn't aware of what the target means..."

Dima beamed.

"We need to make sure Kirill goes down first." The darkness in his eyes swirled like a hurricane, his pupils dilating at the prospect of shedding blood. Fucking psychopath, that one.

"And how are we going to convince my father that Kirill is the enemy?"

I chuckled darkly. "I'm going to rise from the dead."

It was ridiculously easy to slip past Kirill's defenses. The men guarding his compound were no more than Wal-Mart security guards when it came to alertness. Bone cracked beneath my hands as I separated the guard's brain from his spinal cord, his body falling lifelessly at my feet.

There were only ten guards in total, with two active sweeping along the perimeter that Ivan had already taken care of. It was sloppy. Kirill believed himself to be untouchable, especially since he believed I was dead.

Satisfaction welled in my chest, knowing I had been the

reason he had so many guards before. The moment he learned I was dead, he had loosened his security measures.

Big mistake.

Now I was a viper in his nest.

Silent. Deadly. Ready for the kill.

Andrei's two guards stood outside of Kirill's office, ready for action. Their eyes scanned the hallway, continuously on alert. These were the only men we would spare.

Raised voices drifted down the corridor. The two brothers were arguing.

Good.

Neither of them would hear us coming.

"Go," I whispered into the comm line. Within moments, the men at the door slumped against the wall. Ketamine darts were highly effective in times like these.

Nighty night, fuckers.

"You expect me to believe this bullshit?" Andrei roared, his voice sharp like a crack of thunder. "You're a disgrace, *brother*." He spat the word, as if it was a foul taste in his mouth. "There are dozens of accusations here. With proof. You expect me to believe that none of this was you? That your filthy, greedy hands haven't tainted our name with this shit?"

Kirill laughed cruelly.

"Tainted our name?" he asked in disbelief. "We are the *Bratva*. Not some fancy fucking corporation. We spill blood. Our name is meant to spread fear. You have made us into nothing but docile little lambs. No one respects the Tkachenko name anymore. No one fears it like they should."

"You can't run an empire off of fear," Andrei snarled. "Father did that, and look how it ended for him. Too many men switched sides. They weren't truly loyal, just afraid."

"Fear keeps them in line," Kirill hissed. "I have tried telling you this."

Andrei sighed. "We can't rule like that."

"If we did, maybe our enemies wouldn't be making up lies to tear us apart." Kirill softened his voice, but I could hear the calculated manipulation a mile away. "They see our weakness, and now they are exploiting it. We can't allow them to do that."

"Maybe you are right." Andrei's dejected tone moved something within me. This man had fought for so long to stay true to some kind of value among a world where values were a weakness exploited by the enemy.

Andrei was fighting against a tide of men who had only known how to rule through fear. Men who, with the guidance of Kirill, perpetuated that cycle behind their *Pakhan's* back. It was pathetic. Tomas has shown me that loyalty isn't earned through fear. It is earned through dedication to your community. To your people.

Knots wound in my stomach, bile chasing up my throat at the thought of Kirill running the *Bratva* empire in Russia. The Tkachenko family ran everything. Even Tomas paid loyalty to them after his freedom from his own *Pakhan*. If Kirill managed to gain that kind of power, he would tear everything Tomas built apart.

The war would be brutal and bloody.

"He isn't right, *Papa*." Right on time. Ivan strode through the large mahogany double doors with his head held high. His crisp black Bespoke suit was tailored to perfection, and he wore it like it was a second skin. He might have given up the luxury of being a *Bratva* prince, but he never forgot what it was like. "*Uncle* is just trying to manipulate you. Again."

"Ivan." A chair scraped against the wooden floor. Andrei was standing now. I could just make them out through the crack in the side of the door. The photos I had seen of Andrei must have been older. The man in Kirill's office was more distinguished. Older. His dark hair was tinted with gray strands that hung in his face. His salt and pepper beard and mustache were neatly trimmed.

Andrei Tkachenko exuded power effortlessly, unlike his brother, whose power came from intimidation.

"Hello, Father." He bowed his head in respect before lifting his eyes. The resemblance between the two was uncanny. The two were closer to brothers in appearance than father and son. Then again, they were only around twenty years apart, and Andrei appeared far younger than his age.

"What are you doing here?" Kirill spat. "How did you get past my guards? *Guards!*"

No one came.

There was no one left but me, and I wasn't ready to reveal my hand just yet.

Let him sweat a little.

"No one is coming, Uncle," Ivan told him quietly. "It's time we had a nice family chat about everything you have done. Don't you think?"

Andrei's gaze darted back and forth between his brother and his son.

"What the hell is going on?" he asked, his tone dipping.

"Everything you received is accurate intel," Ivan told his father patiently. "It has all been verified by multiple sources. None of it has been tampered with or altered in any way."

Confusion flitted across our father's face. "How do you know about what I received?"

Ivan smirked. "I sent it."

"You little fucking..." Kirill spat, but Andrei held up his hand to silence him. The man's face turned an angry shade of purple, his beady eyes bulging from his head as he glared daggers at his nephew.

"There is so much you don't know," Ivan continued, his

eyes on his father, barely acknowledging that Kirill was having a mini stroke next to them. "So much I tried to warn you about. But you were blinded by his perceived loyalty that you couldn't see through the cracks in his façade."

"He is my brother," Andrei reminded his son. "The man who helped me avenge the death of your mother. If it wasn't for him, your grandfather would never have fallen."

"If it wasn't for him," Ivan sneered. "There would have been no war."

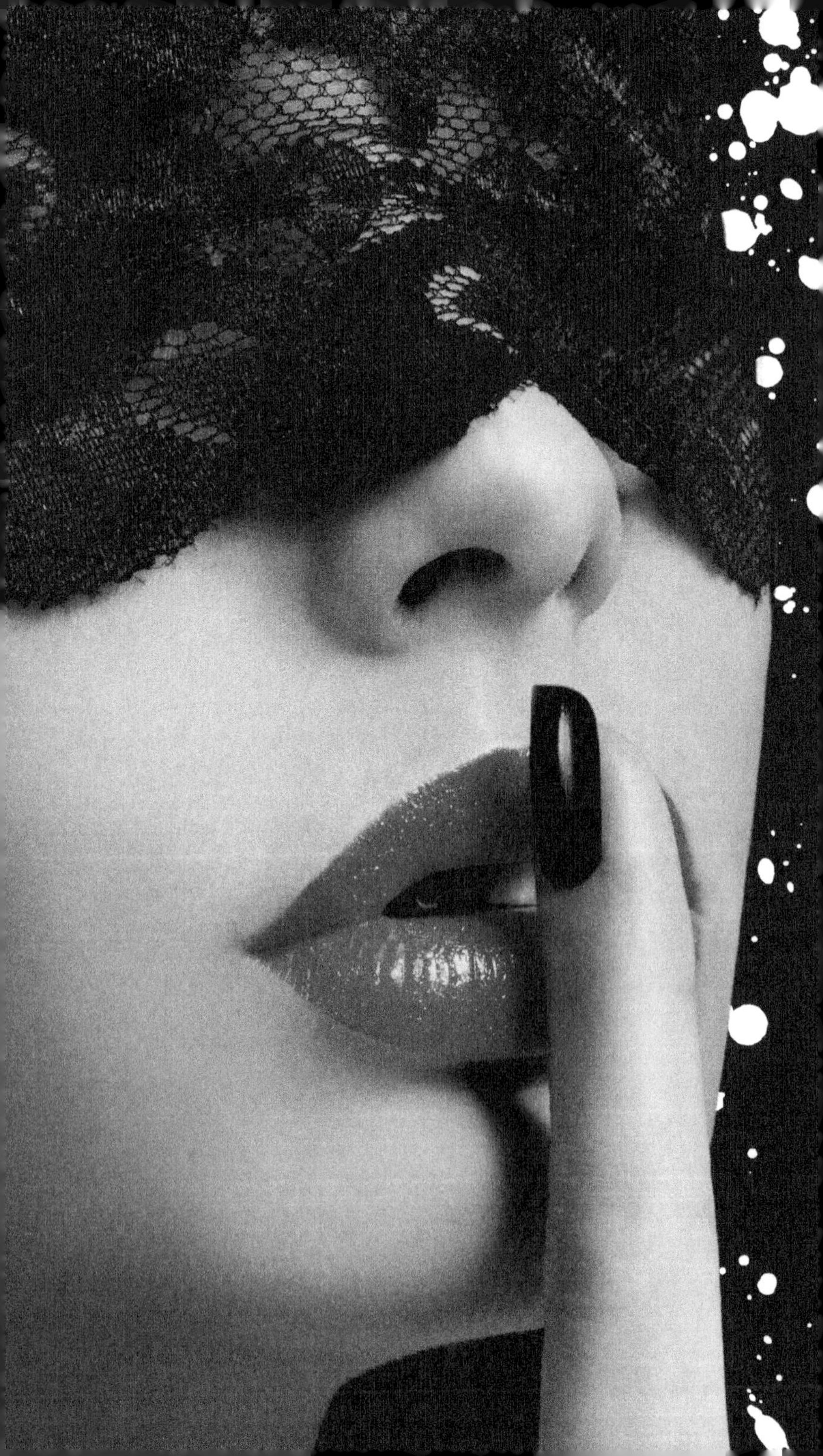

CHAPTER NINETEEN

Kirill paled.

I relished the look of fear on his face as it slowly dawned on him that he wouldn't be walking away unscathed. Not this time. At my sides, my hands clenched and unclenched rhythmically. It was hard not to sink my fist into his pug little face.

"Your grandfather murdered your mother while she was pregnant," Andrei insisted. He was blind to the truth. The love he had for his brother was strong, but I could sense his doubt. See it lurking behind his steel-cut eyes. "He had proof."

"He lied." Striding into the room, hands in my pockets, I kept my gaze on the man who had raised me. The man who had abandoned me without a second thought. He tore my family apart. Murdered my mother and left me to the wolves.

"*Khristos*," Andrei murmured under his breath. Lips slightly parted. Eyes wide. He stared at me as if he was seeing a ghost. The ghost of my mother. There was very little of Andrei Tkachenko in me besides the color of my eyes and the mark I bore on my wrist. Otherwise, I was a spitting image of the woman who bore me.

"Impossible." Kirill stared at me in abject horror, his face paling even further. "You're dead."

My gray eyes darted to his. "You should have realized by now how hard that really is." I reminded him. "After all, you are the one who sent assassin after assassin to kill me since I was a child. *Father*."

Andrei's gaze swept to his brother. "You said he was dead."

"He...he was," Kirill stammered. "Father killed them both. I saw it with my own eyes."

"The lies of a snake are the sweetest," I sneered at Kirill. "Aren't they?"

"He killed Antony, Andrei," Kirill spat, straightening himself up. He would not go down lightly. Not without trying to take me with him. "I have proof of that."

Lifting my chin, I eyed my birth father. "He is right," I admitted honestly. "I was thirteen, living in the shadow of the Bolsheokhtinsky bridge, when Antony attacked me in the dead of night. I defended myself. It wasn't until his last breath that I realized who he was. When he asked me to forgive him and called me brother."

Andrei's darkened gaze turned to his brother. "You told me Antony was killed by the Fedorovs." Kirill audibly swallowed, the fat of his neck tightening, his pulse thumping, his pupils pinpoints as his fight-or-flight instinct took over. He was sweating, his eyes wild as he took all three of us in.

"Why don't you tell him what really happened, Kirill?" The utter disdain I had for this man rolled off me in waves. This would be his last stand. He wouldn't escape this room. Not alive. "Tell him how you are the one who stole our mother. Forced her to be your whore after you got her addicted to drugs. And then, when Andrei called you up to take part in his regime, you overdosed her with those very drugs. Kicked me out on the streets.

"Tell the brother who trusted you how you sent Antony to kill me. Whispering in his ear that I was the bad guy. That he needed to prove himself by killing me. How you set Ivan up so that his own father would lose faith in him. Why don't you tell him the truth for once? That all you wanted was the power the Tkachenko name gave you so you could move your human cargo without worry. That you are nothing more than an ugly, fat traitor to your blood. You are nothing more than dirt beneath his shoes. A coward. A loser. A—"

"Enough!" Kirill roared, standing, silver cross cane gripped tightly in one hand. His knuckles were turning white, his face the color of dark beet juice. This was the man I knew growing up. The one who easily lost control, and when he lost control, he made mistakes. Just like he was now. "You know nothing, boy," he spat. "Nothing about being the outcast. The bastard child. I worked just as hard as Andrei and was given nothing for it. Nothing. While Andrei got everything. So, I made my little side business and built my army."

"I treated you like a true brother." Andrei shook his head, disappointed. "Never once did I treat you as anything less than pure blood."

Kirill sneered. "Please." He rolled his eyes. "Father was right. You are weak. Allowing yourself to draw lines and enforce values. You were so drowned by your grief after the loss of that whore and her child. You made our father look weak when you married her. She was nothing. Her children are nothing."

"I should have seen this sooner." Andrei sighed deeply. There was a flash of anger behind his stormy eyes, but he was the picture of calm as his brother ripped him apart with his words. "His influence over you was greater than I imagined. I thought..." He shook his head lightly, never taking his eyes off Kirill. You never give the enemy a chance to catch you unaware, and Kirill was now his enemy. "I was a fool to believe you were a better man than him."

Kirill scoffed. "You only saw what I wanted you to see." He jabbed, his dark smile triumphant. "And now." He lifted the gold embossed lighter from his desk and flicked the spark wheel. The flint ignited, and I surged forward, ready to sacrifice myself for the father I'd never had a chance to know. We tumbled to the floor, my body shielding his.

Nothing came.

No pain.

No blood.

Chest heaving, I drew up, eyes scanning and alert.

Kirill growled and ignited the lighter again and again, but nothing happened.

"Fucking—" Glass shattered, raining down around me. I swept my arm up to protect my face, the rest of my body still shielding the man beneath me.

"Boss? Are you okay?" Dima's voice was panicked in my ear. "Boss?"

Growling, I stood up, offering Andrei my hand. He took it, and I helped him to his feet.

"We're good, Dima," I told him. "Looks like we've got a guardian angel out there."

"Well." A soft voice filtered in from the doorway. I turned to see Kenzi leaning lazily against the frame, her brown hair in a tight bun, clad in black from head to toe. "I wouldn't say I'm an angel." She shrugged. "But I definitely feel guardian-like right now."

"Who the fuck are you?" Ivan spat as he drew his gun.

Kenzi eyed it wearily, a perfectly stenciled eyebrow raised at the man.

"Really?" She scoffed. "I'm pretty sure I just blew my cover for your ass." Before Ivan could utter another word, Kenzi shifted. Her moves were swift and precise as she shot forward, wrenching the gun from my brother's hand, and disassembling it within a matter of seconds. "A thank you would be appreciated."

Andrei barked a laugh from behind me.

"Leave it to Kirill to hire an assassin." He shook his head. "Man can't even get his hands dirty to kill his own brother." He spat at Kirill's body. It laid slumped against the bookcases; head lolled to the side with a giant bullet hole straight between his eyebrows. "Could have merely injured him, though. Would have been useful to interrogate him."

Kenzi groaned. "Everyone's a critic," she muttered. "You're fucking welcome."

Andrei smirked. "Thank you, *malen'kiy ubiytsa*." Little assassin. It was fitting.

"I hope that wasn't an insult." She winked at him. "Because it sounds sexy."

Andrei laughed, full and deep.

"He is right, though," I sighed. "Whoever is running the Chameleon Agency, maybe even the Dollhouse, he knew who she was."

"She?" Kenzi tipped her head to the side. "That's disgusting. A woman trafficking and using other women? Definitely gonna need to revoke her chick card."

Ivan snorted. "We'll help you revoke her life card, if that helps."

"Sounds like a plan to me."

"We still need to figure out who *she* is." I walked to the other side of Kirill's desk.

"He might not have known who she was," Ivan pointed out. "They never called each other by their real names."

"True," I said as I pulled out one of the desk drawers. "But she knew about Andrei and about me. Which means she knew who *he* was."

"If Kirill didn't know who she was, he was certainly searching into it," Andrei spoke up. "My brother wouldn't stand for having someone being able to hold things over his head without the ability to reciprocate."

"So somewhere, he has a file with his own research on every member," Kenzi mused. She turned to Andrei. "He's a paranoid narcissist. Where would he hide his most valuable intel?"

Andrei cringed, casting a disgusted look at his brother's dead body.

"Not it," Kenzi shook her head emphatically. "Count me out of that one."

Ivan chuckled. "I doubt he hid it there."

Andrei shrugged. "Never know."

Kenzi grunted, unamused. "Imma say it's not."

"Most likely it's in his safe." Andrei smiled at Kenzi and winked. "Where could it be—"

"Got it," Kenzi sing-songed from the other side of the room. Ivan shook his head, bewildered.

"How do you move that fast?"

Kenzi shrugged. "Superpowers." She winked.

Of course the man would hide his safe behind his own self portrait.

Narcissist.

Kenzi hummed while she fiddled with the dial, her eyes closed as it spun on its axis. It took a few tries, but several moments later, locks clicked into place, and the door swung open.

"Voilà." Kenzi dipped a dramatic, flourishing bow, her arm swinging out in a grand gesture.

We all chuckled. "Very well done," I praised her. She beamed up at me like a kid who'd just received her favorite toy on Christmas. Fuck. I forgot how little love the Ward women had grown up with. Ava had told me that there was no doubt in her mind that Kendra loved her daughters. But it wasn't a mother's love. Not the love she received growing up from her own mother prior to her death.

Kendra's love was obsession. Obsession with perfection. Her daughters were a chance for her to relive everything she no longer could be. Young, with pure, untainted beauty. Hope for the future. Now one was dead, and the other was slowly working her way to becoming the next Harley Quinn. When I'd spoken to Vas last, he'd confirmed my suspicion that the twins weren't Ward's biological daughters. They belonged to his brother, Dante.

It explained how Elias so easily gave up one daughter and Christian so callously had the other killed.

"Well," Ivan held up the large, unorganized file that was overflowing with handwritten notes and crumpled papers, "this might take you a while."

"We have one thing going for us, though." Taking the file from him, I flipped through it, giving the contents a cursory glance. "The woman who calls herself Caesar is in Seattle, and whoever this Sulla is, they have to have people they know in common."

"The canes are one way we know how to identify them," Dima said. He'd joined us in the office after he'd secured the perimeter. "However, that style of cane is popular."

"What is with these names?" Andrei asked. "Caesar? Sulla? Are they cosplaying as Romans?"

"Two points to grandpa for knowing what cosplay is," Kenzi cackled.

Andrei shot her a glare, which just made her crack up more.

"We think they're code names." Ivan rolled his eyes. "So far, they seem to all be Roman generals. Caesar appears to be the one pulling the strings."

"Who we know is a woman."

Ivan nodded. "Yes. We know that Kirill is Marius. We still need to identify the one who calls himself Sulla, and who knows how many others there are."

I turned to Kenzi. "The woman who trained you," I asked. "Madam Therese. She has a cane as well. Did you ever hear her called by another name?"

Kenzi took a deep breath and thought about it for a moment. "Maybe. I didn't recognize it as a name, though. Agricola or something. Thought it was some kind of salad mix."

"That's arugula." Dima laughed. Kenzi punched him in the arm and muttered at him to shut it. Laughing, my enforcer rubbed at his arm, pretending to be hurt.

"Well, they sure are a narcissistic bunch." Andrei snorted. "Caesar, I'm assuming, is after the great Julius Caesar. Funnily enough, Sulla was a large influence on Caesar's reign as dictator of Rome. I'd imagine whoever this Sulla is, they know one another outside of the circuit they are running."

"We know the Dollhouse is a separate entity from the Chameleon Agency," Dima mused. "It's been around longer. So, the question is, did Kirill start the Chameleon Agency first and become a member of the Dollhouse, or was it the other way around?"

"Does it matter?" Ivan wondered.

Andrei nodded. "Your grandfather used to talk about a

secret society that called themselves the *Potestas Omnis*. Which translates to—"

"Power Over All," I murmured. Andrei's lips tilted into a proud smile as his gaze swept to me.

"That's a horrible name for a secret society." Kenzi scrunched her nose. "Might as well call themselves Impotus Omnis."

Ivan snorted a laugh while Dima cackled loudly and fist bumped her.

Children.

But it was good to see them laughing through hard and uncertain times.

"As I was saying before I was unjustly interrupted," Andrei winked at Kenzi to soften his words, "what if my brother inherited the position after proving himself? When did this Chameleon Agency pop up?"

"The FBI has been tracking them for several years. Interpol even longer," Ivan informed us. "From what I dug up as Agent Archer, the earliest account goes back to the mid-1980s in St. Petersburg."

"Around the time my father banished Kirill and the war began."

Ivan nodded. "According to the Interpol database, there was a significant uptick in missing and solicited women during that time. Some of the solicited women they found, usually dead with their throats cut, bore the mark of a Chameleon. That's why they started calling it the Chameleon Agency. The name stuck."

"I'm surprised he didn't choose a snake," Andrei snarled. "Better suited, if you ask me."

"Snakes can't hide in plain sight." I coughed, clearing my throat at the thought of what a true chameleon the man was.

"Chameleons were made to blend into every environment around them. A mirror effect."

"And I let him." Andrei leaned his head back and huffed out a frustrated breath.

"Everyone did," Ivan placated his father. *Our father*. It was hard to see the man before me and call him father when the man I had always known to be him was lying dead just a few feet away. Was this how Ava felt when she discovered the truth about Elias?

"He didn't fool you." Andrei placed his hand on his son's shoulder and leaned in until their foreheads were touching. "Forgive me, my son, for being so blind."

Ivan closed his eyes and breathed. The breath was slow as he let years of anger and resentment toward his father fade away. "I will always forgive you, *Papa*. All that matters is that we are here now."

"Yes, we are." Andrei smiled and then fully embraced Ivan. "And I will never let someone create distance between us again. I swear it to you." Ivan nodded, and I could see him struggling to hold back the tears of relief and joy that clung to his eyes like droplets of water on the leaves after a rainstorm.

Everything was washed anew.

Clean.

A fresh beginning.

But who knew what would come next.

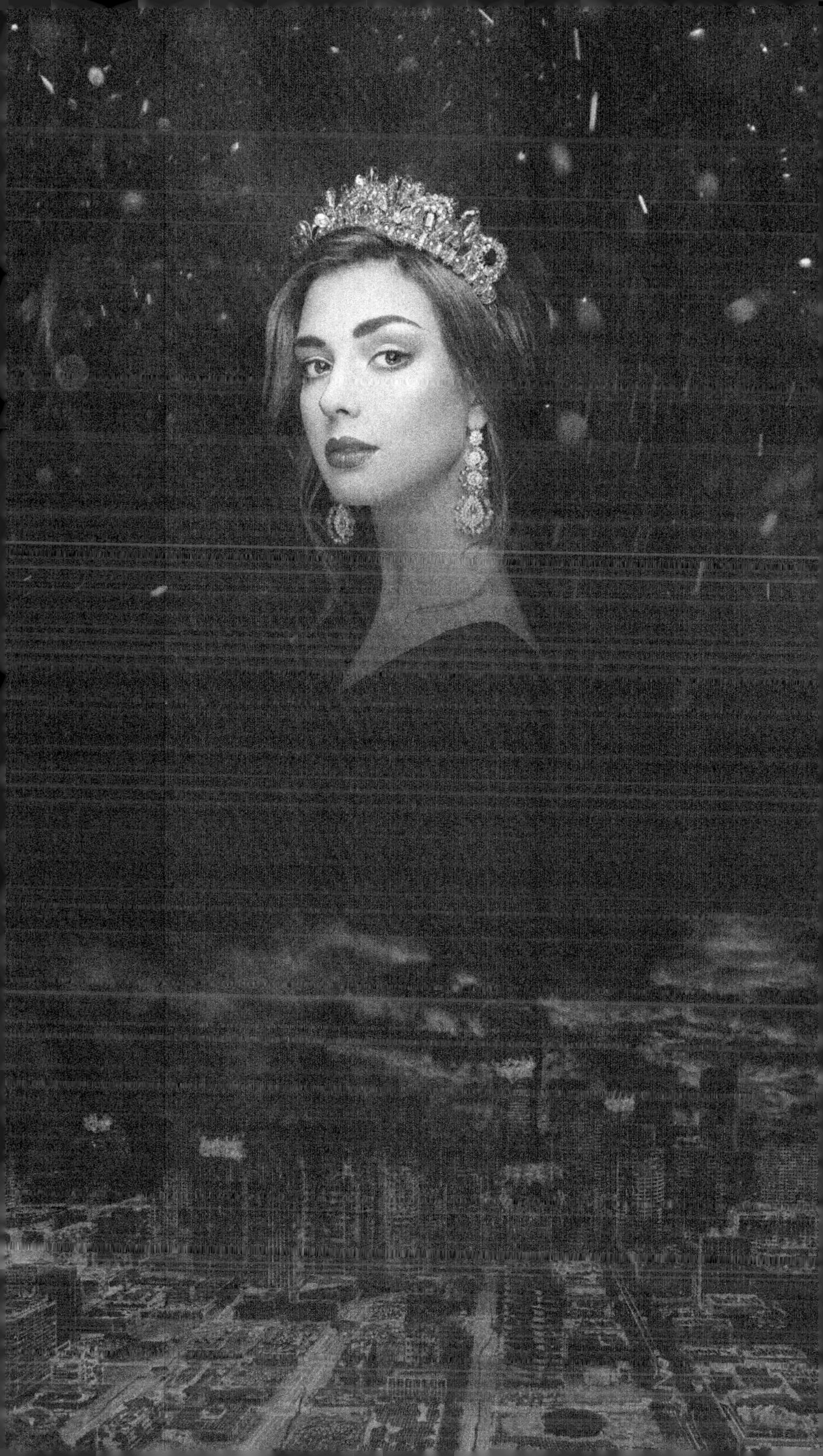

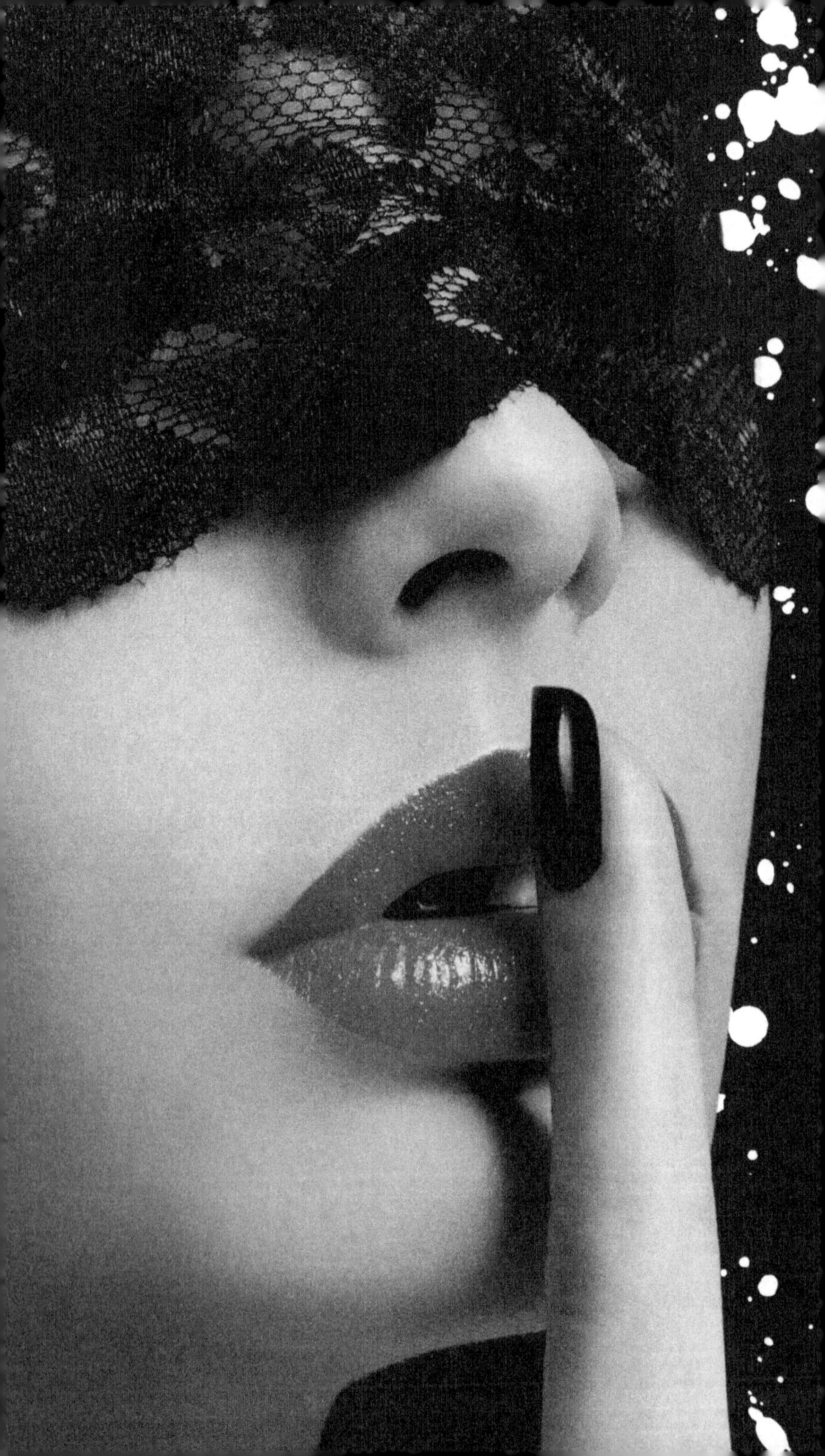

CHAPTER TWENTY

"Did you or did you not lie to me, Red?"
It wasn't really a question. I knew she had. Libby's intoxicated state and the fact that the sisters were both covered in the neon glitter that came with that fucking Club Neon, told me she had. They had both been ordered not to leave the penthouse without an escort and that they certainly weren't to go clubbing. It was dangerous with Christian out there looking for her, for one, and Libby was only nineteen.

I cared less about the latter than the former.

Despite my anger, my cock ached as I looked down at Ava lying on our bed, belly down, her skimpy ass dress riding up her legs. I could just see the bare crest of her ass peeking out from beneath the hem.

Fuck.

How many other men at the club had she given this view to?

"It was my bachelorette party." She smiled sleepily, her head resting on her folded arms. It was early morning, but I was too wired now to go back to sleep.

"And you were told you could have it here," I reminded her

darkly. Ava blew out her lips and swatted an arm at me dismissively.

"You got to go out to the strip club." She yawned. "At least I went to a place where people kept their clothes on."

Frustration bubbled beneath the surface, and I let out a pained groaned as I shut my eyes and pinched the bridge of my nose. "I was at work, Ava, not out partying."

The woman shrugged like it didn't matter, but I could sense the tension around her.

Was my Little Red jealous?

Climbing onto the bed, I grabbed her hips, pulling her toward me as I flipped her onto her back.

Her emerald eyes flew open, lust clouding them as she took in my half-dressed state. Her top teeth sunk into her lower lip as she shyly spread her pretty legs for me, exposing her sweet, delectable pussy to my gaze. Ava had grown more confident sexually over our time together. She was still often embarrassed, a pink hue dancing up her cheeks, but I wouldn't give that away for the world.

Her innocence in the bedroom was refreshing.

"Now," I tsked at her. My hands trailed up her outer thighs, pushing the dress until it was scrunched at her waist, and I had a full, uninterrupted view of what was mine. "Do you honestly think you deserve a reward from me?"

Ava nodded her head enthusiastically, and I chuckled at how cute her eagerness was.

"Orgasms, please." It was a demand. A sweet one, but a demand, nonetheless.

My palm slapped her pussy, causing her to jolt and moan.

"You don't own your orgasms, sweet Red," I reminded her. "I do."

My girl growled. She didn't like that statement.

Shedding my pants and boxers, I threw them to the side,

unbothered by where they landed. Sex for me had always been something more clinical than passionate. The one woman I had chosen to get close to when I was younger had betrayed me, and since then, all I had ever done was pump and dump, uncaring if the woman got off or not.

Ava was different. She was my wife for all intents and purposes. I enjoyed sex with her and wanted nothing more than to bring her to the height of pleasure.

Fisting my cock, I asked, "Who owns your orgasms, Red?"

Ava glared at me before looking away, her nose in the air. Brat. Slowly, I stroked myself. The urge to plow into her was hard to resist, but she needed to learn who was in charge. I let the fingertips of my free hand trail down her already slick slit. Bringing them to my mouth, I tasted her arousal, sweet and decadent.

She cried out when I slapped her pussy again. "Who owns your orgasms, Red?"

Burying her face in her hands, she murmured something I couldn't quite hear.

"What was that?" *I pressed my thumb down, putting pressure on her clit, rubbing it in slow, torturous circles.*

"God," *she groaned into her hands, arching into my touch.*

"Not him, baby," *I laughed.* "Show me your eyes."

I paused my touch and waited for her to obey. Ava didn't hesitate to follow my command, knowing I held the key to her pleasure. Then again, she was always good at following orders in the bedroom. Sweet as a kitten as she writhed and moaned beneath me.

It was everywhere else that she fought me tooth and nail over.

"Who owns your orgasms?"

Her pupils were blown wide with unrestrained desire. Her

cheeks were flushed, her body squirming beneath me, seeking out contact.

"Tell me, sweet girl," I encouraged, lining my cock up with her entrance. I would lose control if I went any further.

"You do," she whispered shyly. I smirked.

"Damn right I do."

Ava cried out as I buried myself to the hilt inside her in one long thrust.

"Fuck." I ripped her dress straight down the middle, exposing the rest of her milky white skin. Her nipples were already hard for me, diamond peaks ready to be bitten and sucked.

"Move." She planted her feet on the bed and thrust upward to get me to shift. I smirked, holding her hips down to the bed. Ava whimpered.

"You're not in control here, Red," I reminded her. "You may be getting my cock instead of my belt, but don't push me. There is still time for me to change my mind."

Pouting, she brought her knees up to her chest and wrapped her legs around my torso.

"Good girl." I pulled out and plowed into her again. And again.

She screamed my name, her nails digging into my shoulders, but I wouldn't be stopping. I pivoted my hips to fuck her deeper and harder. Her sudden cry of pleasure causing me to smirk. Bingo. I leaned forward and took her hardened nipple into my mouth and bit down. Ava let her mouth fall open as she gasped for breath, the pain mingling with her pleasure.

"More," she cried out, pulling her knees up further, letting her ankles dip from my back.

"Fuck you're tight," I groaned, her slick juices coating my cock, causing my hunger to deepen even further. I wanted her.

Couldn't get enough of her. Ava consumed every part of me, and it sent a thrill through my body, knowing she was mine.

Only mine.

Moving to her left breast, I suckled her nipple into my mouth until she was groaning and writhing beneath me, her body arching into mine. I was setting a brutal pace, nipping my way up her chest, sucking at the pulse point on her neck. When I reached her mouth, I devoured it. Lips, tongue, and teeth. The two of us clashing together like thunder and lightning.

The kiss wasn't sweet. It was animalistic and possessive.

Ava was meant to be mine.

"Oh, god." She sobbed when my thumb gently stroked her overstimulated clit. I wanted her to think of me tomorrow whenever she moved. I wanted her sore.

"Who owns your orgasms, Ava?" I whispered hotly in her ear, swiveling my hips. The tension was building in my balls, and fuck, I couldn't hold back anymore. "Who owns you?"

"You do," she breathed.

"What was that?" I pinched her clit.

"You do!" she cried louder. "Matthias."

"Come for me, baby." I pinched her swollen clit one last time, edging her over the cliff we were both hanging from. "Come with me."

My balls pulled tightly, my abdomen clenching. She cursed, tossing her head from side to side as she unraveled beneath me. The rhythmic pulse of her pussy sent me toppling off the edge with her. Her cunt creamed my cock as I slid feverishly in and out. Her legs clamped around me as her orgasm swept over her again and again.

"Fuck, Ava," I cried out her name as I exploded inside her. I thrust once more before I was completely lost to ecstasy.

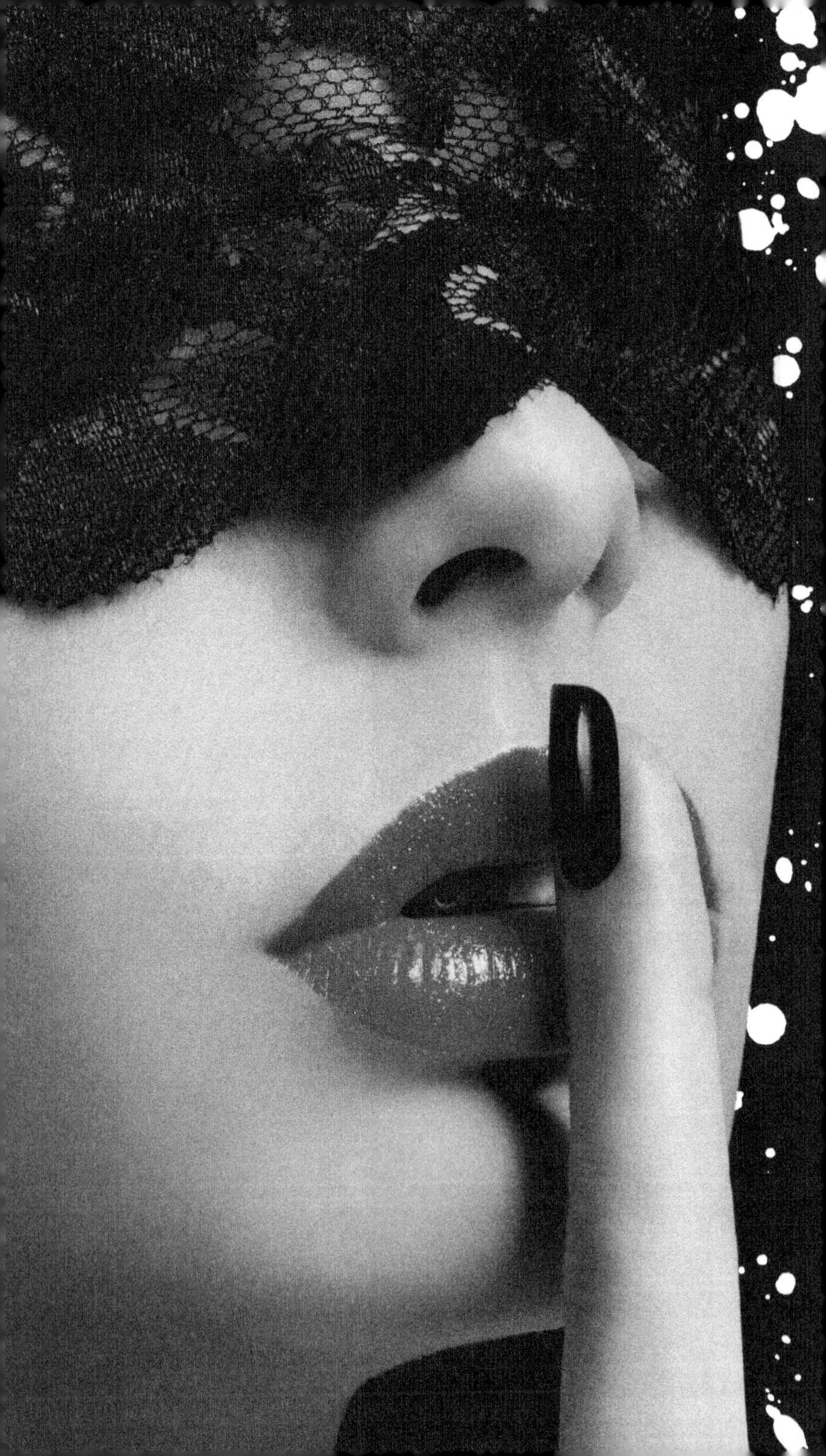

CHAPTER TWENTY-ONE

The night had been restless.

Sleep evaded me like a bad breakup in a small town. Still there, but just out of reach.

Fuck, I missed Ava.

Her heart. Her soul. Her cunt.

Those pretty lips wrapped around my cock.

Sighing, I took a sip of the lukewarm coffee the new flight attendant had set in front of me twenty minutes before. His name was Roger. He was about fifty years old and completely temporary. I'd officially hired him as a butler for the penthouse. Mia had been doing the job of two people for several years now without complaint, but there was even further strain on her with Ava.

Dima was pouting at the back of the plane, his headphones lodged in his ears as he tapped out a beat to god knows what. Roger, apparently, wasn't his type.

The plane was blissfully quiet as we took off from the private airstrip in London a few days after Kirill's demise.

Ivan was staying behind to clean up the London faction. His father had awarded him the title of *Pakhan*.

Our father.

I had to keep reminding myself of that. We hadn't had much time to talk since Kirill's death. We had all been too busy planning for what was ahead. The known and the unknown.

Known: Kirill had indeed been the one to start the Chameleon Agency.

Unknown: How Kirill became involved with a secret society.

Had he been approached prior to his start in human trafficking, or was that what caught their interest? There were still too many unknowns when it came to the egotistical *Potestas Omnis*.

What a fucking ridiculous name.

"Have you ever heard her voice before?" Andrei played the conversation Kirill had with the mysterious Caesar. Kenzi listened intently, but there was no flicker of recognition on her face.

"No." She shook her head. "But Legionnaires usually don't have contact with anyone other than their handlers, if they have one."

"Did you?" I asked curiously.

Kenzi shrugged. "For a little while." She sighed. "Her name was Venus."

"I thought you didn't have names," I asked.

"Only the most trusted operatives get names," she divulged bitterly. "Usually Greek or Roman deity names. It's their reward for doing their job without asking questions."

"You don't sound thrilled about that."

Kenzi snorted derisively. "When you first arrive, they try to pit you against each other." Her eyes took on the faraway look she got when she was dissociating from her past. "The better you are, the better your ranking, and the only way your ranking goes up is by defeating your competition."

"The other operatives."

Kenzi nodded.

"The first day," she took a stuttering breath, "they separated us into groups of four or five and stuck us in a room with a handful of melee weapons. Then told us only one of us could come out alive."

Andrei cursed under his breath.

"They said it would desensitize us to violence." She chuckled bitterly. "I didn't realize dying was the better option."

She didn't say any more after that, and neither of us pushed her. I had a feeling I knew where her story was going, and I respected her too much to force her to relive that.

"Venus was my handler for about six months before I proved I was capable on my own," Kenzi continued, answering Andrei's original question. "Now, it's a text message with a name and photo. Sometimes, like with Kirill, they want it to be done at a specific spot and time, but mostly someone just wants the job done."

I nodded.

"You can't go back," I pointed out the obvious to her. "You know that, right?"

Rolling her eyes, Kenzi shook her head. "No shit, Sherlock," she deadpanned. "But it was completely worth it."

"How did you—" Andrei was interrupted by Dima calling Kenzi's name. Mark was on vidcom for her.

"Be back." She got up from her seat and moved to the back of the plane.

Andrei and I sat in silence for a few moments, neither of us knowing what to say. This was the first time we had been alone together.

I tapped my fingers against the seat's armrest.

Fuck, I was nervous.

I never got nervous.

Then again, I never imagined I had any immediate family other than Kirill. Andrei had decided to accompany me back to Seattle with Dima and Kenzi. He said he wanted to help, and the moment I had graciously accepted his offer, he was on the phone with his *Sovietnik*, making plans to have men sent from Russia to assist.

I thought he was also looking to connect.

Not that either of us knew how to do that. It was pretty obvious where I had inherited my lack of social skills from.

"Ivan says you are *Pakhan* of the Seattle *Bratva*." Andrei broke the silence. I shifted my gaze from the open scenic window to find his gray eyes staring at me intently. It was like looking in a mirror. "I know Tomas Ivankov well. He is a good man. A good leader."

I dipped my head. "He is," I agreed, unsure of what else to say. Andrei licked his lips anxiously, his own fingertips tapping silently against his knee.

More silence.

Fuck, I didn't know how to do this. People. Connections. That was Vas's thing, not mine. He was amiable and charming. Before Ava, the only people who saw my humorous and talkative side were my brothers.

The men of my inner sanctum.

The ones I would give my life for without a second thought.

Tomas had taught me to only show my true self around those I trusted most. The men and women under my command weren't my friends. I may have considered them family and would be cordial with them, but over time, they would think of me more as a comrade and less of as their

SHATTERED EMPIRE

leader. It meant they could come to believe they could skirt the laws I laid out.

It might have seemed cold and uncaring, but the line I had to draw in the sand as *Pakhan* kept everyone safe.

Not through fear, but through respect.

"Your mother..." He trailed off, unsure of how to express what he wanted to know. I smiled at him.

"She was warm and caring," I told him. Even when Kirill had her drugged, she managed to shift the haze aside whenever it came to me. "When she smiled, it was like the whole world lit up. Her laugh was like—"

"Sunshine on a cloudy day," he remembered wistfully.

I nodded. "It was rare, but yes, exactly that."

"Did she ever speak of me?" There was hope in his eyes, and I hated to be the one to extinguish that. So I lied.

"A few times." I cleared my throat. "But it was often vague. I grew up believing Kirill to be my father, and I think that was what kept us safe from him. For a time."

"If that bastard wasn't dead, I'd kill him again," Andrei snarled. "To think my own brother betrayed me from the beginning."

"You couldn't have known the depth of his hatred," I assured him. "He obviously had help."

"I shouldn't have let myself be so blinded by grief," he admitted, his shoulders drooping slightly. "Maybe then I would have seen his treachery. I would have been able to save you and her."

"I wouldn't be the man I am today if you had. We can't change the cards fate has dealt us, but we can learn to master what we are given. My life was hard. Always looking over my shoulder. Waiting for the moment I would slip up and that would be the end." I paused, taking a deep breath before continuing. "I often was cold and hungry. But I learned to fight. To survive. And that was what I was doing when Tomas found me. Just fighting to survive. He gave me the chance to be a part of a family that cared. That had my back. Tomas will always be my father. The one who gave me every opportunity."

Andrei's face fell as I talked. He thought it was too late to be my father. Tomas had been there every step of the way for me as I grew from a boy to a man. He was my father in every way, but that didn't mean there wasn't room for another family.

Swallowing back the lump in my throat, I continued. "And the one greatest thing he taught me is that family is whoever we say it is, and we can always have more than one."

His eyes were wet with unshed tears as he stared at me. After a moment, he gave me a sharp nod.

"I will earn the right for you to call me father." His voice was hoarse, brimming with barely restrained emotion. "I will show you I am worthy of that name."

I smiled at him and nodded. "I look forward to getting to know you."

"Good," he cleared his throat and sat back comfortably in his seat, one leg crossed over the other, "now, tell me about this wife of yours."

Chuckling, I relaxed against the leather of my own seat and proceeded to tell him about the goddess of a woman who had bewitched my soul.

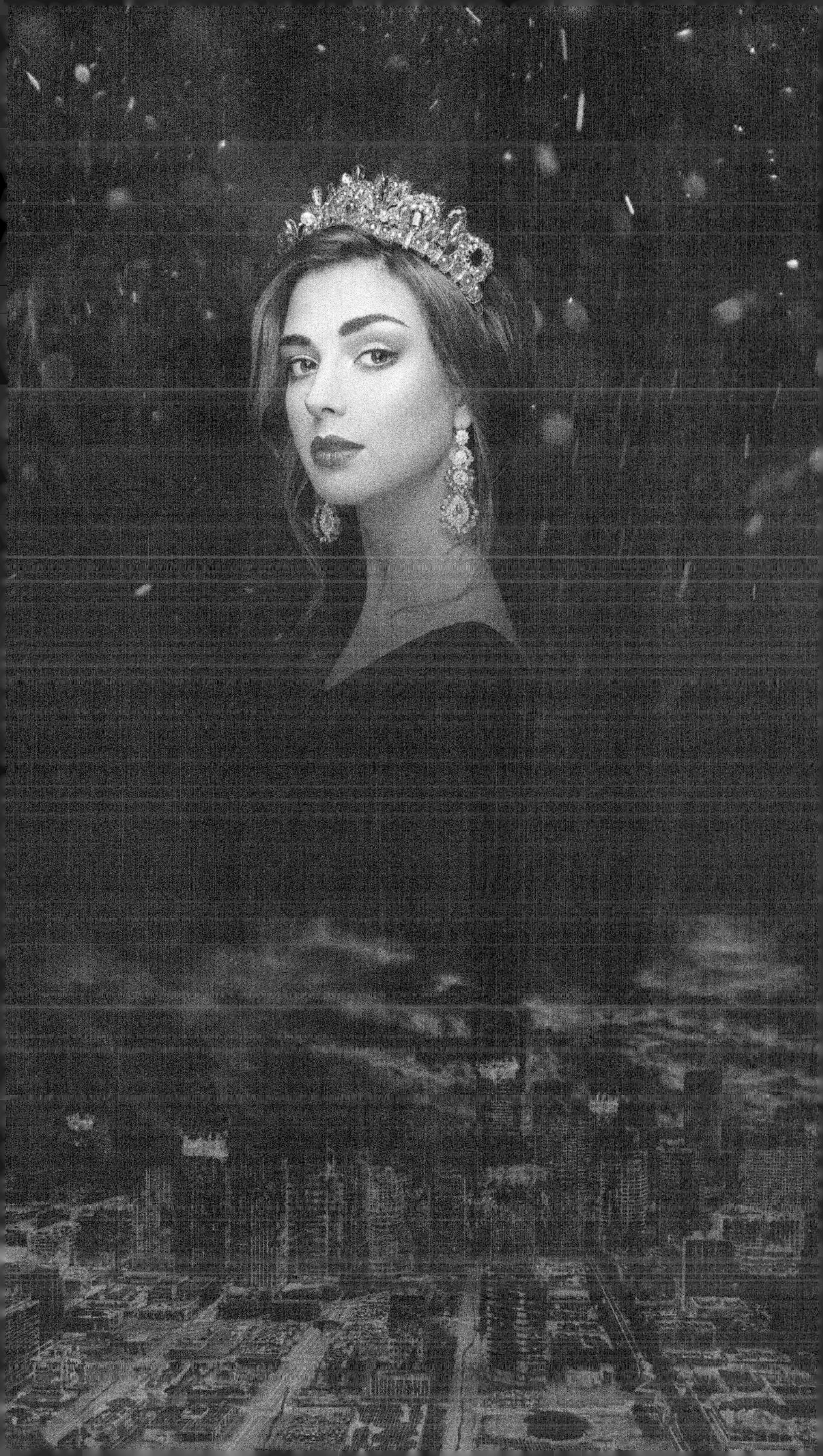

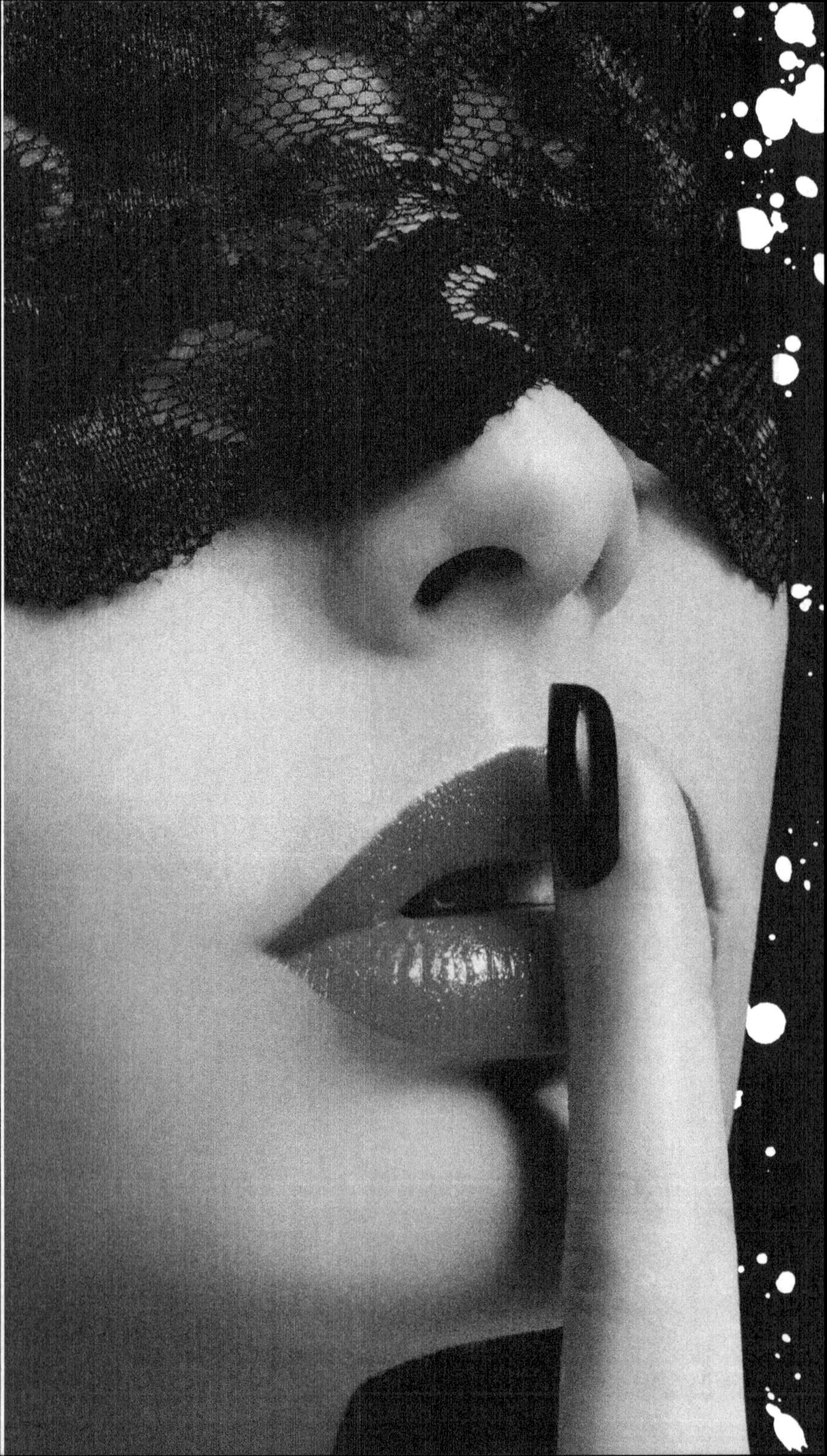

CHAPTER TWENTY-TWO

We landed nine hours later at the small SeaTac airstrip where my hangar was located. I barely slept the entire flight as Andrei and I worked on getting to know one another. In one word, it was surreal. Tomas filled the void Kirill had left within me as a child, and I'd never wanted another father. To have the chance at getting to know the father that would have loved and kept me if he could have shifted something inside me.

Something I wasn't quite ready to name.

Maksim and Nikolai awaited me as I stepped off the plane and back onto the blessed terra firma of the city I called home. The two men greeted me with wide, bright smiles and firm hugs. None of us had ever been separated from each other for longer than a week at a time. Five weeks was nearly unacceptable.

"Your woman is causing quite the stir." Nikolai smirked at me. "And she's learned a few things since you've been gone."

Vas had been keeping me apprised of Ava's every move. Not that I would interfere, but I did have him caution her a few times about her actions.

It hadn't worked.

"I'd honestly wear a bulletproof vest when you decide to tell her you're still alive," Maksim joked. "On second thought, maybe something to protect your legs. She's got a thing for shooting out kneecaps."

Andrei laughed boisterously behind me. "I like her already." He clapped me on the shoulder. "And you said she was sweet and naïve."

"She was," I muttered.

Nikolai smirked. "Then this idiot went and made a fool of her. On top of that, he faked his death."

"Nothing worse than a woman scorned."

"Where is she now?" I slid into the backseat of the G-Wagon.

"In Portland with Vas and her father," Maksim reported. "Looks like O'Malley's niece stole some evidence from her mother's case from lockup for her."

I wish I could have been there for her.

"How did O'Malley get Kavanaugh to agree to a sit down?" It was well known the two Irish families had a long, blood-filled history with one another.

"O'Malley threatened to withhold the evidence pertaining to Ava's mother if he didn't agree."

"And no one is dead?"

Nikolai laughed.

"According to Vas, everything is groovy." Nicolai pitched his tone at the last word. It made him sound like a blond-haired surfer boy named Crash who smoked pot. Or Shaggy from Scooby-Doo.

"Get me something more than groovy," I told him, mimicking his tone. Andrei smirked at me, and for the briefest of moments, I wondered how he saw me.

Would he think I was a good leader?

Would he accept how I ran my organization?

Part of me felt like a teenager again, begging for approval. I wanted my biological father to be proud of what I'd built.

"Where to, boss?" Maksim asked as he pulled through the gate and onto the main thoroughfare.

"Let's regroup at the penthouse and head out from there," I told him. "Let Damon know to have the helicopter fueled and ready to go in two hours."

Maksim nodded.

Sitting back in my seat, I sighed. It was good to be home.

"So," Dima broke the peaceful tranquility that had settled over us. "Who's gonna tell Ava about Kenzi being a badass ninja and you miraculously being raised from the dead? 'Cause," he tapped his finger to his nose, "not it."

The whole car—save for Andrei—followed suit with a chorus of "not it" ringing through the small space.

Fucking children.

My biological father laughed heartily before shrugging and sticking his finger to his nose.

"Not it."

The whole car broke into a fit of laughter.

Yes—it was certainly good to be home.

"Your woman has a thing for kneecaps," Vas groaned into the phone. "She's obsessed with them."

I chuckled. Apparently my sweet, defiant wife had turned into a bit of a psycho. I would be lying if I didn't admit it turned me on.

A lot.

"Doesn't surprise me." The noise of the helicopter was

nothing but a dim sound in the background with the headset on. "Look who she lived with for half her life."

"Kenzi is a bit of a psycho herself," Dima grunted next to me. Kenzi slapped him across the head, and he grinned. "Just saying." He shrugged.

"What's our next play?" I asked my *Sovietnik*.

"About that..." Vas trailed off. "We can't target Cartwright yet, but we're working on it. Your wife has a business date tonight, and she fired me, but otherwise, we're doing pretty good. The entire restaurant will be filled with—"

"Did you say date?" I interrupted him. "Why the fuck is she going on a date?"

"It's not a *date* date," Vas explained. "She's meeting with Joseph O'Neill's son, Conrad, to discuss merging our assets."

"Conrad O'Neill is a narcissistic abuser," I growled, the corner of my lips turning up in a snarl. "Why the fuck are we talking about merging our assets?"

"We aren't *really* going to merge our assets." Vas's eye roll was audible. It didn't take a genius to realize he was irritated that I wasn't catching on quick enough for him. "We needed him to believe that so he would go to dinner with her."

"The only person she should be going to dinner with is me."

"Well, you're dead," Vas deadpanned.

"If he lays one fucking hand on her..."

Vas chuckled. "She'll go straight for his kneecaps, trust me."

"Vasily..." I warned.

My brother sighed. "We needed a way to get to him, and dangling her out there was the only way to get him to bite," he tried to assure me. "She can handle herself, and she has been for more than a month now."

SHATTERED EMPIRE

Sighing, I pinched the bridge of my nose and blew out a breath. "I know."

"Plus, I'm a little hurt that her date was what you focused on first." He sounded affronted. "I tell you she fired me, and you don't have one ounce of pity for your best friend."

"She didn't actually fire you," I pointed out.

"Well, she sure as hell thinks she did," Vas grumbled. "All because I won't tell her where Dima is. Something about trust. Okay, maybe there are a few other reasons, but still. I've never been fired before."

"I heard McDonald's is offering a fairly competitive wage," Dima crowed. "You'd look so cute in that uniform. Maybe even Wendy's. We could dye your hair and give you pigtails."

"Hm, I could also smash your face in and make you look like that man from the Goonies."

"Hey," Dima gasped. "Don't knock Sloth. He was the best part of the movie."

"Children," Kenzi groaned. "Can we please get back on point?"

"Since when does Nikita get to butt in on conversations?"

"Jesus," I groaned. "We'll be there in about ten minutes. Make sure everything is ready."

"Got it, boss." Vas paused before hanging up. "Are you going to see Ava or..."

Was I?

I hadn't thought that far ahead yet. My mind had been focused on things other than how I was going to approach Ava about the fact that I had been alive this whole time and hunting down Kirill.

She was going to be pissed.

I wanted nothing more than to take her.

Make her mine all over again.

But something was stopping me, and I didn't know what it was.

"We'll talk about that later."

"Sure thing." The line clicked off, and he was gone. A wave of regret hit, crashing me against the jagged rocks of the shore.

"Really?" Kenzi raised a brow at me from across the helicopter. "We'll talk about that later?"

I sighed.

"Are you saying that you know exactly how you're going to approach her and spill your guts about being an assassin?"

Kenzi shrugged. "It's not that hard."

"Yeah?" I asked. "Go ahead. Tell me how you plan to explain all that before she goes in for the kill."

She snorted but then bit her lip nervously.

"Exactly." I pointed my finger at her. "Don't pull that holier than thou shit without thinking it through yourself."

"What does it matter how we tell her?" she questioned me. "Either way, she's going to see it as a huge betrayal."

"Probably run off to Daddy's," Dima piped up.

"And that's after she guts you," Maksim snorted.

"We're all fucking comedians today," I groaned. "Why don't we all sit silently and think our private thoughts?"

Andrei snorted. "This is certainly going to be the best vacation I've had in a while."

Great.

"This guy's a douche," Dima growled into the comm line as we watched Ava's dinner with Conrad O'Neill. He wasn't wrong. The man reeked of the worst kind of narcissism and misogyny. They had barely sat down before he started into his personal exploits about sheiks and presidents.

It was nauseating.

"Can I kill him?" Andrei growled when the man had tried to order my wife a salad.

"Only if you can make it look like an accident in front of all these people."

"Poison always works." Kenzi smirked. "I'm sure I could sneak some in. Also, these people are Sully's men. Wouldn't matter if we made it look like an accident or not."

"Right then," Andrei chuckled. "This will be good."

"I have to admit," Maksim grinned, taking a sip of his wine as he watched the video screen of my wife dining with that fucking bastard, "she has definitely turned into a badass."

"Must run in the family." Dima winked at Kenzi, who rolled her eyes dramatically at his poor attempt at flirting.

"So does the sudden urge to murder people." She winked right back at him and ran a finger across her throat.

It wasn't too long before their dinner arrived. Pride swelled within me as I watched Ava break down the O'Neill boy bit by bit. She wasn't the kind of woman he was used to dealing with. They were just empty, airheaded bimbos looking for their next sugar daddy. It didn't bypass my attention that he wasn't aware she was the CEO.

He thought we'd sent him the company whore.

A mistake he was currently regretting as Ava laid into him about his company's sudden drop in shares and his habit of overspending.

"Oh, shit." Dima guffawed. Conrad O'Neill had gone to leave, but my wife wouldn't be dismissed so easily. Without blinking, she'd dug her steak knife into his hand, cutting through the skin like it was supple leather.

"Did I say you were dismissed?" She crooked her head to

the side, her eyes wide and innocent. My cock jumped to attention. He called her a psychotic bitch, but my body and mind were calling her perfect.

My perfect little psycho.

I didn't think my cock could get any harder.

Then I watched her knife his other hand. I lied. I was harder than granite now. Fuck.

"Let's go," I said abruptly, standing from the table in the small room we'd rented to run surveillance. "Now."

Maksim stood and murmured to Dima over the comms to follow.

"Are you seriously going to leave?" Kenzi darted in front of me, blocking my path.

"Yes," I growled. I wasn't about to explain to her why I needed to go. That seeing her sister like that was driving me to the point of madness.

"No." She stood in front of me, arms crossed against her chest, eyes adamant. "You need to wait and own up to what you did."

I stared down at her in fucking disbelief. Is that what she thought I was running away from? She thought I felt guilty about leading Ava to believe I was dead? Or that I didn't want to face her wrath?

The woman couldn't be more wrong.

It had nothing to do with either of those things.

What I didn't want to face was the one thing I had always refused to. My feelings for her.

My love for Ava bordered on possession and obsession. The more I fell for her, the harder it was to keep control of the animal inside me. I didn't call her Little Red for no reason. I was the Big Bad Wolf, and I wanted to devour her.

Every. Single. Inch.

But the more obsessed I became with my love for her, the

more I was afraid of losing her. Not her love, but her life. Every woman I had truly cared about had either died at the hands of an enemy or at my hands for betraying me.

The deeper I fell, the deeper the wound would be if either of those two things came to pass. I knew I had to face my fear of that, but it was often simpler to ignore it. I wanted Ava. There was no doubt in that. And I loved her. But showing her that love gave her access to a vulnerability I wasn't ready to exploit.

"You're scared," Kenzi taunted me. "It's written all over your face."

"Easy, *malen'kiy ubiytsa*," Andrei cautioned. Even he could see how thin the rope was and that it was about to snap.

"Why?" she snarled. "My sister loves you. Even now, in your death, and you can't muster up the balls to face her. Why? Huh? What are you so afraid of?"

"Don't push me, Kenzi." My face darkened as I stared down at her.

"I'm not afraid of you, Matthias," she sneered. "I stopped being afraid a long time ago. You don't want to face her? Fine. I'll do it for both of us."

"Shit," Maksim cursed. He reached out to grab her the moment he saw her body shift into gear, but he was too late. She was a slippery assassin, that was for sure.

"Dammit." Running a hand through my lengthening hair, I tilted my head back and closed my eyes. "Fuck." Deep breaths, I coached myself, deep breaths.

"She's right, though." Andrei spoke up from beside me. "Not about you being afraid of her rage. But you do need to face her."

"You don't know what you're talking about."

Andrei smiled sadly. "You're afraid your love for her will ruin you both." His eyes were brimming with sadness and loss. "You've been hurt time and time again. I can see that. I *know* that. But you can't hide behind that wall forever, Matthias. At some point in time, it's going to have to crumble. Give yourself the chance to truly love her. Because if you don't, you'll lose her for good, and it won't be to death."

His hand clamped on my shoulder and squeezed.

"Think about that, *moy syn*." Then he left.

Moy syn.

My son.

He'd called me his son.

"Hey, boss." Dima interrupted my thoughts. The pride that welled in my chest at being called Andrei Tkachenko's son. He'd told me he would earn the right to be called father. It would appear I didn't have to earn the right to be called his son, and that broke a piece of the wall I had so carefully constructed when I was younger. "You might want to catch up with Kenzi. She took your Martin."

"Point?"

"Umm...your wife is currently hauling ass after her?"

Shit.

"Tell Vas. And make sure Sully shuts down the police radios. I don't want them being followed."

"Got it."

Badass indeed.

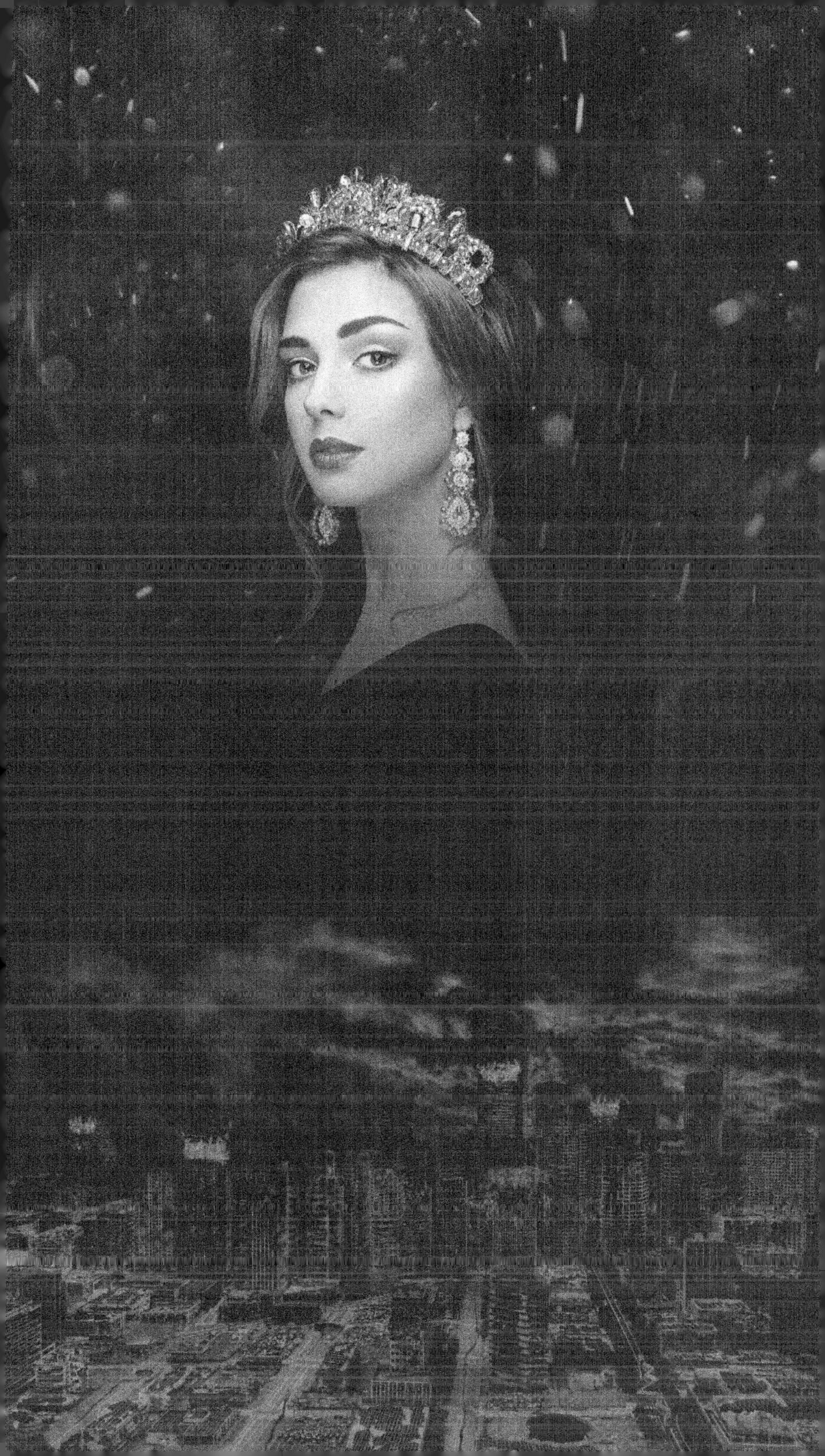

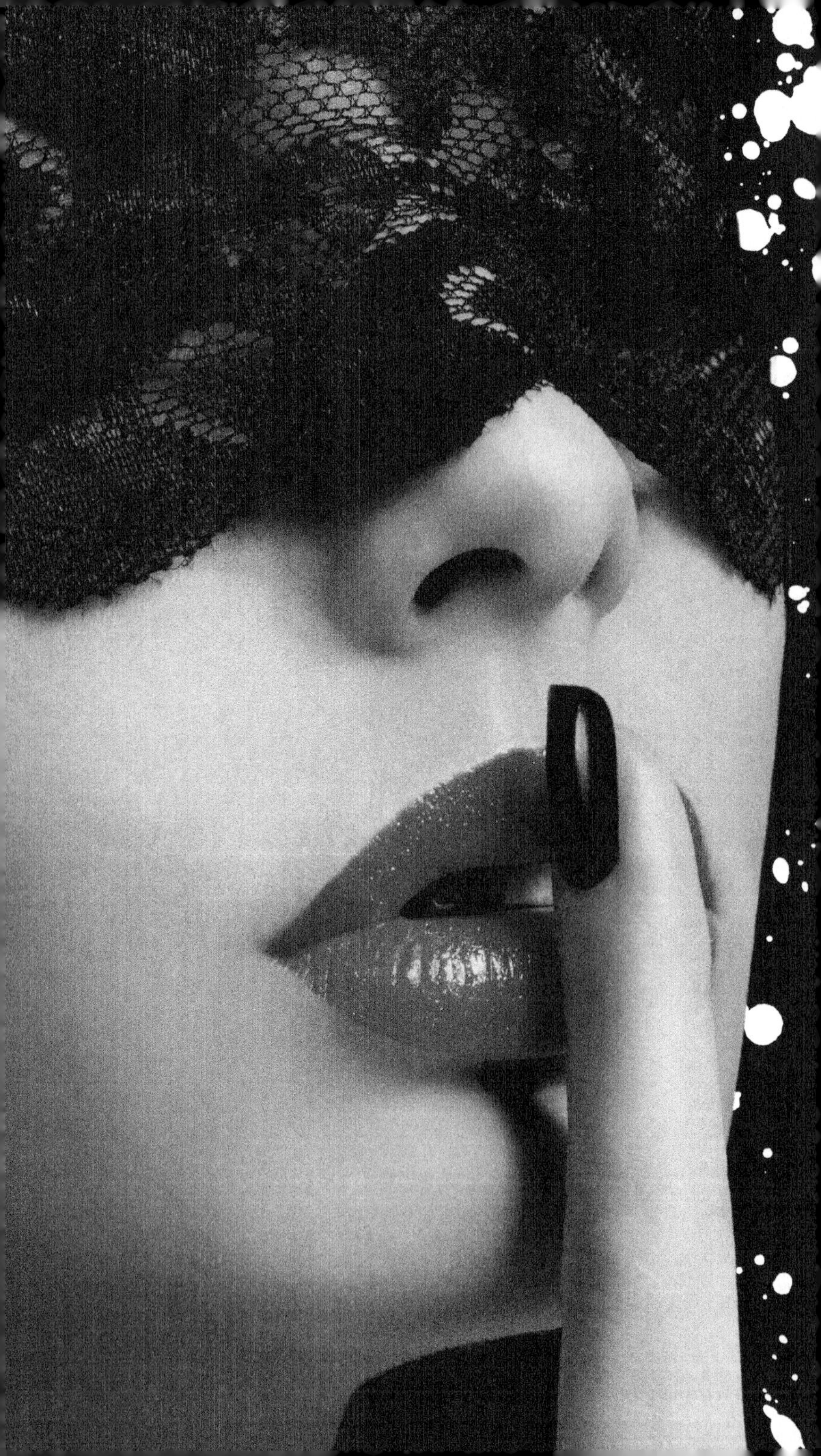

CHAPTER TWENTY-THREE

The rain was pouring down from the open sky, lightning flashing across its star-dotted surface by the time I caught up to the pair. It was lucky for me that my Aston Martin had GPS, otherwise I would never have thought to look in such a desolate place.

The barn was old and decrepit and eerily familiar. Wood beams lay carelessly in the overgrown grass that had turned brown without constant care. It could barely be called a structure. More like a skeleton of the past.

How had Kenzi known about this place?

"If I'm a psycho," Ava's voice drifted through the open doorway, her pain seeping through the howl of the wind to pierce straight through my heart, "you made me so by murdering my husband. The one man who cared for me."

I did care for her.

Even if I hadn't always shown it.

My chest tightened when I thought about the last night we'd had together. The gala. It was where everything changed for us. I knew it would hurt her seeing Serena on my arm. What killed me was seeing the resignation on her face throughout the night. There wasn't one ounce of anger when she saw Serena on my arm. No tears. Just the look of someone who had given up the fight.

That was a look I knew too well from men who fought in the ring in Russia. The look that came right before the death blow.

Her sudden refusal to fight made sense once Vas had learned she'd signed the divorce papers. Papers she was never meant to see. Taking Serena to the ball had been meant to put distance between Ava and myself. To show her I couldn't give her what she wanted. My love. The move also allowed me to set up the needed hit with Kenzi. Serena's family had ties with Kirill's men. Once she was sure I was dead, she scuttled back to her master with that important information.

She didn't live long after that.

"Fuck." Kenzi cursed painfully. That had me paying attention. Ava had managed to get Kenzi on her back, a knife to her throat as she screamed down at her.

Fucking hell.

The pair wasn't paying attention to me as I strode through the barn. My footsteps were quiet, muffled by the hay-strewn floor.

"You. Took. Everything."

Everything. That one word nearly broke me. She thought I was her everything, and I had treated her as if she meant nothing to me. Even if the opposite was true, she had never known that. I had never let her.

"Then do it," Kenzi hissed, baring her teeth as she taunted her sister by moving her neck further into the blade.

"Enough!" My command echoed through the barn. Ava hesitated, and I took that chance to grab her under the arms and pull her off her sister. The knife in her hand clattered uselessly to the ground, and I was immediately swept up into her familiar scent.

Jasmine.

"Enough, *Krasnyy*," I whispered, my lips brushing the shell of her ear. God, she felt exquisite in my arms. Her body wasn't as soft, but I could still feel her curves in all the right places.

She cried out in denial, her sobs shaking her body as she fought my hold. "Stop," she pleaded desperately. "Stop. Please."

But I wouldn't.

"Red."

Ava was too far gone. This was why I wanted to wait. The shock of seeing me alive was too much for her on top of the adrenaline that had been coursing through her system. It wouldn't be long before her body would give out when the high ran out.

She was hyperventilating, her eyes wide with fear and distrust as she clawed and kicked wildly in my hold. I tried to soothe her. To reassure her, but nothing could calm the frantic race of her heart.

"You should have waited," I hissed at Kenzi. "This was what I was hoping to avoid."

Kenzi shrugged, holding one hand to her still bleeding nose. "At least I faced up to her."

"And almost got yourself killed by her, too," I snarled. "Good job. If I hadn't shown up in time, you would have ended up with a knife through your chest."

"I had everything under control." She bit her lip nervously when Ava's body suddenly went limp. Her body had finally given out on her, but she'd be fine. Well, except for the killer headache she would have when she woke back up.

"Fuck no you didn't."

"Yes, I did."

"Get the hell out of here, Kenzi," I growled. "We'll talk about this later when she wakes up and is feeling less homicidal."

"Good luck with that ever happening," she muttered as she limped toward the exit. Kenzi paused, looking back at her sister passed out in my arms. "This place has memories," she whispered to me. "Painful ones. You might try and dig a little into the past while you can. Might find something useful."

Then she was gone.

For fuck's sake.

Another cryptic warning was all I needed.

Gently, I laid Ava out on a small bed of semi-clean hay. Not that it mattered much since she was covered in it herself, but I couldn't bring myself to just lay her out anywhere.

Then I did exactly as Kenzi told me, and I started to dig.

PART THREE

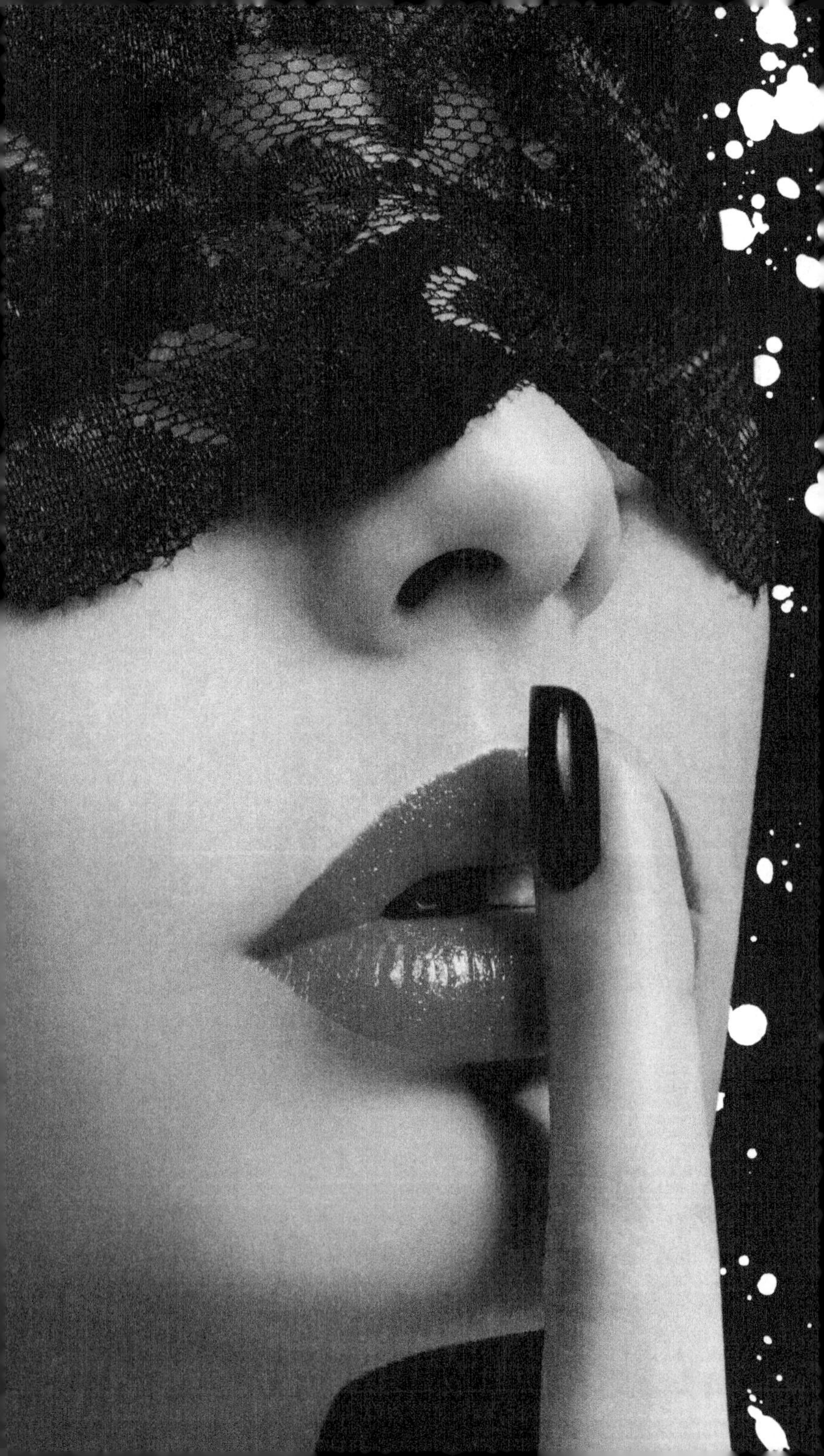

CHAPTER TWENTY-FOUR

A solitary scream pierced the stagnant air.
    I huddled closer to my wolf, hugging the stuffed animal in my arms with all my might. The door to my hiding place was locked from the outside. I couldn't get out. Tears streamed down my cheeks. The sound of crashing furniture could be heard from downstairs.

"Stupid bitch," a woman screamed. She was closer now. The sound of her voice coming from my left, where the stairs were. "You had everything I wanted. Everything. Why couldn't you just lose for once in your fucking life?"

"Stop." My mother's voice was shaky and terrified, but I could hear the sheer determination behind the terror. She didn't want to die. She couldn't. My mother wouldn't leave me all alone. "What have I ever done to you? We were friends. Best friends."

The other voice scoffed. It was dark, filled with a burning hatred. There was a soft lilt of an accent to her words. Like Mommas. "Please. I was never your friend. The only thing I wanted was what was promised to me."

"And what was that, Mar?" mother asked tearfully.

"Liam and your empire."

It was Momma's turn to scoff. "Liam would never have you," she sneered. "And no one but blood can inherit my empire."

Mar laughed. It was dreadful and full of corruption. "Everything's about to change, Kat." The woman was still chuckling. "The McDonough empire is done for. No more of this ethics and value bullshit your father tried to implement."

"You honestly support trafficking women and children?" My mother was disgusted with the thought.

"Why not?" the woman asked. "I was." There was a pause.

"Didn't know that, did you, little Kat?" Mar mocked. "There are plans in place that run far deeper than you will ever know. Soon, the world will belong to the corrupt, and those who stand in our way will perish."

"You should really see to that god complex you've got going," my mother snarled. The woman just laughed again.

"I am a god," the woman whispered. "They call me Hera."

"They should have called you delusional."

That's when my mother screamed again.

My head hurt like a fucking bitch.

Had I been mauled by a truck?

Mom!

Bolting upright, my chest was heaving, my body soaked with rain. Her scream still echoed in my ears. It was the kind of scream that bordered on terror. It had torn through the house and into my soul like a shard of glass. My eyes widened as I fought to take in air. I could feel my heart rate thundering like a wild drum against my rib cage.

Hands grabbed at me, and I cried out as a pair of arms

wrapped themselves around me, pulling me into a warm chest.

"Shh. It's okay, Red," a voice whispered in my ear. "I've got you. You're safe."

Pine and leather enveloped me, and for a moment I allowed myself to relax into the familiarity of his body against mine. I clutched at the arm banded against my chest, holding me tight to him as I sobbed.

Problem was, I didn't even know what I was crying about.

Remembering the last moments of my mother's life. Something my psyche had apparently kept buried for all these years. Or the fact that the man I loved was holding me to him like a lifeline. As if I'd disappear if he let me go.

The man I'd thought was dead.

"Let me go," I croaked. His arms tightened for a moment before releasing me. That was new. He rarely ever did as I asked, only doing what he wanted.

I pulled myself up from the ground, not bothering to dust myself off since I was still soaking wet and brushing at wet hay was as useless as mopping rain.

"*Krasnyy*," he whispered.

"No." I shook my head to clear my thoughts before facing him. Even wet and covered in dirt, he was still the most handsome man I had ever seen. Devilishly rogue. He looked like a fallen angel. The devil in a three-piece suit. "You don't get to call me that." Pain and sadness shredded at my insides.

How could he do this to me?

Leave me like that?

I really had meant nothing to him.

"No." His voice was adamant, his face serious as he gazed down at me with an emotion I couldn't quite pinpoint. "You mean everything to me."

A mirthless laugh slipped past my dry, swollen lips.

"Then why did you do it?" I nearly sobbed. "Why did you draw up those divorce papers? Why did you take Serena to the gala? Why did you let me believe you died?" By the end, I was screaming, my voice gravelly and hoarse. I pushed at his chest with every accusation, and he took it. He let me move him. The immovable force.

"I'm not going to apologize for the mistakes I made, Ava," he whispered to me. "I made my choices, and I don't regret them."

His words were like a slap to the face, and I physically recoiled.

"What I do regret," he told me, his eyes still soft as he stared down at me, allowing the space to stay between us. "Is not seeing that the mistakes I made hurt you so much and how much that hurt me."

"You really expect me to believe that?" I bristled. The gall of this man. "Do you know how many times I opened myself up to you? Even after you forced me to marry you, I opened myself up to you. Even after you lied to me, I opened myself up to you. Hell, I even opened back up to you after you shut me out and called me a traitor. And you *still*, still shut me out again and again. The gala? That was the last straw, even if you hadn't faked your death. And this time—there won't be any fixing it."

He smirked, pushing himself closer to me, invading my space with his warmth and smell.

"Do you honestly believe I am giving you a choice, Red?" His eyes sparked like thunderstorms. "Because I'm not."

"Fuck you." Turning on my heel, I dashed out of the barn toward my father's Ferrari. The rain was pelting down from the sky, and within seconds, I was soaked to the core. I didn't care. I was too hurt. Too angry.

Growling, I searched my pockets for the key fob, coming up empty.

"Looking for this?" I spun around to see him dangling the key fob in his hand, a smug smile stretched across his ugly mug.

Okay, it wasn't ugly.

Not in the slightest.

No. I was pissed at him and not thinking about how handsome he was.

"Are you going to give me the key?" I asked, my voice dulled by the howling wind and rain. The fucker smirked and shook his head.

"Okay then." I flipped him off and began my long walk back to civilization. Fuck him.

"Where do you think you're going, Mrs. Dashkov?" The wind had dampened his steps, and I hadn't heard him approach. "I'm not done with you yet."

"Go to hell," I spat at him.

"Only if you're there with me, baby." He smiled down at me.

"Sure," I told him sweetly. "I'll be the one roasting you on a spit."

"I love it when you talk dirty to me," he growled before his hand shot out to grab the back of my neck. His mouth came down on mine with enough passion and fury that it honestly might have melted the polar ice caps. Excitement and desire rippled through me as his tongue forayed into my mouth, taking no prisoners, and leaving nothing unexplored.

Okay, I was mad at him, sure. But that didn't mean we couldn't indulge in a little hate sex.

That's normal.

Right?

Whatever. My mind didn't seem to care any longer when one hand drifted behind my neck, pulling me closer and deepening the kiss.

"Fuck, baby," he breathed when he pulled back. "You taste so good." He nipped at my earlobe. "Just like I remember."

"Stop talking and fuck me," I snarled, thrusting my hips against his jean-clad erection. He chuckled darkly.

"You don't make the choices here, Red." His voice dipped seductively low, and a spark of desire shot straight through me. I shivered. "I might need to remind you of who owns you."

"No one owns me."

Yeah, that might have sounded more believable if it hadn't come out like a breathy moan. In my defense, his hand had slid into my jeans and sunk directly into my pussy. I hadn't felt him pop the button to them.

Fuck, I was already soaking, and the smug grin that stretched across his face told me he knew it, too.

Suddenly, he removed his fingers from my aching pussy and flipped me around, pressing me against the trunk of my father's car. Seconds later, his fingers returned to their original position as he placed a hot kiss to my shoulder blade. I bucked against his hand, desperate for more, but I wasn't in control here. Just how he wanted it to be.

Matthias's hard length was crushed against my lower back, and I salivated at the thought of having his cock stuffed inside me, replacing his fingers. Unfortunately, he seemed content to keep the slow, torturous pace of his finger banging. So I did what any woman would do. I reached my hand back and rubbed his length.

He stiffened but didn't stop teasing me with his fingers.

"Come on, wolfie," I egged him on, applying just a little more pressure. He groaned and scraped his teeth over my neck. "Show me what you say I've been missing." I screamed when his free hand twisted my right nipple harshly.

"This is my show, baby."

"Keep telling yourself that."

"Fucking hell," he muttered to himself when I squeezed him tightly again. Matthias could have easily removed my hand and kept it immobile, but he hadn't. That was something to file away for later for future Ava to deal with.

His withdrew his fingers again and shucked my jeans and underwear down to pool at my ankles. "Put your hands on the trunk, baby," he commanded, "and don't move them."

My pussy clenched at the low tone in his voice and the hint of punishment he laced into it. The Ferrari trunk was slightly higher and squarer than the hood. The noise of the rain dropping against the car and the howling wind through the open grass and tree-lined forest knocked out any subtle sounds.

The sensory deprivation had my body on edge, waiting for his next move. It wasn't until Matthias's hard cock stroked against my clit that I realized he had undone his pants.

"Matthias," I whimpered, pushing back against him, begging him to fill me. The fucker chuckled, then slapped my ass. I'm not ashamed to say that I moaned like a wanton whore as he did it again and again until my ass was no doubt a pretty shade of cherry red. The heat of my ass was intensified by the icy raindrops, providing that needed bite of pain.

He filled me with one forceful thrust, making me scream out his name. Matthias didn't give me any time to adjust before he grabbed my hips and started fucking me with reckless abandon.

His body slammed into mine again and again, his massive cock stretching me as he struck my ass, groaning as my cunt pulsed around him.

"You love that, don't you?" he whispered in my ear. "My dirty Little Red loves having her ass spanked."

Fuck.

"It's been too long, baby," he groaned. "This isn't going to be long." Which was perfectly fine with me. I was already standing at the edge of a precipice, and when he tweaked my nipple through my drenched silk shirt, I cracked.

"Such a good girl," he cooed in my ear. "Taking me like a fucking champ."

"Matthias." I could barely get his name out before he pinched my oversensitive clit and sent me spiraling over the edge again, bringing him along with me. We fell, shattering against the rocks into a million pieces, just like our marriage. Our love. We were never meant to be, and I knew that.

"I love it when you scream my name," he breathed. "Moan it. Curse it. You're mine, Ava Dashkov and I will prove that to you repeatedly until you believe it."

"You don't need to prove it," I whispered brokenly. "Because it's never going to happen, Matthias. You broke me, and there isn't any way I'm going to allow you to do it again."

"We'll see about that, my little psycho."

For a moment, neither of us spoke. We stood, leaning against one another, relishing in each other's warmth as the rain continued to pour down around us, our breaths heavy and ragged. I leaned my head against one of the arms bracketing me and just let myself relish the fact that he was alive.

With a reluctant sigh, he withdrew, tucking himself away. He bent down and shimmied my panties and jeans up my legs, buttoning me back in place. The evidence of our union lost in the deluge around us.

Then he kissed me.

Soft and slow. Full of sorrow and affection. He'd never kissed me like that before. Like I was precious. Like he loved me.

Nope, I wasn't ready to analyze that just yet.

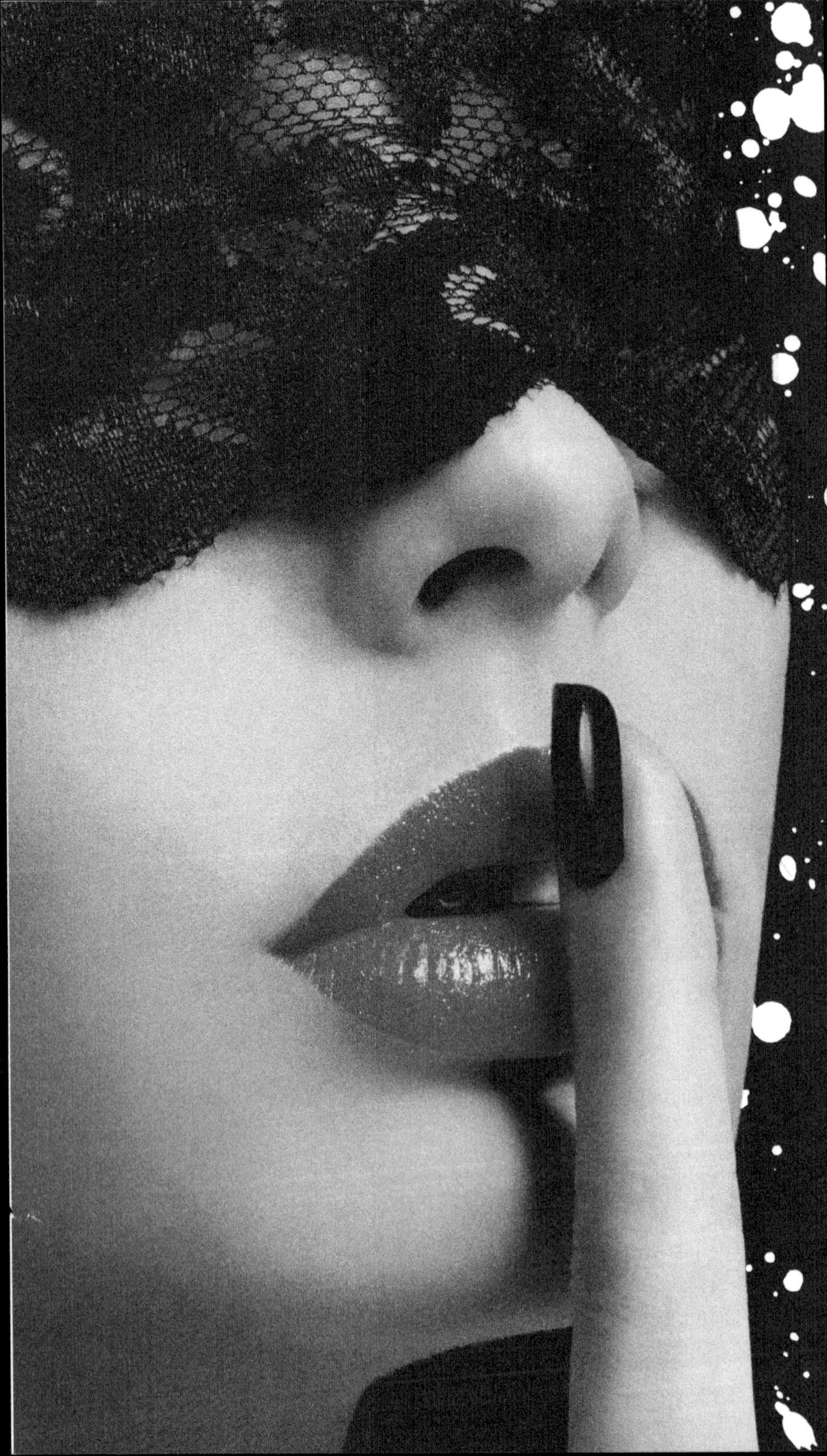

CHAPTER TWENTY-FIVE

"I've been searching this barn since Kenzi left." I stiffened when he said her name. If he noticed, he didn't say anything. "She made it sound like there would be something here, but so far, I haven't found anything."

"What did she say?" I asked, pulling away from him slightly. It didn't get me far since I was still blocked in on one side by the car.

"She said this place had memories. Painful ones," he repeated. "Then she told me to dig up the past while I could."

"Did you find anything?"

"Other than it being a normal horse stable," he huffed. "Nothing."

Stable.

That term still sent a shiver through me whenever I heard it. It was sad how such an innocuous word could have such a dark and powerful impact on someone.

Wait—stable.

Elias wouldn't have been the only one to have a horse stable set up to traffic women. From the look of the barn before me, this one was far older than the one he had set up.

Matthias wouldn't have known to look for a hidden door because he'd never been to the stable back home. Striding past him, I made my way down the center of the dilapidated building and counted out the beams where the horse stalls would have been. If this was a place where they held trafficked women, then they would have placed the door at one end of the barn, most likely in the last stable. There was only ever one exit and entrance to make it harder for women to escape.

Elias's had been larger than the one we stood in now, but the length of the barn had been tripled to hold more women.

I stepped into the last stall on the right and moved the hay around with my feet, ignoring the mice and spiders that scattered at the motion. When I didn't find what I was looking for, I moved to the other side.

And bingo.

It was barely noticeable, even after all these years. The boards had been cut to look exactly like their surroundings, and the handle looked to be nothing more than notched wood from horses' hooves. Grasping the underside of the wood-carved handle, I grunted as I lifted the heavy door.

The smell of mildew and rotting eggs filled the air. We coughed, the scent strong, even with the fresh rain.

"Let me grab a flashlight," Matthias said.

"Don't worry about it." I shook my head and flipped a small metal switch that rested where the stairs began to descend. The whirring of a generator filled the cramped space below our feet before the lights crackled, flickered, and then turned on. "Gross." I pulled a face as I stepped down onto the rotting wooden stairs.

They creaked with my weight, and I took my time as I descended into the first hallway, taking it slow. The steps were covered in a thin layer of mildew, and I didn't want to trip. Looking around, I let my eyes take a moment to adjust to the dim lighting. The concrete walls were covered in mold, and combined with the warm yellow of the lights, it had the space feeling cramped and dark due to the tinge of green.

"This place looks like it has been abandoned for years," Matthias noted.

"How did Kenzi even know of this place?" I wondered. "In fact, how are the two of you so chummy?" I pushed forward, refusing to look back at him.

"Mark had been monitoring dark web chatter," he admitted. "Not much goes on without him knowing, especially when it pertains to the *Bratva*. There were several dark web pings about a possible assassination attempt."

"So someone leaked the information?" Who would do that? Or even know? Did that mean that the Dollhouse had a leak?

"Kenzi did," he told me. "She wasn't the docile little assassin they thought she was."

"I wasn't the target, was I?" I asked.

"No," he assured me softly. "There was no way anyone would believe that an assassin would get the drop on me directly. Not when I am so well protected."

"I was your weakness," I whispered, mostly to myself.

There was a beat, and then he whispered back. "Yes."

Kenzi never believed Christian. She never wanted to kill me.

"She loves you very much, Ava." Matthias voiced my thoughts. "Kenzi hated that we didn't bring you in on the plan."

"Why didn't you?" I asked.

"Because you needed a push," he admitted. "You've

always been someone's pawn. I wanted you to become your own person. Even if I told you about our plan, I could have easily made you the queen of my empire, but if you knew I was there, behind the scenes, you would have never taken it into your own hands. You would have questioned every decision and leaned on me for support. I didn't want that, and it wasn't something you needed. What you needed was to be pushed out of your comfort zone."

"I might have gone a little overboard." I shrugged my shoulder shyly, glad the dim lights hid the flush that crept up my cheeks.

"Oh, I've heard everything about you, my little psycho." There was a smile in his voice. "It was a turn on hearing about your little exploits. My hand and I were very busy imagining all the ways you kept kneecapping people."

"I didn't kneecap the last one."

He chuckled. "That's true."

We fell into a companionable silence as we walked along the long stretch of hallway, peering into the worn, cleared out rooms. I didn't know what the hell Kenzi was talking about. There wasn't anything here. Not of any worth, anyway. So she found an old trafficking barn; good for her. I was about to suggest we turn back when something caught my eye.

"I know that symbol." I pointed to the all-seeing eye carved inside of the Seal of Solomon. "Vas showed this to me. It's the crest for this secret society thing."

"*Potestas Omnis*," Matthias breathed, coming up behind me.

"You've heard of it." Duh, Ava, obviously he had.

"We'll compare notes when we get back," he said, running his hand over the symbol. Pressing onto the wooden door, I pushed. It slid open with a groan. The room was empty, just like the others.

"There might be hidden compartments." I ran my hand up and down the brick on the right side of the wall, stretching tall before moving toward the floor. He followed suit on the other side. Inch by inch, I searched for any type of false or loose brick.

"Pay dirt," Matthias called out. He shifted one of the bricks from its spot. It didn't look like the rest of its counterparts, which had grayed with age. This one was certainly duller, but it was slightly misshapen, most likely from weather damage. The fake brick was barely a few inches long, and the other bricks on either side of it had been carved out to make room for something else.

A small wooden box.

Carefully, he removed it from its hiding place and handed it to me. The design was Irish. I had seen something like this before, but I couldn't place where. On the top, molded from silver, was the Celtic love knot.

My breathing stilled as I opened the lid, the wood of the box soft from being exposed to the elements for who knows how long. Inside, there were small trinkets and baubles, things a child would have. I removed them, one by one, and placed them in Matthias's outstretched hand. Rings, a baby tooth in a small, clear baggy, a lock of red hair, some crayons, a photo of a baby and a young woman I didn't recognize.

"Oh my god," I gasped.

"What is it?" Matthias leaned in to get a better look.

"Holy fuck," he whispered. "That can't be—"

At the bottom of the small box, beneath the first photo, was a grainy photo that was dated March 1990. It wasn't hard to recognize the young girl in the photo with her long strawberry blond hair and brown eyes. She had the same angular features now as she did back then. Was even wearing the same necklace she'd worn in all the photos I'd seen of her.

"Marianne." I finished his sentence, horror rushing through me. The girl in the photo couldn't be any older than twelve or thirteen. Not long before my mother became friends with her. "I don't understand."

"Let's get this back to the hotel, and we can go from there." Matthias emptied the trinkets in his hand back into the box and shut the lid before ushering me out of the room.

The rain had stopped, the sky empty of clouds, allowing the stars to shine through. It was such a peaceful place for such tragic memories. This time, we weren't alone. Several of our men waited for us, along with my father and Sully.

"You two were taking too long, so we thought we'd come and find you." My father approached me. His eyes scanned my body, checking for injuries.

"I'm okay," I placated him. "We found a few things that —" God, how was I going to tell him? He hadn't taken it very well the first time I had suggested Marianne had something to do with Mom's kidnapping and murder. How was he going to take this?

"Where did you get that?" he asked, pointing at the box in my house.

"Umm," I stuttered, holding the box tighter in my hand. This was the proof I needed to bring my mother's murderer to justice. I wasn't going to let anyone take it from me. Not even him. "In one of the rooms downstairs. It was hidden in a wall."

"That's impossible," he told me harshly. Matthias growled at him and stepped forward.

"Watch your tone," my husband snarled at my father. Goosebumps broke across my skin at his protectiveness over me. The fucker was still in the doghouse, but damn if my body wasn't catching up to that.

My father's shoulders fell, and he looked contrite as he

said, "Your mother had one exactly like it," he explained. "It was handmade, and a family heirloom given to her by your great-grandmother. There are only two in existence."

"Who has the other one?" I asked curiously.

"Your grandmother."

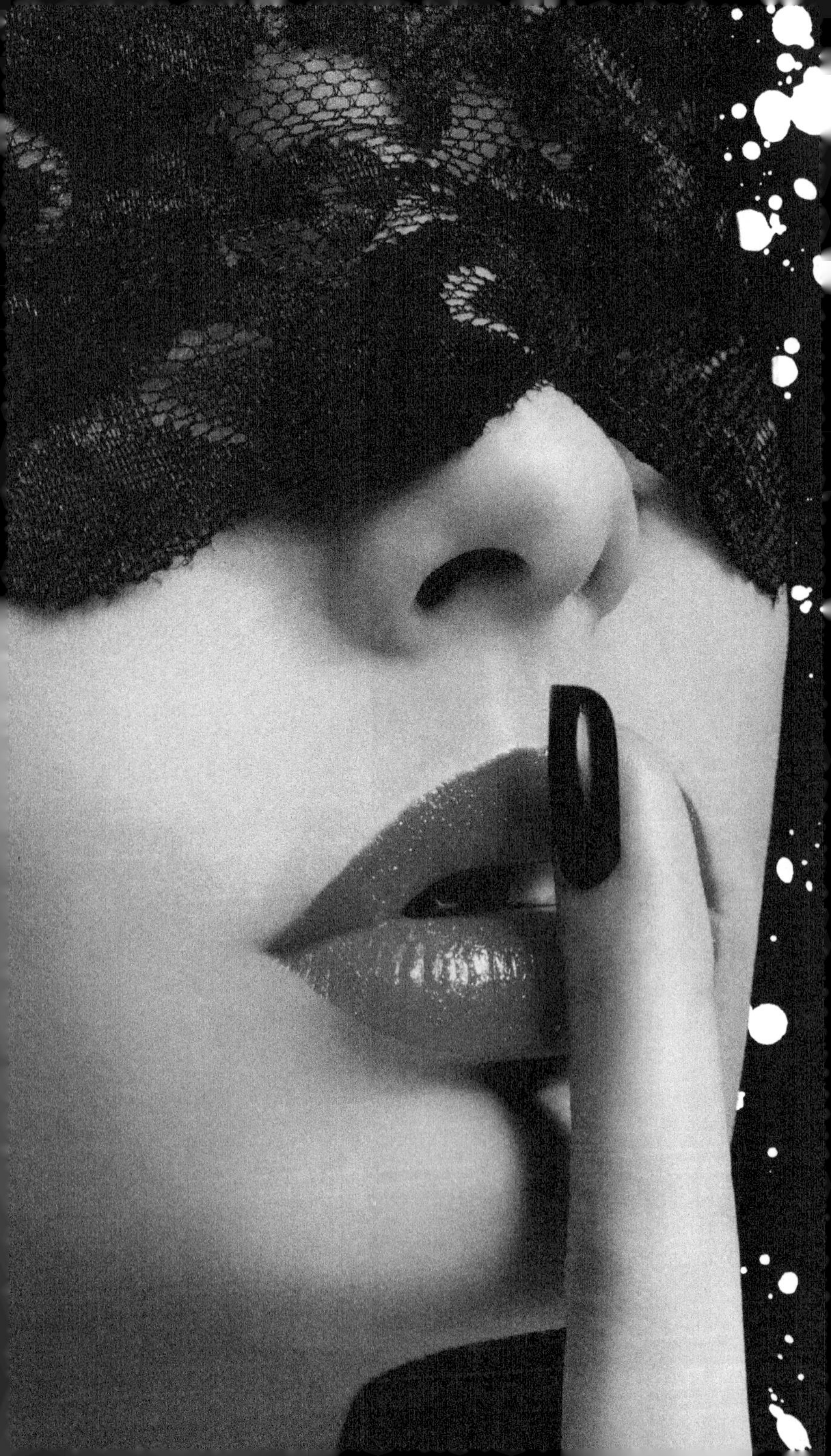

CHAPTER TWENTY-SIX

"Does she still have it?" Ava asked her father.

Liam shrugged. "As far as I know," he said. "I've never actually seen it. It was just what your mother told me when we were children. Your great-grandmother gave it to her upon her birth."

My wife was silent for a moment, and I recognized that the gears in her head were working out a puzzle. I hadn't missed the look in her eyes when she saw the box. Like she recognized it, and the minute she remembered where, her eyes lit up like fire.

"We need to go back to my old house." She snapped her fingers and smiled. "That's where I've seen this before."

"Where in the house?" I asked, because if one of her mother's enemies had seen it, they might have taken it.

"In one of my hiding places in the kitchen," she told me excitedly. "I always thought it was a recipe box."

I nodded my assent.

"Vas." We both called for him at the same time. This could get awkward. My wife looked at me askance as Vas stepped forward with a broad grin.

"Yes, bosses." He gave a dramatic pause before adding the extra -es on the end. Fucking asshole.

"You and Maxim follow us to the house," Ava ordered before I could get a word in edgewise. It was fine. This was her mission, and I'd let her have that.

For now.

I wasn't sure how I planned to take back over the *Bratva* when I came back, but I knew I didn't want Ava near it if I could help it. I did, however, want her to become the face and full-time CEO of Arctic Security. She'd proven several times over that she was intelligent enough to be able to run it.

Even if she had learned about the company less than a week ago.

"Sully, you're welcome to join if you wish," she told him. Sully nodded and leaned over to whisper to one of his men. "Matthias, my father, and I will take another car."

"Does that mean I'm not fired?" Vas joked, but I could see the seriousness behind his eyes. Vas was the closest thing Ava had ever had to a best friend that wasn't one of her sisters, and for the last month or so, he had been lying to her. Withholding information. Keeping secrets.

"Still on my shitlist," she muttered darkly as she brushed past him. Vas's shoulders slumped.

"She just needs time," I told him, handing him the key fob to Liam's Ferrari. "See you there."

Vas nodded, looking like someone had kicked his puppy.

Ava would forgive him a lot easier than she'd forgive me. That I was sure of. It would just take time for her heart to heal.

The drive to Ava's childhood home was quiet. No one was sure what to say. My wife gripped the small box tightly, as if she was afraid someone would take it from her. I understood her reticence to let it go. This was her smoking gun. It was going to be whether her father believed her that mattered.

I stared up at the two-story family home, and for a moment, I wondered what Ava's childhood here was like. She never really spoke of her time with her mother, and that was my fault. I'd never taken an interest in her past as she had in mine.

Over our time together, she had revealed snippets every now and then, but I got the feeling that most of her memories from this time were repressed. I just wasn't sure if it was purposeful on my wife's part, or if someone had forced her to do it.

She wasted no time throwing open the rickety front door and barging inside like a woman on a mission. Ava passed directly through the living room and into the large, homey kitchen. This was where Ava's love for baking had come from. On several occasions, I had caught her and Mia baking up a batch of cookies or brownies. Sometimes even cakes.

Mia told me it helped her feel safe and secure.

Now I knew why.

It reminded her of a time when she *was* safe and secure. A time before Elias and Christian. A time before me. If I could change my Little Red's history, I would do it in a heartbeat. Even if it meant we had never met.

"Here it is." Her voice was calm, barely above a whisper as she opened the door to the small closet hidden at the side of one of the pantries. If she hadn't pointed it out, I would never have known it was there.

She passed the first box off to me, and my heart swelled instantly that she trusted me enough to keep it safe for her. At least I hadn't lost that completely. Ava may not have fully trusted me in some areas, but she knew all I wanted to do was keep her safe.

The box she held in her hand now was different.

Newer.

Carved from a tree called Rowan that was native to Ireland. On the top was the same symbol as the one I held. The Celtic love knot.

Gingerly, she opened the lid and peered inside.

"That's the promise ring I gave her when we were fifteen." Liam's throat bobbed with emotion as he looked at it. Respecting my wife by not simply grabbing the ring, he waited for her to hand it to him. "We always knew we were going to get married. She made me promise her after she got dumped by Mason Walsh in the second grade."

Ava snorted a laugh as she picked up the next thing.

It was a lock of her hair and a baby tooth.

"Your mother said it was tradition to put a lock of your first-born daughter's hair into the box and her first baby tooth. It is said to promote a healthy relationship between the mother and daughter as they move forward in life."

My wife pulled a face, but she gently set the two baggies down on the counter with care.

"My baby photo," Ava whispered as she took the small thumbnail out and handed it to her father. "Mom said I was born with a head of hair and the brightest emerald eyes. Used to tell me it was like looking at one of the fairies."

"It's genetic." Liam smiled down at her. "The only person not to be born with green eyes was your grandmother. Hers were brown."

Ava nodded absently before taking a few more trinkets out of the box that Liam explained were gifts he'd given her over the years. Many from when they were small children.

The last thing in the box was a folded-up sheet of paper with Ava's name on it.

She pursed her lips, her hand shaking as she lifted it from the confines of the box. A photo slipped out, but she didn't pay it any mind. Her entire focus was on the letter. Slowly, she started to peel back the pages when a sudden noise caught our attention.

"We need to go," Sully yelled from the front of the house. "Now."

Gunshots echoed around us, windows exploding as bullets surged through them. Ava gasped and tucked the note away in her jean pocket before throwing her mother's trinkets in the box and snatching it up from the counter, along with the one in my hand.

"Head down, baby," I reminded her as we dashed out of the kitchen to the front door, where Sully's men fired off round after round from their ARs at the bypassing cars. I recognized the make and model.

Platinum Security.

Fucking idiots. They made themselves easily identifiable, and that was a mistake.

"Get us to the helipad," I ordered our driver as we slid into the SUV.

"My stuff," Ava said.

"The men will grab it," I told her. "We need to get back to Seattle. I don't have the manpower here to take on Cartwright and O'Neill."

Ava spun her head to look at me. "How did you know about Cartwright?"

"You think I didn't keep track of everything while I was gone?" I asked her incredulously as I picked up my phone to make a call. "I was in constant contact with Vas and my other men. So was Dima."

"Dima was with you." It wasn't a question. She knew he was. It was all starting to come together for her. How much we had all kept from her. "Motherfuckers."

"Dima," I barked into the phone. "Grab my father and get to the airstrip. We've been compromised."

"Father?" Shock spread itself across her face. There might have been anger there too, but I was ignoring that.

"We'll take the helicopter with Liam," I told him. "Grab Kenzi, too." Then I hung up.

"You wanna fill me in on what the hell is going on?" My wife huffed. Liam chuckled beside her. I narrowed my eyes at him.

"Don't pretend like you are innocent in all this, Kavanaugh," I snarled. "This was, after all, your idea."

"What?" Liam grimaced at her sudden shriek. That one broke the sound barrier for sure.

"Matthias told me about his umm...other father?" He shot me a questioning look before continuing. "When we got word about the hit put out on him by that very man, we came up with a plan to make it look like Kenzi succeeded to draw him out."

"Other father?" She looked over at me.

"It's a long story, *Krasnyy*," I told her. Ava's response to that was to stare up at me expectantly, arms crossed, and snarl. "We've got plenty of time."

There wouldn't be any moving forward if I couldn't be honest with her. I knew that.

"Okay," I began. "Let me start from the beginning."

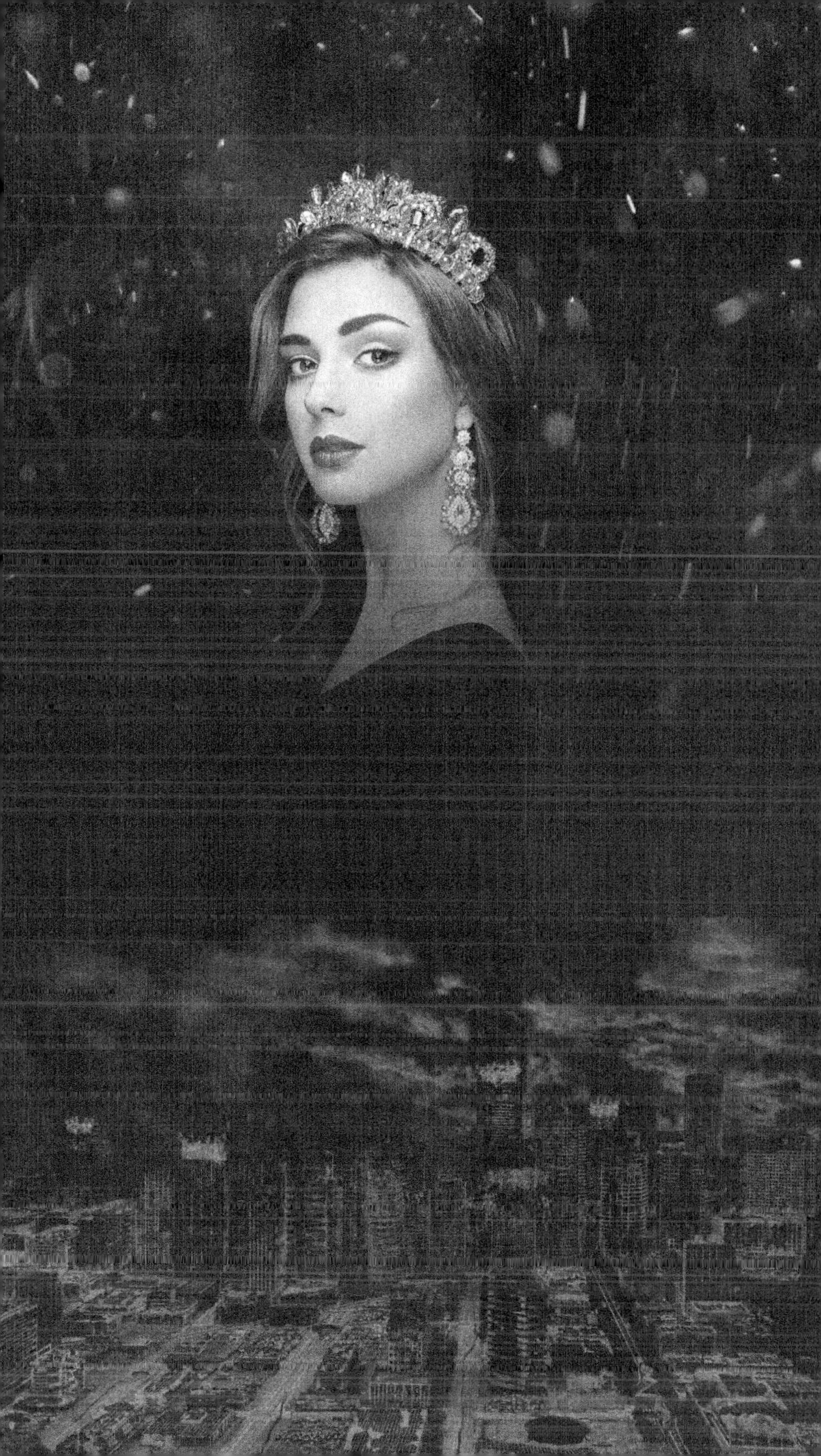

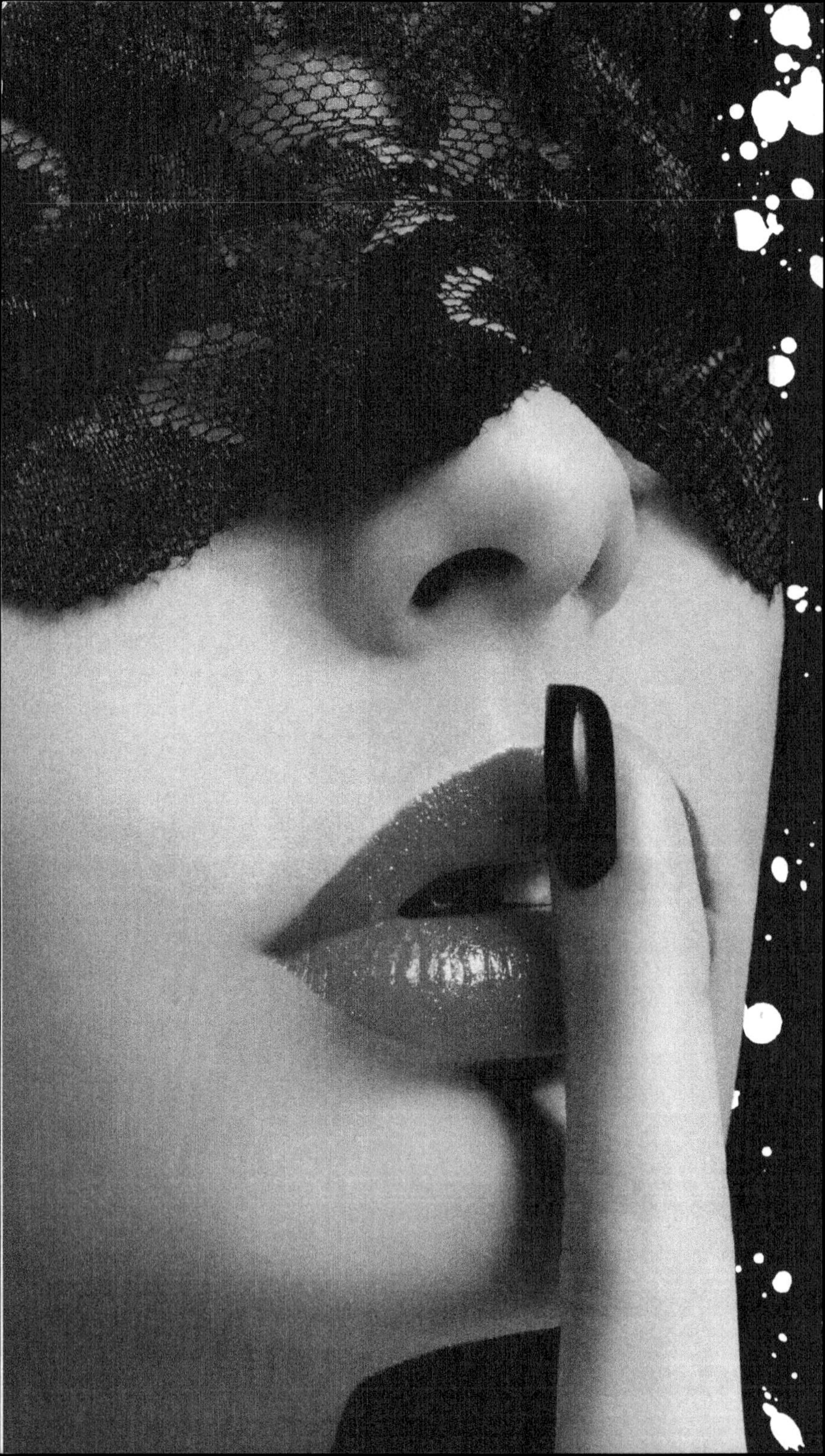

CHAPTER TWENTY-SEVEN

Matthias had a family.

Archer's name was really Ivan, and he was Matthias's brother.

Kirill, the man Matthias thought to be his father, had started the human trafficking ring we knew as the Chameleon Agency, and he had been a member of the stupid secret society thing.

Oh, and he was dead.

And his biological father was here to help.

Because he was the head of the Russian *Bratva*.

Like *the* head honcho.

The *Pakhans* of all *Pakhans*.

I was going to be sick.

The helicopter ride had been short. An easy ninety minutes, which had been plenty of time for my husband to catch me up on all the shit he had been doing as a dead man. The Archer/Ivan thing still got me, though.

I owed that man a swift right hook to the jaw.

Twat waffle.

"The penthouse might not be secure," my father told

Matthias. "But we're going to need all the evidence from the vault if we want to piece everything together." Matthias nodded in agreement.

"Have your lower-tier men move to a safe house," my father said. "The rest of you can come stay with us. I doubt anyone would look for your there."

Except someone would know we were there. I went to say something, but Matthias's elbow jabbed me in the side. "Sounds good," he agreed. "I'll have Tony drive you."

Nodding, my father kissed my forehead gently before striding out the lobby doors. All my time here, and I had never known there was a helipad on the top of the building. It was cool in a billionaire tycoon kind of way.

"Wait for me outside with Kristian." Matthias tilted his head at the burly security guard that monitored the lobby doors. He was a good guy with a sucky name. Not that I held it against him. I just refused to call him by it. Opting for Kris instead. The man didn't seem to mind.

"Okay," I whispered, clutching the boxes to my chest.

"Good girl." And there went my panties. Matthias bent down and kissed me softly before following Maksim and Vas into the elevator that led down to the subbasement level where the vault was held.

"Ma'am." Kris opened the glass door for me and tilted his head toward the large fountain area a little farther from the building. "There's a bench just over there we can sit at until they return."

I grinned and nodded. "Thanks."

He led me to the large wooden bench that sat just in front of a small fountain that was the building's focal point in the front. The building was as much of a business hub as it was a home. Not just for me, but also for many of my men.

No, not mine any longer. Matthias's.

A small part of me mourned the loss of being *Pakhan*. I doubted Matthias was planning to let me help him run anything. Not that I wanted to run anything with him.

He'd lied to me. Kept secrets. I'd wept for him, killed for him, and he wasn't even dead.

We may be getting along now, but that didn't mean I would just crawl back to him. I'd tried that before and look where it got me. Nowhere. When he thought I'd betrayed him, I did everything I could to draw him back in. To get him to trust me again and build back some of what we had before.

I had pursued him.

If he truly wanted me, he had to come after me. Woo me. And there was no way in hell I was going to make that easy.

But that was something for future Ava to deal with. After a large cup of coffee. Maybe two. Right now, I was more interested in the note addressed to me in my mother's handwriting. Licking my lips, I pulled the paper out of my pocket and unfolded it.

Mo Réalta,
If you are reading this, then my time has come, my
precious little star.
I don't want you to be sad.
Death is nothing to fear or mourn but something to
rejoice and cherish.
You are ten now, my heart.
I don't have much time. They are coming for me, and
our time together will soon end.
I love you. I want you to know that. Because what I am
about to tell you may very well break your heart, as it
did mine so many years ago.

There are dark forces at work, my star, that I hope will never taint your sweet, gentle soul.
When I was eighteen, I was taken by a man named Elias Ward, who works for a devil. A man with two faces.
I didn't notice at first. The changes were so subtle that I barely saw what was right in front of me.
Until one day, I did.
You will never meet your grandfather, God rest his soul, for the man who wears his face is nothing but a lie.
A con.
One that has been going on far longer than I could have ever anticipated.
Oh, my star.
I escaped the man who took me, and I ran back to your father. The love of my life.
Unfortunately, I was ill advised and later betrayed. But I wouldn't figure this out until several months later.
Elias stole me again, and I was resigned to my fate until one day I found out about my little miracle.
Mo Réalta.
Now it was life or death. If Elias ever found out about you, he would have forced me to end the pregnancy.
With some help, I escaped again.
I went back to your father, but he had already moved on.
With the one who betrayed me.
She wasn't who she appeared to be, my heart.
Over the years, I have struggled to find out how she was involved, and I think I finally found it.
The connection.

If only I had put it together sooner.
I found the old barn. The one exactly like Elias's.
They train girls there to be sex slaves to wealthy men and women.
But she was more than that. She was a plant. A fake.
At the same time, she was so real.
Not everyone is who they appear to be, and you'll find that those who appear the weakest are, in fact, the strongest.
I never expected her to betray me. But she did.
And now they are here.
Remember, I love you.
Forever.
Your father's name is Liam Kavanaugh. His father was my father's right-hand man. He is a good man, my star. Find him. Tell him my story.
And one day, I hope you find a man just like him.
A mix of monster and prince.
A warrior.
A partner.
I love you, Mo Réalta.
Remember what I've told you and—

"Run!" Kristian shouted next to me, drawing me out of the reverie my mother's letter had pulled me into.

There was a sudden explosion. A cracking sound rent the air, and the next thing I knew, he was tackling me to the ground, and everything went black.

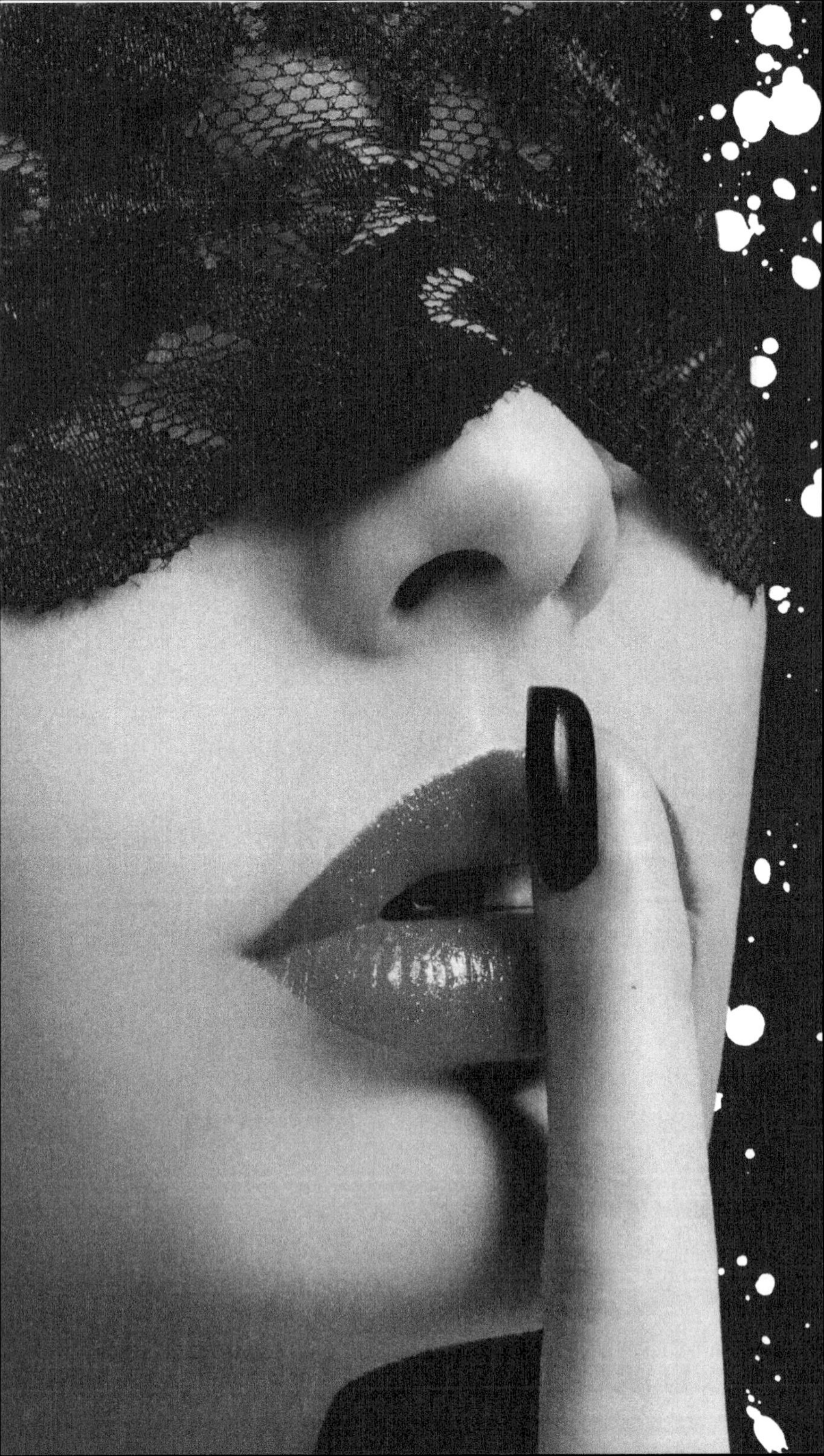

CHAPTER TWENTY-EIGHT

A sharp sting of pain radiated through my chest as I came to.

My eyes fluttered furiously, like butterflies trapped in a glass cage, fighting against an invisible weight. I coughed and sputtered, the pain increasing as I struggled to take a breath. My chest felt like it was caught in the grasp of a boa constrictor. The cracks in my lips split even wider, blood pooling in my mouth as a hoarse cry rose in my throat.

Fuck.

It was like someone had pressed the mute button on the controller. The only sound I could hear was the ear-piercing ringing that tore through my head, sounding like one of those ungodly mosquito tones. Slowly, I managed to open my eyes, the invisible weight pressing against them slightly dampened by my fierce determination to live.

Dust and debris had settled over my unprotected face. I lifted my equally dusty hand to wipe at it, being mindful of my injuries, but it was like trying to wipe away mud with more mud. It just became worse.

A low, keening whine spilled from my lips unbidden as I struggled to move the weight of my own body. My chest heaved in ragged sobs, tears spilling down my dirt-marred face as I crawled through several feet of debris toward the still body of Kristian, my guard. He was half-buried in the building's wreckage, his dark face covered in a heavy layer of white dust.

I reached out with a shaky hand to check his pulse.

Nothing.

He was dead. Just like the rest of them—and now I was truly alone.

The old me would have become numb. Would have curled up in a ball and let fate take over.

The old me was tired of war. Matthias was gone, again, and this time it looked like it would be permanent.

The King. The Ruler. Fallen to his enemies.

There was no surviving that explosion unless they were in the vault and I had to have hope that they were. Their lives were in the hands of fate.

What else was there to do but give in to that fate?

Except this wasn't a game of chess where the fall of the king meant the end of the game. I

No. This was war. And the war wasn't over until the queen was dead.

And I was the fucking Queen.

Or so I wanted to believe.

They were alive.

I had to cling to that hope as I looked around.

My empire was crumbling around me, and I was surrounded by the enemy.

No, literally, I was surrounded by no less than twenty men, the barrels of their guns pointed directly at me. I was impressed they thought they needed twenty men to take me in.

"Hello, dear." A woman's voice filtered through the air, unbothered by the rising smoke and dust that covered the air.

I never expected her to betray me.

"Hello, Grandmother."

SHATTERED REVELATIONS

MATTHIAS

Secrets would be revealed.
Loyalties would be tested.
It was all coming to an end.
She was only meant to be a pawn.
Someone I could use and throw away.
But Ava wormed her way under my skin.
Now, she was my queen.
Ava and this city were mine.
I'd do anything to protect them.
To keep them.
Even if I have to burn it to the ground.
Together we are unstoppable and nothing would stand in our way.
Or so we believed.
New revelations come to light
And the game is about to change.
No one is safe.
Not even us.

ACKNOWLEDGMENTS

Oo...another cliffhanger.

Sorry not sorry.

This has been the best journey of my life. But also the hardest. Thank you so much to all of my Alpha, Beta, and ARC readers. You give me such motivation to finish writing Matthias and Ava's story.

Your love for them keeps me going.

To the AMAZING BETH at VB Edits. You constantly amazing and surprise me with your dedication and friendship. Thank you for always being there for me.

To my Alpha Robin who answers all of my phone calls and listens to all of my rantings and ravings about my stories and brainstorming with me and calling me out on my bullshit. You are the best.

Well...Until next time my Wicked Readers.

Thank you all from the bottom of my heart.

> *"If not you—who? If not now when?"*
> *-Arnold Schwarzenegger.*

ALSO BY JO MCCALL

SHATTERED WORLD

Shattered Pieces

Shattered Remnants

Shattered Empire

SHATTERED WORLD STANDALONES

Shattered Revenge - Coming Soon

KAVANAUGH CRIME FAMILY

Stolen Obsession - Now on Vella

Twisted Crown - Coming Soon

Crooked Fate - Coming Soon

CAGED HEARTS SERIES

Savage Thievery - November 2022

Savage Ultimatum - Coming Soon

TWISTED FAIRY-TALE

(Part of a Shared World Series)

Claimed by Them - February 2023

STALK ME

@jomccallauthor

BookBub
Amazon Profile
Goodreads
Wicked Romance Book Box

Printed in Great Britain
by Amazon